SANDRA'S SYNDROME

MARK MERKLEY

SANDRA'S SYNDROME
Copyright © 2025 by Mark Merley

ISBN: 979-8-9929159-0-7 (Paperback)
  979-8-9921174-1-7 (E-book)

Library of Congress Control Number:2024925434

Published By:

Sun City, AZ
markmerkleyauthor.com

Publisher Provider:

Additional Advance Praise for Sandra's Syndrome

"What a blockbuster! So many moving lines. Indeed, God the Narrator. I found it to be a real mystery page turner. As a man who has battled with insecurity over exclusion of who he is, I treasured the empathetic accounts of the pain and sadness of my LGBTQ brothers, sisters and n-binaries. Mark is up to date on the genetics of gender identity. I'm sure the book will awaken religions and individuals to a greater sense of aliveness. Mark speaks boldly and lovingly about Mormonism. Attachment to tradition is serious – You have done for Mormons what Irshad Manji did for Islam and Bishop Spong did for Christianity. I am amazed and encouraged. Thank you."

Tom Reemtsma

"Sandra's Syndrome is one of the finest books I have ever read. The story captivated my mind long after I finished reading. The main characters are incredible, and the plot is over the top. I will be asking questions, often, until the next manuscript is written.

Liz Ridings

"*Sandra's Syndrome* with its engaging perspective is intelligent, well researched, and finely written. I loved the characters and I fell in love with the family. So relatable. I enjoyed each page!"

Dr. Jamie Rees

A beautifully written story of a complex love affair from college days to family life, retirement and death. I LOVED READING IT."

Shirlee H. Shields, PhD

"I finished reading your manuscript. Thank you for trusting me with it. I found the story very compelling. I enjoyed reading your book. I felt engaged with the characters and the challenges they faced. It was a page-turner that kept me wanting to read more and learn about what was going to happen."

Susan Hamada

"As in writing poetry, words speak the emotions, thoughts and beliefs of the author. It is up to each reader to agree, disagree or have no opinion. However, as you read this book open your hearts and minds without bias, to understand the story to its very depths."

Sam De Leeuw, Poet Laurette;
Five-time IWMA Female Poet

"This page-turner is a must read! A true heroic love story with modern, complex understandings of gender and biological sex. Readers will laugh and cry and never want it to end! I truly loved the book."

Becky Johns, PhD

"WOW! WHAT A RIDE! *Sandra's Syndrome* is unlike any book I've ever read. It was thought-provoking, imaginative, compelling, and intriguing, all at once ... some of it did make me uncomfortable, but even the most difficult issues were capably handled in this book.

Kathryn Jenkins Oveson

Intermountain Medical Center of Intermountain Healthcare. The people, mentioned above, diagnosed myxofibrosarcoma, a malignant cancer in my left forearm; provided 25 radiation treatments and labored almost 18 hours within four separate surgeries to retain and rebuild my arm. These people and I shared smiles, much laughter and a few tears during our times together.

My left arm will never be what it was before I had this malignancy removed. Yet I am playing softball, basketball, and shag balls for the Seattle Mariners each Spring Training in Arizona. Google 'Meet the Mystery Outfielder.' Adam Jude of the Seattle Times is a far more impressive writer than I am. He will provide insight into my character. I intend to write more stories regarding the characters within *Sandra's Syndrome*.

Pastor France Davis ... thank you for your random phone calls. You know I am an individual who lost my faith long ago. Your friendship and caring spirit to enquire of my welfare is magnanimous. You give me hope for endless possibilities, unlike my people who told the NAACP in the 1960s, "We have decided to remain silent." I hope time will allow us to shake hands and give each other a hug as we did each time my students visited to hear your sermons. You are the best public speaker in the State of Utah. "I love ya, and there ain't nothin' you can do about it."—May we live long enough to stand together as the people of my Church say, "We are no longer silent," and speak humble words of apology with supportive explanations.

Preamble

It is easy to take over from those who have not thought ahead.

—Li Quan (General)

"IN THE BEGINNING …"The first millisecond of what is mistakenly referenced as the Big Bang, God's voice, third-person omniscient, was heard. It is the voice that now speaks to you and throughout this story. God's narration is its own personality in literature. A character within stories, to guide readers through worthwhile journeys. Is it male or female? – Interesting question.

The voice informs readers. Occasionally, to make a point. The omniscient voice is possessed with emotions, just as you. The Narrator intends to share broader considerations. Pertinent sources are footnoted. While reading, challenge the omniscient voice. Conclusions are your own, especially when discussed with other readers. Nonreaders of the story are irrelevant; don't waste your time. Self-inflicted ignorance is not to be praised. Readers expect meaningful endings from those deeply in love—so greatly in love they climb heights never thought achievable.

Please climb. Explore higher elevations. Discover meaningful insights. Love shared within exalted elevations is a power unknown to most.

June 8, 1978

New beginnings are often disguised as painful endings.

—Lao Tzu

"MORMONS JUST REVEALED BLACKS can hold the priesthood!"

Sandra turned from the counter clerk, alarmed by the shout. A Black student removed his headphones from a radio that blasted the news for curious listeners. Mormon Church leaders announced the latest casualty of a policy that supported Jim Crow racial segregation. A hot topic of discussion among groups of students and faculty at Arizona State University.

She dashed past people who stood in line to obtain transcripts. Eyes focused on her. Tall, shapely, athletic. Dark, long, thick hair. Full lips, high cheekbones. Clear, bronze skin with raven eyes. Jocks described Sandra as *hot*. Rarely flaunted her charms. Always modest with class. Acute observers saw a fit, well-conditioned woman. Racquetball, her forte. Competed with men. They best approached her skills.

"Do you think our protests influenced the Mormons?" a classmate asked aboard a shuttle bus.

Sandra shrugged in doubt. "I don't know." In her mind she argued, *No one protested on my behalf.*

With transcripts in hand, she proceeded home. *I must learn of this news from Salt Lake.* A glance at the bottom line of courses reflected her academic performance as a Sun Devil: 3.95 grade point average.

The only blemish, public speaking. Advisors counseled to pursue advanced degrees from Ivy League schools. She had other plans.

Conversations at bus stops and on buses focused toward Salt Lake City. *Negro men now have the right to bear, exercise the priesthood.* Everyone expressed joy as victors over an indomitable, insensitive enemy—religious oppression.

Sandra was reared as a Mormon in Surprise, Arizona. A somewhat densely Latter-day Saint area in the Maricopa County, Phoenix area. She found her parents glued to television broadcasts, radio stations, each anxious to learn of the dramatic development. Its impact. Sandra absorbed reports, every newscast that relayed the word of God received by the prophet, Spencer W. Kimball.

She grew irritated. *It came too late. I must have my explanation for what I am.* Her face angry, determined.

Sandra never felt guilt shouting protests alongside ASU students when LDS-funded Brigham Young University athletic and academic teams visited campus. *They claim innocence for gullible, racist behaviors. While enrolled at BYU graduate school, I will research my separation by our religion and its God.*

A TV commentator explained, "This revelation allows worthy Negro men to participate and officiate in Mormon Church ordinances. In harmony with the recent revelation, Black members, husbands with wives, may enter LDS temples, the most sacred places on Earth, at least to Mormons, with full fellowship seated next to mostly Caucasian worshippers."

"Why have I been forsaken?" Sandra asked her father.

"Why does Heavenly Father exclude me?" she questioned her mother.

"Answers will come," her father replied. "Opportunities will be made for you."

"It will happen," her mother attempted to encourage.

Sandra felt betrayed. *Black Africans, once segregated, now in one fell swoop instantly included in all Mormon temple ordinances. Those temples symbolize my hope to be in love, marry **for time and all eternity**.* Everything she thought dear continued outside her grasp. *Heavenly Father failed to hear my prayers, or speak to the prophet.*

Luke exited the Provo LDS Temple near Brigham Young University. He humored elderly patrons who walked to parked autos. Not a place for an intelligent, six-foot-one, muscled, 185-pound, quick-witted young man to discover romance.

As the engine started, the radio buzzed with news from Salt Lake City. "A revelation received by President Spencer W. Kimball has ended segregated practices and policies in The Church of Jesus Christ of Latter-day Saints." He listened intently as commentators reported. "A hundred and fifty years of Church segregation is suddenly reversed. Heavenly Father now accepts Black people fully, without exclusion."

Luke silenced the engine, stepped outside the car, and seated himself on the hood. He pondered deeply the new revelation and gazed at Mount Timpanogos, picturesque against the backdrop of blue skies capped with snow from the previous winter's storms. *Timpanogos did not achieve its grandeur from the sky or clouds alone. Internal forces deep beneath allowed this giant to grow. God builds His temples upon mountains as havens for Saints to escape contradictions, inconsistencies.*

The Church will say, "We are not bigots. We didn't know any better, 'til God told us not to be racists." His hands waved with frustration, got back into the car. *We obeyed doctrinal, divine commands. Yeah … I'm sure.*

Luke swiftly bolted. Indignant, yet strongminded.

Young LDS women are prepared in their early teens for temple marriage, usually to a returned missionary. Sandra sat unmoved through such lessons. Unlike young women from Mormon congregations, Sandra obtained a BS from Arizona State University. She enjoyed arts, humanities, yet above all, math. Less than four years out of high school, the majority of her female LDS classmates mothered a baby, some two.

Academics encompassed Sandra's life. Although a participant in school activities, she remained aloof, rarely dated. Once a movie or dinner ended, the boy was never again entertained. Just her way.

Sandra never contemplated marriage, though she craved romance. She told each eager young man who knocked on her door that she would remain unmarried. Church leaders could not dissuade her. Resolutely Sandra stated, "The Lord has His ways. I have my choices."

Get to BYU. Obtain a master's degree. Understand male dominated LDS behavior and habits.

Luke walked-on to play one season of BYU baseball before a Mormon mission in Toronto. The two-year layoff proved too much in his third game home in March. Positioned at shortstop, he backhanded a ground ball deep in the hole and made a long throw from the outfield grass to first base. Luke felt intense pain. Believed his arm separated from his shoulder. When the next batter dug in, he prayed, *please, Lord, don't let him hit it to me. I'll catch the ball. I can't throw it.*

The inning ended. "My arm is dead," he reported to Coach Pullins. His final game. The injury never healed. Sports medicine of the 1970s was limited and expensive. Luke's hope to become an Academic All-American? Forsaken.

Classes and work occupied his time. As a gym rat, he kept in shape with basketball, racquetball, weights, laps. Romantic interests were a series of trials. Mostly errors. Women attracted to him witnessed a keen personality, sense of reason, debate experience. Humor aided his magnetic appearance. A wordsmith, he led with smiles and common sense. Few ladies caught his attention, though he often looked.

Make a living. Get your degrees. BYU graduate school.

Sandra and Luke were each eclectic, clear thinkers. Tightly tethered to LDS Church doctrines and policies, the culture of Mormonism that embraced them. Each were taught the words, "In the world, but not of the world." Separately, they formed a similar adage: "In the world, not of the world. Nor out of the world either." Brave, forward forms of thought emerged within not only them, but an entire society.

Luke would say, "An Idaho potato has greater value to a person in need than the gospel of Jesus Christ. That potato is damned persuasive. After all, a religion that cannot save a man temporally has no power to save him spiritually." An argument he never lost.

Sandra boldly asserted, "Mormons cannot be reasoned thinkers while worshipping a conflicted God." Her logic stood guard over a deeply hidden secret.

LDS members, Sandra and Luke included, rightly rejoiced the change of racial acceptance amid distractors who balked at the 1978 revelation. Latent biases held sway inside the hearts of Church members. Not merely that of race relations alone. Equally untenable? The issue of homosexuality. With the newly received revelation, hope flourished as newfound considerations forged a more benevolent intelligence.

A grand time to be alive. Doors opened in 1978 for a triumphant love story told by two valiant, imperfect heroes.

BYU – September 1978

We are not human beings having a spiritual experience.
We are spiritual beings having a human experience.

—Teilhard de Chardin

LUKE LOATHED LATE BEHAVIOR. *Punctuality is an admirable trait.* On-time behaviors allowed him to sit on the back row in a large room with forty desks. *The proverb that says sitting on the front row, near the teacher, assures a higher grade is a buncha crock*, he told himself. *My GPA is the only proof I need. Seated in the back permits me to observe and evaluate class members. In the event of an emergency, advantage is in the rear. Closest to the exit.*

Students took seats. He glanced at the clock. *Class begins in four minutes.* Luke never wore a watch or rings. Too cumbersome, unnecessary. Then, like a sunrise, Sandra entered.

Who is that? Luke probed Sandra's frame, smooth complexion, dark eyes, and Mediterranean skin. Long, thick hair framed an enchanted face that needed a smile.

Wow! his entire soul shouted. Luke assessed her dress. A three-quarter-length, red-and-gray, button-front outfit. *Typical attire befitting BYU Honor Code standards for modesty. Her amazon features are exceptional, not wanton. A female warrior. Delicious to my eyes. Arousing? Definitely! Though not shameful. She's a stunner.* Sandra's breasts called to him. *Come to me, speak with me, touch me.* Luke tried to resist. Could not.

7

That guy on the back row has his eyes on me, Sandra thought. *Why do men obsess?* With closer inspection, she assessed. *Six-footer. Athletic. Good posture. Speaks well of him*, she concluded. *I wonder? As smart as he looks? Can he play racquetball? I can beat him. I'd like to try. Improbable*, she concluded. *Impressive though* ... smiled, then stepped into an aisle of desks away from him.

Maintain the impression of being cool, unimpressed, Luke advised himself. His heart raced. *Act unaffected. Be attentive to other matters. But what? All that is unusual, so rare, is near—leaving me!*

Sandra placed her possessions on a desk, took a seat. Eyes focused forward to await the instructor. Her playful side thought, *I'd enjoy a conversation with him*. Her disciplined mind overpowered a curious heart. *Don't risk exposure. Control impulses.*

"Hello. My name is Luke."

Surprised, she turned. "Sandra," quietly said with uneasy embarrassment. No attempt to shake hands or further a conversation. *He moves quickly.* Her eyes completed an observation of his face and physique. *More impressive the nearer he is.* She readjusted herself. Fixed attention toward the chalkboard.

Luke tried again. "Your dress is gorgeous."

"It's not the dress you admire," Sandra coldly objected.

"Okay ... When class ends, let's go to the Cougareat. Share a bear claw, soft drink. Crazy name for a pastry shop—BYU Cougars." Luke chortled. "Get it?"

I got it. She glared. Saw only Luke's smile. *Charming.*

Professor Graham entered the room, interrupting Luke's fixation on Sandra's natural allure. He also interrupted Sandra's fixation on Luke's noble, albeit boyish—or perhaps boorish—approach.

She concealed her appreciation for Luke's efforts and waved a hand to urge him back to his seat. Luke abandoned the back-row desk. Remained next to Sandra. He had no desire to jump desks or step over students to return.

Our heroes uttered silent prayers. Luke acknowledged Heavenly Father. *Thanks for creating such beauty. You do great work, Lord. Please forgive me. Why do you put someone so tempting in front of me, then say, "Don't be aroused"?*

His heart thrashed. Stomach leapt. He wrested to control unwanted impulses. *She is sexy,* he mused between glances. Raced through moral, spiritual instructions to avert his eyes from Sandra. It didn't work. Her face, lovely; form, exquisite. The dress displayed her ample gifts. An unforgivable presence beguiled Luke; but meant no intent to embarrass himself, Sandra, or students in the classroom. There was more, something unexplainable that came from her.

Sandra's prayer was angry. *Why, God? I've asked thousands of times. Why am I what I am? I don't know this guy. He seems likable, handsome. You require our paths to cross; I can do nothing to encourage affection. I am what I am, like you. Why did ...*

Dr. Graham uttered a spiel about the newest class of graduate students, the future, great expectations, accomplishment. Of course, the gospel of Jesus Christ, all things must be done with the Spirit of the Lord, establishment of Zion, dispersed Israel ...

Luke glanced again toward Sandra. *She's a testimony builder, for sure. She could prove there is a God.* He shook himself. Attempted to purge sensual thoughts. *Good things happen sitting on the back row. Ugh. I left my stuff there.* Luke gazed at the rear exit. His belongings rested on an empty desk. *I hurdled two rows, five bodies. If the class could see what I'm seeing, nothing would get done. She's gotta know the influence she has over me. What is happening?*

A lifetime of religious instruction and a two-year mission inundated Luke to conclude that sensual thoughts are criminal. *A man of God should not entertain temptation. Melchizedek priesthood holders should turn away from the devil's temptations. She is no devil. She is beautiful. Has brains or wouldn't be in grad school. Wonder if she has a testimony of the Church? If not, I'll give her mine.* Caught in a cycle, Luke looked then turned away. *Look, no turn away.*

Sandra continued her conflicted self-dialogue. *Could he or anyone truly be interested in me? Not if they knew. All any man wants to see is what this dress shows. I told Mom it's too loud. She made me bring it. I'm here, wearing it at BYU, marriage capital of the world for Mormons. On the other hand, Luke seems nice, certainly courageous. I'm being watched. He keeps looking. I hate what I am. I should ask, find if he's genuine or someone fake, shallow? ... Yes, that's what he is.*

Dr. Graham droned mundane, routine words of academia. It meant little. Sandra's mind mired with ideas of desire. *To have someone look at you, to touch like romantic partners, must be a thrill. Argh, curiosity is an aggravation. I'll never know romance. It's best if this guy leaves me alone. He cannot succeed. Why these thoughts … these feelings?*

The class period ended. Students exited.

Sandra stood face to face with Luke. Her dress now his new favorite piece of clothing. "That is a beautiful outfit. You wear it well. You should model it for the designer."

Pleased, Sandra reminded herself to limit interactions with Luke. *This is a mistake. I need to get away. I cannot be provocative. Do not invite danger.* She fought back tendencies to look at him. Her other side reasoned, *0.it's good to gather information. If I initiate approaches, I will pay for it later. Keep your distance. Control curiosity. Too great a price.*

"Thank you," Sandra surrendered. "It's polite to compliment my dress. Me." Sandra seemed composed but struggled inside herself. She walked to the exit. Fled the room, Luke in pursuit.

"Your shoes. They're … lovely," he blurted.

Sandra halted her escape, became impatient. "My shoes? You're focused elsewhere. It's not my shoes you see."

"You're right. I'm looking at you. Women are impressed when men compliment their shoes. I'm doing my best … There's something unusual about you. Open a window for me, please."

Sandra searched Luke's face for a clue. She turned sharply. Took steps of escape.

"When's your next class?" he called.

"Why do you ask?" Annoyed, yet pleased.

"Let's go to the Wilkinson Center. Your first time on campus?"

"No. First semester of classes."

"Wilkinson Center. Largest building on campus. A popular place. Students gather for classes, concerts, dances, plays, church services. Bookstore is there. Bakery, soft drinks, snacks, the Cougareat." Luke grinned. "Cafeteria, dining services, commissary, theaters, auditorium, BYU apparel, bowling alley, bank, ping pong, TV room, shops … has it all. My treat! A drink or mid-morning snack. Let's learn more about the class of 1980. Get acquainted." Luke smiled again.

"Thanks, I have commitments." Sandra executed her getaway. Hurried down the hallway.

Luke raised his voice. "I do love that dress."

She reached the end of the hall, made a right turn. Gone. No nod or wave.

Next class period, Luke arrived earlier. Placed his gear on the desk nearest the exit. On alert, he waited for Sandra. She entered. He waved for her to sit next to him. Enthralled.

Sandra was pleased to see his enthusiasm. Although attracted to Luke, she kept a bitter secret deep inside her. *Safe territories must be maintained.*

Luke opened plastic containers filled with grapes, apple slices, and orange segments neatly aligned on her desk. "It's a peace offering. I apologize for the tension I created. You make a wonderful first impression. Please, accept my apology."

Sandra wanted to compliment him. She resisted. "Luke, I have my issues. I'm sure you're a good person. You are considerate, but it's irrelevant. I cannot be a cordial acquaintance. Can you accept that?"

"May I share a thought?" Luke asked. "Do groups outperform individuals?"

"They do."

"Let's organize a group of three or five of the brightest, talented individuals. We'll prepare for assignments, assist one another, study for exams together. Good idea?" He offered Sandra the grapes.

"Smart idea. I see your point. I am an excellent researcher and writer with quantitative math and statistical skills. What do you offer?" She'd voiced a challenge. *Top that.* Sandra popped a grape in her mouth.

"Theoretical, bibliographical research capabilities with strong rhetorical talents … plus a good curveball." Luke winked. Crunched an apple slice.

Sandra smiled. Considered Luke good-natured. No matter how well he behaved, she built barriers. Nevertheless, Sandra consistently caught his attention.

Sandra and Luke occupied desks next to each other with the **back-row rowdies** who comprised their study group. He arrived early, ready to engage conversations with Sandra, if she allowed. It gave them chances to interact. Sandra, the heart of his daydreams.

Sandra and Luke's interactions were observed by students in class, who good-humoredly cheered and jeered them all semester long. Onlookers concluded that Luke cared for Sandra. Obvious too, Sandra was distant, unapproachable, chiefly toward Luke. Few women attended BYU graduate school in the late 1970s. Plenty of gentlemen sought dates with Sandra, but she pushed everyone away. No lifejackets.

Eight class periods into the semester, Luke placed a Hershey's Kiss on Sandra's desk. Acted unaware of her entrance into class. She sat. Looked at the Kiss. Scoured the room for a perpetrator. Luke spoke to a fellow rowdy, his back toward her. Sandra unwrapped the chocolate, placed it on her tongue, leaned across the aisle, slapped him on the back. "Good play, buddy. Thanks for the Kiss."

Luke spun toward her. "You're welcome," he replied. "I assume I'm the first to give you a Kiss."

"Nope. And you won't be the last. I prefer sucking Kisses." Alarms sounded in her mind. *Geez. He'll think I'm opening myself. I can't encourage his flirtations.*

"I have more Kisses." He hoped she would interact.

Stubbornly, she stared forward and continued to savor the sweet chocolate. *End it now. It's gotta stop*, she cautioned herself. Looked at Luke. "I spoke before thinking. The Kiss is accepted. Stop flirting."

Frustrated, Luke placed another Kiss on her desk. *Why does she act this way?* Seconds passed. "I'm gonna tell my buddies I gave you many, many kisses today." He tossed Kisses on her desktop. They rested against her forearm. She gazed forward. Professor Graham lectured.

Sandra cared for Luke more than he could imagine. She enjoyed his notes. Each surprise left on her desk. He made inroads, but she could not allow him to continue.

"A chocolate Kiss isn't the only pleasurable taste we may share," Luke requited.

"I don't kiss boys. Especially you, Luke. Your cutesy double entendre," she whispered just loud enough for him to hear. Placed a finger to her mouth and sternly shook her head to quiet him. Swinging back, her attention concentrated toward Dr. Graham, yet she daydreamed, *kisses*.

Students packed to leave. Luke asked Sandra, "Where are you headed?"

"To the library. I reserved a carrel. This campus has more students than places to study. It's an investment."

"Do I have permission to walk with you? Please don't push me away," Luke earnestly pled with hands in prayer. "It's a short distance. We could turn a profit from it."

"Turn a profit?"

"A rowdy in our group offered me five dollars if he saw you walking with a guy on campus. Half is yours," Luke explained.

"Wait … You made a bet—"

"Okay, Sandra. You get 20 percent, but I'm not going any higher."

"Luke. Did you really make a bet?"

"No, I didn't." Luke looked into Sandra's face. Confessed. "I'd enjoy talking to you without being in a classroom. Please? I won't cause problems. Scout's honor." He raised three fingers.

A suggestion beyond her rules. *If not Luke*, she surmised, *another guy will be eager to replace him*. Sandra felt confident she could control Luke. Could she control herself? Luke smiled with a hopeful face. Sandra scowled. "Okay. Don't make a habit of it."

Luke returned the scowl as the two sustained their stares until Sandra broke into a smile.

She threw her wadded Kiss wrappers at him.

"See. We can have fun, good times." Luke smiled. "Let's walk… and talk."

Their first stroll together between classes to the massive Harold B. Lee Library. Sandra showed Luke a carrel tucked into a secluded part of the fourth level. It was dark. Ominous. Yet quiet.

During their walks, Luke listened to Sandra's political views, ideas of social changes, and Church viewpoints on doctrine, history, and culture. Sandra, an entrenched Mormon, challenged with progressive ideas toward gender equality and acceptance for outlier groups. He listened, agreed, argued. Captivated with her beauty and intelligence, he daydreamed.

She sparingly revealed personal family history. "My parents are shields, protecting our well-being." Luke appreciated Sandra's voluntarily self-disclosed personal information. Any increments within her history.

Outspoken regarding numerous issues. Closed off about her personal life, she warned suitors of her singularity, saying, "I am what I am. Never question that." Doors closed whenever Luke stepped too near Sandra's privacy. Luke progressed mere inches near the secret she hid. She pushed him away.

These heroes traversed walkways weekdays and weekends. Attended classes, chatted, engaged group research, collected bibliographies, and, on occasion, sat together at Forums and Devotionals. Their labor consumed time. Knowledge became gold nuggets. Critical thought grew with a purpose, especially as they deliberated with the rowdies.

In addition to their studies, Luke taught two adjunct classes, acted as Dr. Portman's graduate assistant, and worked part-time at a bank in downtown Provo. Sandra, a quantitative math whiz-kid, assisted Dr. Clawson as a graduate-student researcher. An enormous asset in the department.

Frequent encounters between Luke and Sandra were incredibly stressful. Their hearts focused in one direction; their minds, notably Sandra's, another. Although resistant to Luke's romantic gestures, she took interest with certain pleasure at his attempts. *If.*

Adventure—fantasies of love and companionship—filled their daydreams. The distractions became nearly intolerable, though they entertained themselves.

Luke sometimes approached with hints of romance, but Sandra rebuffed him with assorted obstructions. Her rejections stung. It hurt to see Luke wince. She felt it warranted. Deemed the actions *for his own good.*

Sandra felt inexplicably drawn to Luke. Believed his approaches forbidden, too intrusive. She insisted on distance between them. Luke determined to find connections. Each approach met with pushbacks. Constant frustrations.

Despite foolhardy skirmishes, heroes cannot be deterred. Destinies are required to be played. A love story is beset with challenge, misunderstood behaviors, fear, eventual reclamation. Like a Shakespearian play. Tragedy, error, woe—necessary elements.

Touches are, as the word implies, touch and go. Test, see. What can you do? How far? Curiosity, wanting to touch, is painful for two healthy, intelligent, attractive university students. The desire to know how a person may feel. Soft and accepted? Firm or forbidden? Smooth, pleasurable? Each considered some touches as needed. Others unwanted. Add a religious oligarchy that suggested innocent, curious touching behaviors will lead to thermonuclear war—sex and babies. Oh, my ... **Battles raged.**

Sandra, with each step, every conversation, persisted as a daily distraction for Luke. Impressed that she applied minimal makeup to attract attention to herself. The attraction? Her natural and intelligent self.

Enamored with Sandra, Luke desired connections. He replayed a daydream: holding her in his arms, kissing her too-seldomly-seen smile. *How would she feel in my arms?* The conclusion from his daydreams, *exceptional.* Luke felt desperation. He hoped, confidently, that she desired to be touched by him.

Though restrained, each desired to touch the other with hands, lips, hearts. To kiss Sandra was Luke's dream come true. In her mind, she imagined his kisses too. Sandra welcomed his presence but avoided eye contact to deter unwelcome touches. Her treatment toward all boys. Tempted, always. An inexperienced young lady. She

daydreamed to hold Luke, touch his hands, embrace romantically...
kiss. When thoughts continued too long, they ended with spoken
words. "Enough. This is not my fate."

Invasions of personal space grew. Sandra occasionally patted
Luke's shoulder to compliment him. He enjoyed her touches. He
feared to go where Sandra may object but continually tempted.
They learned of unwelcomed touches ...

Sandra and Luke were alone, studying for an examination,
seated closely to each other. He felt her warmth. No words. No
gestures. They scribbled with pens. Eyes focused on notes, papers.
The room deathly silent; the clamor in their minds like a freight
train. Neither wanted to go, nor could they remain.

One of us should do something.

> *What is his cologne? He smells wonderful.*
> *What should I say? How shall I escape him?*

What does she want me to do?
She knows I'm here. Why is she ...

> *Lean left, bump him. Say, "Sorry." Leave. Fast.*
> *Why am I the person I am? Why?*

She wants to be kissed ...

Luke took the initiative. No longer able to resist, he grabbed her
fingers, lifted them, kissed her hand.

Flustered by the touch, Sandra abruptly pulled back. Rose to her
feet. "That is wrong, Luke. Why?"

"I couldn't help myself."

"You do not have permission to touch me. Not like that."

"I've seen kings and presidents kiss hands. Nothing improper.
C'mon ... my intent is innocent," Luke defended himself.

"We agreed, Luke. You violated our trust."

"Sandra, we're seated close to each other. I felt your warmth. You felt it too. What can I do to compliment you without getting bitten? Something meaningful exists between us."

"Luke, what must I do to get through to you? I like you. I think you're a good person. There is much any girl would find charming about you, but there can be no romance between us. Respect my demands. I won't say anything to anyone. I don't want to cause trouble. It is wrong to touch me that way. It's not innocent. Respect my wishes. Cease your approaches for my affection. I am what I am."

"Sandra, I'm dumber than a sack of rocks. I don't see or understand you. I'm willing to learn. Hell's bells, help me. You say, 'I am what I am.' What does that mean?" Luke reddened with irritation.

"I need to leave," Sandra said. "Thanks for your help. I appreciate your assistance in our studies ... assignments."

"Please, don't go. I'll buy lunch. Dinner, tonight? Anything, please." Luke unabashedly sought forgiveness.

"It's kind to offer. No. I have much to do." As Sandra left the room, she admitted her attraction for Luke with the customary self-caution. *I enjoy him. He is well-intentioned, but I cannot allow this. He cannot do this to me.* She fled. *I don't want to hurt him. Stay on task. End the daydreams.*

The pattern so very common. Predictable. Hope extended, then rejection. Luke's last advance far too much. Confused, the door he hoped to open slammed shut. Small gains instantly taken back. Luke, shaken, would regroup, reassert himself. Nature and spiritual forces never fail to make connections. This episode of rough weather helped shape the grandeur of their landscape, like Timpanogos, towering over them.

Steps Toward Understanding

A man who does not think for himself does not think at all.

—Oscar Wilde

EARLY MONDAY EVENING, LUKE ventured to Sandra's carrel. He hoped to resolve matters from their altercation. They were distant, silent with each other for days. Classes and group studies strained.

He bounded up the noisy stairwell, entered the silent fourth level, passed yards of bookshelves to the dark, windowless Lee Library walls, and saw her seated silhouette at the carrel.

Luke sucked up his guts. "Thought I'd be the lone person here tonight. No family home evening for you?"

Sandra turned to observe Luke—tall and handsome—behind her. Pleased to see him, she displayed no trace of concern. *Keep your eyes away. Face forward.* "Graduate studies are demanding. I don't need excessive, redundant home evening lessons." *Every Monday night I've been pestered by the Church. Monday Night Football, popcorn with Mom and Dad—that got us closer instead of incessant church lessons. BYU won't let me escape it.* "Nor do I wish to hear tear-stained testimonies, eat brownies, gobble snickerdoodles, or drink Kool-Aid." Sandra spoke without eye contact.

Luke chuckled. "We stand on common ground. I wanna puke each time some naïve idjit asks Heavenly Father to bless all high-fat, non-nutritive foods and sugar-sweetened drinks to 'nourish and

18

strengthen our bodies and do us the good we need.' What sacrilege bullshinola. They're asking God to turn water into wine."

"People never think about what they say," Sandra agreed. "Church duties and gatherings are an annoyance."

"We're agreed again. Do people ever consider what they say? How they behave or think?" Luke asked, curious to hear her answer. As well-read in doctrinal topics, scriptures, Church history, and social behavior as she was, he wanted Sandra to look at him, engage in a lively conversation.

"I need to study, not answer your questions." Sandra possessed ideas to express but felt vulnerable. *He's far too appealing. Don't look.* She wanted to see him, yet acted unaffected. Postured, attuned to her studies in the carrel.

Luke tried once more. "Professor Douglas quoted Russell. Highly relevant in my opinion: 'Most people would sooner die than think; in fact, they do so.'"

"Bertrand Russell is atheist," Sandra advised. "No one on this campus will consider his words valuable. Besides, Sheldon and Hutchison have stated similar words."

"Okay. But the reasoning is accurate. On this campus, it's apparent. Unless the mouthpiece of God on Earth—our prophet— tells people what to do and think, it won't happen." Luke sighed. "It's the difference between dogmatism and critical thought. How else would Black people gain full fellowship in the Church unless President Kimball sanctioned it as a revelation from God?"

"It's called hegemony, Luke. Our acceptance of domination upon the masses by the powerful few or individual. In this case, it's the Church or the prophet. It's how those in power maintain control. Go away. I'm studying." Her hand motioned for him to skedaddle.

"The only way faithful members will not attend church is when the Brethren tell them a disease, a virus, or idea threatens their families at spiritual get-togethers. The real diseases are teachers, leaders, who are more dogmatic than sensible."

A distant voice demanded, "Quiet."

"Your voice is carrying. This is a library … your way of impressing women? Leave," Sandra urged in a hushed tone.

Luke defeatedly nodded. "It's family night worldwide in the Church. Let me take you to a place where we can eat food that doesn't need to be blessed, or altered, to properly nourish us. We are scholarly, persuasive individuals. Let's discuss issues. You needn't worry," he whispered. "I won't kiss your hand. Promise." Luke wanted her with him … eternally.

"Thank you. I will remain here." Sandra said. *Yes*, her unspoken response.

Luke's a daring thinker, she thought. It pleased her. *Time spent sharing ideas or resolving conundrums is tempting.* She waved her hand. *He should leave.*

Luke, disappointed, exited the library. A light rain fell as he hustled to the Wilkinson Center, ordered a cup of soup and half a turkey sandwich on wheat to go. He sneaked the food past the library security guards.

Luke stood again behind Sandra's carrel. "I wish I knew why you push me away." His sudden presence startled Sandra, but she did not turn toward him. "I'd love being your friend if you'd allow. I want to know you."

"It's nothing you did. It's my issue," Sandra said. She focused on her papers. Faced away.

"You can shoo me away. It won't change how I feel, my opinions. You have intellectual, spiritual, and physical beauty. You need to be told that. No cause to be dismissive toward me or others. There are many on campus who believe the same." Luke paused, stared at the back of her head.

"Here, this will help keep you going. We'll walk tomorrow." Luke dropped the smuggled food and bottle of water in her carrel.

She sensed his departure. Uttered a voiceless *thank you*. Emptiness overtook her. She wanted to give him a hug. A big one—for his kindness, compassionate affection. Warmly drawn to Luke, she fought encouragement. She rubbed a tear from her eye and returned to studies.

Sandra sought answers for her unexplained attraction to Luke. *Is it merely his height, demeanor, athletic build? Professors and students are drawn to him. His words? Luke is a collaborator in the delivery of group presentations and written assignments.* She tried to discount his goofball sense of humor. *He continually has people chuckling while engaging their labors. A fun guy. His leadership and influence are mysteriously offbeat.*

Sandra challenged him as they walked. "As a returned missionary you often swear. Why?"

"I blame my grandmother. She's the first person I heard utter a profanity and flip the bird, all in the same sentence." He pantomimed the gesture.

Where did he graduate from high school? Odd usage of grammar? She smiled.

"A wonderful grandma," Luke continued. "Tough as nails. Knew what bears do in the woods." Luke avoided oncoming students who crowded the walkways crossing the quad. *Stepping on the grass is forbidden at BYU.* "Loved wine, beer. Even received her temple endowments. Grandma never minced words. Had a tender heart. Give you the shirt off her back, if needed. Very kind. She died some time ago. Wish you could've met her. You would've liked her, Sandra. The two of you would've made great friends. We have a big family reunion near her birthday each year."

"Did you profane on your mission?" She stepped into Luke to avoid those headed the opposite direction. *Feet do not touch the emerald grass.*

"Yes. Like J. Golden, Brigham Young, other noted Church leaders. They all profaned. Any athlete or frustrated leader has used 'em. So what? Twain said, 'Under certain circumstances, urgent circumstances, desperate circumstances, profanity provides a relief denied even to prayer.' As Isaiah implied, why make people 'an offender for a word.' We understand words have no meaning except what we assign to them."

"You use weird expressions," Sandra noted. "How'd that start?" She avoided oncoming walkers.

"There are times I get my *mords wixed* up." Luke chuckled. "That's a Spoonerism. Named for a British clergyman ... last name was Spooner. Routinely transposed the sounds of two differing words while preaching, like saying 'mood fart' instead of 'food mart.'" Luke laughed at his own Spoonerism.

"See, that's why you are so goofy. Have you been doing this long?" Her final query. She side-stepped a coed that ran through the congested throng.

"Most of my life," Luke replied. "Think I'm goofy? You should hear my buddy, Sam."

"You're articulate, persuasive, an excellent writer—" Sandra began but was interrupted by Luke.

"Got a B+ in technical writing. Dr. Portman said the course would prepare me to write a thesis." Luke held up a thumb.

"Don't interrupt," Sandra fired back. "In our study group, or when responding to Professors Graham, Douglas, or Whitton, you argue with brilliance. You're a golden boy, yet you do, or say, the dumbest things, like Spoonerisms."

"Please, don't call me a golden boy. Alexander, Wilson—they're the golden boys. You're one of them. You know it."

Sandra grabbed Luke. Stopped their walk. People bounced off them. She stared at Luke with tension. "Boy? What do you know?"

Luke realized he said something unpleasant, raced to recall his words. Prepared an apology. "Sandra, gender has nothing to do with this. Our culture, BYU, Mormonism, world governments are weighted toward the masculine. I'm complimenting you. There are only three women in any of our graduate classes. You're the best, male or female. The best of us all. Smartest and best. You say I'm goofy. You never explain 'I am what I am.' It's all queer." Irritated, Luke walked briskly ahead.

"Okay. Sorry. You used words I didn't understand. I mistook your compliment." Sandra hurried to keep pace with his speed.

"I'm not all that bright. Wish I was more like you … I'm a washed-up jock trying to get a master's degree."

"What do you mean, 'washed-up jock'?"

"I wanted to be an Academic All-American baseball player. I'm not either one, if that's grammatically correct. I don't play baseball any longer. I'm not academic. – We should discuss why you denigrate, push me away?" Luke accelerated.

Sandra ran, pushed him off the walkway under the Tree of Wisdom sculpture. "You wouldn't believe me if I told you." A finger on his chest. "I am the furthest from any women you've met. More conflicted than you."

"Give it a try. Did you ever think I am attracted to such a woman? Speaking of egos, where'd you get yours? What makes you think you're so special? Should someone—"

Sandra grabbed his arm, shook him. "I know what you want. It's not G-rated. My parents told me to watch for guys who think with that goal in mind. I am special. So special you should shout just to stand next to me." A heated Sandra glared.

"Hmmm ... really? Did your parents forget the lesson on humility, kindness, appreciation for the best efforts of people?" Luke said, a bit winded. "Can we be friends?"

"Okay ... friends we can be. I like your qualities. Kindness toward me. We can take advantage of each other. Please, make no mistake, I'm speaking of our academic gifts. Leave romance and sex out of it."

Luke stood in contemplation. "Can we be real good friends? Best friends? Talk to each other about problems or matters unrelated to BYU? I have wonderful discussions with best friends. No romance, okay. Let's put academics and grad school in the same category. Agreed? Best friends have meaningful conversations. Okay?" He offered his hand for resolution and flashed the smile she slyly enjoyed.

Sandra didn't want to let him know she welcomed the idea of best friends. Luke occupied her thoughts more than she divulged. *A step inside each other's circles has multiple advantages.*

They shook hands to confirm their agreement. "Best friends."

"Nice grip," Luke complimented. "May I say, your hand feels terrific. An electrifying handshake."

Sandra pulled back. Slapped at his hand. "You are a goofball," she said, smiling.

Luke clicked a pen, then pulled a card from his shirt pocket. "I never told my best friends how hot they look," smiling. "This is my card from the bank. I'm writing my home number on it. You're welcome to call, anytime. Girls can call guys now."

Sandra continued to smile while Luke scribbled. She took the card and nodded.

"I'm not asking for your number. You can give it to me when I've earned your confidence. I'm the bank's collector." Luke grinned. His eyebrows bounced. "Should you call the bank ... please do. Leave your name. Say you wish to speak with me. The bank will think you're a delinquent account. Which you are." He snickered. "I resolve delinquencies."

"Thank you," Sandra shook her head. "I have no debts that need your assistance, sir."

"I need to get to the bank. Let me walk you to the library entrance." They rushed. "Thanks, Sandra. I hope you'll consider me the bestest friend ever. I want you to know, I fell in deep like with you that first day you walked into class."

"Luke, you're skirting near romance."

"I apologize. I'll take control of that matter immediately. Sometime late tomorrow."

"Luke," she protested.

"I need to hustle. You're my best friend. Talented, bright, caring. I hope to be a bridesmaid at your wedding."

Sandra suddenly thunderstruck. *What does he think? Know? Mixed metaphors, analogies? Confused or cunningly sly? What is he? Gold? Pyrite? Glass or diamond?*

"See you in class tomorrow. Wear my favorite dress. It's gorgeous. Bye." Luke hurried away.

Puzzled by his words, she shouted, "What do you like about that dress?"

"What's in it."

Seated at the carrel, Sandra contemplated their discussion. *As intelligent as Luke is, he's unaware of his inferences. Yes, he wants romance, contractually consigned to limitations. Friendship has greater benefits than detriments for each of us. Particularly obtaining degrees*

together. A best friend is valuable. I've fallen in like with him too. No more. Stops where it is, right now.

She opened books, scattered papers, and ... giggled.

A Star Shines

All truths are easy to understand once they are discovered;
the point is to discover them.
The laws of nature are written by the hand of God
in the language of mathematics.

—Galileo Galilei

SANDRA, A TRUE ODDITY among so many male graduate students shone like a bright star. Her light led mariners home on a dark evening under unruly skies.

Dr. Clawson raised two fingers above his head. *Two minutes until the class period ends,* Sandra alerted herself. Dr. Clawson intently observed Sandra's instruction skills along with her overhead projections of hand-drawn formulae that explained quantitative mathematics to validate statistical conclusions. Sandra made math understandable. No one adrift. As the alarm sounded, men applauded. A returned missionary from Japan shouted, "*Subarashii, masuta sensei.*" Sandra rubbed away her overhead scribbles. Paid little attention to the all-male class who cheered.

"Wow. Excellent, Sandra." Luke praised her as he unplugged a Hewlett-Packard calculator from a wall socket. "You make math fun. You done good."

"I done what?" Sandra asked.

"You done good."

"Luke, this is why you can be so … I don't know … confusing? Where do you find these expressions?"

"I'm complimenting your golden boy qualities. Accept my praise. You're the brightest," Luke openly admitted. "Look how Clawson fawns over you."

Sandra tensely gazed at Luke. "Why the awkward use of grammar?"

Luke smiled. "In high school I had a bishop whose elderly mother came from Europe, the old country. Didn't speak a word of English. She'd sit in church, understood nothing from speakers or teachers. Everyone in their family was totally dedicated to the gospel."

Sandra grew frustrated. "I asked, why the awkward grammar?"

"A simple, good man." Luke briefly turned melancholic. "Dairy farmer with a PhD in cows. Little formal education … worked so hard the skin of his hands permanently embedded with grime, unable to be washed clean." Luke rubbed his own hands. "His soiled hands were the cleanest I've known. All my buddies in high school, everyone, understood. Whenever we'd receive awards at school, he'd say, 'Ya done good.'" Luke hurried them both. "Let's get outta here. The walkways are crowding."

"Did he know his grammar was improper?" Sandra rapidly kept pace with Luke.

"He was a bishop. Like Jessie Evans Smith would sing, 'he that hath clean hands and a pure heart.' Milked cows twice a day, every day, including Sundays, holidays, through wind, snow, and rain. Nothing deterred him from those cows. He sat through our church/quorum lessons, falling asleep from fatigue. He'd wake in time for closing prayer. Compliment the instructor. Told a story. 'You done good' coming from him meant exceptional. We'd smile. I doubt he knew his grammar was wrong." They exited the building and headed to the library amid droned conversations and footfalls of students on the walkways.

"I'd like to meet this bishop."

"Wish you could … he died." Luke paused. "Sorry, I'm sentimental. We're alive. You done good, Sandra. Like you a ton …

Especially when smiling at me." He put his hand to her upper arm, lightly rubbed, smiled with a nod. Walked to his next class.

"Thanks for telling me about him. Be careful who you like," Sandra cautioned. She stood alone. Watched him leave as passersby on the walkway navigated around her. *Tell me more stories.*

General conference passed. So did the World Series, Halloween. Daily activities included papers, exams, projects with due dates. Another daily routine? Attempts to access Sandra's heart. All adeptly squashed. Her words well-rehearsed with impenetrable walls, spoken as though she anticipated when each of Luke's tries would occur. Luke, however, persevered.

As best friends, their conversations were fun and, at times, enlightened. One cold morning they strolled to the library to gather data. Luke spoke with pride, "I've been a Yankee fan my whole life. They won their twenty-second world championship this season."

"Really? Go Dodgers," Sandra teased.

Chagrined, Luke continued his tale. "In 1960, I was a little guy, home alone watching game seven of the World Series on TV. Bottom of the ninth, Yankees tied with Pittsburgh, 9-9. Pirate second baseman Bill Mazeroski comes to bat. Hits a walk-off home run to win the series." The whole time he spoke Luke acted out the pitch, swing, home run trot, and emotional conclusion.

"I was devastated, crying uncontrollably. My mom came home, saw me in tears. And asked, 'What's wrong?' I gasped through my sobs, 'The Yankees lost the World Series. I can't believe God would let the Yankees lose.'"

Sandra smiled. *An overgrown boy. Cute. In need of a hug. It's endearing, yet I cannot be his consort.*

"So, Sandra, anything that makes you laugh? Gives you goosebumps? What makes you happy?"

She thought briefly, understood it wasn't an *I gotta run* moment. "I suppose the gospel. I find great interest in the Church. Unique ideas, temple architecture, controversial history, pre- and post-mortal doctrines. I don't consider it perfect, honestly, I have challenges. It's unusual, though. Totally American. A certain satisfaction with it."

"Agreed. The Church is acting much better with race relations. The latest revelation took its time getting here," Luke responded.

"My dad took issue with the revelation but consented. His history is in southeast Missouri. He raised his arm to the square during conference." Sandra smiled

"As did my parents," Luke affirmed. "My parents still adhere to racist views. I continue to question myself with race, other discriminatory attitudes. — Sandra, in addition to the Restoration, what gives you a kick?"

"A kick? Pounding your butt in racquetball. That would make my day complete," Sandra teased.

"You would gain pleasure humiliating me in some athletic competition? Is feminism on trial? What's wrong with a kiss?" Luke asked.

Sandra laughed. "You've already given me Kisses. The chocolate ones. I prefer your butt in a sling."

"I'm a good athlete," Luke admitted. "I have — what? — three, four inches on you? My stretch and reach are longer—"

"Look, if you're too afraid," Sandra interrupted, quickening her steps, "I can find someone—"

"Gal, let's make bets on the outcome," he said, skipping ahead of her.

"Okay. Nothing to do with romance. Money is best." Sandra kept her smile.

"You're no fun, Sandra. I hoped for a kiss." Luke taunted with feigned tears.

"We're best friends. Let that suffice," Sandra demanded.

The romance part was tough, for each of them.

What could be tougher? An open time to play racquetball. All courts in the Richards Building were occupied with classes. Individuals reserved times to play when courts opened. Our heroes considered their classes, study-group obligations, research, work schedules. The only available court time, 2 p.m. Friday, the day after Thanksgiving. Fewer people on campus.

Thanksgiving

People are usually more convinced by reasons they discovered themselves than by those found by others.

—Pascal

LUKE INVITED SANDRA TO share Thanksgiving dinner with his family. She declined.

A four-day weekend gave her time to prepare for exams and complete written assignments. *Luke and his family are off-limits. I prefer to stay in Provo. Flying to Phoenix, returning to BYU inside a few, short days, is too costly. Christmas break allows me to fly home and remain a full two weeks before winter semester begins.*

At 4 p.m. Thanksgiving Day, Luke arrived at Sandra's off-campus apartment. Uncertain she'd be home, Luke hesitated in the well-worn hallway outside her door. *I'll start to tap dance if a guy's inside.* He prepared for her reaction to his uninvited appearance. *Nothing good ever happens unless you risk.* He crossed himself as the doorbell rang.

The door swung open to a neat but lived-in apartment. Cleanliness surely not a top priority with academics or godliness. She stood at the door in sweatpants, BYU sweatshirt, unruly hair, with ASU maroon fluffy slippers. A textbook in hand.

"What are you doing here?" she asked almost angrily. "How do you know where I live?"

"Sandra, you are alone today. I brought you Thanksgiving dinner. Happy Thanksgiving." With a cheery smile, he raised a large wicker basket full of goodies.

"How do you know I live here? Have you been following me? Should I call security? Seriously, Luke. This is an invasion. What's the word? **Stalking**."

"Sandra, please, we're best friends. You know I'm not a stalker. I only wanted to do something fun. You're away from your family. It's the gospel thing to do. I'll tidy your place. Consider me a person who loves and cares for you."

"You should care for me a little less." Stunned, taken off-guard, she fought to find the appropriate words.

"I'll make it good. Please taste the sweet potato pie. Besides, I want you well fed for tomorrow's epic battle. No excuses when I kick your racquetball butt." He lifted the heavy basket to his eyes and smiled for acceptance.

Curtly, she held out her arm with the book in hand. "Welcome. The pie better be good, you jerk."

Seated on stools at the countertop, they looked at empty plates. Calm. Content. Pleasant conversation replaced surprise and frustration.

"My intent wasn't to upset you, Sandra. We're best friends. Right? I know you're alone. I wanted to give you a taste of Thanksgiving. Afraid I'd find you here with a fella. Go home brokenhearted with all this turkey, food."

"So," Sandra inquired, "a student in one of your classes, who lives in this complex, saw the two of us in the library?"

"Yes. Asked if we're sweet for each other. It's a Mormon university. She thinks I have a crush on you. The way I act when around you. Boy, is she off base or what?"

Sandra knew Luke's fondness for her. Casual observers could see it. His behaviors most predictable. But Sandra, thus far, blocked every available port of entry into her heart.

"I need to have a conversation with that person," Sandra casually responded. "The pie is wonderful. Thanks."

"Well, people are supposed to fall in love, get married here. It's BYU. Happens all the time," Luke argued. "She's a few doors down. Sees you comin' in, goin' out all the time. She gave me your coordinates."

"Coordinates. A *Star Trek* term. I love *Star Trek*."

"As do I," Luke confessed. "I started watching reruns my freshman year at the TV room in the Wilkinson Center. Had no idea what I missed. My dad wouldn't let our family watch it at home. Suggested problems with Blacks, Asians, not to mention females as officers in command over men. Equality is not the future he wanted to see."

"Are you calling your dad racist? Sexist?"

"Spent his childhood in a rural community. Different time," Luke answered. "I've been his son more than twenty-five years. I am as much a bigot as he ... hopefully less. Mormons, Black people, white supremacy—all are connected. It's a part of our history, teachings."[1]

"Will Mormons recover? Can we accept Black people in our flock of white sheep?" Sandra questioned.

"We're what our parents learned from prior generations. Religiously taught to behave, think as we do. Good or bad, we learned it from them. The recent revelation has forced changes. My dad will be bothered to see a Black couple or an interracial marriage take place in a temple. It should improve BYU football and basketball. We'll see. A Black bishop or female supervisor would be difficult for my father to accept or even recognize."

"My family never missed *Star Trek*. Spock is my favorite character. He's the reason I took a philosophy course in logic at ASU. All we did during the semester was algebra, geometry, trig, a little calculus." Sandra brushed aside crumbs. "I even earned three math credits from the class."

"Three math credits, huh? Attaboy, girl."

Sandra stiffened. Her eyes rose, guardedly frozen on Luke's face.

---

[1] Joanna Brooks, *Mormonism and White Supremacy: American Religion and the Problem of Racial Innocence*, Oxford University Press, 2020. Interview aired with Dr. Brooks, June 12, 2020, KUER Radio, Salt Lake City, UT.

He smiled like he'd amused her. Luke innocently continued the conversation. "I've wondered what our world would be like if we were logical Vulcans like Spock on *Star Trek* rather than making decisions based on human emotions or ancient writings. Modern revelation, like Kimball's, opened the door for Blacks to enter mainstream Mormonism. It should help us keep pace."

"Spoken like one of the golden boys in the department," Sandra implied.

"I ain't no golden boy," Luke snapped. "I told you who the golden boys are. For that matter, I think you're the best of us all, not to mention the most beautiful."

"Again? Why do looks play into it in any way?" Sandra protested.

"Come on, Sandra. Research indicates that trust and leadership are more readily given to the attractive, tall, athletic mesomorphs. You possess all those traits with a brain to match. Hell, female prophets existed in the Bible.[2] You should be the next prophet. Or a bishop. You'd be a damn good one too."

"You have no idea. I'm equally qualified as any man," Sandra stated confidently, without hesitation. "Knock off the profanity, dammit. It's not the Mormon way."

They smiled. He looked at her. She looked at the countertop. Her eyes avoided his.

"Sandra, you are too cool. Whenever I'm with you, I see a remarkably bright, foxy person. You can be intimidating, a bit rough, but there is so much about you that any man would lo—"

"Don't you dare say love," Sandra shouted. "I know you look at my breasts. Guys have difficulty differentiating lust with love. *Star Trek* we can love, but you don't know me or what I am. Tell me, Luke, would you love me if my face were scarred or I lost a hand or fingers in an auto accident?"

Luke swiftly seized her head and looked straight into her eyes. Sandra resisted, prepared to strike him, but was captivated by his eyes locked on her own. "Would you love me if I were scarred?

---

[2] Sarah, Miriam, Deborah, Hannah, Huldah, Abigail, and Esther. Hebrew Bible adds Rachel and Leah for a total of nine. Where/Who are the great spiritual ladies of the latter-days?

Only one hand? Your question is valid. It's also a two-way street ... I'm convinced love and trust overpowers fear."

Luke released his hands from her head. Sat back. "Does it really offend you? Or are you actually pleased when I look at your beauty? Men never want women they marry to change or age. I understand your question. Men want women to remain as young and attractive as the day they married. Men rarely understand what babies do to a woman's body. There are scars you can see; those you can't."

Who hurt you? Sandra wondered. Without pause, she said, "I caution you. My dad taught me how to knock men into tomorrow who touch me like you just did."

"I'm not violent. You know that. I made no attempt to kiss you or express my affection in any way. I needed to make a point." He paused. "Your eyes are as pretty as your other body parts. Does it offend you when I look too long at your eyes?" He smiled. "Scars give people nobility, beauty, handsomeness; otherwise, their value is unrecognized."

"My point, as you grabbed me—"

"I held your head." Luke paused. "When we speak, please, look into my eyes," he declared.

"Okay." Sandra gathered her thoughts. "LDS members, especially BYU students, are too focused on marriage. Get into it totally unprepared—stupid—it's wrong." Quietly she said, "By the way, your eyes are nice."

"I don't disagree, I mean, about marriage," Luke clarified. "President Olsen told me during my mission departure interview that when I returned home, marriage is my next duty. I should 'hasten the day.' This last general conference, I attended my mission reunion. President Rekdahl, my first mission president, said that if we weren't married or engaged to be married by the time of our next reunion, we weren't fulfilling the Lord's errand. We'd reap great disappointment."

"Are you proposing to me? Sorry, pal, I'm not your salvation in this matter. You have no awareness of what I am."

"Not proposing," he smiled. "But keep the option on the table... both my mission presidents are General Authorities. These men have power. Tons of ethos. I supported the belief that General

Authorities knew more about how I should live my life than I do. But no longer ..." Luke's voice trailed away.

"Why would they give such crazy counsel to gullible missionaries?" Sandra asked, "How do they know if a kid without a degree is ready to marry?"

"Rekdahl is too full of himself. One of my former companions who sat next to me at the reunion said, 'He's full of shit' when Rekdahl told us to be married inside six months."

"You see, members can disagree with General Authorities. It is healthy for members to state challenges," a provisional Sandra approved. "Just because a man is a General Authority doesn't make him a qualified marriage counselor."

"'Tis better to marry than burn,' I suspect," Luke smirked.

"I'm certain the Brethren feel missionaries should marry quickly when returning home or they'll have premarital sex," Sandra said. "Future church activity and spiritual cleanliness is in jeopardy."

"Marry as soon as you get home so you can have guilt-free sex. Now that's brilliant counsel. Don't concern yourself whether you are prepared for marriage, have a degree, earning an income, or possess parenting skills. If not, you'll go home, have unmarried sex, and risk eternal damnation." Luke's sarcasm was clear.

"What is your solution?"

"Condoms."

"Whoa. That's radical. The sex act is improper."

"Really? It isn't true. Sex is proper, a natural, biological act. It's how we propagate our species. Built into us." Luke found Sandra's eyes and spoke decisively. "The way people think about sex is stigmatized by all religions. Our own church included. We all know people who feel dirty when they have sex, even three years into a marriage."

"Agreed, Luke. It psychologically, emotionally, and spiritually damages people."

"The Church is mistakenly advising you'll go to hell, suffer eternally if you have sex today. Marry in the temple tomorrow morning, you can have sex nine different ways with that person, go to church, take the sacrament, function in church callings—you're as pure as the driven snow." After a slight pause, he asked,

"Sandra, is sex evil? Bad? Satan's playground? We have learned in Graham's classes the ultimate touching behavior in the study of nonverbal communication is sex. It is constantly vilified by our own church leadership."

"Only when you're unmarried," Sandra said, confirming the LDS position. "Sex is special when done within the confines of marriage."

"*Confines*. Nice word selection, Sandra. Is sex a prison? Sex has been happening for centuries, millennia prior to religions having their sordid say in the matter."

"Relatively speaking, we're not that far removed from Neanderthals." Sandra found Luke's eyes, "Our intelligence limits with whom, when, where, how much, even why we have sex. I suggest Aristotle's golden mean. What is the balance between excess and deficiency? The who, when, where, how much?"

"If you provide answers to that—how religions regard sex—you'll be the first latter-day prophetess. Thank you, Sandra. Looking into your eyes, I now see your finest intellectual beauty."

"A female leader? Hah. Men would rather be castrated." Sandra laughed. "As Mae West learned, 'Too much of a good thing can be wonderful.' Again, your eyes are nice, handsome."

"Thanks, gal. Who knows? Heavenly Father already has answers. He's an omnipotent know-it-all. Kimball can ask the question and receive a revelation. That's the Mormon way. Trust me, I have reasonable questions I'd ask the Almighty." Luke opened his arms to Sandra. "I'm just saying, sex is painted as joyless, even evil, by those likely never engaging the act. Babies, legitimate or not, are called 'blessings.' Welcomed into the Church, baptized, sealed to families in the temple."

Luke excitedly tapped the counter as he continued, "Here's my example: I have an uncle who impregnated his girlfriend their senior year of high school. Shotgun marriage. Never served a mission. Later became a bishop, now a stake president. What did they do wrong? Babies happen. God bless 'em. Stop calling it *illegitimate*, *a mistake*, or *sinful*. Call it an act of love. Which it is. Possibly a bit off course, but within safe harbors."

"They could've taken precautions," Sandra responded. "I suppose rubbers are not easily made available to the righteous. Certainly not encouraged, as you propose."

"Convince my uncle their eldest love child is a mistake. No child or set of parents should be shamed for their conception."

"Thanks for helping me see the vision in your eyes. You are a golden boy." She grinned.

"Are you sweet-talking me?" Luke hoped for a kiss.

"We're best friends, Luke. I'd prefer your sweet potato pie recipe."

"Okay. Okay." He shook it off. "You'll find this interesting. A small group of experienced elders stood in front of the big wall in our mission headquarters where pictures of all the missionaries are pinned. Some two hundred pictures, all paired and organized into companions, areas, districts, zones, and leaders. While looking at the wall, President Olsen, out of the blue, announced, 'We'd have great leadership in this mission if it weren't for masturbation.'"

Sandra spontaneously laughed aloud. "Oh my ... did he really say that?"

"Why *soitenly*," Luke said, imitating the stooge, Curly. "We laughed and giggled nonstop the rest of the day. Truth should be as obvious. Missionaries are horny. Can't keep their hands off themselves. Put 'em in dry dock for two years, they become creative. The stories I could tell ... anyway, Olsen, in one sequence of zone meetings, separated the elders from the sisters. Sister Olsen took the lady missionaries to the Relief Society room. President Olsen sat the elders in the chapel. Even the married couples were included in the riot act. 'Stop masturbating!'" Luke's hands waved in the air.

Our heroes laughed aloud, chuckled, then fell into silence.

"Do you masturbate?" Sandra asked matter-of-factly.

Luke looked at her for some seconds. "I'm not going to say I haven't. I met elders on my mission who are peeping Toms, pedophiles, experienced sex prior to their missions, during their mission, or had/have sexual hang-ups, issues after missions. One thing the Church has difficulty addressing is sex and sexuality ... to answer your question ... I never resigned my leadership positions while on my mission or at home as a consequence of masturbation."

Another flash of quietness ensued.

"Do you want to ask if I masturbate?" Sandra asked unashamedly.

He looked into Sandra's face for an instant. "Don't need to ... already know."

"You know?"

"So do you. But I'm enjoying the conversation. I'll confess, I can't lie on my stomach and think of you at the same time."

Both snickered.

"There you go again. How do you do it?" Sandra asked.

"Do what?"

"Find humor in a terribly tense situation or circumstance. Being goofy?"

"Sandra, I'm not as confident as you suppose I am. I use humor to avoid confrontation. Embarrassing myself. Exposing my weaknesses, faults. Discovered it years ago. Rather have people laugh at or with me than be exposed. Humor and laughter are capable allies. When my intellect fails, laughs and giggles buy me time for escape. It's useful when going into danger. You call it goofy. It's my standard for self-protection. Better than dodging. Another Mormon thing to do."

"What faults or weakness do you have?" Sandra dug deeper.

"Look who's talking? Miss 'You Don't Know Me. What I Am,'" Luke challenged.

"I know my own standard for self-protection," Sandra emphasized. "It's best no one knows me. What I am."

"Bullshit, Sandra. I've heard you say that far too often. Professor Graham taught us that everyone hides tons of things about themselves from others. Risking self-disclosure is the only way to gain trust in leadership, small groups, or interpersonally. Fear controls us. So, what is it you fear? That I could love you, be a closer friend?"

"It goes beyond fear. Quite far. Yeah, I share the same opinion as Graham. We each hide plenty of garbage about ourselves. Before you marry someone, discover what they have hidden. Sometimes we discover what a person has hidden far too late—well into marriage. On the other hand, there are tons of issues that best remain hidden. My situation runs deeper—wider—than you can imagine." Sandra held her ground.

"I try to understand you. You're not as tough as your posturing suggests. I'd like to know you. What you are. The most unique person I have ever met."

"Unique is overused—" Sandra faltered for words. "Well, tomorrow is the day we go to battle. Are you ready for racquetball, sport?"

"See you there. We can ride together if I come get you."

"No. I'll meet you at the courts. I'll be on time."

"Best efforts. One hundred percent at all times. Your terms. Correct?"

"Best efforts. One hundred percent always, but I'll make a deal with you." Sandra pointed a finger at him. "If I win tomorrow or remain inside five points of fifteen or eleven per set, you cease your challenges, stop pursuing me, trying to discover who I am. Give up your attempts for my attention. Love. Romance."

"Should I win"—Luke confidently folded his arms— "you'll tell your story. Open your heart for us to share love. Is that it?"

"Deal."

"Deal it is. You never should have impressed me the first day of class. You and that dress."

Luke returned home. Prepared himself for bed. Momentarily struck by his mirrored reflection. *I'm nearer thirty than twenty.* Male returned missionaries usually married between the ages of twenty-one and twenty-three. The adage in Utah: Mormons marry young, dumb, and poor. *We marry well below the national average in age (young), without a college degree (dumb), and with low incomes (poor). Each factor of young, dumb, and poor has a dependency upon the other. Spock would advise to marry later rather than sooner, get a degree, and have a job that pays well. Owe no debts for diamonds, gold rings, tuxedos, dresses, food, a big reception before conceiving children. "It is logical."*

Sandra reasons more clearly than I. Luke pointed at his mirrored image. *On the other hand, her story must be heard. What does she fear? Keep hidden?* Loudly he sung, *"Vincerò. Vincerò. Vincerò."*

Sandra pulled down the sheet and blanket of her bed. Dutifully knelt to deliver her nightly prayer as she did since childhood in a saintly LDS home. She confronted her reflection in a mirror near the bed, pondered an angst-ridden argument oft repeated to God. *Look at me. I neither enjoy nor appreciate this trial. Luke has touched my heart. He's unwelcomed. I could love him. But how? Tomorrow, Luke's loss at my hand will continue my torture, this infliction you forced upon me. Isolation. Despair. Are you a kind Father? Is there a Heavenly Mother to comfort or aid me?*

Like you, I am what I am. One day you must answer the reason for what I am inside. Unjust trials, from a kind, loving, benevolent Father in Heaven demand explanation. Hiding what I am is an offense, spiritually. Justice for all like I am expect restitution.

Fist clenched, she stared at her reflection. *No more secrets. I want to be loved for who, what I am inside. A miracle, not a threat. I pray not to be wasted as a piece of junk.*

The Kiss

To love and win is the best thing;
to love and lose is the next best.

—William M. Thackeray

SANDRA BOUNDED DOWN THE stairs of the Richards Building practically empty because of the holiday. The facility housed the racquetball courts. There Luke stood. On time. Early. *He can be so irritable.* She knew his behavior of punctuality should not be criticized. *It embellishes his golden boy persona.*

Luke's athletic tone was on full display. His gym trunks and sleeveless shirt gave Sandra pause. His muscular arms and legs were not as hairy as she imagined. *Baseball players hit homeruns with their butts. The best rear-ends are displayed by baseball sluggers. His fanny punched out a few homers*, she imagined … giggled.

Luke smiled as Sandra approached. "Hi. We've got court seven. Mickey Mantle's number. My lucky day."

"I know Mickey Mantle. Yankee centerfielder. Hall of famer. Hit 536 home runs in his career. Nothing about today has a thing to do with luck," Sandra said. The epitome of gall.

Luke stared at Sandra in her BYU-sanctioned gym outfit for women. Usually ill-fitted, uncomplimentary. Not so for Sandra. Worn with class. The minor violations applied to the outfit were not egregious—simply folded higher up her thighs. *Well done.* The definition in her calves and upper legs led to a rounded, firm backside. *Wow. What a sight.* He observed her legs in class those days she pushed BYU policy and wore shorter skirts, revealing an athletic, shapely tone. Her outfit tried but could not conceal the glorious profile of her breasts. Thick, long hair tied into a ponytail. Sleeves rolled to the shoulders. *Ready for competition.*

"You look sharp," he praised.

"Not too bad, yourself," she replied. "Let's get to it."

Sandra won the first set of the best of three with a 15–12 score. Luke expended more energy than expected. *I will lose Sandra's heart if I do not win the next two sets. Far better player than anticipated,* she's *a superb female athlete. Well-conditioned, finely coached, and skilled with experience.*

"Where did you learn to play this game?" Luke asked in near desperation. "I didn't think this was your first time on the court, but… Wow! You're wonderfully talented."

"My dad is an athletic instructor at ASU. How'd you think my BS degree was funded? My dad and scholarships. He made sure guys never took advantage of me." She motioned to the door. "Wanna leave?"

Luke stared at her. Their standoff lasted just seconds. *Okay. It's time to hit the high C note.* He bounced Sandra the ball and assessed her racquetball play from the first set. *Rarely retreats from the service lane. Slaps her shots low off the wall. Force her out of the service lane. Place better caroms into the corners. My advantage? Size, reach. Her strengths? Everything. Weaknesses? None … I'm in deep shinola.*

Set two, an intense battle. Each serve followed with multiple volleys. Weakly struck balls rarely scored points.

Sandra reasoned, *Keep working him. He's battered. His legs are weakening. His lungs too.*

Make her run. Force her back. Hit lower off the front wall. She wins anything higher. Luke determined, but troubled.

Sandra took full advantage of his weaker, backhanded slaps. He labored for each point earned. Luke managed a 14–13 edge, and held serve. With hope, he entered the service lane. *I have to win this set—now,* he determined with a flawless serve deep in Sandra's backhand corner

She slapped the shot hard, midway up the front wall. Luke forced back. The ball hit the floor ten feet from the back wall. Luke struck the ball far too high off the front wall. Sandra charged, placed a low, soft shot two feet up the wall. The ball died.

Luke charged the wall at full speed. He slid as he would feet-first into third base. Tapped the ball gently to the wall, eighteen inches above the floor. It bounced straight back at him. *Get out of the way!* He lifted his right leg high in the air, still sliding, twisted to avoid contact with the ball. He flailed his legs as the ball flew between them, over his chest, finally smacking the floor in a series of small bounces behind him.

"Outstanding," Sandra shouted. She stood close to midcourt more pleased than Luke. "We'll need to watch KSL Sports for highlights."

Still on his back, he rolled. *A yard from the front wall. I played it well,* Luke praised himself. He panted, out of energy. "You're right. I'd watch that video replay."

Luke, exhausted, grumbled. *I won the battle. It's cost me the war.*

"Need a break?" Sandra teased with game control. "Honestly, that was a great play and I've seen a few."

"You should've returned my shot. I wasn't on my feet. I couldn't recover."

"My dad would've chewed me out for not charging the wall. I didn't think you'd get to it. My error. Won't underestimate you again." Sandra smiled. "Ready for set three?"

Luke won set two 15–13. Match tied. Sandra's upbeat, but underhanded compliments, disconcerted Luke. Win it or lose it, their future together awaited the next set of play. Legs spent; Luke pounded, was weak and prone to mistakes.

Luke reasoned, *If I don't win set three 11-6, I've agreed to walk away from Sandra. Although I'm in good shape, I wasn't prepared for this or her.* He took deep breaths and encouraged himself. *Balls to the walls.*

No one knows what that expression means. Spoken when victory or defeat is on the line.

Outgunned, overmatched, Luke braced himself. He thought of Vince Lombardi's famous expression, "Fatigue makes cowards of us all." Luke petitioned the Lord. *Help. I need a wondrous event. Now.*

Nothing happened, it seemed. Sandra dominated. She retained a 6–2 lead and service. Should she score the next point, the deal Luke truly hoped to win—her love—totally squandered.

"You understand," Sandra stressed, "I'm within five of eleven. I could let you win nine straight points. I am under no obligation to explain myself. You're a good guy, Luke. You understand?" She held the ball toward him. "With this point, you will leave me alone. Academics only. No romantic behaviors or words. No double entendre, innuendo, Hershey Kisses, notes, treats, contraband food in the library, unwelcome visits to my carrel or apartment, or humorous flirtations. No further inquiries. Got that?"

I'm heartbroken. "Serve the ball. Miracles happen," Luke feigned confidence. "Haven't you seen a seagull eat a cricket?" – A beaten man.

"Science says there are no miracles. Oh, excuse me, that's Spock's line." Sandra grinned.

"Let's play." Luke prepared for his last stand.

"Okay … The priesthood has spoken. You're the man … You have the power."

She dropped the ball, slapped the serve. It rebounded to his backhand side, hit the floor, Luke drilled the ball over her head. As usual, Sandra positioned within the service lane struck the ball. It came to his forehand. *I'm hitting this ball as hard as I can. Blow it past her.*

Luke crushed the ball then saw its trajectory—directly at Sandra! Her eyes focused forward, the ball hit her right leg, behind and above the knee. She screamed, leaped into the air, no awareness of the ball's approach.

Damn. Luke rushed to her.

Sandra bounced in all directions. She groaned, writhing in discomfort, prepared to exact vengeance.

"Sandra, I'm sorry," he said, appealing to her sympathy.

"You hit me on purpose!"

"No, I didn't." He grabbed her arms to balance weight ... it didn't help; she stumbled to stay upright. "If I tried to hit you, I woulda missed." Her right foot curled behind her. She hopped on one foot. Her hands searched for the injury.

"Stay down," Luke demanded. He supported her weight until she came to a seated position on the court. He scrambled to her right side and glanced at her face. Tears welled; no eye contact. Sandra's pain was intense. "Let me look at it." She rolled toward her stomach.

Luke gripped her right ankle, then straightened the leg. An angry, crimson circle glowed above the knee.

"What can I do?" Luke hoped Sandra could answer, but only muffled groans heard. Her pain, his doing—*think*.

"Lie flat. I have an idea," Luke directed.

Sandra, face down on the floor, angrily shook her head. Frustrated, in need of relief, she muttered under her breath, "What the hell."

Sandra felt Luke's hand on the back of her knee below the impact site. *What's he doing? If he starts any funny stuff, I'll hit him so hard, he'll never wake again. The pain is bitter.*

She sensed his face close to her leg. Unexpectedly, she felt the coolness of his breath. He blew on the inflamed circle. The act strangely comforted her. He continued to blow unhurriedly across, over, back, covering all areas that seemed hurt. No urgency, just several cool, uninterrupted breaths. Then, without an alert, his lips touched the wound. He kissed the part of her that hurt so terribly.

Sandra's heart leapt. Mind exploded. Tremors pulsed through her groin. She all but moaned from the pleasure, expelling a sigh of relief. He continued the kiss until she relaxed, tension escaped. *Don't stop, please*, she wanted to say. *This sensation must last forever.*

Luke innocently discovered a part of Sandra she never knew nor experienced. The pleasure of their connection at this crossover was pure, euphoric, almost heaven. The experience included more than words could describe. Compassion, and thoughtful empathy. He tenderly lifted his lips from the wound. Remnants of peace, calm and assurance remained.

"Did that make it better?" He asked quietly.

Sandra didn't know. Her first impulse—*say yes*. She refrained. The tremors wonderfully ecstatic, nearly sexual, truly pleasurable. Silently, she relished the final seconds of joy– confidence.

"Do you feel pain now?" Luke urgently asked.

The question surprised her. The pain vanished. The diversion was excellent. "It still tingles a bit. Thanks. What is that technique you used? You need to author a medical paper."

"I broke my arm in junior high. The doctor blew on my arm as he set it. My mom says kisses make owies go away. I didn't know what else to do. Are you okay? I'm so sorry, Sandra. I never want to hurt you. I wasn't trying."

"I know. Thanks for the rescue." She faced him.

"Don't be upset, please … I enjoyed the kiss, uh, your leg … kissing the owie."

Luke attempted to share the exquisite experience he felt when his lips met her skin. A mysterious connection. Sandra spoke to him, internally. His mind, heart, all senses harmonized. The energy pleasantly powerful. He didn't want the kiss to end. Rather, to last forever. *She might protest.* A glorious sensation, practically erotic. He enjoyed her presence inside his consciousness. Overwhelmed with affection, empathy entered him through this simple, immaculate touch.

"You taste good," he confessed then shied away. "Though a bit salty."

Seated, Sandra focused eyes toward his. For the first time she looked directly into Luke's soul. She gave an appreciative smile. "I'm done for the day."

Her eyes smiled. A new, brilliant expression. Luke hoped Sandra's eyes would smile forever. *I love her.*

Luke clasped her arm with one hand, placed his free arm around her waist, then lifted. He didn't release his hold. The two walked to the exit. Sandra protected within his arms. Her face pressed against Luke's chest, with an arm around his waist. He dropped his cheek to her head. It felt splendid. She swung her free hand to Luke's open palm. Sandra never held so closely by a man.

Embraced arms, hands clutched, our heroes began their first steps together as companions.

Luke carried their gear to his car. Assisted Sandra into the front seat. They rode the short distance to her apartment. She walked without much discomfort. The welt, however, would take time to heal.

Luke assisted Sandra to her apartment and softly said, "I'll hustle back to the Richards Building to shower. Let's go to the Brick Oven. Pizza and garlic bread sticks. We'll have bad breath for three days." He chuckled, waved at her, and trotted down the hall.

Sandra no longer guarded herself. Certainly not with Luke. She watched from the door as he disappeared. *I want to be with him, share stories, laugh, play, pursue our scholarly work together. I love him… but, how can I? When he's told what I am, he'll run. If not, what compromises will he accept? For that matter, how much can I withstand? Is love truly enough?*

Her mind calculated the odds. She drooped her head. *I should have died as a baby.*

First Steps, Taken by Two

Even the greatest was once a beginner.
Don't be afraid of taking that first step.

—Muhammad Ali

LUKE GESTURED WITH A bread stick. "When I saw the ball flying at you, a hundred different thoughts went through my mind. None of them hinted we'd be here, together, eating pizza and bread sticks. I assumed you'd never speak to me ... **Ever**... that scared me."

"Yeah, you should've felt it. Hurt like hell. I thought my leg would require amputation."

They laughed. Their eyes now locked; the conversation paused.

"Remember when you asked what make makes me happy?" Sandra posed.

Luke nodded.

"It's been a wonderful day. The owie, too. None of it possible without you." Her fingers caressed the back of Luke's hand.

Luke took Sandra's hand, raised it to his lips, and kissed her fingers. She caught her breath. *It is a relief not to be confrontational or defensive.* In her early twenties, Sandra never knew or felt the intimate touches or kisses of a man. Now, in one day, Sandra had been kissed innocently on her leg and hand. She received Luke's kisses without protest, anger, or contempt. Luke's touches gave her comfort, happiness.

"You won the match, Sandra," Luke admitted. "You had the upper hand. Total control. I'll concede. Don't shut the door on me. I want to know who, what, you are. Secrets are tough to keep. You could've told me about your dad," he paused. "What else is hidden?"

She smiled. "Surrender accepted. I'll tell my story. Done properly, though, preparations are needed. It will take time."

"What can the matter be?" Luke asked with simple curiosity. Truly unaware. "You can't imagine what's in my mind. How long do I wait? Is it really that big a deal?"

"Can we finish the semester first? I need to speak with my parents. My whole life they have been my biggest means of support. It won't be long, I swear. Please? I'll tell you the whole story. I need time, okay?"

Luke recognized the unusual circumstance. Stepped too far into neutral territory, he felt her discomfort. "Okay, I won't press the issue. I'll be patient. I'm simply curious."

After an awkward pause. Luke said, "Look at me." She peered at Luke. "On one condition." Luke gazed with one eye crossed. Stupid grin.

She laughed aloud. "Stop it." *Whap!* She swatted his chest. *What a goofball.* "What's the condition?"

"It's the holiday season. Lights are shining at Temple Square. Let's go. It'll be fun. It's beautiful. An official first date."

First date? I'm deeply inside unfamiliar territory. I've dated. Not like this. I need to think. Adjust to alien conditions. There's gotta be a Star Trek episode that dealt with this. She peered at Luke, saw his anxious look.

"Sure. It's a date." Sandra smiled brightly. Then nodded her head.

Luke parked the car, rushed to Sandra's apartment. Knocked enthusiastically.

Sandra immediately opened the door. Dressed in a warm jacket. Prepared for a cold night at Temple Square.

A perfect gentleman, Luke opened the passenger door for Sandra. He watched her lithe body take a seat. "Buckle your belt."

Heroes on the road to Temple Square. The hour-long drive to Salt Lake filled with taped Christmas music.

"Wanna hear a missionary story?" Luke offered.

"Sure."

"In my initial interview with President Rekdahl, first day in the field, he informed me who my companion would be. I looked at this guy's photo on the mission wall. Thought, cool guy. Then Rekdahl disclosed information, 'You're six-one, 185 pounds. You played high school football, baseball in college.—Your companion is aggressive. I don't believe he'll pick a fight. You're the same size. I need you to be tough. Get him out of bed. Obey mission rules.'"

"How'd you respond?" Sandra asked.

"I said, 'Yes, President.' Next day, I got off the bus. There I was greeted by my first companion, the district leader, and his companion."

"Did the two of you ever fight?" Sandra asked.

"No. The first week was good. We got up at 6:15 a.m. Showered, studied, ate breakfast, spent each day fully in line with mission rules. We're encouraged to visit the homes of members. He wanted to visit homes with teenage girls. Stay too long. The third week went downhill fast. He wouldn't get out of bed. On Saturday, 'preparation day,' we played basketball with missionaries from our zone at the local church. This screwball elder knocked guys to the floor, picked fights. One time, he attacked a smaller missionary in our apartment. Two of us wrestled him off the guy. It shook up the poor kid."

"What did you do?"

"I wrote letters to Rekdahl. Chatted by phone with my district leader. I described my companion as neurotic. I finished a psychology course at BYU right before my mission. I'm sure that impressed everyone. The junior companion diagnosing his senior companion as neurotic, in need of counsel. Rekdahl must've laughed aloud. A nineteen-year-old greenie advising him. I asked Rekdahl, 'Who is the senior companion in this area?'"

"Is this normal in all missions?"

"Me advising a General Authority? Everyday." Luke chuckled.

"No. Missionaries behaving badly?" Sandra asked, swatting his shoulder.

"Ongoing. I've seen it all. Too many elders, even the sisters, need babysitters. I was three months too long with this psycho companion. Good thing neither of us carried guns. Here's my point... I tell you these stories of masturbating, pedophile, peeping Tom, screwball missionaries from my mission—endeavoring to convert people to Mormonism—each scarier than you, Sandra. What can you say about yourself that would turn me away? —I trained six greenies."

Sandra silently understood Luke's supportive intent. The eventual outcome of her self-disclosure could be catastrophic. She yearned for a happy ending. That they could live happily ever after. *Fairy tales, like religion itself, rely heavily on fantasy. Implausible assertions. Reality, truth, each claim victims.*

The battle in Sandra's mind raged. *Luke will shut me out.*

Luke parked north of Temple Square. Our heroes walked through the north entrance onto the temple grounds. Perfect, clean, bright lights sparkled in the night air.

"Are there really a million lights decorating the square?" Sandra said doubtfully. Not her first visit to Temple Square, but the first visit to view Christmas at the Square. This disciple of Spock would not be easily fooled.

"I've heard that number too," Luke confirmed. "I doubt a million, but certainly a few hundred thousand, I'm sure. Who cares? The lights are cool."

The temperature was thirteen degrees Fahrenheit. Snow on the ground. Patches of ice on the concrete paths. "Watch your step. Arizona folks like you aren't used to these conditions." These heroes were well-bundled with heavy coats, multiple layers, and head gear. Luke sported a knit cap and a long, black gentleman's coat; Sandra, a hooded jacket.

"To tour the Square could take hours," Luke said. "Should the cold become too much we can retreat to the Visitors' Center or other buildings." They viewed the Christus statue, along with modern Church displays and museum artifacts. Then, into the cold.

"Wanna learn how to keep your hands warm in frostbite weather?" Luke asked.

Sandra suspected a prank. "What you got up your sleeve?"

"It's not up my sleeve. It's in my coat pocket."

"Really? What is it?"

"Remove your left-hand glove."

She did as Luke directed with suspicion. "What's going on?"

"You'll see. Guaranteed. Your hand will not get cold."

Her glove removed, Luke took it and placed it inside his full-length winter coat. She balked.

"Put your bare hand inside my coat pocket," he said, patting his right side below his waist.

She obeyed. He bit the tip of the middle finger of his right glove and removed it.

He snatched the glove in his left hand and stuffed it in his coat's left pocket. Luke's right hand plunged into the pocket where Sandra's hand awaited. His fingers found hers. They interlocked in a gentle grip.

"Impressive," she smiled. "You seem to have experience with this routine."

"My freshman year, our branch from the Y came to see the lights. Rose's hand in the right pocket. Colleen in the left. My first experience with future plural wives—" *Whap!* Sandra struck Luke's shoulder. They grinned.

"Don't say anything like that ever again. You chauvinist." Sandra giggled. Placed the side of her hooded head against Luke, while firmly gripping his upper arm with her free gloved hand. Luke placed his left hand on her gloved hand as they walked the exhibits of lights, Christmas scenes, and music.

Sandra enjoyed their date. Luke provided all kinds of first-time experiences, warm, interlocked fingers included. Unknown how long these encounters would last, she remained careful, shrewd. Kept avenues of escape available. *Luke is a blessing*, she repeated to herself. *I've never felt so found; except I am still lost, greatly lost. I do not want him to run from me.*

"The Tabernacle is open," Luke observed. "Would you like to see inside? We can get out of the cold for a while. Warm ourselves."

"Good idea. My hands are warm, but the rest of me is chilled."

They approached the east entrance of the Tabernacle. An usher stood bundled in what appeared to be twenty layers of thermal wear from head to foot. Luke asked, "What's happenin' here tonight?"

The upright sleeping bag responded, "The Choir is rehearsing."

"That means we can't enter," Luke responded.

"You can enter. Don't speak aloud. It might disturb the rehearsal."

The usher pulled open the door. Sandra and Luke entered and removed their head gear, gloves, opened their coats. They welcomed the warmth of the Tabernacle. A large number took refuge from the cold, scattered among the bench seats under the Tabernacle dome. Sandra looked at the massive organ, after that caught sight of the choir director. "There's Jerold Ottley," she excitedly whispered.

"He loves baseball. A big fan."

"You don't know that. What is it with you and baseball?" They spoke softly.

"Serious," Luke breathed. "Seen him at Derks Field. Don't go there just for the hotdogs. He's a big baseball fan. I bet he can play a mean saxophone."

"Be quiet. They can probably hear us whispering all the way up there. You know how acoustically sound this place is."

"Sandra. *Acoustically* with *sound?*"

She *whapped* him.

The choir rehearsed two songs. Ottley directed, issuing comments and specific instructions. Often, he said, "Stop. Try those bars, again…"

Warmed, our heroes prepared to leave. Ottley said, "Selection 14, Handel's Hallelujah Chorus. Let's polish it."

Sandra sat upright with anticipation. Pages turned. The choir prepared to sing.

Sandra leaned forward, a hand on the bench in front of her. Placed her feet firmly on the floor. Ottley lifted his baton. At the stroke of the first note, Sandra rose. The choir powerfully delivered the masterpiece. Sandra, robustly, sang in sync.

Luke, with spectators scattered among the Tabernacle benches, arose. King George II supposedly flew to his feet when hearing the Hallelujah Chorus sung at the inaugural performance of Handel's *Messiah*. Now, a common tradition throughout the world. Sandra's voice strong, quite good, but not alone. Visitors in the Tabernacle sang emboldened. Forceful.

Sandra pressed Luke into the aisle. Briskly, they approached the rostrum. Sang fully without hesitation. Luke kept pace to the barricades that prevented sightseers from climbing the rostrum. All full-throated participants. Others, with Luke, sang steps behind Sandra.

Ottley heard the united voices and turned to view the spectacle. Sandra stood below the choir seats. Everyone in the Tabernacle on their feet all sung with passion. Ottley's direction continued. He motioned the Choir to follow. Repositioned, Ottley led the unified voices through the finale of the Hallelujah Chorus.

The Tabernacle audience erupted in cheers. *Are we allowed to cheer in the Tabernacle?* Luke wondered. The sight of Ottley's applause dispelled all doubts. Luke clapped. Surprisingly brilliant.

As people quieted, Ottley addressed listeners, "In all my years, I have never experienced an occasion like this. Remarkable. Perfection. That piece needs no further rehearsal." He opened his hands as if to say, *It is done.*

The choir began to clap again, pointed toward audience members. A few specifically motioned in the direction of Sandra. The congregation returned the praise. Principally, Sandra. She smiled openly. Nodded. Hands clasped with joy.

Luke saw Sandra's elation. Her behavior totally unlike the resigned person she demonstrated at BYU. It gave him pleasure to see her spirit unchained, released from the burden she hid. His hope? For Sandra to live each day free with happiness. They embraced.

Still jazzed by the event, Luke spoke as they journeyed home. ". . . absolute coolest. Look what you did, Sandra. Wow! Even Ottley was impressed. What gave you the idea to go down the aisle? You have a first-rate voice. What else are you holding back? First racquetball. Now this. Can you truly blame me for how I feel about you?"

She squirmed in her seat at his questions. The hidden secret, a great threat. Luke wholly unaware of her severe discomfort felt from his questions; however, her smile, joy, and expressions, most genuine. Happier than at any other time of her life.

Sandra shrugged. "The music is thrilling. Moved me. I've sung in church choirs. No formal training. Just as spontaneous for others as for me." Without thought she reached for the same hand she clasped all night. Connected, again.

Silent seconds passed until Luke's eyes glanced to the seatbelt in the middle of the car's bench seat. "You can sit next to me."

Getting the gist of his intent, Sandra unbuckled with lightspeed, scooted herself next to Luke, buckled again. She settled into him while he wrapped his arm around her with a warm squeeze. She rested a hand on his leg—an act that young adults, teenagers, married couples do commonly. It came naturally for her with Luke.

On cloud nine despite her secret.

"Sandra, I love you." Luke waited.

Until now, Sandra always became irritated when *love* was mentioned. Nestled snugly under his arm, she voiced no objections. He continued, "I can't say *I love you* without saying your name. I can't say your name without saying *I love you*. The words fit, frontward or bassackwards."

Sandra tried to suppress concerns. At the same time, she felt elated, laughed quietly. "Your goofiness again." Sandra pressed her face against Luke's chest. "You are the only man to say that to me."

"Oh, please, don't say that. You're so bright, beautiful. There had to be dozens."

"You're the first, truthfully. I've never allowed anyone to be this close. I'm terrified."

"Okay, I'm confused. The competition for your attention had to be there. The group of guys I run around with would have fought for a chance to win you over. Why be afraid?"

"I didn't—I couldn't allow it to happen," Sandra answered.

"What do you mean? I thought girls like being told they are loved by men. Especially by a guy they love. Why not you? Folks in Arizona are not much different than folks in Utah."

"Guys aren't different. *I am different.*"

"Really?" Luke looked puzzled. "Different simply cuz you're gorgeous, cerebral, athletic? Is it your math skills? Oh, guys are intimidated with your backhand service shots."

"There are details you don't know. When you learn"—she hesitated before continuing— "you'll run away from me. I never should have allowed you to get this close." Sensations with streaks of awareness from their experience on the racquetball court flooded Sandra's mind. She recalled Luke's kiss on her welted leg. *Exceptional. I love him.*

"So be it," Luke said. "Now that Blacks can hold the priesthood, so what? Is your mom or dad Black? Is that it? Hell, my dad will be upset, but I love you, Sandra."

She grinned at him. "When your lips touched that nasty owie, I nearly climaxed. But the thing is, I better understood you … Us … I became aware of many concepts. Surreal," she flustered.

"I was struck by it, too. What happened to us? Do you know?" Luke sought for a resolution to their shared experience. "I've been cautious to say 'kiss.' Friends will think we did something kinky. It was harmless, nothing that needs confession to a bishop or church leader. A tremendous flood of information. I—I don't know what to say. I've felt strongly since first seeing you. But Sandra, when my lips touched your wound … I fell in love. I need you."

"When you kissed my leg," Sandra disclosed, "I knew, then, there, to tell you about me, as scary as it is."

Over the next twenty-five miles our heroes shared all their ideas, knowledge, and impressions learned from the kiss. Their spectrum of empathy deeply enlarged. So much gained from an experience that took so little time. They concluded the event, without spoken words, as *spiritual.*

Sandra caressed Luke's hand. "I'll tell you the entire story, but not yet."

"When?" Luke asked, flushed with frustration. "Sleeping will be difficult for me 'til I hear what this is all about."

"To hear all that is to be understood," she said somberly, "well, sleep could be a long time coming."

"What can it be? Why is it such a big deal?"

Future events were settled at Sandra's apartment door. The next day Sandra would fly to Phoenix for the holidays. Luke planned extended work hours at the bank through the holiday break.

"I care for you deeply," she said, hugging Luke tightly. "This will be difficult. My parents have been alerted. I'm obligated to tell them of you. My feelings and thoughts. I will share everything."

"Sandra, you're not dying, are you?"

"I'm not dying. It's as serious as death, though. You'll understand." Her eyes dampened. "I have your phone numbers. I'll call you. Miss you already." Sandra hugged with all her might.

"Sandra, whatever is explained, I doubt it will change a thing."

"Luke, it won't be long. I want you to know. My parents and I will talk. It's our first order of business. You'll hear my story. I promise."

"Are you a secret agent? Is that it? … You know James Bond on a first name basis? Oh my, you haven't had sex with Sean Connery, have you?"

She giggled, swatted Luke's back. Tightened her arms around him.

"Keep this up," he said, "I'll spend the night here. Think of all we'd need to confess."

She looked into his eyes. Quickly slapped his butt. "You play a good game, buddy. See? I'm not alone on this team. I can make you smile, too."

"I don't want you to go away. To Arizona or from me. When can I kiss you?"

"I'll miss you, Luke. You are noble. I've done more, gone further with you, than any man. When we are next together, I'll share my secret. We'll discover whether love is enough." She buried her face into his neck with a final hug, then turned sharply into the apartment. Closed the door.

Luke hoped to kiss her. Sandra's final barrier, however, could not be crossed.

Luke passed mailboxes as he walked to the car. *This is a federal offense. I'm not concerned. She'll know I was here. That I care for her. No better reason to be arrested.*

He reached deep into a pocket of his coat, collected two Hershey Kisses. As he approached Sandra's mailbox, the Kisses were deposited. Their lips never touched. Yet Luke felt like a victor. He gave Sandra two sweet Kisses.

Family Conversations

The truth is rarely pure and never simple.

—Oscar Wilde

TALL, DARK, WITH AN athletic demeanor, Sandra's father met her at the Hughes Airwest gate. They hugged.

"Where's Mom?" Sandra asked.

"Home, baking for Christmas day. This is our individual time to talk. I wanted alone time with you. I'm anxious to hear the jeopardy we're in."

"Of course."

The warmth of Arizona, her classes, and the cold temperatures at BYU dominated their small talk at the luggage carousel. With Sandra's suitcase in the trunk, father and daughter rode home.

"From phone conversations it seems we're connecting with this young man." Brazenly pleased, he said, "Your mother and I, despite your efforts, knew this would happen."

"I'm sorry, Dad. I didn't want this. I don't want you harmed. But you seem pleased."

"Sandra, we're hopeful. We don't know much. Only what we've gathered from phone conversations. The holidays will allow us, as you say, 'to discuss the issues.' Your mother and you will consume much of that time. If I don't see you again, I love you."

Her father knew ways to comfort tensions. She felt protected at home, in their presence. His words resonated with security as they sped onto I-10. He squeezed her hand.

"Dad, I'm scared, confused."

"What scares, confuses, you?"

"Everything is so unlikely. It's freakish. I'm not supposed to be in love."

"Who said that?"

"No one. It's not my fate."

"Okay. Stay grounded." He waved a hand for her to continue. His eyes locked on the road.

"Dad, I'm on a high cliff. I don't know if I can survive the jump into the water below. This could kill me."

"It won't kill you."

"Please," Sandra pled. "The potential for harm to you, mom, me is tremendous."

"Tell me about Lucas. Or is it, Luke?"

"Luke. He's a fun person, on the goofy side. Persistent, to a fault. Extremely intelligent. A leader. Innovative. At times deviant. I like that about him. A returned missionary. He went to Toronto, Canada, on his mission. Loves baseball. Played semi-pro ball, then later at BYU. Works for a bank. Says he loves me. I really like him." A second passed. "Okay, I love him," she conceded. "What am I doing?"

"Sandra, sooner or later matters of the heart take over. We're prepared. You are too. He seems to be a good person. What is there not to love?"

"Dad, he could betray us. I've tried to avoid this. Now he's here." Sandra thumped at her heart. "Like Elvis, I'm all shook up." She looked straight through the windshield, shaking herself. "Heard that last comment from Luke."

Sandra's father chuckled. "Sweetheart, we've had this discussion. Nature has its way—"

"Dad. Nature is my enemy," Sandra strongly protested. "If discovered, think of the consequences. How can I live with this? How might it affect our family? Dammit."

"Sandra? Did BYU teach you profanity?"

"I blame Luke's grandmother." She hesitated. "Then you ... then racquetball."

"Luke's grandmother? Got to hear that story." He grinned. "Sandra, you're at a crossroad. It's time to go over the bridge."

"Oh, my gosh, Dad. You're as bad as Luke. Is this how men talk? When I do something Luke likes, or when complimenting me, he'll say 'attaboy, girl' as if it is laugh-out-loud funny. Inside, I'm not laughing. It's unsettling."

"We're under some stress. Relax. This may not be as bad as you're thinking. That's all I'm trying to get across. Sandra, it's good having you home. We miss our conversations with you." He merged north onto Highway 60.

"I have Mom's math skills. I've calculated the odds for success in all this. They're not good," she bellowed.

"People win lotteries. I don't think your odds are poor. What did he do? You stopped all other attempts. What caused you to tell him about yourself?"

"He kissed my leg—the owie." Sandra fell back into her seat. She looked out the window. "I literally was moved."

"Uh-huh, heard about that. The kid's got talents. Can't wait to meet him."

"Dad, you're not helping."

"I believe I am. Luke was beaten, then he hit the ball into your leg..."

"He didn't try to hurt me. He was really upset about it. The pain was horrible."

"Luke kissed your wound? Yuck."

"On the spot where the ball hit me." She touched under her right knee.

"The pain went away?"

"When his lips pressed on the red welt, the pain vanished." She momentarily lost herself in the memory of those magical seconds.

"Wow. Now you say the odds aren't favorable. For all you know, Luke could be a future Church president or Captain Kirk's fifteen times grandfather. Did you compute that? He might be meant to play a part in your life."

"*Star Trek* and mixed metaphors are not relevant," Sandra lashed back.

"What is relevant? Religion? Politics? Have you kissed him?"

"Dad? Why do you ask? It's personal. Isn't it? You know how dangerous touching someone is for me. For each of us."

"I understand the behaviors of touch. Your calculations. Leave your mother and me out of it. I'm not troubled, at all, that you're in love. It's a risk factor. Part of your journey of self-discovery. I have tenure. We don't require your protection, Sandra!"

"I'm terrified to kiss him. He keeps my hands warm. Wraps his arms around me. I feel safe with him. He's kissed my head, my hands. Our mouths have never met. Not yet."

"Hmmm. Words alone may not tell you what you need to know."

Sandra was carried back to Luke's kiss on her leg, their discussion. *That touch communicated like no other experience. It transcended all that is familiar.* Silence passed inside the car as she attempted to understand the kiss.

"Thanks. Dad, I love you."

"I love you, too, Hon. So does your mother. Give Luke some latitude. Look how far he has come to know how wonderful you are." He made a left turn into a cul-de-sac. "Let's say hi to Mom." He steered into the driveway of their home.

Sandra entered through the kitchen door from the garage followed by her father loaded with a suitcase and packages. "Hi, Honey, I'm home. Look who I have with me," Sandra's father playfully shouted.

Home smells of Mom's holiday pumpkin bread. Sandra thought, *Good to be with Mom and Dad.* Their home comfortably adorned with bright colors, comfortable furniture, and Christmas decorations. Memories of her childhood with comfort grew. The feel of marble tile. Thick carpet under her feet. The sights of familiar fixtures. Christmas songs, flavors. Her parent's encouragement and laughter created hope.

Sandra's mother clapped her hands. She rushed to hug Sandra. The three stood in a group hug.

While her father carried the suitcase to Sandra's room, Sandra asked, "Mom, when can we talk?"

"The house is stocked with food. We're here. Whenever you want."

Her parents resettled Sandra into their home. Diverted by their diplomas as she passed them in the hallway. Advanced degrees for each. Sports training for her dad; mathematics, her mom. It comforted Sandra to see them, their home, her room. She sat on her bed.

"Your dad said you enjoyed a good discussion on the way home."

"Insightful. Dad has me thinking concepts I've not considered."

"Explain."

"He suggests there are factors to be understood that come to you without words. I took it as an awareness, or knowledge, taken from a shared experience between two people. Like when two people kiss. Luke and I have spoken about our only kiss. When he kissed the owie."

"Whoa. Your father and I need to discuss that concept tonight," she tittered, seated on the bed next to her daughter.

"I understand why your students like you." She paused. "Mom, I've never kissed anyone. Not like Luke's kiss. Whoa! Luke didn't even kiss my lips. I was in pain. Lying face-down on a racquetball court."

"Luke has gifts. Consider them," her mother said. "Other factors could be at play in all this."

"Mom, I care greatly for him. When he kissed my leg, the wound, I moved here." Sandra placed hands over her vagina.

"Oh, my. Lucky you. Parts are working." She grinned.

"It was"—her hands gestured to find the right phrases, metaphors— "too wonderful for words. Did Dad do that for you?"

"Well, Honey, your dad is skilled. I don't—"

"It—Luke is—" Sandra searched for expressions. "He is wonderful, Mom. Look at what we're discussing. I don't have any experience with this. Is this normal? If so, no wonder babies happen. The experience was amazing, otherworldly. I want him to love me for all that I am. I made that decision when he kissed the welt on my leg. I love him. Will he love me, Mom? He tells me that he loves me, but our lips have never touched." Sandra's voice weakened. She slumped. "Mom, how can I? How can we?" Her posture crumbled. "Luke doesn't know."

Sandra's mother tightly hugged her. "From what you've told us, Luke seems reasonable. He cares for you. The answers must come from him."

"There's the rub. He doesn't know what I am. Against all odds, doctors, everyone else—I've not allowed anyone to get this close … until now." Sandra resigned, "He'll abandon me once he learns. I can feel the pain already."

"You don't know that." Sandra's mother wrapped her with comforting arms. "We understand the risks. Consequences to be taken. We'll share them with you, come hell or high water. Your lone choice is to invite Luke inside your circle of experience. His heart will be tested. He'll make his decisions. He can take it, everything about you."

"It will be a bloody mess. I've tried to avoid it at all costs. The rejection already chokes me. The damage could be immense. The math doesn't favor us, Mom." Tears escaped Sandra's eyes.

"Again, you don't know. Suspicion has its own harmful costs. Cards are placed on the table to discover winners. He could kiss away that pain too." Her mother's arms steadily held Sandra.

"Luke could do great damage. I could ask for his silence," then paused. "Down the road he could betray all of us."

"Your father and I have discussed this particular episode of your life. It's not going to be easy. We're ready to share the dangers. You're not alone."

"I knew since the kiss I had to tell Luke about me." Sandra sighed. "If he rejects me, I could never return to BYU. Seeing him there, our colleagues and group associations, with all he'd know about me, it would be more than I could bear. Mom, I've calculated, again and again, the success of this disclosure. The odds are always against me … it hurts." Sandra looked defeated.

"Heaven will help. Heavenly Father is already involved. Favorable things happen. Trust in Him. Ten-coin tosses, ten heads in a row."

"Mom, those words don't make me feel confident. I love the Church, but I am what I am. God has yet to answer our prayers.

Luke showed me a scripture where Job, in his big test, wanted to argue with God, as would I. Sometimes the trials we are forced to endure are immoral. I want to argue my reasons. Like Job, I want to argue with God and his questionable behaviors."

"You'd win the argument. The prophet would help if we could get his ear. He changed things for Black people and the Church ... Sandra, consider this. Your dad has already agreed. You should tell Luke the whole story here." Her mother pointed to the floor.

"Here? Why here?"

"Home court advantage. Besides, all the material, information, and data are here. You say Luke is intelligent, aware, and knowledgeable. It's all here. It's better than taking it all to BYU with you. In the event backup support is needed, your father and I are here."

"Luke will think I'm stalling or lying if I put this off any longer. I need to tell him when I return to BYU."

"No. Tell him now. Invite Luke to spend the New Year here, in Surprise. We're all here. Safest, best place. We'll pay for his flight to Phoenix."

"Oh, Mom, you've already spent too much. You can't—"

"You're an only child. Money isn't important. We would've spent the money on two or three kids if we'd had 'em. We're okay."

"Luke is working. I don't know if he ..." Sandra's voice trailed off as she thought. "You're right, Mom. It would be best to tell him here. I'm sure—yes, he'd spend his own money to—"

"Enough, do it now! Ask him to celebrate the New Year with you. It would be fun for us to meet him. We have room. That will save money he'd otherwise spend at a hotel. Hurry, call—" Her mother pointed out the door to the phone.

Sandra called the bank to speak with Luke. *Thrilled* to hear her voice. Luke accepted the invitation, more than happy to spend the New Year with Sandra. He teased her, "I'm gonna hafta break a few dates—"

"If there, I'd whap you," Sandra said swatting the air. They laughed.

Luke purchased airline tickets. Schedules were settled. Luke called and spoke briefly with Sandra's mother. He gave Sandra his itinerary for the trip. The return flight to Salt Lake included seats together. The bank's travel agency proved helpful.

Sandra and her parents greeted Luke at Sky Harbor International in Phoenix. After giving Sandra a big hug, he graciously addressed Sandra's parents. Gave them each a belated Christmas gift of nuts and chocolate. He clutched Sandra's hand, took a few steps, and cleverly wrapped his arms around her waist in a bear hug, lifting and spinning. He whispered, "I love you, Sandra. Wanna bite you."

"Luke, stop it." *Whap!*

Luke dropped Sandra to her feet. Sandra's parents smiled at them. "She made me do that," Luke said innocently. "She always makes me do what I don't want."

Sandra looked at her parents with gestures like *I don't know what to do with him.* They grinned.

Restarting their walk, Luke put his arm around Sandra. "I missed you. I'm happy to be here. Thanks for having me. Your parents are generous people. I'll be good."

Sandra put her arms around Luke. "I think they just fell in love with you." She gave him a big squeeze as the two walked stride for stride.

Sandra and Luke sat in the backseat of the car. Sandra's parents took their places in the front. "Thanks, again," Luke said, "for the invitation to celebrate the new year in Arizona. Greet a stranger at the airport, provide transportation, offer lodging. Do it all with openness, warmth. It's queer but appreciated."

All three turned toward Luke as Sandra exclaimed, "See what I mean, Dad?"

Christmas leftovers were placed on the dining room table. The four passed food while they engaged conversations. Luke, naturally, entertained. He appeared comfortable in their home. He pointed to an item in the living room accompanied with a question, "Is that a Friberg painting?" He waited for Sandra to look. When she turned, Luke took food from her plate and placed it on his own. Sandra's parents chuckled. He winked at them with a grin until Sandra discovered his antics.

"My schedule is so demanding at BYU. Sandra's unending calls. Hangs around me all day. Never leaves me alone." The family laughed quietly. Luke came back to earth. "Thanks, everyone. You're very kind to invite me to your home. I miss Sandra, even if it's just a day. Life's dull without her."

Sandra delivered a soft, customary swat to his upper body. "I missed your slaps too." Luke hugged Sandra. Kissed her head. Sandra's parents were impressed with Luke's ease to express affection toward Sandra in their presence. They were equally fascinated to observe how comfortably Sandra welcomed his affection. A sight unseen until this occasion.

Sandra smiled at Luke's oft-used, self-deprecatory humor. She, with equal ease, enjoyed his warmth. On the other hand, she mused, *What does he say that is jest? How much is real? Will he accept me?*

Sandra feared the hours of the next day. Her secret would be exposed. The disclosure meant life or death, happiness, possible heartache. For the final time, she computed the numbers. Her heart sunk.

"I'm going to bed." Sandra uneasily stood. She hoped the new day would be the dawn of a brighter life. Her chances seemed slim. With a forced smile, she said, "We have a big day tomorrow."

Aware of what awaited. Sandra's mother went to her as she walked to the bedrooms and gave Sandra's cheek a kiss. Her father followed with a big hug. Whispered, "I love you. We all love you."

Luke drew near. "Sandra, I'm really in the dark. I'll be here when the sun rises. I'm your best friend. Don't forget it. Smile ... Love your smile." They embraced.

She looked at Luke without speaking, flashed a brief grin, turned into the hallway, and walked to her bedroom.

Always darkest before the dawn.

Telling Conversations

A good friend keeps your secrets for you.
A best friend helps you keep your own secrets.

—Lauren Oliver

Two CHAIRS SAT AT a table in the living room decked with scrapbooks, texts, papers, and what looked like journal publications. Sandra and Luke faced each other.

Sandra succinctly started her story. "I am a man."

Luke sat silently, perplexed. "Come again?"

"I have been male my whole life."

"Sandra, what are you saying? You're joking."

"Not joking, Luke. Unknown to my parents, I was born with a genetic syndrome that has the effect of making a male emerge as female at birth. It impacts sexual development. First explained in 1970, scarcely eight years ago. The condition is referenced as 46XY androgen insensitivity.[3] It is complex. I'll do my best to explain."

Luke raised a hand like a student in class.

With exasperation, Sandra responded, "Yes, Luke?"

---

[3] 46XY androgen insensitivity is an actual genetic syndrome. Internet information sites and links will substantiate all conversational claims between Sandra and Luke regarding this condition. Search youtube.com: Biology of DSDs (5) Complete Androgen Insensitivity Syndrome and A Woman Shares What It Was Like Growing Up Intersex | The Oprah Winfrey Show | Oprah Winfrey Network

"I'm sorry. Your shape and movements are not male. I don't wish to be flippant. Please forgive my choice of words. You already know I'm an egotistical hotdog, but—what the f***? Please, just continue." Luke motioned.

"Yes. You are an egotistical hotdog." She regained her confidence and began anew.

"I appear female. I have notable breasts, shapely body, long legs, even a vagina—an ideal woman. Genetically, however, I am male. Androgen is a hormone receptor that is found in both males and females, but a mutation in the AR gene that encodes proteins causes ..." Sandra deftly explained how the X and Y chromosomes in relation with androgen-insensitive receptors affected her birth and postpubescent growth as a woman.

Sandra showed Luke pictures of herself in grade school. A sweet little girl. "As a child, my parents recognized subtle abnormalities in my genitalia. At age eleven, I developed sizable breasts but never menstruated. I was screened by specialists who provided no answers but confirmed my abnormalities.

"An obvious indication of the syndrome is the absence of pubic and underarm hair." Sandra raised her arms. Luke saw no underarm hair or stubble. "I'm not showing you my private region."

Luke waved a hand, shaken by the intimacy from the barrage of information, yet intellectually curious to learn of Sandra's syndrome.

"Specialists in 1970 finally provided answers." Sandra opened journal pages, complete with photographs, charts, diagrams, depictions. Explanations followed with a conclusion, "Complete androgen insensitivity is irreversible. My condition is permanent.

"I have no ovaries, fallopian tubes, or uterus. As a teenager, undescended testes inside my abdominal area were removed at a clinic in Los Angeles. Doctors consider them unnecessary, a health risk in my adult years. My parents encouraged surgery to enlarge my narrow, shallow vaginal pouch. They believe marriage with pleasurable sexual behavior will be a part of my healthy, adult lifestyle." Sandra behaved like the outcome was *impossible*.

"Plastic surgeons recommend a partner with a five-inch, no larger than six-inch erection. Nothing larger." She peered straight into Luke's eyes.

He acted unaffected but astonished with Sandra's disclosures. Stunned by her openness, straightforward approach and explanations with deep personal details. His mind raced to keep pace with Sandra's narrative.

Sandra reiterated, "I outwardly look and act female. That is what I am. How I behave. However, I am male. I have never experienced cramps, a period, nor will I. I will never become pregnant, bear a child, suffer menopause. As the man I am, I consider myself equally qualified to bear the priesthood, lead, and serve. Test my blood. Ironic, isn't it? I don't have the preferred chemical/hormonal balance or body parts to accompany my masculine genetic makeup. I am a child of God but have no place in Heavenly Father's heart. I am a man parading as a woman. I had no choice in this. I can't participate or fulfill roles in either gender. I am conflicted. Is that understandable?" She paused, bluntly emphasized, "I won't use the f^{***} word like you did. You should be ashamed, Luke."

"Do you want me to leave?" Luke gravely asked.

"What?" Sandra asked, uncertain of Luke's question.

"Is it your intent that I leave? Never return?" Luke probed.

"Of course not. Have I made myself unclear?" Sandra was puzzled.

"I thought I prepared myself for today. Wow ... I was clearly off-target ... ready to learn, respond to anything. But I'm staggered. Do you want me to leave?"

"Why do you keep asking?" Sandra needed to know.

"Are you a homosexual? Is that why you kept pushing me away?"

"I am not homosexual," Sandra responded. "I'm a girl attracted to boys, in every way. Please, help me to help you understand. Genetically, I am a male. It wasn't my choice to be born a boy with complete androgen insensitivity. As I have explained, it's a genetic syndrome. I have behaved as a girl my whole life. I want to fall in love. Marry *for time and all eternity*, like you."

"You're the best-looking man I've ever met," Luke complimented through his confusion.

Upset by his words, Sandra attacked. "Luke, what is it you want to say? Or for me to say?"

"From the first day I saw you, I've done my best to win your attention, approval. I have no doubt what you have told me is true.

I wish to speak with your parents ..." With uncertainty he asked, "Is this some elaborate ploy to make a final pushback? Force me to go away? Never return?"

"No. Not at all, Luke." She stretched her arms across the table and clutched his hands. Looked directly into his face. "What I have told you is true. That's why my parents invited you here. For you to learn the truth about me. The effects this syndrome has on my family.

"Hear me, Luke. My biggest fear is you'll run from me, voluntarily. I've calculated you'll point fingers at me with words like *queer* or *homo*. I can explain all this to you. I can't understand it for you." She released her grip.

Luke could not speak. He stared at Sandra in silence. A thought suddenly struck him. "Are you attracted to men? I should ask, are you attracted to me? Or does this thing you have confuse your sexual sense of male and female?"

"Luke, I am genetically a man. Yet, I am more female than most women because I have complete androgen insensitivity." She reached for Luke's hand placing it to her face. "I've been charmed by you since that morning we first met in Graham's class. I don't want you ever to leave me. But I cannot change what I am. We'll never make a baby. We can try. I'll give 100 percent best efforts. It won't ever happen. I'm a woman, literally trapped in a man's DNA code." Sandra faltered. She released Luke's hand. "I'm sorry. I'm talking as if you want to spend your life with me." She placed hands over her eyes, hiding tears.

"Why keep pushing away? Setting me aside? Sandra, I love you. Why wouldn't you trust me?"

"Who could I trust?" Sandra asked, hurt by his questions. She wanted to run, hide. The anguish felt from multiple defenses to turn him and others away damaged them both. She tried to explain.

"For now, Luke, I'm the egotistical hotdog. I'm an intelligent, eye-catching woman, albeit a man. A guy, like yourself, is enthused by what he sees. You make a play for my heart. I give my heart. At the same time, confess, 'I am a man.' You say to me, 'I can't be with a man who looks like a woman. It's all wrong. God would never allow it. My role is to be a father. Why didn't you tell me, everyone else, what you are so we all can avoid you? You're queer!'"

Sandra rested, assessed Luke's response to a very real scenario. "Luke, please understand. I don't want you to go. Not ever. Yet, answer me. Why would you stay? I cannot be a mother as we're taught in church to do. You cannot be a father with me." Her voice cracked.

Sandra fought to keep her composure. "In all these journals, charts, graphs, there is not one, not a single article to help someone cope with this syndrome. *Nada*. My mental and emotional welfare is neither discussed nor considered. I am a cypher. The Church, its members, are more concerned with what happens after death rather than our quality of life on Earth."

"You have a place—"

"Do I?" Sandra angrily snapped. "What if you looked like a man on the outside, but inside—you were genetically a woman? How would you behave in the world, our Church? Go with the men to priesthood meeting? Or with the women to Relief Society? Sisters would call you the best-looking woman they've met. Got it? … Do you get that tasteless insult?" She angrily barked.

"The first time I heard, really understood the word *queer*, a doctor described this condition inside me. He said, 'You're queer.' So, I'm queer." Tears fell from Sandra's eyes.

"I apologize, Sandra. I had no idea I hurt you. I'm an ass. I didn't realize my words wounded your heart. I'll amend my vocabulary." Luke rose to his feet. He wanted to go to Sandra.

Sandra lifted her hand to stop him. "Stay where you are. I am not finished. I do not want or require your pity." Luke felt her power and settled back into his chair. To provoke her, he knew, would be unwise.

As Sandra wiped tears from her face, Luke interceded, "May I ask, since you posed it, does this syndrome emerge where someone who is genetically a woman looks like a man?"

"Rarely, if at all. Not as it does for those like I am. Think about it, Luke. Would you go to your bishop if you knew you are genetically a woman but look like a man? Would you ask to be ordained to the priesthood, serve a mission as an elder, bless the sacrament, be a bishop? You can't father a child. How would you explain it? Be received? What of dating?"

"I see the complexity of your argument," Luke admitted.

"As I am, how shall I behave? What do you say to a bishop? How do you enter a temple? I am a freak of nature. I've lied on every application that asked *male or female?* Luke, how should I respond? Explain myself? The Book of Mormon says all liars go to hell."

Luke sat silently, unable to reply or gesture.

"My parents understand. They've explained that men sit separately from women in temples, like priesthood, Relief Society. Where do I sit? Where do I go? Do I sit with the brethren or the sisters? Do I tell people, Church members, possible employers, or teachers I am genderqueer? Luke, where is my place? Which restroom? I need to know."

Unable to respond, Luke sat unmoved, without a syllable to utter.

"Job unjustly had the shit kicked out of him. God playing God with a person's life. Just for the purpose God and Satan could settle a bet—a wagering game. Which of the two, The Father or Satan, is more unkind, wickeder? A trial of Job's faith? Well, I'd trade trials with Job. I don't know where to sit when I go to church. I challenge God's moral character, integrity. Where is my place? I do not feel welcome. Not at all, Luke. Not in the least.

"One conclusion I have gained from all this is that God cannot be trusted. I am a statistical error. It proves that evolution among all living species is quite evident. I would have preferred to win the lottery rather than be completely androgen insensitive (CAIS).

"Luke, let's consider how we'll behave at BYU, what our LDS Church activities would be like if we become romantic partners. How will we get through that process? Should I have kept my secret hidden from you? Avoided all your curious questions? Lied to you about why I cannot conceive a baby? How would I explain myself should you discover my secret years into a marriage?"

Still frozen, Luke sat expressionless. He had no responses for Sandra's questions.

"Now that I've told you what I am, let's suppose we wish to marry in a temple. What do I say? 'Hey, Bishop Brown,' who doesn't know anything about genetics or this syndrome, 'I wanna marry this man, but I gotta tell ya, I'm a man, too, literally. Test my DNA.' Do you want me to lie, Luke? Bat my eyes like a homecoming queen? Tell 'em what they want to hear? Pay the price when I get to the judgment bar in the hereafter? I'm a man. Though I look hot for a guy, I can't make babies. That's what men and women are supposed to do. As Mormons say, '*Multiply and replenish the Earth*.' Luke, we can't make babies, or become a family.

"I've lived with this confusion since I learned I am queer in these matters. Do you find fault with the way I push guys away from me? You?

"I've always feared someone at school, junior high or high school, would discover what I am. I'd have to endure teasing from everyone, not just at school but church too. Would Church members or God tolerate me? Be compassionate? They're all nice on the outside, but really? What's the true spirit of Church members? I know what's inside me. Do they know what's inside them? You can't move out of town each time someone learns what you are. Points fingers at you. Whispers vile words.

"When you say to me, 'Attaboy, girl,' I almost panic, worried that you know of my syndrome. Right now, I'm terrified. You know"— she gestured at Luke with an open hand— "You know what I am." Sandra thumped her chest. "You tell your parents, brothers, sisters, friends, colleagues at BYU …" Sandra lost emotional control for a time. "If it slips out somehow, somewhere, what becomes of me? Luke, you've got me by the short hairs, if I had any. Now that I've told you what I am, you have power to destroy my life. Hurt my parents. I'm so frightened, I'm shaking."

Luke sat frozen. No responses. His only option? Receive and store Sandra's disclosures. He scolded himself. *My thinking is flat, two-dimensional. I've studied three-dimensional thinking. I suck at it. Today is proof how little I think three-dimensionally. I have no dimension at all.*

Sandra continued her story, "Depression and doubt have been my constant companions. So often, I wanted to die. I'm not suicidal. Too big a coward for that. Mom and Dad kept watch over me.

Protected our secret. If what I am became publicly known, death would be my only choice."

Luke interrupted. "Sandra, don't say that. You're special."

"Wish to hear what I've thought about that? If I'd died prior to the age of eight years, I could've gone straight to the highest degree of the Celestial Kingdom. It's Mormon doctrine. I could've lived happily next door to Jesus on Golden Rule Avenue, somewhere in the Gamma Quadrant on the planet Kolob. But here I am—Dying before I turned eight years old would have made me special. Instead, I'm queer." She slammed her hand on the table. "Got that?"

"I will tell no one what you have shared with me. Sandra, I won't tell God Himself." At that instance he thought, *Or Herself?*

Sandra continued her pent-up aggravation. "Who has the skill, understanding, or experience to counsel me? This is all recent scientific discovery. It's not like explaining diabetes or cystic fibrosis. What do you want me to do each time I am to explain myself or perhaps fall in love? So much 'for time and all eternity.' I want to participate in our concept of eternal love, marriage. But how, Luke? How? The concept is grand. Where's the open temple door for me?" She gravely questioned.

"What if I told my branch president at BYU of my syndrome? What do you think he would say? He teaches Shakespearean literature. He would recommend, 'Get thee to a nunnery.' Wrong church with bad advice."

"You're not the Lone Ranger. How many are like you?" Luke asked.

"One in twenty thousand, about the same as natural redheads. That makes me the sole androgen-insensitive person at BYU, two at the most. In the entire Church, there could be two or three hundred like I am. The numbers are small. Who really cares? I believe the Church would exile me. Those like us. Until Civil Rights pressures came along, Blacks remained excluded. How will I ever be accepted by the Church? Who will advocate for my syndrome like those who advocated for Black people?"

"How much of you is male? How much of you is female?"

"Specialists consider me 'the ideal woman,' every bit a girl. Except for my DNA. I suppose 95 percent female, 5 percent male." Sandra shrugged her shoulders with an open palm.

"Your story must be told," Luke said.

"How? Expose myself? Be labeled queer? Do what we've done today? Undergo rejection, separation, segregation, isolation? I've had years to think this through. Hell, you likely want to fly home to Salt Lake right now. My dad will take you to the airport if you want to leave." Sandra looked straight into Luke's eyes. "When you kissed that wound on my leg, I felt wonderful. The days since the kiss have been great. Absolutely grand."

Sandra flopped to the carpet with expressions of defeat, eyes flooded over. "How can we continue all this?"

Luke rose from his chair, fell to the carpet. Spooned himself next to her. He felt her body tremble. Fear. Risk of rejection. Disclosure of a deeply hidden secret left her exposed, unprotected, vulnerable. He asked, "Have you finished what needs to be said?"

"Pretty much. For now. There's far more," she said as Luke wiped tears from her face with his handkerchief. "There are overlooked episodes of my life with this stupid syndrome. When prompted, I'll share more. Should you stay ... should you really care to hear it."

"Great. Are you hungry? I bet you're thirsty. We need a break. Then, we can learn more about your incredible story. Let's take some stretches."

Sandra sulked, somewhat irritated by his upbeat behavior.

Luke opened his hand and reached over her head. She grasped. He rolled, lifted Sandra and wrapped his arms around her. Perplexed by his embrace, she hugged him, burying her face in his shoulder. A kiss struck her head. She anticipated Luke would show early signs of retreat, attempts to escape. Instead, he was warm. Accommodated her needs.

Calm before the storm, she thought. *This likely won't end well. Should he remain, **he must earn it**.*

Sandra's parents sat at the kitchen table before a full spread of food and goodies as our heroes walked into the kitchen.

"Eavesdropping? Did you hear everything?" Sandra asked.

"Nothing we haven't heard from doctors and you. Besides, your father felt if Luke behaved badly, he'd intervene."

Luke saw a metal Louisville Slugger propped against her father's leg.

Sandra's father grinned. "I play on the ward softball team." He shook the bat. "It can also be used as a weapon." Humorous, certainly, though on red alert to see Sandra's father with a bat that doubled as a weapon.

"Before swinging that bat at me, may we speak?" Luke politely asked.

Sandra retreated with her mother. Luke, lemonade in hand, sat on a lawn chair at the backyard patio that overlooked the family pool. Sandra's father approached with a tray of food and his own drink.

"How ya holding up?"

"Feel like I've been kicked in the balls, which I've learned is a questionable metaphor."

"Don't feel uneasy. The three of us have gotten our own chuckles with what we've stumbled over. Having Sandra in your life, with all her attributes, will give you a broader view of the landscape."

"No idea the harm I spoke. If I were her, I would've smacked me in the mouth. I am so stupid. Unaware, totally … I hurt her. Can she ever consider me a person of value?"

"She loves you. Told me herself. She's impressed with you. She'd like to keep you nearby. She also told us about the kiss. You eased her pain."

"The kiss, huh? Unexplainable. Made up a new word to describe that experience: *transcenditory*.[4] It exceeded any other experience in my life. So much knowledge and understanding were gained

---

[4] Transcenditory: An event surpassing knowledge and understanding that is poorly and wrongfully described with mere words alone; exceeding a level of awareness equal to self-actualization. A transcenditory experience is shared between couples, or within small groups. The experience communicates subtle meaning(s) toward many issues, but enhances tolerance, compassion, and reason. The significance of a transcenditory experience is

from that touch. Most remarkable. Certainly pleasurable. A release of pain. Never has so much happened, greater intuitions and realizations, as when I kissed Sandra's wound. I received a greater awareness of Sandra, herself. I learned I love Sandra from that kiss.

"Sir, I've kissed my mom. Sought out my dad for a goodnight kiss. Kissed a few girls. Kissed nieces, nephews, grandparents. In high school, I kissed a catcher on the face after he hit a walk off homer." Luke reflected, "I hurt Sandra when she took that racquetball to her leg. It was killing me … I needed her back, without pain…" Luke paused. Pondered. "Your daughter, uh, son is …" Luke faltered, unfamiliar with the proper address for Sandra's gender.

"Luke, she is what she is. Our daughter. Think of her as she is in your heart."

"Your daughter is an angel, sir. *Special* is an inadequate word. When I kissed her wounded leg, we shared something … exceptional. Some kind of communication. She came to me. I found her here," he tapped his chest. "In my heart."

Sandra's father grinned. Thought reflectively, *Young and in love. I hope they appreciate their wondrous connection.* Finally, he said, "Sandra is more than unique. Can't be argued."

"Sir, how did Sandra react when she learned of her syndrome?"

"Confused, naturally. Very much still a child … filled with contradictions. Balancing Church instructions and doctrines with this odd condition. Raised as a daughter, abruptly told you are a boy. It was difficult. Church gender instruction was—is—a gross challenge. You hear discussions of marriage to a man, motherhood, families, then discover your parts do not function. Your gender is muddled up. We recognized moods would shift as she aged. We were concerned with self-harm, emotional and physical distress. Suicide, certainly."

"Sandra mentioned it. She loves the Church with justifiable complaints," Luke concluded.

"Honestly, Church gender-specific discussions about motherhood, children, and families made us account, then remove,

---

understood by only those involved at the moment it occurs. Most often described as 'a spiritual encounter.'

pharmaceuticals. School, friends, classmates—greatly difficult to control. That's when I taught her racquetball. We spent a ton of time together. Her mother did far more than I ever tried. We did our best to make home enjoyable. Tolerant, open for discussions of all kinds. Home became her safe place. Shelter and refuge. Never a place of ridicule or criticism. Music, laughter, no limitations. Sex, drugs, rock-n-roll were understood as deeply as gospel principles, along with other issues. Humor always a top priority. Followed with hugs. Overall, I'd give our efforts a B or B+."

"You did well in that endeavor. She speaks highly of you."

"Luke, in my mind, she loves you for the same reasons. Calls you goofy. That's why you've gotten this far. You make her laugh. She feels good about herself when with you. Her mother and I appreciate that quality in you. You never know how far a bad joke can go. The good it can do."

"Thanks for the vote of confidence," Luke countered. "I assume Johnny Carson is a bridge too far."

"Don't give up graduate school." They both chuckled.

Sandra's father provided an addendum. "The kiss is a connection of some kind between the two of you. A transcenditory moment, as you call it. Tactile behavior needs greater study, like hugs … a specialty research."

"Sir, I owe your wife and you an apology. Sandra has enlightened me. I realize how greatly I embarrassed myself. Unaware, inept words. I need to recover. Sandra, your wife, you."

"Luke, don't beat up on yourself. We understand. I'll select my words as best I can. You dodged an unexpected high, inside pitch thrown at you. You're dazed, might be angry, ready to fight, but you're still at the plate. Sandra didn't want to throw that high, inside pitch. She had no other choice. You can hit the next pitches. Do you love her? Will you leave? If you leave, will you guard her identity? How long? She doesn't want to be exposed, or suffer ridicule. Her hope is simple. You'll never divulge what she is to anyone. This is important to her."

"Yes, sir. I understand. I give my word. I'll die rather than betray her in this matter. People are more prone to ridicule small numbers of unique individuals. It's unfortunate."

"I do not say this to influence your decisions, Luke. This could take some time for you to decide. She cares for you. Deeply. She needs someone to share this burden she carries everywhere she goes. A friend, a person of interest she can clearly trust. It is her greatest hope. Whichever way you proceed, do it honorably. We are prepared for aftermaths. I have my bat." He smiled at Luke.

"I hope you never swing it at me." Luke returned the smile.

Luke walked back inside the house along with Sandra's father. Sandra and her mother sat at the kitchen counter.

"Did the two of you solve the world's problems?" Sandra's mother asked.

"Didn't talk about you two. Those damn Yankees," Sandra's father responded.

Each person smiled at the joke. They acted unaffected by the tensions felt from Sandra's disclosures.

Luke walked behind Sandra. Wrapped his arms around her. He kissed her thick head of hair. "Excuse me, I'll return shortly," he whispered then walked to the hallway and into the bathroom. He needed alone time, however brief, to think. Draw conclusions. His decisions, literally, impacted eternity.

I've been in here too long. Act. Now. Luke placed his forehead against the closed bathroom door, inhaled, sighed, reached for the knob. As the door opened, Sandra's mother came from the bedroom across the hall. She gripped his elbow as they stood in the hallway. "What's going to happen?"

"I don't know. Do you?"

"Are you getting cute with me?" Sandra's mother snapped.

"Please, ma'am, I mean no disrespect. I was thrust from pitch darkness into midday sun. I'm in need of help, some consideration… geez, do you go at your husband like this?"

She led Luke into the bedroom. "Sandra's happiness is in your hands. I want to know how this will playout."

"You're concerned parents … what is it with his bat, now you? Sandra must decide her own happiness," Luke stressed.

"What double-talk is this? Are you walking out? Leaving?"

"People are mistaken. They believe someone else has power in the matters of love, happiness. They do not."

"Where'd you come up with that idea? Is BYU teaching this crap?"

"Please. Sandra has told you and your husband that she loves me. She's never told me. It hurts. I've wanted to kiss her, here." Luke's fingers patted his lips. "She won't let me. That hurts too. I now understand why she's behaved as she has since I met her. The only kiss we've shared? Her wounded leg. I'm not here to make your daughter happy. I am powerless to do that. I'm here to find happiness with her. It's Sandra's decision to be happy. Not me or Disneyland. She's got to make her own way. That includes steps toward me. She must earn happiness herself. So, if you'll excuse me."

Luke walked out of the bedroom but paused in the hallway. He turned back into the bedroom. Sandra's mother stood grimly silent.

"Ma'am, did you buy that three-quarter-length, red-and-gray dress for Sandra?"

Surprised at the question, she answered, "Before she went to BYU."

"Great. Will you take me to the shop where you bought that dress? It's my favorite. I'd like to buy Sandra another. Will you help me?"

"Yes. The store isn't far. We can go later. Tomorrow?"

"Alright. You're cool. Sandra will be thrilled." Luke began to leave, stopped, and looked back at Sandra's mother before saying, "I hope." He gave Sandra's mother a hug to reestablish good will. "Please, don't tell your husband I gave you a hug in your bedroom. He'll for sure swing that bat at me."

He marched out of the bedroom toward an uncertain fate.

Sandra and Luke found themselves seated at the table.

"First order of business. I assure you, with all my heart, I will never betray what I know about you—this androgen-resistance condition—to anyone. As Rabbi Becker would say, 'My hand to God.'" Luke held his right hand toward heaven to seal his assurance.

"I want to learn more about this genetic syndrome. I will never, under any circumstance, risk your family's privacy in this matter. I told your father, and I'm confirming to you, I'll die rather than betray this trust."

"Thank you. I know where you live and work. Where you go." Sandra gestured.

Luke thought of a metal bat. A concerned mother. Sandra's gesture. *What a day.*

Luke asked, "Who or what group makes up your primary medical care for this syndrome?"

"There are skilled people here in Phoenix. Los Angeles isn't far. They have great facilities and doctors there. Most procedures occurred in LA. My parents have spent too much. Fortunate I'm an only child. I owe them everything."

"You are wonderful. A gift from heaven. I know they're not disappointed. They made a magnificent baby. Wish they had more like you."

"More boys that look like girls. Some blessing from heaven," she harshly responded.

"Wait, you're judging this unfairly," Luke cautioned. "In high school, a biology teacher told us of babies born with both sets of genitalia, hermaphrodites. Arthur, a Native American from the Navajo tribe, part of the LDS Indian Placement Program, sat next to me. He said, '*Nadle*.'[5] I learned from Arthur that nadles are hermaphrodites or gender confused, like effeminate males. It goes many ways. These people are highly revered among Native Americans and receive special privileges in their society."

---

[5] Nadle: A term that describes "two-spirit people." Sex, gender, and sexuality in historic, contemporary Native American culture (LGBTQ) mainly within the Navajo tribe.

Sandra briskly interjected, "Native Americans didn't understand genetic factors. Why some babies are born with male and female genitalia. It doesn't make me feel privileged or accepted. How do you think the Lord, His Church, will treat me should I be exposed as genetically male? No approval in the 1978 Revelation to assure me, my kind, entry into the kingdom, is there?" Sandra's anger was obvious.

"You realize you're arguing the other side of the issue, don't you?" Luke asked. "The human genome, with its twists and turns, are part of the Lord's plan. When science with sociological research provide answers, changes will take place. Give Native Americans credit for recognizing what religious leaders have yet to see and learn. Acceptance. Tolerance. Even praise. Revelations will come. They are expected."

"Yeah, well, who will ask Heavenly Father to consider such issues? Besides, doesn't God already know? You call God a know-it-all. Why does He like messing with me, Job, starving children, Holocaust victims? Trials, tests, that *must* be endured are a weak response for compassion."

"Your point is taken. I agree with you far more than you think. Job is a fabricated story, nonliteral, along with Jonah and a bunch of other fanciful biblical tales. Let's forget that for a while. Please?"

Sandra nodded.

"You have an exceptional story. I appreciate your reasoned thoughts about details of your life with this syndrome. I now understand your actions. 'Tis noted. None of it has changed how I feel for you. Know this, each time you pushed me away, it hurt ... like sticking me with needles."

Sandra sat up in her seat. She saw tears in his eyes. Heard his shaken voice.

"You've never conveyed your love for me—or even told me if you do love me. I want to kiss your lips. You won't allow it."

Luke's words stung Sandra unbearably. She had hugged Luke, held him, received his warmth, accepted kisses on hands, fingers, and head (don't forget the leg), and even heard his confessions of love for her. Sandra's walls and barriers succeeded. She never expressed her heart's affection for Luke. Walls have their tendency to *keep in* what they want to *keep out*. Overcome, Sandra left her chair to escape the discomfort felt from Luke's words, walked a few steps, and flopped into a recliner.

Luke, unsure where Sandra headed, rose to his feet and stood beside the table. "I want to tell you about my fascination with Asia and Asian women—"

"Okay. Need to hear this. Don't spare details."

"—when in seventh grade, a music teacher wanted us to appreciate opera. Everyone groaned. I paid attention. She told the story of Madame Butterfly. Specifically, she explained what happened when Butterfly sung the Puccini aria '*Un Bel Di Vedremo.*' I simply want to tell this music appreciation experience."

Sandra nodded and waved her hand to continue.

"This romantic teacher dropped the needle on a 33 1/3 RPM record. Told us to listen for the English word *butterfly*. When it neared, she prepared us by saying, 'Now listen.' She softly sang 'Butterfly.' I heard the soprano sing, in English, 'Butterfly.' I was taken by it. The most beautiful piece of music I'd ever heard. Still is. I enjoy the tragic love story … Puccini's composition. Some guys acted like they were puking. I would've been slapped around expressing my preference for opera over Elvis. I should've told the teacher how beautiful the aria is. Should have thanked her for my appreciation of Puccini—"

"What of Asia and Asian women?"

"Yes. Excuse my detour. *Madame Butterfly* and *Turandot* each take place in Asia. Each opera revolve around a beautiful Asian woman. Two greatly loved arias, '*Un Bel Di*' and '*Nessun Dorma*' are heard in Puccini's compositions. What is it about the Asian culture and Asian women that have this effect?"

"My God, you're a hopeless romantic," Sandra criticized.

"Wanna know what I did the night before we played our racquetball game? I sung *Nessun Dorma* from *Turandot*. Well, the final lines: '*Vincerò. Vincerò. Vincerò.*' I will win. I will win. I will win."

"You didn't win," Sandra protested.

"Yeah, I surrendered. I was beaten. Like Turandot took power over Calaf. I love you, Sandra, with the same depth Calaf felt for Turandot. Look where we are."

"It's an opera. Turandot did not have my syndrome," Sandra objected.

"Who knows?" Luke speculated, "Androgen insensitivity wasn't understood until 1970. Turandot, this hot Asian woman, seems a bit extreme in her disdain for men, love, marriage. Beheaded dozens trying to win her approval through Ping, Pang, and Pong's stupid riddles. Why behave so harshly? These men thought of her as beautiful, strong, intelligent. Hell, Sandra, you treat me every bit like Turandot treated Calaf. Good men and princes killed with ice-cold indifference. For all we know, she bore your same syndrome. It's answered my questions about your behavior. Now, possibly answers questions about Turandot."

"I wanted to protect my identity," Sandra insisted. "Trust is earned. Betrayal is the price paid for self-disclosure. I could not risk rejection and the acidic words thrown at me should I be exposed."

"Understood." He gestured with defeat. "In the opera, Calaf lost. But he won. Big time!" Luke raised a victor's clenched fist above his head.

"Calaf was next in line for execution," Luke continued the story. "When asked for his name, Turandot could've replied, 'His name is Calaf.' We never would've heard the great love story of Turandot and Calaf, the tremendous opera, the aria '*Nessun Dorma*,' or Puccini's genius." Luke gestured himself being beheaded.

"What did Turandot say? She said, 'His name is Love.' Wrong answer. Do you see it, Sandra? It is the right answer. A big win for Turandot and Calaf. We're in the same paradox. I love you, Sandra. I'll lose again and again just to kiss your sweaty scars."

"Your assumptions, though interesting, analogous even, fail to provide a conclusion for this man-to-man discussion we're having."

Luke kept the high ground and fired his final salvo. "Here's my conclusion: I am a person of noble heritage. With a good name. Required traits from all who tried to gain Turandot's favors. Say that my name is Love. Should it take an eternity, we'll battle all challenges that lay ahead. Including your syndrome. What say you?... Dammit ... Make it good." Luke stood tall. Prayed his heart would not be broken.

Sandra, in the recliner, gazed at Luke intently for several seconds. Her eyes glanced briefly upward. She rose and walked to Luke. Stood toe-to-toe with him. Their eyes locked. She placed her hands to his face. Pulled his forehead to her own. Pressed her lips against his. A long, deep kiss that took away the breath of God.

Words were unneeded. The kiss communicated their commitment to each other. Devotion, duties, and obligations. All matters they required for the arduous journey and peaks to be climbed together. The kiss, spiritually transcenditory.

The kiss ended. Sandra asked, breathlessly, "What is this attraction you have for Asian women?"

"Whoa. Your mind is unrelenting." Luke took a deep breath and held Sandra closely. "Butterfly and Turandot are notable characters. Butterfly, badly treated, abandoned, then embarrassed by an American officer. She behaved honorably with her final suicidal act. Turandot is a mystery I never understood until today. People never appreciate uncommon qualities others possess. Neither gender nor ethnicity are important. I will cease being a flat thinker. It tells me each person's life matters. Inclusion without exception.

"Thanks, Sandra. You are the best of Butterfly and Turandot. Forget what I said about Asian women. I enjoy the operas. Your life is more meaningful than their stories."

"May I still call you Luke? Or must I say to others, 'his name is Love'?"

They kissed again, longer and deeper.

Overlord

They fight to end conquest. They fight to liberate.
—Franklin D. Roosevelt

Get your ass on the beach. I'll be there
waiting for you and I'll tell you what to do.
There ain't anything in this plan that is going to go right.
—Col. Paul R. Goode, D-Day pre-attack briefing

THE FUTURE IS FRAUGHT with hazard. Of necessity, to make heaven and hell resonate, mistakes must be minimal.

Sandra, her parents, and Luke called themselves *The Big Four*. Each gave an impression of generals and subcommanders seated around a tactical battlefield kitchen table. They engaged discussions to navigate through anticipated obstacles.

"All plans and objectives that regard Sandra's syndrome will have a codename: Overlord," Luke suggested. "It's the same codename given the invasion of Nazi-occupied France. D-Day—World War II."

Everyone approved.

"No one in my family—including my parents—need be told of Sandra's syndrome," Luke declared. "What the four of us know remains with us."

"We four will maintain our security," Sandra's father approved. "The fewer who know of Sandra's syndrome ... will minimize harm and exposure."

"Sandra and I should marry," Luke articulated as plain as water. "That will blanket much."

"Are you proposing?" Sandra tersely asked. "If so, contain your enthusiasm with this creative approach."

"As a matter of fact, I am. Sandra, I love you. I'm not minimizing our love, romance. I want to marry you. We'll make it good." Luke confirmed.

"We should discuss this," Sandra's mother contended. "Where will you marry? In a temple? LDS chapel? City hall? Las Vegas? Tongues will wag. More gossip will spread if you don't marry in a temple."

As the silence rested, Luke exclaimed, "We will marry in a temple."

Sandra blew back. "What? How? We'd be lying to our bishops, stake presidents, families. The deception is immoral, unethical. Should interviews take bad turns, I could be discovered. They would never try to understand. I'll be exposed—called 'queer.' They'd be right."

"Sandra, the deception of morality, ethics, rests with others. If Church members understood, they'd welcome you into the temple with open arms. Our destiny is *for time and all eternity*."

"Sandra, listen to Luke. Hear his thoughts." Sandra's father gestured with an open palm.

Luke sat expressionless and thoughtless.

"Uh, well, Sandra, knowledge progresses in science, less in social behavior, and um ... " As at a debate tournament, his reasoning grew. He gathered ideas. "Can you imagine what people thought in Old and New Testament times when a hermaphrodite child was born?"

Everyone looked at Luke oddly. Sandra's father thought, *Where's this going? What's he thinking?*

"They were shocked. 'What's God trying to do?' they asked. Bronze and Iron Age people didn't understand genetics. Moses, Isaiah, Peter, Paul, and Mary Magdalene were ignorant of facts as true as baptism that we take for granted. It's sad they didn't know about the human genome, the knowledge we possess today."

Luke built up steam and confidence.

"Two—five thousand years ago folks knew nothing about the double helix or general science. Men—excuse me—*people* observed, experimented, and duplicated their efforts to conclude the concrete facts we possess in the atomic twentieth century. Religions linger far behind current-day knowledge. We believe the same dumb fantasies people believed in Old Testament days. We call it righteous while it makes no sense."

Luke steamed ahead.

"Our Church took 150 years to give Blacks the priesthood. Our leaders behaved like it was a gracious act. The Church has a long way to go in this game of catch-up to behave properly toward Sandra. Native Americans are a just society. They regard Sandra as special, blessed. Our duty is fighting within the Church until acceptance is granted. 'Tis a worthy battle to win."

Luke had initiative. Took full advantage of it.

"Worldwide spiritual leaders, including the First Presidency and Quorum of the Twelve, are unaware of Sandra's syndrome—the human genome. Their lack of understanding requires our sympathy and forgiveness. Not our anger or fear. We will marry in the temple. Effect changes. Our leadership and persuasive influence will impact the prophet. All Church leaders and members. People everywhere! We shall be heard. Remembered for the good we hath wrought."

"Amen," Sandra's mother said as she patted Luke's forearm. Sandra's father nodded his head, awed by Luke's two-and-a-half-minute talk. Sandra smiled, shook her head, and blew him a kiss.

Luke offered a silent prayer. *Thank you, Lord. Tithing check is in the mail.*

"Wait." Sandra threw her hands in the air. "How will I answer questions? I don't want to lie."

"You won't need to lie. I've thought to myself how you'd respond," Sandra's mother explained. "Questions are not specific to gender. They ask with words like are you worthy? Are you clean? Do you pay a full tithe? Straightforward questions. So, give them straightforward answers."

"Above all," Luke added, "don't volunteer information. Let them ask questions. Provide short answers. 'Yes' or 'No' is all you need to say. Should a question make you feel uncomfortable, paraphrase what is asked into words you find comfortable. Answer your own self-made question. Bat your eyes like a homecoming queen if necessary. As a man, use the power of your feminine mystique. You'll get through it. I'll be nearby, if needed."

"My church calling gives me access to the temple recommend questions and temple interview protocol. We'll prepare you for all contingencies," Sandra's father assured.

"We'll conduct a few mock interviews. I really don't see complications," Luke said.

"I am queer. I'm not as—"

"Sandra," Luke said, "never say that again. Stop. You are not queer. You're a star. A child of God as much as any person on this planet. It is not you." Luke rose from his chair. "Church leadership and their commitment to ignorance is the issue. We, your parents, you—no one is queer." Luke realized he was on his feet. *When did I stand?*

The three stared at Luke, alarmed by his outburst.

I've embarrassed myself. "I'm sorry, Sandra." Luke fell back into his chair. "I apologize."

Sandra rushed to Luke. Sat on his lap. Wrapped her arms around him. Hugged as tightly as she could. Luke felt pleased she came to his protection. She comforted him. "In the short time you've been here, you've learned about androgen insensitivity, genetics, how all this has affected me. We should've prepared you for the shock. I take all blame."

Luke arched back and regretfully looked at her. "No. What you've shared is understood. I feel the concern you've expressed. I've been exposed to my own conflicted, arrogant attitudes, my thoughtlessness. **Queer**—it hurts me more deeply than you to hear that word. Please, no more words of self-denigration. We just became engaged ... hell, why would you marry an ass? In your own words, someone so damned goofy as I am?"

"I love you. It's your name." She put a hand on his face and looked in his eyes. "Luke, we'll do great things. We're meant for each other. You're Calaf. I'm Turandot. Two very different people who love each other more than what we are. What anyone expects of us." Sandra gave Luke a plush, ardent kiss.

This kiss took its sweet time, Sandra and Luke both reluctant to end it.

"It's time we leave," Sandra's father said, "the events of the day ended. They may want to make a baby." He stood, took his wife's hand, to lead her from the table.

"They can't make a baby," Sandra's mother bluntly countered. "Besides, they shouldn't be doing any of that kind 'til they're married."

"They're not children. Let 'em be. They understand what they can and can't do. How far they can go. Nature figures it out in the end."

"When did you become a philosopher?" she challenged.

"They are likely into something *transcenditory*. I like the word. C'mon, they'll find their own way." They walked to the hallway. "It's been a while since we engaged in behaviors close to *transcenditory*. Let's do our own research." Sandra's father smiled at his wife, opened the door, and extended a hand into their bedroom. Sandra and Luke, still locked in their kiss.

Conversations among the Big Four continued the next day. Where to marry was decided. Subsequent decisions needed resolutions.

"We will avoid lies," Luke advised. "However, we cannot speak openly or volunteer information that needn't be exposed. We are tightlipped, like keeping secrets. The Church, militaries, governments—each and all have similar policies. Without disclosure of personal information, our objectives will be met. Done for a higher purpose. Peace. Freedom from oppressors."

They each agreed to protect the truth within Overlord.

Sandra, Luke, and Sandra's parents conducted themselves like Nimitz, Churchill, FDR, or Eisenhower. Tactical procedures needed preparation. No matters leading to their marriage could arouse suspicion. *Sandra will be sheltered in plain sight of bullies. Our purpose? Initiate inclusion for those labeled uncommon.*

"We are like everyone else," Luke counseled. "No more, no less than any of God's children, the same rights of privilege for inclusion. We don't know why Heavenly Father allowed Sandra to be what she is. It would be nice to know what's in God's all-knowing brain. We'll persuade Gods and humans to understand. Engage compassion with reason."

We pleased Sandra when Luke used the word. Her best friend, now an ally. Alone no more. He understood the cruel world of intolerant partisans that threatened outcasts like her. Hope and freedom owned no restraints. She could expand and risk more greatly. Luke, at her side, presented an image of normalcy with its traditions. She felt delivered from enquiry. Her freethinking behavior, however, would forever invite challenge.

Decisions became unprecedented labor. Details became greatly relevant. The magnitude of their lives hinged on these decisions. *The glory of God is intelligence.* Sandra and Luke possessed abundant intelligence.

"When shall we marry?" Sandra asked.

"In August. During the longer break before fall semester. Write theses as 1979 ends. Defend, spring 1980." Luke formulated.

"Likely undoable," Sandra said. "But let's give it the good old college try."

"Where? Which temple?"

"Mesa," Luke suggested.

"No. Too little time with so much to accomplish." Sandra concluded. "Your family would struggle with the short fly-in-and-fly-out schedule."

"Either Provo or Salt Lake," Sandra's mother suggested.

"Salt Lake," they all agreed. Luke undertook the task to contact President Olsen, his former mission president and current Salt Lake Temple president, to perform the marriage.

Logistics? Expenses?

"Luke and I will budget this event with our own resources. The simpler and smaller the costs, the better. Mom, Dad, you've spent enough—too much—having me." Sandra, through her perils, formed few close friendships. Indeed, far fewer close family members who would be invited or participate in a wedding and reception. It also made Utah the better place to stage the event.

Rings?

"I refuse to wear a ring," Sandra insisted. "The tradition indicates a man's ownership over a woman. I won't have it. Diamonds are not rare or precious. Diamond companies are ruthless. Primarily to women and children who unearth diamonds. I refuse going into debt for gold, diamonds, receptions, gowns, dresses, food, and drink for a single day. It is not logical."

"I now know why I've fallen for Sandra," Luke said. "I don't care to wear a ring or watch. Singlehandedly, with what we'll save, she has paid at least one semester of graduate school for each of us, maybe two. We'll need an explanation as to why the ring part of the marriage ceremony is eliminated."

"We are the atypical couple. We'll find atypical solutions," Sandra concluded.

"Couples who cannot afford rings use strands of cloth when sealed. It's a common practice," Sandra's father said.

"Wedding reception?"

"We'll have a gathering that is intimate, simple. The closest of family, friends, and colleagues," Sandra concluded. "Graduate school makes time and expenses for a reception limited. We'll have an open-house in Surprise, late August."

"What of children? A family? How will this be explained?"

"I'm firing blanks. Low or zero sperm count. It'll take attention away from Sandra." Luke grinned.

"The issue is mine," Sandra prevailed. "Heavenly Father gave me this trial. We'll endure. We needn't concern ourselves until well into our marriage. People may be curious and inquire. No lies. We'll discuss children later. We have time to address the issue properly."

The matter quickly settled.

Sandra's syndrome, with Mormon issues of family and children, persisted as a highly sensitive concern. For now, Sandra felt at ease with her condition and circumstances. Her best friend to stand guard over a secret no one actually wanted to know or cared to understand, but would take opportunity to whisper hurtful words and persecute. Certainly, our heroes wanted to create a child.

Leave their genetic selves for the next generation. Only a miracle could make their prayers come true. Adoption remained their only possibility for a nuclear family. Not immediately, however.

Sandra and Luke, now rapt with each other, fixed their pursuits to earn advanced degrees. Ultimately achieve Overlord. The expression of the day, *upwardly mobile*.

The New Year in Surprise included enlightenment and entertainment. Great fun. The Big Four went to dinner, played games, and shared stories, usually centered on Sandra's experiences. All four shopped. Luke bought Sandra two dresses.

"Your dress at BYU is the best of all, Sandra," Luke confessed.

Luke and Sandra played racquetball on two different days at the ASU facility where Sandra's father taught and trained. A flyer near the courts posted a New Year dance. Luke pointed to it. "Let's go."

"I've never danced with a boy," Sandra confessed. "I danced at home with my parents. To dance with a boy in public would be something new for me. I don't know how."

Luke saw her discomfort. They spent a few hours together in basic training. Sandra, a quick learner, trusted Luke's leads. She enjoyed their close encounters as they waltzed, took Latin steps, or learned to Lindy. Rock-n-roll individual and exuberant. They danced and kissed their way from 1978 into 1979.

Luke sat alone in the family room. He contemplated both joy and sorrow the morning would produce. On the morrow, Sandra and he would battle again the wintry cold at BYU. So much accomplished. Great distances traversed. Life decisions made in Surprise. *All worth it.* Luke smiled inside himself.

Sandra came into the room wearing a long, white robe tied securely at the waist. Hair wrapped with a towel; she carried a brush in her hand. Luke seized the opportunity. "Can I brush your hair?"

"Thought you might. I'll enjoy it."

"You smell good. Taste as good as you smell?"

"Wanna know?"

Luke chuckled. "Quit tempting me, you vixen. I need to count brush strokes. Five hundred?"

"Drop it to fifty or twenty-five; I can't wait that long to kiss you." She kissed his cheek.

Sandra sat on the carpet and scooted back to Luke, who sat on the sofa. He took the brush, clutched her hair, and began to brush, making certain never to catch a snag or pull her hair.

"Once again, you seem to have experience," Sandra observed.

"Three sisters, my mom. Cries of pain when they brushed their own hair. Learned snags are *no bueno*. Brushing hair seemed enjoyable to them when there are no snags."

"It feels good to have someone brush my hair. Thanks, Luke. I love you very much."

Luke smiled, "I hope you will give me every opportunity to brush your hair even during the busiest of times. It will give us the chance to talk, be together."

"I like the idea. Thanks again for the clothes you bought for me. You spend too much money," she cautioned. "We need to finish school. By the way, my mom is more curious than I. What makes that red-and-gray dress your favorite?"

Luke smiled inside himself. He continued to brush. "I've told you—what's in it."

"Luke, please."

"I'll tell you when we're back at BYU—when you're wearing the dress. You can pass the information to your mom then."

"You frustrate me. I want to know now."

"I'll tell you when you're wearing the dress," he pressed. "I have another idea. Forgive my imagination."

"Okay ... By the way, I enjoy this ... you brushing my hair."

Luke took another stroke through her hair then asked, "Has someone ever massaged your feet?"

Sandra pondered. "No. Not professionally, by a masseuse or anything. I rub my own feet all time. Why?"

"Professor Douglas spoke about nonverbal studies associated with interpersonal, marital relationships. Got me thinking. To brush hair and massage feet are menial tasks, though pleasurable, at least for me. They are *transcenditory*. I'm brushing your hair. A behavior that is sensual without being sexual. It expresses understanding beyond words. Makes us each happy."

"The pleasure reduces stress. It calms. There is merit in what you say, an action that communicates a message. Please don't stop," Sandra said. "Keep going."

"I want to test this idea. No matter how annoyed you become with me through careless words or actions, please don't ever deny me the chance to brush your hair or massage your feet."

"Fun. How often?" Sandra asked. "To brush hair and massage feet consume time. You have my interest. Speak. Interesting conversation."

"The Savior washed the feet of His disciples. The act expressed humility, love. Feet are calloused, smelly, and grungy—unless you have a fetish for them. To touch, manicure, massage feet usually require money for someone to do such. However, should a husband say to his spouse, 'Our children have been little shinolas today. Let me massage your feet, then we'll prepare for bed. Cuddle for the night.' To voluntarily engage a menial act done for the pleasure of someone you love – transcends. Again, sensual without intercourse, although a foot massage could lead to sex. Just don't expect or force sex to happen. The act of service for one you love without expectation for some favor in return is *transcenditory*. It communicates a vital message that words cannot adequately explain. The same is possible while I brush your hair."

"A connection. A link is established. Like when you kissed my owie."

"Yes. Douglas reported couples grow apart during marriage. Children and money are big factors for the loss of interest between married people. Even if we never have children in our home, no matter, I never want us to wander far from each other. I hope we say the words *I love you* each day we're together. That our touches will keep us close via the *transcenditory*. Sandra, our behaviors communicate love, hate, bias, charity more eloquently than words."

"We can create a quantitative instrument and collect data. I'll structure the research study," Sandra volunteered.

"Sandra, your hair is remarkably lush, smooth," Luke complimented.

"Those with my syndrome usually have thick, luxurious hair."

"You are fortunate to be such a person," Luke said.

Sandra turned abruptly toward Luke. "I never imagined I'd hear anyone tell me I am fortunate to be what I am."

She pulled Luke to the carpet. He landed on his back. Sandra fell atop him and kissed his lips fully, passionately. Luke plunged his hands into her hair. The two embraced. Kissed. Writhed on the carpet.

Touch remained an integral commitment in their lives. Sensual without the expectation for sexual pleasure. A reward for labor and worthy deeds. Brushed hair, caressed feet, hands held—each delivered messages of concern. Empathetic meanings shared through their touches for labors rendered. The behavior kept Sandra and Luke close, conversant. Words spoken during these cherished experiences gave assurance, praise. At some point, appropriately, sexual pleasure. Touches allowed each to receive and give, charity with needed humility. Acts of compassion that transcended language. *Transcenditory* communication, or spiritual transcendence.

Peaks to Ascend

I questioned God's silence. I don't have an answer for that.
Does it mean that I stopped having faith?
No, I have faith, but I question it.

—Elie Wiesel

"TIME FOR THE IN-LAWS to meet the new outlaws," Luke said. His family suspected an announcement. Luke left work at the bank without prior notice. Flew to Phoenix for the New Year to be with a person named Sandra. The entire family—married siblings, their children, and all—waited eagerly to meet this unknown person.

Luke scheduled the get-together at his parent's home—a smaller, three-bedroom, two-bath residence that ably housed six children, with occasional friends and guests. Couches turned into beds. For one child, the downstairs furnace/laundry room kept a single bed and small table for study in the corner. No one ever complained of meager essentials. The home always clean, neat, and well-stocked. Smelled of fresh-baked bread each Thursday. Mom's day off from work. Their home, like the family, boasted its own personality. Fit, fun, welcome for everyone. Especially the holidays. On this occasion, the atmosphere was roast beef, Sunday, family night.

Sandra entered the small kitchen with Luke from a porch via a side entrance. From the kitchen they saw "the whole famn damily," as Luke whispered in Sandra's ear. They gadded about in the living room. Luke and Sandra walked through the kitchen to approach the anxious crowd in the limited, but adequate, gathering space. The family ogled the unknown guest with curious smiles, awaiting an explanation. Sandra wore Luke's favorite dress. Tall, poised, gorgeous.

Luke stood behind Sandra. His hands clasped her upper arms. Each tense, unaccustomed with the situation. They faced a sizeable family.

"It is good to see everyone; we're happy you're all here. This is Sandra." Heads nodded toward her with smiles. "Sandra and I would like you to share in our happiness. We are pregnant."

Sandra swung about. *Whap!* Slapped Luke soundly on the chest, then turned back to the family and thundered, "I am not pregnant. We're getting married." She pointed at Luke. "Where did you get him?"

"The hospital," one shouted with a grin.

"Training School," another laughed.

"Mental sanatorium in Provo," the last said. "Your choice."

Everyone chuckled, fully enjoyed the humor. Luke's parents welcomed Sandra. Luke received handshakes, high fives with hugs, back slaps. Each family member milled the carpet near Sandra, waiting their turn to introduce themselves. Well-mannered, she took special interest in each person who spoke with her.

The conversations gave Sandra information that confirmed the origins for Luke's distinctive humor. It also provided insight into his good nature. Sandra soon understood, to some degree, the closeness and conflicts that occur in large families.

"I've seen Luke's bare bum more times than he has, I diapered him so often." The eldest sister smiled with a subtle undertone of lament.

Luke's youngest brother, an eighth grader, passed Sandra his own compliment. "Luke's right; you're good looking."

Sandra's heart shuddered. She managed a smile. "Thank you."

If born into this family, I would have been exposed. Not that these people are uncaring. There are so many of them. Sandra felt intensely threatened. *Even now, should a hint of my syndrome and Luke's involvement with me be known, it would be disastrous.*

Our heroes drove back to BYU along Highway 89. Early evening shadows darkened as nighttime fell. Temperatures dropped as the sun quietly fell behind the Oquirrh Mountains. Streetlights, shops, and homes, still adorned with Christmas decorations, bade farewell to the holidays.

"Luke, your family is kind. Fun. They're also large. Will our lives, Overlord, remain confidential?"

"As long as the two of us are secure, Overlord is secure. Mind you, that's not a threat. Even if you left me for a scumbag or embarrassed me in front of the world, I will never expose Overlord. We have a purpose. We'll succeed. Sandra, I love you."

"I love you too." She smiled; her shoulders shook with giggles. "We are pregnant. You really are something." She gently slapped his chest.

"It was funny. Someday, someone will use it again to get a laugh."

The two cuddled ... one last duty.

"Luke, you promised to tell me. Why do you love this dress?"

"You're in it, obviously."

"Enough. Now, please. We have plenty of time before we get to my apartment. What is it you love so much about this dress?"

"Remember the first day of class last semester, when we first met?"

"Yes."

"You won't be angry, please?"

"About what?"

"Are you aware how well this dress drapes your body?"

"It's form fitting. No, I guess I don't."

"Sandra, your shape is beautiful; so are your eyes, face, hair. I can only say, that dress cannot conceal your physical charms, particularly your breasts."

"Luke. You looked at my boobs?"

"Well, yeah. Most of the class period. Certainly, as you first stepped into the room."

"Luke," she protested. "What could you see? What does this dress do to me?"

"While you sat at your desk"—Luke paused for a few seconds—"the top of your dress bloused perfectly for me to see a small portion of your breasts. The way you buttoned the dress, or something in its design ... your shape is scenic. Hubba, hubba."

"Scenic? I felt an impression you, or someone, was looking at me. Is that why you came and sat next to me?"

"No. I jumped desks and students for one simple reason. You smiled toward me while standing there ... at the entrance. I didn't see all I saw until I sat next to you. It's nothing bad, really. I'm a good boy. I kept thanking the Lord for your beauty. You are gorgeous. I hope you're not upset."

"How much could you see?"

"Some breast. Wonderful. Out of this world. I find you very feminine and sexy. What do you want me to say?"

"Luke, I really did not know this outfit or I moved you. The things a woman can do to men." Sandra patted at her chest and tugged buttons. "I thought being genetically male—well—thanks for making me aware I have appeal?" Sandra smiled; a bit lost.

"At times you moved in your desk. I saw nothing. You'd shift weight and your dress revealed heaven. My prayers answered, again."

"I could feel it, your eyes on me. I could feel it."

"Are you upset? Honestly, I couldn't see that much. You have other clothes that are more revealing. I didn't hear or retain much from the lecture that day. You captured my attention."

"You asked my mother to go shopping and buy other dresses. Oh my, this will be a fun story to tell her. She's been as curious as I." Sandra fiddled with buttons. "I didn't show anything to your family today, did I?"

"You and the dress behaved very well today. The new dresses are open collar, with buttons. I thanked your mother for making you. She and your dad made a great baby, Baby. You make people, especially me, smile."

Sandra buried her face into Luke's chest, nestled closer. She silently speculated, *He's an enigma.* She loved his innocence, the ability to compliment without the intent to do so. *He is unaware of his words, the meaning he impresses upon me and others.*

"Sandra, it's not only your breasts I love. Though they are beautiful. It's what's between them."

Bewildered, Sandra thought, *What's between them?* She looked.

Luke spoke effortlessly, "You have a big heart buried deep inside you. Kinder, more caring, than you realize. I'll explain it all. Not today. We'll talk of this before the wedding."

Stilled for an instant by his comment, Sandra wrapped her free arm around his waist and hugged. "I am happy we discovered each other."

"Thanks, for loving me," Luke said. "Remind me of this conversation prior to our marriage."

Night now surrounded them. For the remainder of their drive, they enjoyed silence. Safe within each other's arms, the lights of their love shone brightly.

Department chair, Dr. Clawson, assigned Sandra two separate research grants and a quantitative math class; the first instructed by a nontenured faculty member. Luke continued to instruct two adjunct courses, assisted Dr. Portman, and worked bank collections. Incomes from these sources eased burdens as the wedding approached.

Time passes too slowly for the young, too rapidly for the aged. Late June arrived. Experiences to be shared and ideas discussed as their day to marry neared.

Sandra and Luke committed to stand atop Mount Timpanogos, a sixteen-mile roundtrip hike rated difficult/strenuous to a height of nearly twelve thousand feet. Never attempt to climb the peak in bad weather. Today, the sky sunny with few clouds. At these altitudes, smog is nonexistent. Firm, well-established trails to the peak lead to thin, but clear air. Pine, firs, quaking aspens, conifers, shrubs, and brightly colored wildflowers grace trails through meadows and basins to the peak. Emerald Lake, quite blue, is below the glacier. Steep, 200 feet long waterfalls are seen along the Aspen Grove trail. Along the way, hikers will see mountain goats, deer and birds. On occasion a moose. Rarely, if ever, a bear or cougar. Rugged cliffs, canyons, ridges and monumental mountain scenery.

Sandra and Luke began the hike at Timpooneke in American Fork Canyon. They returned via Aspen Grove in Provo Canyon. Friends started from Aspen Grove. They returned via Timpooneke. Once hikers reach the saddle area of Mount Timpanogos, there is a single trail to the peak. "We'll meet at the summit or on the saddle trail, exchange keys, hike back to the cars, and gather for dinner in Provo."

Luke spent his seminal years in Utah Valley. He grew to adulthood at the base of Mount Timpanogos. *Timp is as majestic as the Tetons, especially the backside. Nothing is more breathtaking than when a full moon rises behind Timpanogos and makes its way into the early evening sky. People stand on porches, assemble stools on decks, or gather in driveways to watch the spectacle.*

Timpanogos secured a special influence in Luke's mind for reasons he wished to share with Sandra. As a young boy, Luke heard the story of a Native American princess.

"Utahna threw herself from a cliff, saving the life of Red Eagle, her mate. The silhouette of Utahna's resting body can be seen by valley dwellers as Mount Timpanogos itself. I have difficulty seeing a reclined body in the mountain. However, a lying body is possible to see as snow blankets the mountain. It looks like Utahna lying at rest under a white sheet."

"Is there any truth to that legend?" Sandra asked. They held hands as they paced the trail.

"It's not even a Native American story. A non-Native American BYU professor made up the story back in the 1920s. There are probably a dozen different versions floating around. A dozen other mountains look like reclining bodies. Timpanogos is special for its heart. No other mountains have a heart deep inside them."

Sandra, the ever-practical logician, said, "I've seen the heart inside Timpanogos Cave. It's a stalactite."

"I get that. But the story, a mountain that looks like a resting princess. A two-ton heart inside the mountain is as impressive as you, Sandra. Well-built, excellently proportioned, intelligent, beautiful."

"Why do these stories have a sacrificial princess? A virgin?"

"The mountain is tall, expansive. You can't look up at Timpanogos without seeing the moon and stars. The stuff of legends. That's what you are, Sandra, a perfect example of nature, and you love me. It's a mystery."

Sandra studied Luke's face, expressions, movements. His goofy words. *Is he aware of his words? Is his goodness so innate that he is unaware? He's the bigger mystery, not I. What is he? Is he thinking? Aware?*

"Luke, stop."

They turned to each other. Sandra held his head firmly. She peered straight into his eyes to find Luke. She wanted to see him, hoped for something *transcenditory*, like the kiss.

Nothing happened. For untold seconds, possibly a minute, she explored Luke's eyes vainly for answers. Finally, she pushed away and shot, "You are insane or a savant. Whichever, please don't leave me, Luke."

"What were you trying to do?"

Sandra kissed his face and tightly hugged Luke. "There are parts of you no one will understand nor explain. I can't. Never doubt my love for you." She kissed his face again.

"Sandra, what do you want me to say? I'm not complex. Not at all."

She snatched his hand. "Let's keep hiking."

"Sandra, can we talk about something personal?"

"Of course. What?"

"Remember when you told me of the surgery to widen and deepen your vagina?"

Sandra giggled. "Landmark day. How could I forget? Why?"

"Specialists said a man of six inches is preferred. Nothing Larger."

"I'm happy you took notes." Sandra smiled.

"I took measurements." He breathed as though he possessed top-secret information.

"When?"

"Last night. I borrowed a tape measure." Luke mimicked pulling a yard from the case. "Before long, emphasis on *long*, I measured—"

Whap! "Quit being cute. What did you learn?"

"I'm not quite six inches …"

"Flaccid or erect?"

"Erect."

"How'd that happen? Did you have a *Playboy*? Details," Sandra goaded.

"It's not difficult. You know whenever I get a boner. You can tell."

"You try to hide it, that's why. Even at church."

"What do you want me to do when you put your hand on my legs or inner thigh?"

"It's so much fun when the sacrament is passed. I have power." She waved her hands near his groin. "I control your mind. Body parts." She spoke as a crazed charmer.

"Geez, Sandra, there are people on this mountain." Luke looked behind and around them. "Every time I think of you, it happens." He pointed skyward. "My unit is positioned directly due north."

"North is that way." Sandra pointed true north.

"Either way, it's good I'm not Wilt Chamberlain. I don't want to hurt you or for us to be incompatible due to my enormous size or lack thereof."

"Aaahh," she sighed. "We'll make do, or do a lot, with what you're packing." She giggled, tickled under his arms.

"Sandra, I want to see you naked. Is it wrong for me to say that?"

"No, it isn't. I want to see you naked too. I can't wait to see and touch you with no clothing," Sandra seductively confessed. "We'll fit perfectly. Thanks for sharing what you've got, big fella."

"Quit teasing me. Men are sensitive about this thing," he timidly pled. "Can you imagine small breasts?"

"Ooh, Luke. Have you been looking at me again?" She feigned astonishment with her breasts postured outward.

"Each day. It's hard not staring. You're perfect. Heavenly Father worked overtime making you."

"Thank you. You're sweet." *There he goes again. Is he thinking? Aware of his words?*

"We have six weeks 'til the wedding," Luke said. "It's like Christmas. It's gonna take forever to get here."

"Wilt Chamberlain," Sandra shook her head. "What is it about guys and their penis size? Or New York skyscrapers? Besides, my doctor has prepared me for the big day. Emphasis on *big* day." She grinned. "I estimated your girth accurately."

"You sly vixen. Love your surprises We'll discover what pleasures us. We'll fit or die trying," Luke drummed.

"I want to look into your eyes the first time you enter me," Sandra announced. "Lights will be on. I want to guide you in with our eyes locked together."

"I've never thought of that. Straight into each other's eyes. I look forward to that." He imagined.

Their conversation aroused them. They stopped and kissed passionately. Luke pressed his lips to Sandra's face. He continued their embrace with more kisses. On her ear, below the ear, neck. Sandra sighed and softly moaned when Luke blew what he called a *bluzzard* on the tender skin of her neck.

Sandra wrestled away from Luke's grasp with a scream. Stunned, she looked at Luke with annoyance. "I've warned you about doing that."

Luke laughed. Ran away as fast as he could, Sandra in hot chase. Pleasantly riled, she sought payback. Luke zigzagged in attempts to escape capture. His laughter ended when she jumped on him and wrestled him to the ground.

Sandra dominated. She slapped and struck him playfully. Tickled under his arms, stomach, and waist. "You deserve this."

"Stop, please. Sandra, I love you."

"Stop laughing. I'll think about it."

"We're going to attract attention. There are other hikers on the trail."

"Those who live by the sword will die by the sword. When you're sound asleep, deep in a delta brainwave, I'm gonna blow on your stomach. Teach you a lesson. You're such a snot." Sandra grinned broadly.

"I did it to protect our virginity until we're married in the temple." Luke twisted with laughter. He made attempts to hold her arms and hands. "If I kept kissing you, your neck, the next thing you know, we'd be naked and doing it here, out in the open, on Timpanogos." He struggled to protect himself. Each laughed aloud.

"I might prefer losing my virginity rather than take a bluzzard from you. How'd you create that silly word?"

"It's a simple, home-grown expression. Sounds like what it is."

"One day, someone will hurt themselves when you do that."

"Yeah, they'll die from laughter." He continued to snicker. "I won't do it again. Certainly not today. Maybe tomorrow."

The two playfully wrestled on long, wild grass a few yards from the trail. Sandra straddled Luke. He reached up and pulled her down. They kissed. The kiss continued while a small group of hikers passed a distance on the trail.

"People could complain to a ranger," Luke suggested.

"What will they say? 'There are two men kissing near the trail.'"

"Sandra, I thought such language and inferences are taboo. I'm shocked."

"No one can hear. Since I have been with you, there are long periods of time I don't even think of myself as an androgen-insensitive person. You are Luke, a man. I am Sandra, a woman. That's the way we behave ... Enjoy each other ... It is what we are. I've learned from you. Sarcasm. Humor. Tools that release great stress. My syndrome has continually hounded me, but I'm not bothered by it when I am with you. I now find humor within myself. How am I doing?"

"Timing and delivery could improve. Don't do it often." He smiled. "We'll have a lifetime to perfect our special kind of wit related to what makes you so special. Just smiles between us. Let's get moving."

Sandra rose, grabbed Luke's hand, helped lift him to his feet. They adjusted their backpacks and soon back on the trail of their steep climb.

"Did Jesus ever smile?" Luke asked Sandra, hand in hand.

"What?"

"Jesus wept. Did He ever smile?"

"Odd question."

"Happiness is the object and design of our existence, as we are taught. We possess the truth of the Restoration. Are we a happy people? Is Heavenly Father or Jesus happy? Do they smile? Share laughs?"

"I believe so," Sandra answered. "What makes you think like this?"

"You do."

"How?"

"Sarcasm, humor. Finding smiles in what we are, what we have. All we do."

"Okay, what's on your mind?"

"Charlie Chaplin struggled with chronic problems of depression, yet his life's work made people smile, laugh," Luke responded. "Don't you find that odd?"

"I find it heartbreaking," Sandra countered.

"Chaplin composed the song 'Smile,'" Luke said. "When you hear the lyrics, it tells Chaplin's story. Jesus never smiled in the Bible. Smiled just once in the Book of Mormon. God is jealous, angry, critical, comin' down hard on people with famine, floods, pestilence, and death."

"We disappoint Him," Sandra responded.

"Possibly. No reason for Him to behave so harshly. Behave so cruelly. I'm not convinced His behavior is appropriate," Luke contended. "God should try a different approach. Have you ever thought God, or those like Him, need a psychiatrist? Better emotional control, behavioral management. Surely an analyst. Someone with whom to discuss His frustrations."

"Luke," Sandra exclaimed, "what is your point? Is there a problem?"

"I grasp my problems pretty well. Even yours, Sandra. Is God taking care of His problems? Personal or whatever? Does He smile? Enjoy a good laugh? Or is He continuously angry, jealous, troubled, unendingly disappointed in the results of His work? He seems to always threaten His children. That's not so loving or kind. If so, He should have created us with lesser intelligence like all other creatures on this planet. To me, it is difficult to punish innocence. After all, ignorance is bliss." Luke smiled broadly.

"An intriguing thought, Luke," Sandra mused. "Are you suggesting happiness is enjoyed by less experienced, lesser intelligent, smaller-brained creatures? Or humans?"

"Homo sapiens, Neanderthal, Lucy, Cro-Magnon—all have been on Earth for hundreds of thousand years. God didn't deliver His commandments and anger toward people 'til the last four to five thousand years or so. Brains require time to develop and grow so God could express His wrath and displeasure. That's my point … If God really spoke." Luke softened his voice, "He's a know-it-all, and He knows we know far, far less than He does. It's scary. Makes Him scary."

"So that I am clear on this," Sandra said, "God should smile. Be more tolerant toward humanity struggling with a three-pound brain that is still evolving. Our brains are still learning to think, interact, and reason, emphasis on *reason*, with an omniscient, omnipotent Heavenly Father … God should show far greater patience."

"While humankind remains ignorant, or shall we say *innocent*, God's simple miracles are impressive, like aspirin or morphine to relieve pain. Myths and superstitions become assured proofs among innocent, lesser experienced, or within the fantasies of untrained minds."

"I understand," Sandra concurred. "Seeing jet aircraft during Moses's lifetime, or during the meridian of time, would've been astonishing to those folks. Something so advanced seen by ignorant, innocent minds establishes hegemony, along with social construction over the minds of naïve people."

"You understand, Sandra, men have larger brains than women." His tone indicated tongue-in-cheek.

"Not by much, Luke. The frontal lobe and limbic cortex of the female brain is generally larger than those of men and are associated with problem-solving and emotional control."

"Hmm. The parietal cortex, which gives the perception of space, and the amygdala, which is linked to sexual and social behavior, tend to be larger in the male brain than the female." Luke grinned.

"Women have ten times as much white matter related to intelligence than men," Sandra victoriously stated.

"Men have about six and a half times the amount of gray matter than women," Luke responded. "It, too, is related to general intelligence."[6]

"Glad you're retaining what we've learned in class. Is this a competition?" Sandra elbowed him.

"Does size matter?" Luke asked.

"We'll learn if six inches is enough on our wedding night, big guy," Sandra nudged.

The two laughed aloud. Held each other tightly.

"Luke, you think strangely."

"No. I think skeptically. That makes me think critically. I am dangerous, according to scholars, when thinking skeptically. You are no different. We're both dangerous thinkers," Luke concluded. "We are contrarians."

"Wow. Are we the second coming of Bonnie and Clyde? People in your gospel doctrine class might be troubled by our dangerous thinking."

"Why? We are merely curious. We challenge. I don't repeat the same words, ponder the same concepts, or plow the same ground every Sunday. Or any other days each week. Neither do you."

"I have been fairly consistent concerning gospel principles my whole life."

"Not in regard to your syndrome. When you told me about your syndrome, you railed against God. You did. The conflicts between what you are and Church policies/doctrine, culture, gender issues, gender identification and so much more. You have frustrations. You want to argue with God. Your arguments are valid, meaningful."

Luke, silent for a few yards, suddenly blasted, "I want to take your dad's bat and swing it at anyone who'd call you queer."

They hiked more strides in solemn silence. Finally, Luke angrily uttered, "You are the most perfect person I've ever met. You are distinct, uncommon." He softened. "Thanks for selecting me as

---

[6] Data cited by Sandra and Luke regarding female and male brains is accurate. Enjoy researching the *differences between female and male brains*. Each gender possesses unique gifts and uses.

your companion. Sandra, I am not androgen insensitive, but I have my own *Q* word. I feel equally threatened by it."

Sandra anxiously asked, "What *Q* word?"

"I question. Expressly our Church," Luke boldly confessed. "Questions endanger me. With my family, friends, colleagues at BYU, Church members, and Church leadership. Definitely God. My questioning mind threatens us both. There is much I support in the Church. However, there's far more I question since I learned of your syndrome."

"Luke, we are interdependent. Yes, I railed," Sandra admitted. "I question Heavenly Father, Church dogma, policies, and cultural practices. You're queer in many ways yourself," Sandra smiled. "I don't think either of us are dissimilar to other members of the Church or people in the world. You take yourself too seriously— just like I probably take myself too seriously." After taking more steps, Sandra admitted, "I fear bullies."

"I understand your conclusion. We're not Lone Rangers. There are several like we are, who fear being discovered. LDS members who say nothing. Hold doubts inside that are unspoken, yet remain silent. They put on a good show of conformity, notably with their money."

"Fair observation, Luke."

"Can I tell you of one or two questions I have concerning God?"

"Not 'til on our way down the mountain," she sternly answered. "Please be warned. Don't get caught placing Hershey Kisses in my mailbox. It's a crime. Nothing is to interfere with our wedding day. Seeing each other naked. Got that?"

Luke smiled, hugged her tightly for two steps, then chuckled. Unexpectedly, he lifted Sandra into his arms, like a groom who crosses a threshold. He looked into her eyes. Kissed her. Very subordinately and matrimonially, Luke said, "Yes, Dear. I got that."

Our heroes reached the saddle. The steeper, more arduous climb to the summit awaited them. The air thinned; temperature cooled. From here to the peak consisted only of rockface. Large, loose, black stones underfoot. The hike began in earnest. The pattern predictable: Climb a few yards. Stop. Catch your breath. Climb a few yards. Stop. Catch your breath. Drink a few gulps of water. Climb a few yards. Stop. Catch your breath. Think, *I should turn, go back*. Climb a few yards. Stop. Catch your breath. Think, *Why am I doing this?* Climb a few yards. Stop. Catch your breath. *Who said this is fun?* Climb a few yards. Stop. Catch your breath. Finally, an hour later, Sandra and Luke stood at the peak of Mount Timpanogos.

"Where you guys been? We thought you'd arrive first," their friends good-naturedly ribbed.

"Sandra's been distracting me. Lollygaggin' along the trail, mainly on the rockface. You know people from Arizona. They're not made like we—"

Whap! "I was forced to carry him the last two hundred yards," Sandra playfully bantered.

Hugs and chuckles.

Sandra and Luke held each other as they looked over and beyond the world before them. "Keep your feet under you. From here it's straight down. In every direction," Luke advised.

"Look at this view," Sandra said, gazing in awe. *A glorious landscape.*

To the east, Heber. Northward, Park City. Below them, the glacier that fed Emerald Lake. Northwest, Salt Lake City and the Great Salt Lake. Those with binoculars or a telescope searched for recognizable sites. They hoped to see the Capitol Building or Salt Lake Temple, the site where Sandra and Luke would be sealed for *time and all eternity*. To the west Provo and Utah Lake. Beyond the Oquirrh Mountains, Tooele, Bonneville Salt Flats, the Great Basin. To the south stood Nephi, farmland, empty terrain. All beautiful, panoramic, colorful.

Cameras clicked. Hikers munched snacks or downed sandwiches. The experience met all expectations. "I've been told to hike here as the sun rises or sets. I've heard the view is magnificent. Should we try someday?" Luke asked.

"Someday." Sandra nodded. She wanted to look in all directions at once. Luke stood behind Sandra with his arms wrapped around her. He guaranteed her balance. *No one as wonderful as she should fall from her grand, gifted place.* He vowed at that instant: *I will do all that is in me to make whole what she's been denied. Even if I must contend with God Himself.*

They watched aircraft fly below them on approach to Salt Lake International. Pointed toward cities and landmarks in the valleys. After rehydrating and eating snacks, they exchanged keys with their friends. Conversed, told stories, laughed. Prepped for the trek down. Luke took a small stone, placed it in his pocket. He stepped toward Sandra, kissed the back of her head as they took a final gaze of the world.

The group reached the saddle area. Sandra and Luke headed to Aspen Grove. Their friends marched toward Timpooneke. "See you at the restaurant," they waved to one another.

The hike to Aspen Grove was easier, faster, and far more enjoyable than the climb to the peak.

"Sandra, I wanna state a point … about God."

"We're on our way down the mountain. Go."

"I have concluded that God cannot experience awe or be surprised. He is an omniscient know-it-all. Obviously drives Him mad, psychologically."

"Okay, my skeptical lover. Explain." Luke's thoughts continuously intrigued her.

"If we, or anyone else, planned a surprise birthday party for Heavenly Father, He'd say, 'I already know you planned this party for me. The slippers you purchased as a gift are a size too small. Could you please take them back and get the BYU blue pair, size ten, the ones I really want? Thanks, I know you'll do it.' His existence is dull, uneventful. It drives Him mad, literally. He knows the punchline before the joke is told, give or take a few million years. What fun is that?"

"Interesting observation, Luke. What else do you question?"

"God cannot feel joy or actual disappointment. As a know-it-all, He already knows who has won or will win every World Series or war. He knew an eon ago that the Yankees would win the 1978 World Series in six games against the Dodgers and knew before the war began that the Allies would be victorious over the Axis powers of World War II. God gets vindictive with people for doing something He already knows has happened … will happen … Lunacy."

"I see," Sandra answered. "We are so sure of our beliefs and practices that we never doubt or question what we do or say. Is that wise? There is no challenge for God. Nothing changes."

"God has tolerance for all lesser creatures, but not for those who are intelligent, but far less intelligent than He, the mortal and inexperienced humans on earth." Luke continued, "The Church teaches that we can become like God. But, individuals shouldn't pursue it. To be omniscient, omnipotent, omnipresent is madness. Are we so certain of our ways and methods, we never question what we do? Socially? Religiously? Including Blacks, the priesthood, and people like you, Sandra."

"I see your reasoning. Scholars, even characters on *Star Trek*, have already explored these issues," Sandra smartly responded.

"God is powerless. As an omniscient, omnipotent being, He knows what the outcome will be for all life on this planet. He has no power to alter the past, change a person's mind. He cannot be surprised or awed by what we do in the future, because for Him, He is angry and insane. He, or God the Mother, will not do a thing except watch Armageddon take place, in spite of humanity's best efforts to prevent it from happening. End of story. He lives an utterly dull, unproductive existence. I do not want to become like God is—I enjoy the wonder that comes from surprise birthday parties, to be awed by a sunrise or sunset. I want to live as if what I do will make God smile for doing something unexpectedly cool, like marrying you." Luke smiled at Sandra.

"It makes me smile to hear what I didn't know you would say." Sandra wrapped her arms around Luke and hugged him as they kept pace down the path.

"Luke, I'm a numbers person."

"That you are," Luke responded. "When married, you'll be responsible for the checkbook."

"I've been thinking about me. Probabilities," Sandra admitted.

"Oh-oh, are we in trouble?"

"I have a few conclusions. Like to hear them?" Sandra marched solemnly.

"I'm a captive audience. What have you concluded?"

"Nature, among all its life forms, will misfire occasionally. I am speaking about genetic misfires."

"True. I've seen a two-headed calf, people with six fingers, other peculiarities."

"Nature hits the mark somewhat consistently. Abnormalities occur from time to time. Inasmuch as I am queer, am I a part of God's plan?" Sandra asked.

"Do you want me to respond? Or are you asking rhetorically?"

"Just asking. Like others with my syndrome, I am meant to die. I have no place in the continuance of humanity or family."

"Sandra, knock off that shinola. You aren't meant to die, not at all. You are someone distinctive, gifted. We've made a purpose for ourselves. It ain't makin' babies, if that's what you're implying. I'd be the one to die if you weren't here to give me life."

Sandra stopped Luke in midstride, hugged him, turned, and restarted their descent down the mountain. "My point is this: Genetic oddities, those who possess them, rarely pass what they are to offspring."

"Actually, they do," Luke countered. "There are dozens of penguin species, similar with differing characteristics for each. Swedes, Japanese, aborigine."

"That's understood. Indicators of evolutionary development. Thanks, Darwin. It is obvious God's genetic system isn't hitting on all cylinders. Not with everyone. Though God is perfect, His genetic system, like Church dogmas, is imperfect. Perhaps that's His plan."

"Okay, I'm interested. Continue."

"I see abnormalities dying," Sandra declared. "God will dispose of those who cannot function in the mainstream. They silently go away. Genetic mutations are often consumed by predators or the inability to reproduce the trait in offspring. I, for one, cannot pass the essence of what I am to a child. Luke, I can't bear a child with you. Or for us. I don't want you to one day become disappointed, dissatisfied with me. To create a child is expected in marriage. 'Make a family' is what the Church demands. It would be wonderful for us to have a baby and pass our qualities to the next generation. I can't. We cannot combine our DNA. Our qualities will end because I am what I am."

"Don't speak that garbage. I love you, Sandra. I know what you are. I'm unconcerned. We'll be a family. Have children. As Spock would say, *'There are always possibilities.'* The future will one day surprise us with multiple possibilities. Have faith."

"Thanks, Luke. I consent to our combination of queer and questioning. We'll surprise the world with all we do. Nonetheless, there'll be nothing of either of us passed to offspring. What we are will end with us," Sandra concluded. "I am happy we're sharing this adventure."

"Who wants to admit they descended from Hitler?" Luke waved his hands. "We're not psychopathic, fascist, or despotic. What we'll leave with the next generation will be our principles, ideas, reasoning. That part of us will be passed to society via *transcenditory* experiences. As powerful as genetics. Maybe more beneficial." Luke spoke persuasively.

"We'd better become first-class writers," Sandra advised.

Luke nodded. "Sandra, I feel some power or entity watches over us. Could be God. I don't know. I'm convinced of it. We are to resolve an issue of greater significance. Our union is under some kind of design. Don't ask me to explain; I can't."

"I've given that idea attention. Our coming together is intentional. At this time, I'll give Heavenly Father all credit for it. It challenges free will ... but there's a purpose ... it could be Overlord. Who knows? I welcome what is to come."

"As do I." Luke released his grip on Sandra's hand and placed an arm around her. "We'll shake things a tremor or two." Luke kissed her head. "From our earlier discussion of male and female brains, genetically masculine as you are, do you consider your brain male or female?"

Sandra thought impartially. "It is a female brain. Understand this, you ever give me another bluzzard, buddy, and I'll neuter you." Laughter and teasing followed.

"Sandra, remember the conversation we spoke the day I introduced you to my family?"

"About my heart," Sandra confirmed.

"This is corny. Forgive me. You are majestic, impressive, as rugged and equally beautiful as this place. I love this mountain, especially when covered with snow. Your heart is one of a kind, bigger than the heart of Timpanogos. You love me. I'm at a loss as to why. My pledge? To do whatever is necessary to keep your heart as close to mine as this mountain has been to me."

"Luke, do you understand what you're saying? Doing for me?" She halted their stroll. Looked into his eyes deeply. "I pledge the same. Your name is Love."

Our heroes, each queer and questioning, kept pace with a fate they did not fully understand. Nonetheless, they remained confident to complete their journey amid personal concerns of fear and threat. A conscious influence gave them a reliant certainty to stand atop peaks. Greater mountains must be climbed. Their gifts demanded courage to play roles unseen and unknown to scale a summit higher, grander, than Timpanogos.

Happy, confident heroes, unaware where their paths would lead. Oblivious of heights they must ascend to attain charitable inclusion for lives God needed humanely restored into His care.

End of Days - BYU

*The key to wisdom is this—constant and frequent questioning,
for by doubting we are led to question, by questioning
we arrive at the truth.*

—Peter Abelard

THE WEDDING FINALLY ARRIVED.

Sandra looked beautiful in her clothing/gown. Dark hair and complexion balanced against white made her radiant, remarkably so when she smiled. They kissed over the altar. In unison family and friends uttered *aaahs* with smiles of pleasure.

Luke greeted Sandra's parents with words of assurance, "Sandra will not be exposed or threatened. We'll care for each other." He whispered words they shared just for themselves, "Overlord is secure. Vinceremò. We will win."

An uncrowded reception met at sundown in Utah County followed by a weekend honeymoon in Park City.

Awesome ... When Luke saw Sandra's naked body. Awesome for each to see the other pristine and pure.

True to their commitment, they looked into each other's eyes as Sandra guided Luke inside herself. The feel of two united as one, exquisite. Filled with delight. They kissed, embraced, felt the other's nakedness. Their acts of intimacy sweet and innocent. Happiness for their companion became their intent. Not just for a weekend of bliss, ***for time and all eternity***.

Sandra and Luke never felt guilt for their sexual pleasures. They welcomed chances to pleasure each other. Neither used sex as a tool of manipulation or power. To tease, absolutely. All they did sensually remained kind-hearted.

Marriage made Sandra a more confident, productive individual. With Luke as her confidant, she no longer remained withdrawn. Purposely, Sandra drew attention to herself—sharply dressed, well-groomed, attractive. Suitors no longer threatened her secret as a man with androgen insensitivity.

Sandra's fears were contained. Hidden impressively as Luke's wife. She felt no limitations to function in work assignments, church roles, service activities, or projects. She lengthened conversations, far less vulnerable to suspicion. Willing to discuss sensitive issues. Self-assured, she defended causes and delivered presentations to students, academics, and leaders. Utilized her platforms to persuasively express arguments. These experiences enhanced her future endeavors.

A cypher no longer, when a gentleman flirted, Sandra showed him a photo of herself with Luke. "My husband," she declared.

"Why aren't you wearing a ring?"

"I am not chattel," Sandra brusquely responded.

Sandra's prayers pled for Luke to live a long life. Her mind calculated the randomness of their union. *Is Heavenly Father playing another cruel game? A continuation of my trial?* Sandra felt shielded while Luke lived. *Should Luke die? God will have exceeded His limits. Heavenly Father*, she hoped, *a fellow partner securing Overlord.*

The remainder of their days at BYU focused on their degrees. However, Sandra and Luke balanced home, work, school, and play.

Sandra and Luke sat for their comprehensive exams in November. Though difficult, each passed. No qualifications for either issued. Sandra eased through the eight hours more ably than Luke. It took an entire Saturday, 8 a.m. to 5 p.m., for them to finish.

Sandra completed coursework in December, finished the first draft of her thesis New Year's Eve, and defended in March. She taught quantitative math classes and assisted faculty research activities until the semester ended. Luke completed classes, wrote his thesis spring term, and defended in July.

Sandra hooded and walked during April commencement. Luke received his diploma in August. Debt-free heroes, they never missed payment of tithes and donations, the Lord's full allowance. *Someone must, somehow, pay for the universe in which we play*, they happily agreed.

Time to escape Utah. They settled permanently out of state. A location far different, more remarkable. Superior for tolerance. Their minds, with new experiences, sharpened like a blade. Problems solved with simple precision, devoid of limitations and restricted thoughts.

The two remarked years later, "The wonderful years at BYU are missed."

Family in Frisco

Paternity is a career imposed on you without
any inquiry into your fitness.

—Adlai Stevenson

SANDRA AND LUKE SETTLED in the San Francisco Bay area to obtain doctorate degrees.

Their commitment to engage exercise, hairbrushes, foot massages, and racquetball were consistent, though irregular. Each commuted to separate campuses. Sandra enrolled at Stanford; Luke, Berkeley.

Sandra was awarded a doctorate in mathematics from Stanford, 1983. Luke received a PhD in rhetoric from UC Berkeley, 1984.

Sandra wrote high school and college math textbooks. Authored three bestselling books: *Mathematics—Moral and Ethical Associations*; *Social Change by the Numbers*; and the wildly popular *Spock—The Logical Connection of Math with Reason*. She became a regular guest on television and radio programs, appeared with Morley Safer on *60 Minutes*, and interviewed by Nick Clooney in Los Angeles. An immensely popular speaker at science assemblies, university conferences, seminars, and symposiums in the United States, Canada, Japan, and Europe.

Her textbooks and pedagogical guides were implemented in hundreds of schools, colleges, and universities. Luke observed, "They want her to speak of math, see it calculated by one beautiful and humorous. It is time to recognize gender identity, discovery, and talent."

Sandra's confidence flourished while married to Luke. Immune from exposure, she drew people to issues. Dressed stylishly with makeup tips applied from professionals who worked in studios she visited; Sandra's natural beauty enriched. Her eyes focused on cameras. She looked directly at those who interviewed her, smiled, spoke logically with lucid diction and interpretation. She epitomized allure with modest simplicity. Throngs were drawn to her gifts of intellect and persuasion. Viewers found her pleasant to hear, as well as see on screen.

Luke's three-dimensional dissertation and new word, *transcenditory*, became a bestseller. Groups of curious readers recognized the need for thought and greater intelligence within decisive moments to resolve problems. Diagrams of 3D thought illustrations with game scenarios taught parents, small groups, business and political leaders to select best-quality decisions.

The term *three-dimensional thinking* became frequently heard in conversations and group discussions. Luke's research listed Sandra as a statistical analyst of data collected. Of particular interest were studies with conclusions that regarded improved interpersonal relationships by those who engaged in foot massages and hair brushing. The data labeled as 'with potential.'

Luke wrote two novels under a pseudonym. The first told the story of a young girl with a dreaded secret. The second involved a boy who questioned the traditional wisdoms of his community's cultural beliefs. Each became Newbery-recommended children's literature.

Sandra and Luke coauthored books on relationships, social acceptance, religion and science, with explanations of thought patterns of the past and those in the near and far future.

Airports and hotels were familiar territories. Sandra and Luke insisted that those who extended invitations never separated them while engaged in their professional duties. One never without the other. Cleverly designed joint presentations. Audiences laughed, cried, learned, and understood. They exhibited their concepts to think, discover problems, and solve problems.

The decade in San Francisco developed Sandra and Luke's social, spiritual, and political opinions. They linked with diverse people—academics, politicians, musicians, advocates, artists, writers, administrators, entertainers, composers, homosexuals, with multiple ethnicities. As individuals ... "straight" and "alternative," their discussions grew broadly enlightened.

Sandra and Luke's curiosities explored what BYU, LDS Church protocol, and their families declared prohibitive. They established connections. Colleagues who remained lifelong friends.

Among these people, they became parents.

Luke rushed into their spacious townhome, liberated from cramped apartment quarters. They lived in a comfortable, nicely furnished home with space to grow. A haven, when needed.

"Sandra," he roared. "I have news!"

"What's put a fire in you?" Sandra sat at her desk scattered with papers. Luke lifted her from the chair and embraced her. Spinning, he kissed her. She wrapped arms and legs around Luke and returned his affections with enthusiasm. They stopped and held tight to each other.

"Wow. The news you have must be good." She kissed his face.

"I received a call from the director over Southeast Asian Immigration. Primarily Vietnamese boat people[7] attempting to settle into the USA."

"The same person who spoke at Berkeley?" Sandra asked, kissing Luke's neck.

"That's the guy."

---

[7] Refugees who fled Vietnam and Southeast Asia after Saigon fell to communism in 1975. The migration and crisis of 'boat people' was highest in 1978-79, and lasted through the early 1990s. Crowded onto boats far too small for the number of people onboard and sailing beyond the safe limits within the South China Sea in the hope to be rescued by U.S. Naval ships. Preyed upon by pirates, many died from dehydration, starvation and drowning.

Sandra pulled back. She peered at Luke inquisitively. "I remember speaking with him. He was a bit personal with us, asked if we're going to have children."

"I know why he asked. We're Mormon, and Mormons have large families. He's curious why we don't have children."

"He knows I'm barren. For all the sex we have, we'd be the parents of eight kids. Oh, how we behave, big guy." Sandra provocatively smiled.

"Well, he asked if we'd be interested in adopting a Vietnamese child."

"Really? What did you say?" The two sat.

"That we'd discuss it. There are whole families requiring sponsorship. Thousands of people needing to be relocated from Laos, Cambodia, Thailand, mostly Vietnam. They all hope to enter the US. Canada has opened its doors. Orphans urgently need adoptive parents. What do you think?"

"We still have educational debt to pay," Sandra stated. "But our books and contractual appearances are substantial. Television and seminar presentations provide consistent, generous incomes. We can do it."

"We've received offers for academic positions. Media contracts here and elsewhere. For some reason, I think it's time for us to experience parenthood," Luke suggested.

"Curious. No one has asked for a specific reason why I can't conceive. Not even your family. They likely think we are too academic, out of touch with the gospel mainstream. However, we don't often see them. It seems a good time to adopt. Our income opportunities will increase. Ventures are growing."

"My parents understand our inability to have children is personal, accepted our explanation that it's too personal for casual discussion. One day the truth will be exposed. Overlord will have its day. Adopting is what we've wanted to do."

Sandra put her arms around Luke. She appreciated his defense of her syndrome. "Thanks, Luke. I love you. Let's discuss making a baby. We've spoken about adoption. We've never spoken of adopting a child who would make us an interracial family."

"What do you think of the idea? What would your parents say?"

"I always thought we'd adopt an Anglo child. My parents will say an interracial child fits into Overlord. Everyone will talk about the child, not about either of us."

"I thought the same pertaining to Overlord," Luke connected. "My parents, primarily my dad, will bristle some if we adopt an Asian baby. But I think they'll accept—even show off—a unique grandchild. We're putting everything into plain sight. No one will suspect a thing. My dad will say—never in front of us, only in his own mind— 'at least it's not a Black baby.'"

"Once we adopt the child, there's a no return policy. We must be certain. Aware of what we're doing."

"Okay. I know your mind, Sandra. List the consequences of this decision."

"Will the child resent the fact that he or she doesn't look anything like his or her parents? Can we accept the child is not Caucasian when everyone around our child won't be Asian?"

"I fell in love with a man. Sandra, I love you more than I love myself. I believe I can love a child who is Asian nearly as much as I love you. I hope the child will love us in spite of the fact that we're not Asian and not common. The child will know I love you more than anyone else. We'll love that child with the same connection. Our love for the child is the bigger consideration. I'm rambling. What's your rationale?"

"I don't want the child to ever get a feeling that it is a trophy we're trying to show off. He or she will be treated like he or she is our own child. No stereotypical, racial inferences. It cannot be tolerated from him or her either. Damn, let's do this so we don't have to use gender-neutral pronouns. I feel like I'm speaking about myself."

"Agreed." Luke smiled. "Let's make a baby."

"We'll have a story that needs retelling—a hundred times," Sandra explained. "People will want to know how we acquired an Asian baby."

"My responsibility," Luke volunteered. "Anything else?"

"Are you ready to be a dad?"

"Are you ready to be a mom, sir?"

"Knock it off," Sandra cautioned. "Don't become too casual. We're merely applying an extra onion layer to our protection of Overlord. The big job is raising a child to be a competent adult. Stay on task."

"Sandra, our intent is to do good. Make the world a better place. I'll get the process in motion. Are we agreed?"

"I'm confident. Our lives will be altered, certainly. You realize that?"

"I'm pleased with the course we're taking. You've already made me a better person." Luke winked at Sandra, jazzed to play the role of a father.

Sandra discerned the dangers of parenthood more than Luke. She entered the game with greater caution, nonetheless committed to save someone who, like herself, would not be common.

Short weeks later, Sandra and Luke flew to San Diego, supplied with all the goods needed to take home a baby: documents, diapers, toys, baby clothes, and food. They rented a car and drove north on I-5 to Camp Pendleton. Marine guards greeted them at the gate. Documents were exchanged for passes and given a map to locate base headquarters.

Military ushers guided them to a large seminar room. Eight adoptive parents sat a distance apart to minimize conversation. U.S. government officials thanked the guests for the children they would take into their care. Assurances were given of medical examinations and vaccinations for their ages.

One official candidly spoke. "Southeast Asians are anxious to become Americans and escape communism. The natural parents of your child, as far as we know, are deceased. Take these children and raise them as your own."

Sandra and Luke learned each child suffered heartbreaking circumstances that led them to America. No details were communicated. Only standard information was provided.

Their names were called. A slender, Vietnamese caretaker warmly greeted them, then led Sandra and Luke to a room. She directed them to be seated on a small couch just inside the room that faced toward the doorway. Our heroes felt somewhat anxious and tense.

"Are you ready to greet your child?" The caretaker's English enjoyed a French accent.

"Scared to death," Sandra said, sighing.

"Ready as we can be," Luke added.

"I've read your file. I'm impressed with your educations. You will be excellent parents to care and provide for this child's future," she said with warmth. "Do you wish to ask questions?"

"Has this baby been abused? The mother drug-addicted?" Luke guardedly asked.

"There are no indications of abuse or drugs. The baby is perfectly healthy."

"How old is the child?" Sandra followed.

"Eighteen months. You get the brunt of potty-training duties." The caretaker smiled.

"What can you tell us about the parents?"

"We do not know. The parents will never cross your paths. I can tell you that Vietnam is a cultured country. Your child is healthy. Physically and mentally."

"Does the child understand any English words?" Sandra asked.

"Again, Vietnam is a cultured nation where French and English are spoken. You are the child's parents. Teach whatever languages you wish."

"We're ready to give birth," Luke concluded with a smile. He looked at Sandra's uneasy face.

"Would you like to know the gender of the child? Or wait until the door opens?"

Sandra and Luke turned to each other and shrugged shoulders. Sandra said, "Don't tell us. We'll know the gender once the door opens—when we 'give birth,' as Luke says."

"Will we be able to tell if it's a boy or girl?" Luke asked. "It's not like you're giving us a naked child. Are you?"

"You will know." The caretaker smiled. "Remain seated on the sofa. Your baby is ready for delivery. Do not be loud, shriek, or scream. Make your movements deliberate. Abrupt or rushed gestures may frighten the child." The caretaker closed the door behind her. A long minute passed.

"Sandra, my eyes are filled with tears. I can hardly see."

"Luke, you're holding my hands too tight."

"Same at you."

The door swung open.

For a few seconds, the entrance remained empty until an adorable little girl in a white dress with a red sash around her waist stepped into the doorway, guided by an adult arm and hand behind her. She wore little calf-high, white socks and tiny, black shoes. Thick, sable hair, neatly cut, covered her forehead and ears. Her Vietnamese eyes and color beamed.

Sandra and Luke emptied the sofa, dropped on their knees, sat on the carpet, while extending their hands toward her. The child touched them; they tried not to be too enthusiastic.

"Hello, sweetheart."

"You are so beautiful."

"Where did you get that pretty dress?"

"She has your features, Sandra." Luke teased.

The caretaker stood at the entrance with a smile. Sandra, seated on the floor, lifted the child to her lap. All three members of this new family remained at eye level. Sandra and Luke wiped away the few tears that succeeded to escape their eyes. They hugged and gently kissed the newborn girl. Love at first sight. The child lifted her small hands and fingers to their faces, confident with two strangers who gave her so much attention.

"What is her name?" Sandra and Luke asked the caretaker who sat with them.

"Her Vietnamese name is Phuong. You may call her whatever name you wish. A document requires your signatures establishing her given name for official certification of adoption."

"Does Phuong have a meaning?"

"Yes," the caretaker responded. "One who recognizes her destiny. Americans say, 'Phoenix.'"

"I like the name. She should keep it," Luke insisted. "She's already accustomed to the sound."

"Agreed," Sandra said. "It is the name her birth parents gave her. It will bridge us with them. Phuong, you are perfect. Such a stunning young lady. I love you already." Sandra gave Phuong a warm hug.

"I don't think we could have done any better doing it ourselves, Sandra."

Nearly overcome, the caretaker left the room. The three remained on the carpeted floor. Talked, played, touched. Everything necessary to become acquainted. Time passed. Entranced by the experience, the family felt a newborn inspiration. They came together, an introduction between souls, bonded eternally.

The caretaker returned. Time for the family to go home. Documents signed; instructions were given with a medical history portfolio. The caretaker gave Phuong a farewell hug and goodbye kiss. Best wishes shared.

With Phuong secured in a car seat, Sandra and Luke headed back to San Diego International for the return flight to San Francisco.

"What do you think?" Luke asked.

"You ask a question whenever you have an observation to state."

"True. I need to hear your opinions of our experience."

Seated on the passenger side, Sandra half-turned with her left arm outstretched to the tiny passenger in the backseat. Sandra's fingers played with Phuong's hands. "We have work ahead of us."

"Yes, we do."

"I'm happy with our decision. We'll be challenged as parents. Neither of us is below average in what we are or have accomplished. We'll be fine. I wish we knew more about Phuong. How she got here, what happened to her parents, whether they are alive."

"I've thought the same," Luke said. "She's a doll. We couldn't have handpicked a more lovely little girl."

"She is gorgeous. When she's a teenager, you will be charged with bodyguard duties."

"We both will be interrogating and patrolling the neighborhood boys. I'll ask your dad to give me his bat."

"You have your own bats. You won't need his." Sandra grinned.

Luke sighed and took a deep breath. "I believe the caretaker gave us a message about Phuong's parents."

"Explain."

"Twice she said Vietnam is a cultured country. Interesting word selection. She told us that Phuong's parents are well-educated. She specified that French and English are spoken there. Reemphasized her good health, mentality. She knew the meaning of Phuong's name."

"Her name could be commonly understood," Sandra suggested.

"Possibly. Phuong is healthy. She is well adjusted for an eighteen-month-old orphan. Didn't fear us when we approached her at the door. A bit wobbly, but for eighteen months, she is remarkably composed, cool."

"Again, I thought the same," Sandra nodded. "They didn't say a word about her ever being malnourished. She has no illicit drugs in her system. From what we've seen, there are no visible signs of abuse or hardship on her skin or body. She acts like a well-trained baby. She might be accustomed to caregivers. Meeting us like meeting two other servants."

"Not to pat ourselves on the back, but I have a few conclusions." Luke paused before continuing. "The caretaker read our file and was impressed with our educations. Our application papers included a list of our publications and income. Phuong could be the child of a diplomat, community leader, educator, or some well-established Vietnamese family. They gave her to us. We are nearest to what she experienced in Vietnam, closest to the people who fed her, took good care of her. They, or US authorities, placed Phuong with us, assured she'll get the same treatment, level of care, and advantages in America."

"We may never know … I concur with your thoughts … things have occurred almost too well. You get a call from the director of Southeast Asian Immigration, the head honcho. We submit our application for adoption, and here we are, two weeks later, with this perfect little angel." Sandra gazed at the ocean. A tear fell. She wiped her face. "I wonder what Phuong's parents did, what troubles they underwent so we could have her in our home."

Luke reached for Sandra's hand. He attempted to divert her imagination from undue guesswork.

"We're conjecturing," Sandra concluded. "Let this be the last time we speak of this matter. Phuong can never hear such speculations. She will be better served not hearing our suppositions."

"So be it. It is on par with Overlord. However, should what we have deduced be true, there are people out there who know us, who have encroached on our lives. Albeit, whoever these people are, they generously manipulated our lives. They blessed us with Phuong."

"It is premature to say we have been blessed," Sandra cautioned. "Phuong is darling. Let's hope no ulterior purposes are at play, whether Vietnamese or American."

"What are you suggesting?" Luke asked.

"If what we have discussed is accurate, let's hope these people are benevolent. We need to be watchful. I don't want any strangers on our doorsteps attempting to take Phuong from us."

"These people know that our intent is honorable. That we're Mormon." Luke floundered. "That sounded wrong. Sorry. They know what we are. Our behavior is predictable. Constitutional law governs this adoption. If what we have reasoned is true, they have entrusted us to be Phuong's parents. We cannot become unjustly fearful. We've done something wonderful. Phuong is our daughter. Suspicion or speculation cannot dwell in our lives."

"The numbers agree, Luke. Everyone involved in this adoption has Phuong's well-being as a top priority. Indeed, should influences outside our awareness be at play, they may be used to guarantee Phuong's protection. An additional guardian of Overlord, protecting our exposure, conceivably assisting us."

"I feel inclined to approach the director of Southeast Asian Immigration. Share our impressions. His nonverbal reactions would say much," Luke said.

"We have Phuong, I don't want to lose her," Sandra resolved. "We'll do well for her. These people, whoever they are, will be pleased she is in our home, that we are caring for her needs."

"The caretaker told us the natural parents would never cross our paths. I hope that is true. We don't know whether the parents are alive or dead. We'll just need to trust their words," Luke concluded.

"Phuong's parents could be incarcerated in a political prison, for all we know," Sandra said.

"Let's hope nothing ever happens to complicate or harm Phuong. I love you, Sandra. I love Phuong. The two of you are the greatest loves to enter my heart. I'm happy. We'll make this work."

"I'm happy too." Sandra shifted her weight toward Luke. "Keep your eyes on the road." Sandra leaned across the console and kissed Luke's face. "I love you. I love what we're doing. Our lives have intrigue and adventure. It's a fun roller-coaster ride."

Luke kissed Sandra's hand. "How are you doing back there, precious?"

Sandra turned to see Phuong asleep in the car seat. "Aaahh. She's out like a light."

Luke glanced in the rearview mirror as their little baby girl slept. "I'm gonna kiss her leg. She may have something to tell us." He smiled. Tensions eased.

"When she wakes, she'll need something to eat or drink."

Our story now has three heroes.

Luke called the director of Southeast Asian Immigration for an appointment. The director claimed a busy schedule with more than a month out of the country in Thailand. Undeterred, Luke asked pointed questions but learned nothing. The director advised Sandra and Luke to live free of suspicion.

"Enjoy your family. We are appreciative that you have adopted a child. May God's blessings be with you." A statement made by the director to soothe LDS standards, something the director believed would appease their inquiries.

Sandra and Luke lost the hope of observing the director's nonverbal responses to their comments and questions. Nonetheless, they behaved as a family. Joyous, yet never free of suspicion.

Sandra and Luke each sought equal time to diaper, bathe, play, and certainly, brush hair. Luke dressed Phuong in a toddler-sized Oakland A's uniform. "She already loves baseball."

"Phuong will eat the right foods, exercise regularly, and be a fit person," Sandra said resolutely.

When Sandra and Luke played, exercised, or rode bikes, Phuong stayed with them. Inseparable, with times coordinated to assure they would be available to care for Phuong. Each were committed parents. Hugs, kisses and play in this family never ended.

Phuong was taught to understand the world and its inhabitants. Mozart, The Beatles, Williams, Davis, Rachmaninoff, Satchmo, Clapton, Mahler—all of them played for her enjoyment. She was embedded with a foundation of music from the gifted, extraordinarily talented composers and entertainers who come along too rarely. Luke did his best. He sung for Phuong at bedtime. "Smile," "Wandering Star (a la Lee Marvin)," "I Only Have Eyes for You," and "I Am a Child of God." Sandra joined to make them duets. As Phuong grew, the songs became trios.

The three played and prayed together. They performed their roles in conventional tradition but far from traditional. Phuong embraced the journey. Few children ever discern the gains or losses experienced in their lives. Phuong matured spiritually, intellectually, and physically. She absorbed much through her behaviors and experience. Sandra and Luke, queer and questioning, instilled Phuong with gratitude for each Q word.

When prayers ended at the conclusion of family home evening, Luke or Sandra shouted, "Hugs." Enthusiastic hugs shared by a family of three. On occasion, Sandra or Phuong yelled, "Hugs." Luke ran and shouted, "Don't hug me! Don't hug me!" Sandra and Phuong chased him until he couldn't escape. They tackled him and rolled on the carpet as they gave him big hugs. Luke always said, "Thank you. Thank you. You saved my life."

In no time, Phuong started saying, "Don't hug me! Don't hug me!" Sandra and Luke chased her through the house, picked her up, threw her in the air, caught her, then gave her hugs, kisses, and bluzzards. In response, she screamed, squealed, laughed, and started again.

Sandra and Luke would often lay exhausted on the carpet when Phuong said, "Don't hug me! Don't hug me!" Too drained to chase her, Luke questioned, "What did you say?"

"Don't hug me! Don't hug me!" Phuong shouted, expecting to be chased.

"I can't hear you … come a little closer, please."

"Don't hug me! Don't hug me!" Phuong took steps closer to Luke, ready to run.

"Did you hear something, Mom? I thought I heard Phuong."

"Don't hug me! Don't hug me!" Phuong shouted as she stood over Luke, flat on the floor. He captured her with hugs, kisses, and bluzzards. Phuong's energy was boundless. Sandra and Luke enjoyed her play, her love, her uncommon traits.

A gift from God.

Return Visit to Zion

> *You are not entitled to your opinion.*
> *You are entitled to your informed opinion.*
> *No one is entitled to be ignorant.*

> —Harlan Ellison

SANDRA AND LUKE FLEW to Salt Lake for the cussing, drinking grandmother's family reunion. Phuong was a big attraction for everyone. Sandra and Luke's renown and doctorate degrees created a split between them and Luke's family.

"Sandra, the size of your family is best. I understand why you described my family as 'so many,'" Luke announced. "They'd never remain silent about a personal matter. They're weird. Don't know it."

"Really? Your family is large. Extended aunts, uncles, cousins. I see your point, though. Could anyone keep an issue like Overlord confidential? Four is simpler for security than seventy outlaws." She smiled. "What makes your family weird?"

"My cousin," Luke gestured, "is wearing a t-shirt that reads *RULDS2*? It's odd that my family wants to seek out those like themselves, specifically by religious membership. My brother-in-law has a baseball shirt printed with *Provo Stake Champions—1986*. It's tribal. I understand that. If you don't know what a stake is, don't know the religion, what does it say?"

"I'm sure Catholics do the same."

"Possibly. Whoever has the best basketball or softball team is the true church or religion. That should settle it. Think of the competition for supremacy."

"War, not softball or basketball, uses that method to solve those problems, even in current times. Competition is ruinous for cooperation, collaboration, or acceptance."

"Noticed how we're being treated? Everyone has been cordial, yet most are distant, even now. The three of us are here, by ourselves. No one, not even the kids who once played games with us, talk to us. They leave once we approach."

"They're teenagers—young adults. We're parents. We're not the same people, Luke. Is it them or us you are analyzing?"

"In my mind, I'll remain a kid forever, the mentality of a teenager. The wonder, excitement, and awe that comes with discovery. Doing something for the first time, like tasting root beer. That's a memorable experience. I want to be there when Phuong makes those discoveries, to experience the same wondrous surprises."

"As do I ... but remind yourself, they will be her own discoveries, her own experiences. Phuong will sense them differently than we, Luke. Her journey will be one of a kind, just as each of the paths we've taken. Clearly, my own."

"Sandra, you're a pragmatist. That's why we'll be bonded for a hundred years, should we live that long. Phuong, as a teenager, will separate herself from us. She's on loan to us until she can pump her own bicycle."

"Luke, your language, metaphors, are unique. You make me smile, although your clarity could improve."

Luke wrapped his arms around Sandra, Phuong on her lap. No three people could be as queer, questioning, or further apart. Nevertheless, no three could be so close and greatly buttressed for storms of challenge. A dissimilar, united family.

"While here, let's try reaching as many people as we can." Luke suggested a hypothesis, "We aren't like these people, not anymore. We're not what they are, not any longer, particularly now, with Phuong. They don't know what to do with us. By now, someone should've asked us to become distributors in their multilevel marketing group."

"What are you implying? They're rejecting us? Or have we separated ourselves from them?"

"They aren't rejecting us," Luke answered. "We've separated ourselves from them. First, in distance. We live in San Francisco. Second, our thoughts, pursuits. We are more attuned to the diversity and social tolerance experienced in the Bay Area. Third, the books we've written, our ideas, experiences, applications. Fourth, our academic degrees. And fifth, how we're understood.

"Part of it is Phuong," Luke continued. "Part is our visibility on television. Of course, part of it is also you, Sandra. We're no longer accepted in the Mormon culture. Wherever we go, people recognize us. Our families see us more often on television than in person. We no longer fit. Wanna test the theory?"

"Okay, but consider that we frighten them for the ideas you mentioned. We do what they fear to do. Risking less chosen paths. Be considerate. Okay?" Sandra hoped to influence a moderate compromise.

"Received and understood. Let's mingle. They'll vacate in no time. I agree to be supportive. We discuss their issues. Not ours."

Predictable topics of discussion arose. Missionary calls, who is where, when they get home, companion problems. Challenges with alien cultures to America, baptism successes/failures, blood of Israel, hard-heartedness of people in certain areas of the country and world. Church travels, jobs, Church history, school, Church activity, BYU football, Church blessings, temple marriages, grandchildren, divorces, signs and wonders, marital problems, the approaching millennium, money, and multi-level marketing.

Luke's family expressed their praise to Sandra and Luke with well wishes as new parents. All of them were drawn, with suspicion, to the dark pearl who shined among the supremely white folk of their clan. Voices suggested that sealed to Sandra and Luke, Phuong would, on the Morning of the First Resurrection, be "white and delightsome" as the Book of Mormon once expressed. Either by the literal blood of Israel already within her or via adoption, Phuong would be changed. She would be seen as white ... the House of Israel.

Sandra responded with poise. "Yes, we have heard those words. We are familiar with Church teachings. Such dogmas are not absolute. Blacks have access to Church blessings, temple ordinances. Yet they may not wish to be 'white' as part of 'white and delightsome.'"

Luke agreed. "I love Sandra for all that she is. I would not want her changed in any way."

Sandra turned to Luke with an anxious look. He skirted too closely to her syndrome.

"If Sandra were Asian or Black, she is the person I love, married. I want her hair, skin color, all her features. Everything that I love. I would not want her transformed into something blonde or Swedish. It's stupid. What is another way to put it? Ah, diversity. Since 1981, the Book of Mormon words changed to 'pure and delightsome.' Not 'white.' Certainly, as a result of the 1978 revelation."

"When we first saw Phuong," Sandra added, "her eyes and sweet and innocent face shone brightly. I do not want her to be anything other than what she is—our beautiful little girl. Asian features, color, everything. When I look at Phuong, yes, she is Asian. Though I don't even think of it. I love her simply as our daughter. There is plenty of room for color in the celestial kingdom. She will never be 'white.' Delightsome? Yes. Grand just the way Heavenly Father made her."

"Intelligence transcends ethnic skin color or characteristics of any kind," Luke concluded.

Family members squirmed. Some inched away amid comments of their celebrity status. Sandra and Luke's words encompassed Phuong, San Francisco, or difficulty with three-dimensional thinking. Everyone smiled good naturedly but with difficulty. An elementary-aged cousin, Abigail O'Neill, let slip, "I told my teacher and class I would see my adopted Chinese cousin today."

Sandra smiled. "Let's take a picture." She motioned for Abby to come near. "Phuong is Asian, like the people in China. The remainder of us here are lighter skinned, like the people in Europe.

To be precise, Phuong is Vietnamese. There is a difference. Phuong could have plenty of Chinese in her. We don't know.

"O'Neill is an Irish name. Abby, I'm sure you have German, Dutch, Polish, and a dozen other people and places inside you. Now we can say Phuong is a part of us. You are a part of Phuong."

"Her name sounds funny; it's not easy to say," Abby confessed. Cameras clicked.

"You're right, Abby. Phuong is a simple name to say, but not for all English-trained speakers. It takes a little practice. Can you imagine how difficult it would be for people in Vietnam to say Abigail?" Sandra over-emphasized *Abigail*. The family chuckled.

"That's why everyone calls me Abby, for short." Cameras clicked again as Abby, Phuong, and Sandra grinned.

"Vietnam. What a grimy place. When Phuong is older, she'll be happy. Feel blessed to have been raised in the promised land of America," a family member said. "How do you like living in San Francisco? All the homos with AIDS?" Cameras silenced.

Another divulged, "AIDS is God's punishment on those queers."

Luke seized Sandra's hand; secured her silence. "I'm disturbed by those words. As disciples of Christ, it is our obligation to be compassionate and sympathetic. The words I just heard show no concern or consideration. All are children of our Heavenly Father, including homosexuals. As the Savior taught, anyone in need of well-being should be in our prayers. Have sympathy. Charity for all."

Nonverbal reactions were unable to be screened by Luke's rhetoric boldness. It took only minutes for family members to disperse. Sandra and Luke expressed their affection, scooped up Phuong, grabbed their personal effects, and vacated the reunion amid hugs, kisses, with expressions of love.

A line had been drawn in the sand with shots fired in a small skirmish between our heroes and beloved family members. They exposed their intent in regard to conflicts none dared to socially confront, or challenge gospel principles. Certainly, entrenched soldiers in God's Army and spiritual commanders are not to aid and abet the enemy. It became clear that greater queer and questioning frontline battles with weapons of greater destruction approached our heroes.

"I try to be patient, Luke. I do my best," Sandra said, hours later. "There are times I want to take my dad's bat and swing at people. I look forward to the day we speak openly of Overlord. 'AIDS is God's punishment.' I can't believe what people say in their self-righteous certainty. It's hubris. Extreme conceit, arrogance."

"Sandra, we tested the theory. We've moved in a direction away from the thinking of my family members. Unless we think as mainstream Mormons with adherence to dogmas, we will constantly be at odds with them. I prefer where we are, our thoughts and behaviors."

"There's still racism, despite the 1978 revelation. Homophobia a decade later." Livid, Sandra protested, "These attitudes inflict pain, separation, segregation. How can our Church suggest we are elect, caring people? We unknowingly spew hate with our righteous words."

"Let me tell you about my mother," Luke said. "Just hear me out for a piece. Mom came home one Sunday from church services in tears. Happened more than once. We asked, 'Mom, why are you crying?' We thought she heard a sad story at church and preferred to cry at home, in private."

"I assume that wasn't the case."

"Nope. She cried because she's a working mom."

"A working mom?"

"When my parents bought their home in the 1950s, my dad's entire annual income paid the mortgage, taxes, and insurance. There was little money left to pay for groceries, education, books, clothes, and other necessities. My mom was forced to work. Our family needed two incomes to remain above water."

"Again, Luke—" She waved her hand. "You make sense. Keep going."

"Some Sunday School instructor alleged that mothers working outside the home would raise delinquent kids. My mom had to work.

A family with six kids on my dad's income alone would fail. Mom felt at odds with the Mormon words, 'The most important work you will do is within the walls of your own home.' Mom worked 40 or more hours a week, as did my dad, all outside the walls of our home. Your mother, like my own, worked their whole lives. They did it to make our homes comfortable, plus they had more than just domestic skills. Their love was willing to challenge Church dogma with careers. They gained friendships and experiences in the workplace."

"You are alluding to Mormonism's one-dimensional, flat perspective of motherhood. If you are not a stay-at-home mother, you will ruin the family," Sandra concluded.

"Bingo. For a time, my mom believed it might happen. When she heard that crap at church, it shook her. Instead of compassion and support, General Authorities, Sunday school teachers, idjits spewed words from the pulpit, beating up on her. Not specifically on my mom, you understand, but spiritual knockout punches just the same. 'I'm better than you. I'm obeying. You're not. I'm doin' what the prophet told us to do.'" Luke enacted a Muhammad Ali knockout punch as he spoke.

Luke changed his stance to that of Elmer Gantry. "'You ain't doin' what you've been told to do, you communist-sympathizing, disobedient, never-go-to-church-on-Sunday, Satan worshiper.' Those words hurt my mom. It's the same hubris, conceit, and arrogance you mentioned earlier that we saw and heard from persons in my family today."

"Your mom lived an incredible life, as did those who fought through World War II."

Luke nodded. "The millions of stories that could be told by their generation."

Sandra summarized the situation. "Your mom worked at a naval station while your two oldest sisters stayed at home with your cursing, drinking grandmother. Your dad was in Europe fighting Nazis. None of your siblings received delinquent records. Even though both your parents worked, you and your siblings behaved well. Without my working mother, my syndrome would have been exposed."

"Tell that to our moms and all working women who get fed a continual diet of crap over the pulpit about a ton of crap most speakers, including the Brethren, are unsympathetic to understand. Our working mothers won a war. Then all these bozos in church say their kids will be delinquents because moms work outside the home. We hurt good folks, like you, Sandra."

"Luke, I understand. Your grammar needs attention."

"Here's my point. I'll say it as an academic … As enlightened with truth as our Church claims to be, it has yet come to terms with its own behavior and manner of communication. Mormons are sacrosanct and esoteric. Sandra, I apologize on behalf of all homophobes everywhere, remarkably within our own LDS Church and culture. To hear narrow-minded words used by my own family is horrifying. It illustrates the deep-seated, one- or at best two-dimensional patterns of thinking embedded in us. At this minute, I can only infer from the fifties and sixties— 'That's just the way it is.'"

"Just because that's the way people think, or once thought, doesn't make it right. Why allow it to continue unchallenged?" Sandra concluded.

"Sandra, I want to swing your dad's bat more than you. The Earth keeps turning. Three-dimensional thought has been discussed and studied for decades. Just recently it's found voices in some universities. Our day will dawn. We crossed swords with my family today. What we heard illustrates the tasks ahead of us. Whether it is gender fairness, homophobia, or 'white and delightsome' racism, nothing will change until people discover compassion for themselves via enlightened thinking and increased experiences."

"What if Phuong begins to think or behave like we did or like Mormons around us still do? Oh, Luke, it makes me ill. How do we keep her from coldhearted thoughts?"

"Defend those unseen, unheard, misunderstood, or uncommon."

Sandra and Luke lived true to their words. They created and collected research data. Sandra's numbers with Luke's rhetorical skills were cleverly and entertainingly delivered through academic journals, printed texts and popular magazines. Their charm, beauty and persuasive reason established meaningful summaries and conclusions that enlightened viewers who watched, and listened to interviews, attended seminars, or tuned into social media programs.

This family of three engaged efforts to defend the unseen, unheard and misunderstood. They, in fact, were part of the uncommon people who lent their own voices to those without confidence to speak, or challenge. Audiences within public, private, and government organizations accepted the information and helped disburse the *good news* to larger groups with greater utilization to understand and make use of human talent far too long neglected.

Income from book royalties, television programs, and presentation tours accrued sizably. Phuong traveled with Sandra and Luke. Her sweet, natural self, encouraged donors and sponsors. She called for parents to adopt a child. Sandra or Luke never whispered in her ears. She gained a reputation all her own. Performed her role as a gifted and well-trained child. She spoke few, but memorable, words.

Audiences were greatly disappointed when Phuong did not appear at gatherings, but children need their play.

Angels Among Us

*Strenuous intellectual work and the study of God's Nature are
the angels that will lead me through all the troubles of this life
with consolation, strength, and uncompromising rigor.
Long live impudence. It was my guardian angel in this world.*

—Albert Einstein

CHANGE IS ABRUPT AND stressful. Everything is affected when a
couple becomes a family. Everything. Stories are told differently.
Money and time are in greater demand. Thinking is challenged.
Sandra and Luke's renown as writers, researchers, speakers, scholars,
and television personalities with an interracial child continued to
capture worldwide attention, but change also took place.

Sandra maintained a presence in academia, teaching quantitative
math at Stanford. She continued to write, consult, participate
with research groups. She investigated data and conclusions,
that included fascinating suppositions. Her name appeared in
articles and journals. Sandra's image, fashionable style, and public
presentations won over audiences at symposiums, conferences,
media events, and programs. Regardless of gender, Sandra finished
in the top-five categories of achievement.

Luke, an executive administrator at UC Berkeley, collected data
from graduate students who completed theses and dissertations.
Classroom instruction kept Luke conversant with three-dimensional

thought and *transcenditory* experiences. Luke was twice awarded teacher of the year. The symbiotic academic relationships allowed Luke to author stories.

One day, students assembled in the classroom as Luke prepared in his office. The receptionist knocked on his open door and said, "Luke, there is a gentleman who would like to speak with you."

"On the phone?"

"No, waiting in the reception area."

"At your workstation? He walked in hoping to catch me?"

"He did. Stepped-in, asked to visit ... what should I do?"

"I'll greet him," Luke answered. "Do you have his name?"

"He gave me a card. I'm not sure how to pronounce the name."

The receptionist gave Luke the card. On it, a Vietnamese name—Nguyen. The address on the card was in the government district of downtown San Francisco. *Yellow alert!*

Luke asked the receptionist. "Do you know this person? Anything about him?"

"No. Never seen him 'til a minute ago."

"Strange." Luke walked down the hallway toward the receptionist's station. In those steps, his thoughts raced. *Who is this person? What does he need? Money? Hope it isn't Phuong's father.*

Near the receptionist's counter, Luke saw a nicely groomed Asian gentleman in a dark business suit, white shirt, and navy-blue tie. He looked impressive and stood as if a leader. Late-forties.

"Mr. Nguyen?" Luke offered his hand in a friendly introduction. "I am Luke. Would you please come to my office?" The man's hand was hard and cold, the grip not firm. The handshake transmitted little information. His eyes communicated far less. Nonverbal conveyances minimal, though Luke saw a long scar below and behind his right ear.

The man nodded. They walked to Luke's office. Each took a seat.

"What can I do for you, sir?"

"I am aware you adopted a Vietnamese child."

"Yes." Luke felt unease, icy and passive.

"It is unusual for white Americans to adopt a Vietnamese child."

"You are here to discuss unusual adoption practices?"

"My visit is not to criticize what you have done. Set aside my words." The visitor bowed his head slightly. "I wish to offer my services."

"What services?"

"Children are curious. One day she will want to know about her people."

"How do you know our child is a girl?"

"You and your wife are well-known. I watch television, read newspapers, magazines. Your daughter's name is Phuong. You pronounce her name properly."

"Forgive me. I am suspicious."

"Why are you suspicious, Luke?"

"I'd rather have you answer that question." Luke stared at the visitor.

The man did not flinch. He sat unmoved, locked with Luke. "Fear makes all people suspicious. A man, like you, risks greatly. Do you not?"

"We are playing chess … you know I care little for money, although it is good to have plenty of it." Luke paused, then said, "I'll move your next chess piece. Love is what I value most."

The visitor stared. "The loss of love, its departure, is tragic. Painful."

"Yes, it is. You can trust, sir, I will watch over those I love with all means at my disposal."

"You and I value love and happiness above all other possessions," the man said. "We both wish to shield children. Individuals we love."

"Who are you? Speak the truth, sir," Luke demanded.

"Friends need assistance. It is beneficial to have partners who will bear burdens that one cannot shoulder alone."

"Friends? This is not your card." Luke brandished the card toward the visitor. "Your behavior does not impress me as genuine. Your choice of words is too good. Your purpose? True identity?"

"I am, as you would say, a guardian angel."

"Whose guardian angel?" Luke smirked. "You're not my guardian angel. I'm not sure I'd want you as a guardian angel." Luke thought quickly. "You speak of Phuong. You'd better give me quality answers, or I will have security detain you."

"Calm yourself. You believe in angels, correct? There is one atop the temples of your religion."

"Point taken," Luke conceded. "I believe in angels. My angels have wings. They are pilots of US Navy and Air Force fighter planes."

"Clever response," the strange visitor praised. "Like an American, you reference military strength. Power for righteous actions. To keep dollars within your possession."

"I don't know you. Not sure I like you. Leave, immediately."

"Your wife and you are intelligent. Instantly surmised the circumstances regarding Phuong. We concluded you deserved explanations and guidance in your future. Yes?"

"Who are you? Who are the 'we' you mention?"

"I cannot answer. Phuong is uncommon, as you already know. Your selection to be Phuong's mentors was purposeful."

"Okay, still playing chess? Why us? Are the three of us in danger?"

"No physical danger. I assure you. I have read all Sandra and you have written, including your novels."

"No one knows I write novels. What—who—I write with a pseudonym. Explain yourself." Luke felt his heart pulse and breath shorten. His irritation with the man grew.

"We approve of your divergent skills. As people of compassion, of reason, you will guide Phuong to discover her destiny. Have I moved enough chess pieces?"

"What do you know? I feel used, manipulated."

"Each person is manipulated, Luke. You recognize its use in your religion. Put the puzzle together. Why protest?"

Luke felt exposed. He tensed, but remained silent until the mystery man spoke again.

"Call the person whose name is on the card. Your friendship will be accepted. Phuong should become acquainted with her cultural and ethnic history while becoming an American. It will do much good for your family."

"You are not Nguyen?"

"Never made such a claim. The card is genuine. Make the connection," the visitor directed.

"Does the real Nguyen know who you are?"

"He will know his card was given to you."

"I'm not—well—how am I supposed to behave normally when a self-proclaimed guardian angel, speaking half-understood words, visits my office? You're frightening."

"Luke, do you understand yourself? You reason quite well, then you drown in waters filled with monsters of superstition. You believe, as fact, religious leaders visited by angels, a prophet who speaks with God personally, given gold plates, uses seer stones. *I* should be frightened of *you*."

Luke sat motionless, silent.

"Don't try our resolve, or my patience. The vote was not unanimous to place Phuong in your home," the odd visitor sternly warned. "You have a child who awaits her destiny. Be competent guides. Phuong requires your love."

Luke was silent until he gathered himself. "My apologies. Your words overtook me. Your presence is unsettling."

The visitor waited for Luke to continue their conversation.

"Will I speak with you again?"

"Likely."

"Sandra will want to meet you ... share a conversation."

"Your attempt for a mutual connection is honorable. But it will not happen at this time."

"What is proper in this association? I have questions."

"You know enough. Maintain your course," the visitor counseled.

"Will we ever know who you are? The underground group you represent?"

"One day, undoubtedly. It would give me great satisfaction for Sandra to sign the books she has written."

"I'm sure she would—wait. You didn't ask for my autograph." Luke paused before continuing. "It's Sandra, isn't it? What do you know?"

"You speak of Overlord."

Luke sat back in his chair, flabbergasted. "No one knows. Only four—who are you? CIA? KGB? What?"

"I am a guardian angel. More guardian than angel."

"How did this happen? You gotta be related to Porter Rockwell. Part of some LDS Gestapo."

"I have established my intent. Time to leave." The visitor rose to his feet and stepped to the doorway.

"No. Stay where you are. You drop a bomb like that then expect to walk away? I'll follow you. Tell me what this is."

"You have students to instruct. Do your work. Do what is necessary for Phuong and Sandra. They are stars."

"What am I? A comet? How will I communicate with you?" Luke felt desperate.

"We will contact you."

"I need confirmation. Give me something. What is happening? Why?"

The visitor looked directly into Luke's eyes. "Phuong."

"Can you guarantee that our family will be unharmed?" Luke demanded.

"I'm confident you would understand my words. I am an angel. We guard a select few."

"How do we trust you?"

"Trust is earned." The visitor stepped into the hallway.

"You say words—perhaps the right words—but leave no meaning."

"Do your work. Love Sandra and Phuong. Angels are nearby."

"At least give me your name, please."

The man walked away. He raised his hand and gave an anemic wave, steadfast in his departure.

Sandra and Luke attempted to make sense of the Visitor—an apt name for this enigmatic person. How did the Visitor know of Overlord? Phone taps? Was their home bugged? A leak among the Big Four? Connected dots led only to greater frustration. They concluded to contact Nguyen for answers.

Sandra called. She reached the office for Vietnamese Affairs in the San Francisco region, an area that included Sacramento, Silicon Valley, and areas of Washington, Oregon, and Nevada.

When Sandra asked for an appointment, the receptionist stated an appointment with Mr. Nguyen would be possible in two weeks. No sooner. Days and times were exchanged until an available hour could be scheduled. The receptionist asked, "Your name, please?"

"Sandra—"

"Are you the Sandra who speaks on the Channel 6 morning television program?"

"Yes, I am."

"You have a Vietnamese daughter?"

"Yes, we do."

"Do not hang up. Please hold."

Less than a minute passed when a man's voice came on the phone. "Hello. Is this Sandra?"

"Yes."

"This is Mr. Nguyen. Will you meet with me tomorrow at 10 a.m.?"

Surprised and somewhat flustered by the turnabout, Sandra scanned Luke's appointment calendar. "Yes. Tomorrow at ten would be perfect."

"Great. I am eager to meet you. Will Phuong be with you?"

"Yes, we'll all be there."

Sandra heard Vietnamese words and unfamiliar vocalizations as Mr. Nguyen conversed with others. He then said, "I am so happy. Please hold for the receptionist."

The receptionist gave Sandra directions to the government district in San Francisco, with parking instructions and details to reach Nguyen's office.

The next vital steps in the mountaintop climb would be taken. Answers would hopefully be received as to who the mysterious visitor may be.

Two Vietnamese women, along with Mr. Nguyen, stood inside the office, anxious to greet and introduce themselves as our heroes entered. Phuong, naturally, created praise and attention. The ladies were enamored with her. Treated Phuong as a princess. Sandra and Luke observed peculiar nuances in Mr. Nguyen's behavior. Clearly, Phuong issued an appeal that drew these people to her.

The office space was small in comparison to the region covered. Mr. Nguyen looked to be in his late fifties, wore glasses, and had a well-trimmed moustache. He bore a remarkable resemblance to the visitor. Directed to a larger room, the ladies suggested they could tend to Phuong while Sandra and Luke spoke with Mr. Nguyen. Sandra and Luke declined the offer, uncomfortable to be separated from Phuong. Sandra partly spread a comforter on the floor with toys and books. She explained their caution in light of recent events with the Visitor.

Luke immediately took the opportunity to discuss their issues. "Mr. Nguyen, a man of your same height, in his mid-forties, with a scar behind his right ear visited me. Do you know this person? I will say, you look alike, with the exception of your age and his scar."

"I know many people," Mr. Nguyen shrugged.

"He encouraged me to approach you. Made clear that Phuong would benefit from our association. The Visitor used the word *friendship* to describe our future. Are you sure you don't have a connection with this man?"

"I escaped Vietnam when the US embassy collapsed in April 1975. A helicopter flew me from the embassy to the carrier *Midway*. I was a businessman in Saigon. Advised American Embassy workers. I know hundreds of people. The man you describe could be one I met either in Vietnam or here in America. We all have scars. Sorry, I cannot help you."

"This man knows information … personally confidential," Sandra uneasily stated. "So private, only Luke and I know. He gave us your card." Sandra slid the card toward Mr. Nguyen. "How can you tell us you do not know him?"

"I know only those I know. Should he return, take a photograph. I then may recognize him."

"The man implied Phuong is special. She should learn about her people from you. Gave us your card. What are we to infer? What makes Phuong different, special?"

"You are troubled. Please, put aside your fears. Let me explain what I can do. Will you allow me?"

Sandra and Luke nodded their heads and sat back in their chairs.

"All children, including Phuong, are special. Americans, along with Europeans, are arrogant people. Actually, each person is unaware of their arrogance. As you say in your book, two-dimensional. Six of every 10 people in the world are Asian. Caucasian, Black people, and other smaller groups makeup the remainder of humanity. However, European and American history, economics, and politics dominate our world. They are the primary influence in global affairs. Sandra, Luke, what did you learn in school about Asia? Asian scholars? Asian achievements? Contributions?"

Sandra and Luke looked at each other. "Chinese dynasties, Marco Polo, Genghis Khan, the Great Wall, Confucius, gunpowder, Silk Road, Buddha, Hiroshima—we see your point. We didn't learn enough … unfortunately."

"European and American dominance had devastating as well as positive influences in Asia," Mr. Nguyen explained. "Included among those influences are communism, fascism, imperialism, capitalism, democracy. My country became a battleground between the Soviet Union and the United States. Communism against capitalism. Vietnam lost. The French, English, Dutch, Spaniards, Russians, and Americans brought their politics, religions, philosophies, and conflicts to Asia. When they departed, one artifact was left behind—children."

"Children?" Sandra questioned.

"A common expression in England and Australia throughout World War II went like this: Americans are overpaid, oversexed, and over here. It continued in Japan, Korea, and Vietnam. Wherever Europeans and Americans go, they leave behind the children they fathered. It distresses me that Americans left their mixed babies when Russian-backed communists seized my country."

"That is wrong." Luke felt sincere regret. "From your words, I gather you disapprove of Sandra and me as Phuong's parents."

Mr. Nguyen raised his hands. "Not at all. Phuong could have no better people than the two of you as her parents. The world is blending. We are each related. In generations to come, we could all look more alike than distinct. However, allow me to be blunt ... should a Caucasian-American child with the potential of Carl Sagan be adopted by Vietnamese parents in Ho Chi Minh City, Saigon, I'm sure you would feel concern."

"Sir, if I can be bold," Sandra said, "is Phuong as gifted as Carl Sagan?"

"I wish I knew. She may be greater than Sagan. Much of what she will accomplish depends on you. It will be her duty to excel. Do any of us know the brilliance children possess or what they might possibly become? Treat each as stars. Their brilliances differ greatly. Those who shine most brightly receive special care and attention."

"You speak like an academic," Sandra said.

"I should. I lectured at Columbia when I came to the United Sates. I was awarded my doctorate from the University of Strasbourg, Alsace, France."

Sandra and Luke looked at each other, impressed with Mr. Nguyen. Nonetheless, they were perplexed and disappointed to remain unenlightened. Who were these characters? What was their influence upon Phuong? Her family history? Who was the Visitor?

"Let's discuss how I may assist in your efforts to nurture your child of destiny."

"Phuong has a destiny," Sandra straightaway endorsed. "Correct?"

"It is her name. All children have a destiny, small or great. Her name is common in Vietnam. May I speak with candor? Am I allowed?"

Sandra and Luke motioned to proceed. Phuong, meanwhile, behaved as a genteel young lady, occupied with books and toys.

"When told popular writers, Mormon scholars from Stanford and Berkeley, adopted a Vietnamese child, we were thrilled. For some, an interracial adoption is offensive. For others, barriers abandoned."

"Our intentions are founded in love," Sandra assured him. "Phuong is neither a social nor political agenda. I cannot bear a child. Family was our goal from the day we married. We love Phuong as though she carries our own DNA. Luke has theorized of connections through *transcenditory* experiences. The three of us are genetically different in countless ways, but we are a family. What that means, what we share, is everything that's human. Phuong is a natural part of us."

"We have determined religions neglect humanity rather than embrace inclusion for all people. Separation, along with favoritism, seem to discourage acceptance for uncommon people. That is junk. It's fear and bias," Luke concluded. "We reject it."

"I have read your books," Mr. Nguyen acknowledged. "There is value in your labors. I hope to become your friend and assist the journey. Allow me to be a link with Phuong's heritage. The people who made her a child of destiny."

Mr. Nguyen outlined a strategy with activities, time sequences to educate Phuong, along with Sandra and Luke, in Southeast Asian history, genealogy, customs, holidays, and traditions. He communicated a need for Far Eastern immigrants to participate in the American culture and processes, best done together via social activities. Their negotiations and discussions were robust, meaningful, and pleasant.

Mr. Nguyen looked at his watch. It neared midday. "One last educational matter, then we shall depart. Would you please share *pho* with us?"

"*Pho?*" Sandra and Luke asked in unison.

"*Pho.*" Mr. Nguyen nodded.

"What is *pho?*" Luke asked.

The office staff entered the room carrying trays of food, followed by children and adults. Phuong squealed and wrestled to free herself from Luke's lap to reach the floor. Although the facility was limited, ample room allowed everyone to mingle, eat, and play.

Phuong went directly to the children, all near her age. They acted like kids, mischievous and fun. Sandra spread the comforter on the floor. Plates of food for each child were placed on the comforter to sit, eat, and play. "Don't worry about the comforter. Let the kids be free."

"I smelled something, a wonderful surprise," Luke said.

Introductions and names were shared. Each person warm and amiable. Conversations were lively while *pho, bun, cha gio, goi cuon, banh mi,* and other Vietnamese foods were tasted. It had been too long since Sandra and Luke smiled, laughed, and kept company without suspicion.

"Do Sandra and you have alone time?" Mr. Nguyen asked Luke. "Time together without Phuong?"

Luke swallowed a bite of *goi cuon*. "Are you asking if we leave Phuong with a babysitter? No, we do not. Our alone time is when Phuong sleeps."

"The two of you need your time together, just like Phuong is now enjoying her time with these children."

"We've been anxious and became suspicious after the adoption. The Visitor mentioned information no one should know except Sandra and me. Our reputations, fears—we trust no one to be alone with Phuong. One of us is with her at all times. It makes our lives stressful. This last hour has been more joyful—festive than we've known for some time."

"For your welfare, and for Phuong, that should change. Reliable people will assist. Phuong is in no danger. Your family is not in danger. You believe God has angels to guard you, do you not?"

Luke hastily swallowed a mouthful of *banh mi*. "Excuse me. You used words the Visitor spoke." Luke attempted to swallow food and speak at the same time to answer Mr. Nguyen. "Uh, yes, I do, I do believe in angels." Luke coughed to clear his throat. "Socio-psychopaths exist. I am skeptical. So is Sandra. We are cautious."

"You enjoy opera," Mr. Nguyen said. "Attend the opera. Play together. Call on me to assist. I will guard Phuong, see for the safety of all. The people you have met today are capable. They will help. We protect ideas and special people."

"We'll discuss your offer. We have your number. Today has been wonderful. Thanks." Luke praised the entire group. "Y'all done good."

"Our pressure," Mr. Nguyen replied.

The two men smiled at their own odd uses of grammar with malaprop.

The Visitor spot-on. A friendship begun.

With Phuong buckled in the car, Luke asked, "Wanna drive?"

"Sure."

Luke conveyed regrets. "We should have done this much sooner. My paranoia kept us secluded. Phuong enjoyed herself today. Right, sweetie?"

"Good times!" Phuong shouted.

"I'm sorry, Sandra. Mr. Nguyen set me straight."

"We should behave more like this every day. Free ourselves, let go ... within good reason. We can't become too wild." Sandra giggled. Luke smiled with her.

Confidence increased. Suspicion decreased. Sandra and Luke reclaimed the right to be approachable. Get-togethers at their home entertained diverse individuals. Their intent? Bridge gaps. Especially toward uncommon people. Create friendship. Interactive tolerance. Mr. Nguyen, neighbors, people of color, diverse groups, members of the Church—all came together. No one imposed their spiritual, religious, or social will upon others. Phuong and children engaged responsible activities with reasoned discussions and performances displayed by skilled mentors. Fun, never indulgent, with non-judgmental concerns. Learn, understand, then enjoy associations with those unlike yourself.

Aristotle's golden mean was observed: *Neither excess nor deficiency.*

Eating habits, study, work, play, sleep, television, entertainment— all activities met with balance and suitable reason.

The **Platinum Rule** replaced the antiquated Golden Rule: *Do unto others as they themselves would have done unto them.*

Compassion instilled a prerequisite for moral thought toward inclusion of uncommon souls. Understand how others think. Behave toward the expectations of others. Know their needs and issues prior to all interactions with uncommon, dissimilar, or unknown souls.

Luke taught: *Don't overdo it. Never doin' nothin' — the pits. You can get yourself hurt treatin' others like you wanna be treated.*

The Most Trying Angel

Many are destined to reason wrongly; others, not to reason at all; and others, to persecute those who do reason. Prejudices are what fools use for reason.

—Voltaire

"LUKE?"

"Yes?"

"This is the director of Southeast Asian Immigration. Do you have time to speak?

"What's on your mind?" Thoughts flashed through Luke's mind. *Fundraising. Celebrity status. A cause. Money.* The hammer fell.

"I have a child who needs a home. Can I meet with Sandra and you to discuss adoption of another child?"

Phuong a kindergartener, neared first grade. Events with the Visitor and Mr. Nguyen never allowed discussions between Sandra and Luke to increase their family to four. A flood of scenarios bounced in Luke's head.

"I gather from your silence," the director continued, "you're unprepared to respond. This is a distinctive situation. I need your assistance. Please?"

Luke rapidly connected dots, processed options, consequences. "Sandra is not home. Can I call with an answer in the morning?"

They decided to speak by phone early the next day.

Luke greeted Sandra with their customary hugs and kisses. Prayers offered and songs sung with Phuong before she fell asleep. Luke briefed Sandra about the call from the director. Sandra felt troubled. Too many unanswered questions and complex characters at play. She escaped to their bedroom, hoping for privacy.

Luke took Sandra's hairbrush and stepped into the bedroom. Sandra, in a nightshirt, sat behind the dressing table, all but her mind prepared for bed. Luke stood next to her and gently placed his hand on her head. He felt the smooth, rich softness of her hair against his fingers. He clumped strands, lifted them to his lips, kissed her hair. He lightly rubbed the strands against his cheek. The brush knew the routine. It glided through her hair.

The two intimately acquainted with the practice. Sandra leaned back and gently shook her head. Hair fell into his control. Luke brought his face forward, kissed her neck and shoulder. He brushed through her hair, stroke after stroke.

"Your hair is gorgeous. I love brushing every lock, each tress."

"Women would never cut their hair if all husbands behaved as you do for me."

"It is one of the greatest pleasures I hold dear from our love. We never argue when I brush your hair. Have you noticed?" Luke smiled.

"Do you say that hoping we will adopt another Asian child?"

"I love you. That's why I brush your hair. Not to avoid arguments… or adopt children. Sandra, you are so hot."

"Thanks for the compliment, Luke. I love you too," she smiled.

Luke finished a stroke, leaned his face into her cheek, and gently kissed her. "So, how should we approach this issue?" he whispered with another stroke.

"Throw some words out there. Get us talking," Sandra calmly directed.

"The Visitor, I believe, worries you."

"Mr. Nguyen is a good person. I trust him. The Visitor is a mystery. Despite this, I feel comfortable with Mr. Nguyen. His angels. We should be alert," Sandra advised.

"Agreed."

"Always thought we'd adopt at least two children. Many times, as an only child, I wished for a brother or sister."

"Good point. Often helpful to have a brother or sister while I grew," Luke said, with continued brush strokes.

"You're not a real parent until you have two or more children. Sibling rivalry, I suppose?"

"We're talking like we're going to do this, Sandra. What if we receive another girl? Or a boy this time?"

"Flip of the coin," Sandra conceded.

"The sooner we get our kids here, the sooner they leave," Luke said, chuckling. "I enjoy our alone time. Mr. Nguyen is right. We need our own maintenance. Date nights are hubba, hubba. Will another kid allow us to enjoy ourselves?"

"Is two too many?"

"Nah. We're earning a great income and investing money. Overlord will impact the world." Luke continued his brush strokes. "Our children will cope with what we are when they are independent from us. They should know of Overlord well before D-Day happens. They need to be prepared."

"Yes. Will two children be our limit?"

"I don't have an answer. Each child we have is like driving a stake into the ground. Mobility, area, means of expenditure, time— everything becomes reduced. More difficult to control and manage."

"Two is the minimum. We'll consider three when or if ... I might get baby-hungry," Sandra said, snickering.

They smiled while Luke took another long brush stroke through her hair. "So, you're willing to meet with the director about number two? Two Phuongs would be spectacular."

Sandra inhaled and held her breath. Quietly, she yielded. "Let's see the director. Discover what's happening."

"I'll call in the morning," Luke volunteered.

"Phuong has become talkative, smart, and very curious. There is something about her that is different. It's not her ethnicity. She is not like others her age." Sandra then questioned herself. "Or are we making ourselves seem important? She could be like all children her age. Maybe we're making something out of what is actually ordinary."

"We detected a rare quality in her the moment we first met," Luke said. "Why say that now? Have you seen or noticed something recently?"

"There is an unexplainable trait in her. It deals with us, Luke. The Visitor confirmed our suspicions. Yet, we might learn with a second child that all children behave like Phuong. Some uncommon characteristic."

"I grew with five siblings. I've seen kids, other people's kids, even our extended family and colleagues. Friends have sensed the same as we. I hope that whatever it is, she isn't a serial killer."

"Oh, Luke, really? She's our little girl, not a psycho. I wish I could understand her brain, hear her thoughts. Do you think she uses Vietnamese words in her mind?"

"I've wondered the same, Sandra. Wish I knew. I have a hunch someone knows. Maybe Heavenly Father. Mr. Nguyen might know but won't say a word."

"Did the director say we'd receive another Vietnamese baby?"

"No. I simply assumed another Asian child. Maybe Cambodian. Thai."

"Make the call. Thanks for brushing my hair; I do love it. Can I ask a favor?" Sandra turned in her chair and looked into Luke's eyes. She bit her lower lip with an inquisitive smile.

"Anything, Sandra. I love you."

"Will you give me a foot massage? I'll wash my feet first."

"Hop on the bed," Luke directed. "I'll get the lotion."

Luke gazed at her face as she smiled in return. He lifted Sandra into his arms and kissed her warmly. They broke. Sandra flew to the bed. Luke grabbed the lotion, hit the bed, and placed Sandra's foot on his thigh to smooth lotion on her toes.

Sandra fell deep into thought while Luke caressed her feet. *Luke's hypothesis is true. A foot massage is far more enjoyable and beneficial for couples than watching television. Little wonder the Church continually requests him to speak, lead, and counsel. Fun and sexy.*

"Sandra, when I saw you enter class at BYU and kissed your owie, I discovered love with vistas as broad as those we saw standing atop Timpanogos. You are wonderful. I love that you allow me to touch you."

"I enjoy your touches. Thanks." Sandra appreciated the care Luke demonstrated with his hands. Luke grasped the tensions of her day at the ankle, pressed them to the heel, through the arch, along the sole, and herded them to the toes, where Luke released the contaminants from her body. It meant the whole world to have Luke hear her words as he pressed the soles and stroked the arches of her feet. He individually touched and rubbed each toe. Exquisite, when followed with a kiss.

As Luke kissed the last toe, Sandra lurched forward on her knees. The bed bounced. She clutched Luke's face and pressed their foreheads together, "Remember how we looked into each other's eyes the first time we made love?"

"Unforgettable."

"Let's do it again. Now."

"No arguments here." Luke swiftly acquiesced to Sandra's desire.

Hurriedly, they undressed, clothes and holy garments strewn on the carpet. Sandra shook her head; hair fell on her shoulders and breasts.

Luke sat on the bed. He gazed a few moments at Sandra's lovely image. She sat on her legs, feet behind, torso and head upright. Her erotic appearance, firm and shapely breasts aroused Luke. Without words or touches, Luke hardened at Sandra's mere presence. The beauty of her face, cascading hair, legs, and skin suggested nothing other than femininity. Hands rested on her thighs, an ideal illustration of a beautiful woman. She hid her masculine DNA very well.

"I'm glad I can still turn you on. You may not be Joe DiMaggio, big fella, but you're everything I need." Sandra giggled, leaned forward, and crawled toward Luke. With one hand she touched his face and leaned in to kiss his lips. Not once, twice. "I love your taste." At the same time, Luke rubbed her back. Her skin smooth; and muscles firm.

"Sandra, you are so beautiful. I'll never run or hide from you … exquisite."

As her eyes watched him grow, she said, "If the ward knew what's happening to their bishop tonight." She giggled.

"PhDs or Mormons, we're doing what all people should enjoy. Romping sex."

Sandra lifted her head toward Luke, "This is our time for pleasure. Allow the world, Mormons included, to discover the Kama Sutra or other pleasuring guides themselves. Kiss me."

They kissed passionately. The feel of their naked bodies enhanced by hands that searched, touched, explored. A loved, trusted companion allowed inhibitions to flee. Luke placed a hand to Sandra's breast. Her breaths accelerated. She writhed when Luke's lips, tongue, and teeth brushed her. She exhaled a soft moan, passionately clutched his hair.

Sandra pushed Luke's back to the bed as her head and hair fell on his torso. She kissed him willfully on his chest and neck. Luke buried his hands in her hair. She placed a hand on his chest and pushed upward. Sandra straddled him. Looked into his eyes as she guided Luke inside her. Each cried sounds of rapture and jointly fell into rhythmic excitement. Luke massaged her legs and buttocks. His hands held her breasts while Sandra continued to satisfy them.

Experienced, bold, they continued their amorous encounter as climax neared. Luke sat upright. Sandra greeted him with an open mouth. They kissed and clutched the other with legs, arms, hands. Gripped hair, skin, muscle. The orgasmic release—ecstatic.

Luke turned Sandra on her back, delivering final thrusts. "I love disappearing inside you. Never disappointed—to see your eyes as I enter—"

Sandra kissed his lips.

"Don't ever leave me, Sandra. Can't live without you. I love you more than anything or anyone."

"You are my soul's companion." She embraced his nakedness to her own. Their skills of lovemaking learned from themselves ... researchers of pleasuring ... being pleasured.

Upon recovery, Luke said, "Sandra, the oldest opera tells the story of a man who entered Hell to rescue the woman he loves. I'd go there for you. You mean that much."

"Luke?" She looked into his eyes with a hand on his cheek. "You'd go there? What the hell am I doing in Hell? Who wrote such a story?"

"An ancient Greek, I believe. Active imaginations, those folks." He kissed her neck and shoulder. He paid attention to her breasts in the delicious after play of climax.

Rolled to their sides, they faced each other. The conversation continued while final acts of pleasure took place. They fondled, kissed, and admired each other's nakedness.

"In the opera," Sandra asked, "did the fellow find her? Did they escape?"

"I don't remember. I'll research it. If they didn't, I'd rather be in Hell with you than live in heaven without you."

"Luke. That's romantic. Is it wise?"

"It would be for me. I could never be happy without you. Heaven would be hell if I couldn't brush your hair, hear your voice, kiss you, touch you. Hell is a place. You are heaven to me. Sandra, you'd make Hell a heavenly place." He kissed her deeply on the lips and embraced her naked body once again.

"Well, Love, I hope I never need to be rescued from there."

"If I searched and found you in Hell and we couldn't escape, I'd follow John Milton's words: 'Better to reign in hell, than serve in heaven.' Sandra, we'd turn Hell into Eden. I don't care where Jesus is. I want you."

They kissed again. From their ardor, the evening's playtime still lived.

Located near each other in the government district, Sandra called Mr. Nguyen to ask if the ladies in his office would watch Phuong while they met with the director of Southeast Asian Immigration.

"Absolutely," Mr. Nguyen responded.

The office staff greeted Sandra, Luke, and Phuong. Children were ever-present since their initial visit. Phuong became fast friends, and there was always an immediate reunion. The kids bounced into the conference room with games and activities.

"We never mean to bring chaos to your work," Luke apologized. "I feel we impose on you too often."

"No. No. We are happy to have Phuong here. So are the children. Our joy," the office crew responded.

"When we return, we'll have ice cream," Sandra offered. "What does everyone want?" Orders were taken.

Mr. Nguyen is a godsend. Sandra and Luke thanked them for their assistance. Luke crafted a simple compliment. "You are the best. Thanks."

"We'll return as soon as we can. It may be an hour, no longer than two," Sandra assured.

Minutes later, they stood inside the entrance of the director of Southeast Asian Immigration. This place was larger, busier, and more sterile than Mr. Nguyen's office. Neither fun, nor warm.

"We have an appointment with the director."

"Yes, Sandra and Luke. It's my pleasure to meet you. Follow me." The sharply dressed receptionist led them to the director's office.

Sandra and the young lady exchanged a conversation. The receptionist spoke of gender issues related to discussions aired on Sandra's broadcasts. Their conversation was detailed though brief. A personal connection, it seemed. The receptionist disclosed, "You are more vibrant, younger, and much prettier than you appear on television."

The receptionist's comment confirmed Luke's assessment. Sandra possessed poise to lead, spoke well among diverse groups, instilled confidence in listeners, and solved problems. The star of this show? Sandra. No jealousy felt from Luke.

The receptionist announced, "Sir. Sandra and Luke." They entered.

The corner office was large, with windows that presented a view of the bay. A desk, sofa, bookshelves, cabinets, and a round table with four chairs graced the room. A world map and workroom whiteboard hung on the walls, along with photos and artifacts.

"Thank you. Please take a seat." The director motioned them to the table.

Sandra and Luke noticed another person with a familiar appearance. An Asian woman, with unsightly hair, looked strikingly similar to Mr. Nguyen and the Visitor.

Luke whispered into Sandra's ear. "This is stereotypically wrong for me to say, but either all Asians look alike or something odd is happening."

"She looks like Mr. Nguyen, but she's unpleasant," Sandra answered.

"Check behind her right ear. If she has a scar, she could be the Visitor's twin."

The director moved from behind his desk to the table. Gesturing toward the unknown woman, he said, "This is Ms. Ngo. She's essential for our discussion."

As Sandra and Luke shook hands with the woman, Sandra asserted herself. "There's a person we know. His office is a short distance from here. He looks like you, Ms. Ngo. Thirty or more years older. The two of you have a strong resemblance. Your father?"

"My father is deceased," Ngo politely replied.

"There is a man who visited me some time ago. You and he could be twins," Luke said. "Do you have a scar behind your right ear?"

Ngo turned her head so that everyone could see. "I am unwounded."

Sandra applied pressure, "Mr. Nguyen, your thirty-years-older doppelganger, says all immigrants from Southeast Asia have scars."

The director intervened. "I sense tension. Luke has shared concerns with me. Ms. Ngo is a trusted colleague. Please, sit. Let's discuss the purpose for being together."

The four seated themselves around the table. Ngo declared, "Mr. Nguyen is correct. We who are liberated have scars. The scars least visible are emotional. We love freedom. Miss our homeland with deep pain. Scars include memories."

Sandra, as a lion, continued the inquisition. "Mr. Nguyen has our daughter in his care. Should we be concerned?"

Ngo stared at Sandra, unmoved. With calm resolve, she assured the couple. "Phuong is in good hands. Of that, I'm certain. She has excellent parents who select trusted caregivers."

"Sandra. Luke. There is a child who needs you," the director said, attempting to bring the discussion back to the topic of adoption.

"Needs us? Why?" Sandra sharply questioned with an eye still on Ngo.

Ngo answered the questions. "The two of you have unique qualities. You are prominent, well-educated, financially capable Americans. Your ideas and thoughts are innovative. The only part of you I dislike is your religion … any religion. Mormons are the strangest."

"No arguments from me," Luke agreed. "We're conceited, self-righteous, unsympathetic, and overly adherent to our doctrines and culture. My own top ten list. So what? Mormons are no different than Jewish, Christian, or Muslim ideologues."

"Mormons claim to be humble yet boast of themselves as elite, valiant spirits. Ms. Ngo, what is your point?" Sandra glared.

"Get off my porch. Away from my home," Ngo attacked.

The silence became thick. A dreadful response.

"Conversion is your goal, your greatest satisfaction. Within or outside your own people," Ngo continued. "Lack of converts is a big disappointment. Peace and well-being for people mean little to you. You do not need missionaries. Should happiness and peace truly exist within your religion, Mormons would be forced to construct refugee centers for all who seek to enter Salt Lake, your Zion," she said, speaking with obvious disgust. "Living women, children, oppressed people struggle for opportunity while you sit inside darkened temples to redeem a dead population … with billions of dollars."

"I'm intrigued. Continue," Luke encouraged

"Acceptance and inclusion are relevant when all think, look, and behave similarly. Agreed?" Ngo asked.

"The world is safer when people think, appear, and behave according to the restored gospel of Jesus Christ. Obey the words of living apostles and prophets. Specifically, those men in Salt Lake City."

Ngo smiled. "You speak what you doubt. Your books. Your stories. Scholars who stress challenge but are bound by flat dogmas." Ngo shook her head. "Would your family of Mormons have welcomed Sandra if she were Black or Asian?"

Sandra and Luke straightened with stunned suspicion. The question probed beyond race. Did Ngo imply Sandra's queer genetic syndrome?

Luke answered, "Before June 1978, my parents would have disowned me for marrying a Black girl. My dad would've been upset if I married an Asian, Latino, or Polynesian." Hesitantly, Luke continued, "After 1978, I believe my parents and family would still object to marrying a non-Anglo-American, non-Mormon, non-white."

"Many scholars prior to the 1978 revelation doubted racial segregation. Why cease the dogma of separation in 1978?" Ngo asked. "Could it be reinstated?"

"What was previously unknown was revealed. It is now God's will."

"Luke, do you consider me an ignorant woman? You speak words that make spiritual leaders appear noble, those who conceal their own doubts with greater skill than you."

"Yes. I doubt scores of spiritual, doctrinal, so-called truths. Verbalizing doubts create consequences for me, for those within any faith-based organization. It is true in politics, social settings, or gender issues. Doubt threatens ... interpersonally and organizationally."

"Is not doubt a rule of science? The handmaiden of faith? Without doubt there is no faith. Doubt is the first step toward wisdom, truth. Is it not?" Ngo calmly provoked.

"Expressing doubt is dangerous. Alienating," Sandra contended. "Doubt separates you, sometimes permanently, from those you love. Not just religion. It separates colleagues in science, politics, and other matters. Free expression of doubt improves decision making. But tell Hitler you doubt his ideas? It is separation, likely death."

"The two of you fear the consequence of separation arising from expressions of doubt. Separation from your family, friends, and affiliation with Mormonism. Is it a greater threat than doing what is right? Do I understand your words? Has doubt improved your decisions? Ethical, moral behaviors?" Ngo coolly questioned.

"Are you playing with a full deck of cards?" Sandra asked. "You may be unaware of issues, Ms. Ngo."

The director interceded. "Sandra. Luke." He paused. "When you called me after adopting Phuong, you asked questions we did not imagine you would consider. Hear Ms. Ngo. Let her continue."

The director opened a palm toward Ngo. "We understand issues in your lives. We are neither evil nor enemies. Your influence with this next child is critical."

"You've taken shots at us and our religion. You are irritating," Luke dryly said.

"Offense is never given. It is always taken. – I've read your books," Ngo responded.

"Thanks for reading. I'm not offended. You speak eloquently, with depth. God knows the end of our stories. Nothing is at risk. We'll do what we do. God cannot be surprised despite what we do. We'll do our best. Yet I emphasize, no surprise endings, not for God. He already knows how each story ends. Including politics, economics—all world events."

"Luke, are you an ignoramus? Listen to yourself. You have reasoned God's life is dull. His omniscience allows Him no awe or surprise. Omniscience makes God insane ... you concede to it. Why agree with a conclusion you consider false?" Ngo asked.

"I've shared that idea only with Sandra. How do you know what only the two of us have discussed?" Luke felt unsettled.

"It's not difficult to see your doubts," Ngo said. "Far more than just the two of you who think skeptically. Like you, too few ever express their doubts when they should be reasoned with bright, open minds. Fear keeps doubts hidden from righteous leaders. Most share doubts only with God; rarely are they expressed to qualified counselors. Unfortunately, spiritual leaders, family, and friends dismiss or evade words of doubt. You can express doubts to strangers in an airport. They leave ... never seen again."

Sandra spoke. "Luke and I have settled these issues between ourselves. We have not disclosed our conclusions or intents to our families or fellow Church members. When the circumstances make possible the practice of intelligence over superstition, dogma, we will stand on the battlefield to win that war. How does all this affect the issue of adopting a child?"

The director bluntly addressed Sandra. "This discussion is extremely relevant."

"Please explain," Sandra requested.

"The child is beyond what people will accept in greater parts of the world. Chiefly America," the director explained.

"And among Mormons," Ngo insisted.

Sandra frustratedly asked, "What are you implying?"

"The child's mother is Vietnamese. The father is Black," the director proclaimed.

Sandra and Luke's postures froze. They sat upright from the slap received. They expected to receive another Phuong. The words blew through them like a blade so sharp it could not be felt. Nevertheless, heroes wounded in battle.

Phuong was acceptable among their friends, family, Church members—an innocent soul who escaped communism, rescued by white Americans who could not bear offspring ... a noble story that made headlines. A mixed Black/Asian child that followed the Civil Rights Era of the 1960s and 1978 revelation would be intolerable.

"Details are unimportant," the director continued. "It is best you possess fewer specifics. The child was born in Guam. Vietnamese refugees are processed there to enter America. A Black US Army officer and Vietnamese woman conceived the child. The Vietnamese woman died, as did the officer. Benefits will cease when the child reaches age five. The boy is presently three years, nine months old."

Sandra growled. "Nearly Phuong's age."

Though interrupted, the director droned, "The mother was considered bright. The father's aptitude and intelligence scores ... above average. Medical histories will be supplied, should you adopt."

"Why this child? Why us?"

Ngo began a lengthy response. "High-profile white Mormon parents with an adopted Vietnamese girl. Now a mixed Black-Vietnamese boy. It will promote racial acceptance and integration within mainstream white America. This boy needs attention. He is odd by virtue of his racial mix. Black parents are reluctant to adopt him. Few, if any, Asian parents will tolerate the mixed child. You have gifts that will help this boy understand his nature. He should not bear blame or disgrace for what he is. You will encourage him to honor his ethnic heritage, not be ashamed of it. Black Amerasians remaining in the Far East are impoverished, street children. Americans do little or nothing to care for their

Mark Merkley

castaways. In Vietnam, they are treated no better than dirt. It is our hope Americans will adopt more children when they observe your compassion, magnanimity."

"Should we adopt this boy, you will provide us with information. And not just about him. We need support. Who is Phuong? Why is she special? Why were we selected to be her parents? More detail. Why this boy?" Luke demanded

Ngo sighed and looked at her hands. Her dark eyes passed from Sandra to Luke. She took a breath. "Vietnam possesses a long history of dynasties and monarchy rule. Phuong is a descendent of royal blood. That's all to be said. Some from our country believe Phuong's noble blood is to excel in America. Her natural parents did not survive the violence in our homeland. As her American parents, it is expected Phuong will be well-treated, educated, and given experience. That she will become distinguished culturally and socially. Share common with uncommon. Privilege alongside humility. A mixed brother, that is obvious. Sandra, you are the star to guide not just Phuong but this boy toward acceptance for that which is more greatly uncommon."

"You know of Overlord." Sandra snapped.

Ngo nodded. "Your medical records in Los Angeles revealed your syndrome to us. You are"—she paused slightly—"tremendously unique. Uncommon among all who are common. As Jesus, the Son of God among mortals."

Sandra sat visibly stunned. Shocked to discover her vulnerability was exposed to possible bullies, unknown people. Expressionless, hurt, no power to even move her eyes. She was now filled with anger, tears.

"Excuse me." Luke signaled for a timeout. "That last statement is a leap. Sandra and I need to speak privately."

Heads nodded. Sandra's did not. Ngo and the director rose from their chairs to leave. As they did, Ngo imparted to Luke, "Phuong is learning of humor. An interactive comfortableness among diverse people, cultures. Well done." Ngo smiled.

Luke accompanied Ngo and the director out of the office and closed the door behind them like he owned the place. He walked back to Sandra, still slumped in a state of disbelief at the table.

"Sandra, this room is bugged. Who cares? They know largely everything. I need to hear your thoughts."

"You first. I'm playing catch-up. Outside of doctor-patient confidentiality, I thought my parents and the two of us were the only ones who know my syndrome. These people know. They know Overlord," she frightfully stated.

With demonstrative hands, Luke paced without slowing. "Should we adopt this boy, my dad will shit-a-brick to have a Black-Vietnamese grandson. We could never return to Utah. Who in all the white suburbs of Provo, Utah County, or anywhere in Utah would include the boy? Our diverse family? There are so few Black people in Utah ... fewer Asians? I prefer San Francisco. Los Angeles would be a good fit. Sandra, say something. I'm rambling... again."

"The boy is nearly four years old, likely potty-trained. We've lost a great portion of our own personal impact on his formative years of cognitive learning. Phuong is progressing. She's on course with us. But—but—they're required to report the boy's experience, his training. Oh, Luke ... people know about me. Us. They know what I am, dammit." Sandra dropped her head to the table. Hopeless and defenseless.

Luke sat next to Sandra. Placed his arms around her. "We have options. Let's consider the possibilities, then make decisions. One possibility is not to adopt."

"Yes, we could walk away with Phuong." She wiped her face. "We are not obligated to adopt this child. We can wait. Adopt a younger child, a newborn." Sandra hesitated, then became angered and determined. "My god, Luke. We're considering this child as if it is a potential abortion. Except he's real. We have culpability."

"Sandra, do you consider this a moral decision?"

"I consider the boy a living person." Sandra drew back. "To turn away our love for this child will haunt our thoughts well into the future. He's in need. Is our concern his color? Ethnicity?"

"We have means, capability," Luke said, thinking aloud. "The right decision is to act. You know my father ... despite his racism... would lift the boy into his arms if he saw him in danger, even with his ethnicities. I see my dad sheltering and protecting the boy.

People—our family—will understand. We'll help them empathize, sympathize, and accept our decision. He'll be our son."

"Our hope is to change people, Luke. The whole purpose of Overlord is to consider higher laws, honorable acts of tolerance, and compassionate behavior." Sandra's demeanor shifted to conviction. "Luke, get those bastards back into the room."

Ngo and the director took their seats. The four sat in silence and gazed with icy stares. Sandra broke the silence. "We'll adopt the boy. Does he have a name?"

"Jordan," the director answered.

"Thank God it isn't Malcolm, Kareem, or Muhammed," Luke mumbled.

"Luke." Sandra swatted the back of her hand against his arm. "Be kind. He could be Parley P., Thomas S., a Mormon name with the customary initial." Sandra turned, "When will we receive him?"

"He's in Guam. We'll sign documents. He can be in San Francisco next week," the director explained. "He speaks English, although you must be patient. Assorted Vietnamese people have cared for him. He'll need attentiveness for some time."

"I'm certain you wish to exploit us as public figures," Sandra said.

"Correct," the director verified. "Your popularity will find sponsors, donors, adoptive parents."

"For a price." Luke firmly spoke.

"What will that be?" asked the director.

Luke pointed at Ngo. "We don't know this person. She looks like two others we've met. Give us answers. Secondly, your intelligence work is remarkable. We want access, updates, information. Privacy for our family. Sandra's syndrome remains classified. Full partners on this team."

"From the beginning, you've always had access, been partners. Our highest confidence. You've never asked nor tapped into it," Ngo said.

Sandra hissed. "Look, I don't like your arrogance. Your answers say nothing. We'll give Jordan guidance. He'll be loved and cared for like he is our own blood— inform us. Tell us how, where, what, when, and why. Don't say, 'Always had access. You've never tapped into it.' Bullshit. Where are the wiretaps? Give us a phone number. The name of your association. Exchanges. Hell, I'll sit on a bench in Golden Gate Park. Drop an envelope; I'll walk away with it."

"Is that what you want? A game of spy versus spy?" Ngo asked.

"We want awareness, understanding," Luke demanded. "You know our secrets. Who are you? We have a right to know. Access to your intelligence. We expect confidentiality."

"Parts cannot be discussed. You have been of interest to us since your days at BYU. Much will be shared ... you are remarkably bright. Intelligent. Yet, your behaviors indicate great innocence, lack of experience. Inability to discern when matters are clear. In your words, 'dumber than a sack of rocks.'" Ngo stared at Luke.

"BYU? Really?" Sandra suspiciously enquired. "What can you discuss? We'll determine what is sufficient."

"We are altruistic. What academics, like you, label a philanthropic association. We never do harm. We assist and aid humankind. Guardian angels. It is holy work, royal endeavors." Ngo turned the discussion in a new direction.

"Was it right that Catholic missionaries entered Brazil or Peru? Destroyed their architecture, art, customs and burned historic records? Replaced their languages, customs, and cultures with their own religious dogmas? Have you read and studied published anthropologists ... historical sociology and subjugation?"

Luke responded, "European incursions in America and Asia, exclusively in the name of God and what is holy was evil ... continues to be evil. Mormons, Jehovah's Witnesses, any circus-tent, door-to-door evangelist should stay off your porch, Ms. Ngo. I apologize on behalf of all Mormons, Catholics and religions everywhere. It is immoral, unethical behavior to purposely convert people. Should something be of value, it will be pursued. Like a pearl of great price. Religions needn't force, subjugate people in new places, or sell God's benefit package like a used car."

"We're progressing well." Ngo nodded and asked, "Are we to meddle in the matters of God?"

"God seems to ignore the death of children. Abuses upon the innocent," Luke said. "I abhor the biblical story of Abraham and his son, Isaac. I question sacrificing a savior, the only begotten, or slitting the throats of animal scapegoats ... mandatory acceptance of biblical writing as absolute truth. There is no logic or reason in it."

"Have religions ever claimed logic or reason among its virtues?" Ngo questioned again.

"Good point. Rarely." Sandra snapped. "That is why Isaiah and Joseph Smith each advised to reason in groups. Job wanted to argue with God. Confrontation and discussion are comfortable companions. Logic and reason are persuasive. Change is always possible. Afterall, dissent is the basis of all critical thought."

"Does God understand quantum mechanics?"

"Yes," Sandra and Luke responded.

"When did God know of relativity or quantum mechanics?"

"From the beginning," Luke answered.

"Did Abraham or Moses understand classical physics or quantum mechanics? Did God reveal that knowledge to them?"

"Old Testament writings do not confirm they did. Not at all," Luke replied. "Ancient Greeks understood the concept of atoms. Hebrews in the Bronze or Iron Ages knew nothing of physics, quantum or classical. They didn't understand Newton's laws of motion, complex mathematics, or disease-causing microbes. The sophistication of Relativity $E = MC^2$ or quantum mechanics was not generally understood until the late nineteenth century, early twentieth century."

"What about medicine? Dentistry? Metallurgy? Bacteria? DNA? Viruses? When did God reveal these issues through prophets or religious leaders to benefit humanity?"

"Luke, I understand Ngo's intent," Sandra said, settling the fray. "God will not interfere in spiritual, social, or scientific development. Humanity is expected to discover it themselves. It is our victory when we, the people of the Earth, complete the math. Compose symphonies. Construct instruments, tools, and machinery to do it all."

"Well done, Sandra," Ngo complimented. "God has left breadcrumbs. Clues. As evidence is discovered, conclusions and decisions are made. Hence, 'Let us reason together.'"

"You speak familiarly with scriptures. Like you know God," Sandra observed.

Ngo confessed. "I know God as well as you ... very little."

"Why this pleasant discussion?" Luke asked.

"Revelation is myth," Ngo argued. "Truth is a burden of intelligence. Akin to reason. Truth has never been obtained from a burning bush, oracle of Delphi, or inspired, holy writings of prophets, imams, gurus, popes, priests, pandits or rabbis. Conclusions are best understood when self-discovered," Ngo nodded her head. "People achieve awareness and knowledge from humankind's efforts to discover truth. As those written in your books, Sandra and Luke, **revelation is a problem that requires a solution**. Mysteries in need of reasoned, mathematical answers, from intelligent and curious minds."

Sandra turned, "I see it! God can be surprised, Luke. Heavenly Father and Mother would enjoy a surprise party. It keeps them on their toes. Acquire languages, use words, run and sequence the numbers. We employ logic and reason. Spirituality is science—scientific discovery."

"Religion's usage of math and science is largely absent. Yet, religious people become scientists. Scientists truly create miracles. Not from revelation, but from reason. Awe-inspiring achievements which use knowledge, mathematics, experimentation and logical conclusions. Do not ask science for explanations of religious fantasies or dogmas. They are incompatible." Ngo sat back.

A long pause followed.

"We've a son to adopt," Luke said. "Sandra gathered your intent. I am dumber than a sack of rocks. Vaccines could have occurred centuries ago had Heavenly Father declared it to prophets. But who would've believed it? Understood processes? Or even do the right thing? I allowed myself to remain ignorant, holding to a belief that a person who claims to be a prophet, seer, or revelator could simply ask God then receive instant answers. That is backward and lazy. Revelation is damned ugly. It is our struggle to continually challenge dogmas with intense debates. In particular, those we religiously worship—I want my son, now!"

Sandra moved her chair close to Luke. "Everyone has difficulty seeing through fantasy," she said, placing an arm around him. "Luke, intelligent people juggle superstition and science every weekend, in all religions." With arms around Luke, she turned to Ms. Ngo, "We want Jordan in our home, immediately."

Luke stared at Ngo. "Sandra and I have been of interest to you since BYU? Why?"

"Sandra, you are queer; Luke, you silently question. Each of you possesses parts of each word. Together, a formidable pair. Similar to Joan, Abraham, Albert, and Martin. Your lives will change the world. Humanity may finally, one day, escape the Dark Ages."

"Phuong and Jordan have roles in this endeavor. Correct?" Sandra asked.

"Relevant players. They will prevail," Ngo summarized. "We'll assist your climb."

Strategies were discussed with deeper explanations. Achievable goals with objectives.

Ngo delivered her final recommendation. "Remain close to Mr. Nguyen. An angel of great worth. Phuong and Jordan will benefit from his compassion."

"Have we addressed your questions?" Ngo asked.

They nodded. "We have a daughter to rescue. Mr. Nguyen needs a break," they exclaimed.

"Sandra's syndrome is to remain concealed, until the world is to be told," Luke insisted.

Angels or not, *Consortium* became the term for the Visitor, Mr. Nguyen, and Ms. Ngo. Partnered with Sandra and Luke, they were dedicated to liberate then include people labeled queer or questioning by archaic religious and social tormentors.

"My hairbrush will be on your pillow tonight." Sandra grasped Luke's hand and wrapped his arm around her waist. "The Consortium is impressive. Use caution in our words. Don't say the right words to the wrong people. Or vice versa," she said. "Got that?"

"Yes, babe. Got that."

"Let's buy ice cream and get back to Mr. Nguyen's office. Phuong's brother arrives next week. How will we explain this to our parents?"

Later that night, Luke watched as Sandra finished brushing Phuong's hair. He found Sandra's hairbrush, as promised, on his pillow. Their conversation and lovemaking broke new grounds.

Jordan's Arrival

...a little child shall lead them.

—Isaiah 11:6

SANDRA AND LUKE OPTED to take Jordan home from the airport. A lounge above the terminal allowed privacy and personal time for the family to become acquainted with Jordan. The lounge included chairs, sofas, and two tables. One table offered finger sandwiches, fruit, veggies, treats. The second, larger table, provided room to sit, dine, and converse.

Mr. Nguyen agreed to act as an interpreter, if needed. He suggested a small number of children be nearby, attended with parents. He explained, "Jordan is not an infant. He may speak unfamiliar words. Children will—"

A usually calm and confident Sandra felt unsettled. "Mr. Nguyen," she implored, "Luke and I want to be the first to greet and speak with Jordan. We need this as our family time ... Jordan will come to know the children, you, and their parents in due time," She tried to explain. "I hope you understand." She wanted Jordan's arrival to be perfect.

"Yes, Sandra. We're here to support your family." Mr. Nguyen placed his hands over his heart. "We will remain quietly distant. Should you feel we are needed at any time, we will respond ... at your request."

"Thank you, Mr. Nguyen. Everyone has been kind … this is so intense."

Mr. Nguyen smiled and nodded his head. "This hour will be a memorable time."

Luke, as well, stammered, "It's unnerving. We'll give birth to a boy … like an ultrasound … but this kid can already speak."

An airline runner was assigned to lead Jordan and his chaperone to the lounge. He carried a walkie-talkie to update a second airline employee in the lounge as events happened.

Sandra and Luke took cues from the receiver. They hoped to duplicate the Camp Pendleton experience. A small sofa was placed near the open, double-wide doors. Sandra and Luke sat on the sofa; hands held in anticipation. Phuong, unconcerned, stood occasionally and waved at children seated with parents behind them.

The receiver did little more than hold her walkie-talkie. The runner's voice declared, "Jordan and Sgt. Steele will arrive in thirty seconds."

Everyone stirred and prepared themselves to witness the arrival. Sandra excitedly hugged Phuong. "Jordan will be here soon."

"Happy day," Phuong said, grinning. Sandra and Luke sandwiched kisses to her cheeks.

Luke turned to Sandra, looked into her eyes. "Another milestone, Sandra. I love you."

Sandra smiled as she heard rustling. A fit, young, red-haired US Army sergeant stood at the entrance in service military attire. He faced into the room. At the end of his outstretched arm, a boy fought to run away.

Sgt. Steele took a knee. Like an older brother, he constrained Jordan in his arms and spoke softly into his ear. Confidently, the soldier lessened his clench. The boy turned and gazed into the room. Jordan stood protected at Sgt. Steele's chest.

Sandra and Luke were instantly taken by Jordan's Amerasian handsomeness. Jordan received the best of Asian and African-American features. On this day, at this tense occasion, his eyes filled with tears and fear. Sandra and Luke went to their knees from the sofa.

"Hello, Jordan. I am your mother. So thrilled to see you. We want you to be happy. Please, hold my hand?" Slowly, Sandra held her hand toward Jordan.

The boy shook his head demonstrably.

"Jordan, I'm your father. Let's be friends. I have a ball. Play catch with me." Luke rolled the ball gently toward Jordan.

Jordan wrestled to be free. Tears streaked his cheeks as he shook his head, cried, and twisted against Sgt. Steele, whose arms and chest held him in place.

No freedom. No escape.

There was little chance for smiles, balloons, cake, or a happy ending as Jordan's screams became louder. His efforts more furious to escape.

The tension and horror of this frightful scene mounted.

He jerked powerfully. Cried out, desperate, deeply upset.

Calm and resolutely, Phuong walked between Sandra and Luke toward Jordan, who thrashed, grunted noisily, and struggled to run away.

She placed a finger to her lips— "*Shhhhhhhhh*"—approached the wildly agitated Jordan.

Fearlessly, she continued her approach. All the while whispering a peaceful "*Shhhhhhhhh*."

Phuong took more steps toward Jordan and placed her free hand near his face. Softly, she repeated, "*Shhhhhhhhh*." Finger at her mouth.

Jordan stilled himself.

Her openhanded touch to his head and face dispelled tensions. A finger pressed against her mouth as she uttered another "*Shhhhhhhhh*." Jordan fell silent.

As she stroked his face, Phuong continued to whisper "*Shhhhhhhhh*" until Jordan completely settled.

With a final "*Shhhhhhhhh*," Phuong spoke Vietnamese words.

Jordan nodded his head.

Phuong looked to the back of the room, called, "Tuan. Cam." She waved a hand to say, *Come here.*

Two children, a boy and girl, ran to Phuong and Jordan. They conversed in Vietnamese and English. They touched Jordan, rubbed his head, arms, and patted his shoulders.

Sgt. Steele released his arms from Jordan and left the little ones to themselves. The soldier rose to his feet, took a step back, but continued to maintain guard over the children, his eyes constantly on the youngster in his watch.

A consoled Jordan was now under Phuong's care.

Mr. Nguyen approached Sandra and Luke and knelt next to them. "That was extraordinary."

"Yes, it was," Sandra agreed. "What did Phuong say to him?"

"She said, 'Be still my brother. You are home.' That's all I heard."

"Did you teach Phuong to say those words? Make that shhhh sound?" Luke asked.

"No," Mr. Nguyen responded. "I did not. The children may—"

Sgt. Steele came forward, still impacted by the event. "I presume you are Sandra and Luke."

"Yes, we are."

"The first encounter between children of this age and adoptive parents is an unknown thing," the soldier said with a slight southerly accent. "We do the best we can, but I've never seen anything like what just happened ... I'm glad I witnessed this." Humbled, Sgt. Steele silently turned his focus ... "Please forgive me, sir. Sgt. Rulon Steele, sir." Sgt. Steele stood at attention, now speaking with military discipline. He exchanged a firm handshake with Luke.

Luke, still under Phuong's influence caught himself, "Yes ... my wife, Sandra. This is Mr. Nguyen, a dear friend. Phuong, the savior of the day, is our daughter."

"It is my pleasure to meet you and your family. I deliver greetings and appreciation from my commanding officer in Guam. Your service and support are recognized. Your benevolence is graciously accepted."

"Thank you, Sgt. Steele. Please, feel free to relax in our presence, military protocol included. Be a part of our family."

Over the next minutes as the children interacted, Phuong never strayed from Jordan. She introduced him to all the children and guests, directed him to the table with food, chatted, and ate together, never releasing her grip from his hand.

Sandra and Luke, anxious and tense, waited nervously near the sofa. They believed it a strategic move. *Remain subtle. Don't be large or prowl.* Their hope? *Phuong will lead Jordan to us.* She acted as the link from the world Jordan escaped to their family. They understood how well Phuong played her role.

Seated on the carpet in front of the sofa, Sandra and Luke sipped water. Passed time patiently as Phuong guided Jordan to everyone in the room. Each greeted and introduced themselves. Finally, Phuong led Jordan to Sandra and Luke.

"Jordan, Mom and Dad."

"Hello, Jordan," Sandra and Luke said, greeting their son in unison.

"Welcome to our family."

"Sit on Mom." Phuong patted Sandra's upper leg with her open hand but still clutching Jordan with her other hand. She led him toward Sandra's lap. Jordan, now calm, sat. Phuong released Jordan's hand and fell into Luke's lap. The four sat as a family, though guarded. Sandra feared to move rapidly. Jordan could protest any attempt to place her arms around him. She rested a hand to his arm and gently rubbed. Silence overtook the room.

"Hugs!" shouted Phuong as she reached around to Luke and hugged him. Luke responded as if at home, with enthusiasm, followed with tickles. Phuong playfully laughed.

Sandra did not attempt to respond enthusiastically. Unsure, she lightly put her arms around Jordan. He turned to receive Sandra's hug. Warmly holding him near, tears welled in her eyes. Sandra and Jordan's faces touched as she whispered, "I love you, Jordan. I—we—will protect you." Jordan's arms wrapped around Sandra's neck. She welcomed his hug.

Luke held Phuong in his arms. Motioning to their daughter, he said loudly enough for only Sandra to hear, "A little child shall lead them." Sandra gazed at Luke and mouthed the words *I love you* as she hugged their son warmly. Phuong and Luke embraced them. A family united, deeply in love.

This unusual family possessed intents far-reaching and sublime. Each held gifts to battle the armies of ignorance. The challenges from social and religious tormentors. Change ultimately wins. In all quests, fatalities are expected ... even calculated. Our heroes, no exception.

Luke searched for Sgt. Steele as the gathering waned. "Sergeant, I want to ask—"

"Yes, sir." Military discipline intact.

"It is expensive for you to travel with a lone child. Rarely happens, I suppose."

"VIP treatment, sir."

"VIP treatment," Luke acknowledged with a humble blush. "Sandra and me."

"No, sir." Sgt. Steele relaxed the military delivery. "Your ego is speaking. The VIP is Jordan, sir."

"VIP?"

"Sir, yes, sir. Very Impoverished Person, sir," Steele whispered to mask any embarrassment. "The term we use to describe people and children with exigent circumstances."

"Big words."

"USC graduate, sir."

"Southern California?"

"No, sir. University of South Carolina." Steele smiled.

"Thanks for cutting back on the military dress. BYU and Berkeley." They bumped elbows.

"Y'all won the NCAA football title in '84."

"Wasn't there when it happened. How'd you get into the Army and this work, Sergeant?"

"My dad was a Korean War vet. Said the Army made him a man. It would do the same for me."

"Did your father see conflict in Korea?

"Yes. Fought in Pusan. His life saved by a battle buddy. 'A Negro named Rooolon,' as my dad would explain it. That's how I got my name. Rulon." Sgt. Steele grinned.

"Great story."

"At graduation, I enlisted. Finished basic training and stationed in Guam, which is actually a nice place. Been helping place immigrants since I stepped on the island more than two years ago."

"The work, I'm sure, is brutal."

"Yes, sir. It is," Steele admitted as if defeat approached.

"What can you tell us about Jordan?"

"Sir, I have no information to give. Relevant data for your needs has been provided." Steele's military tone remained intact.

"I understand your restrictions. I know you accompanied Jordan from Guam. How did his parents die?"

"Sir, I do not know. That's the truth, sir." Stated with complete military etiquette.

"Okay. Look. You've done this work for some time. Please, what can we do for Jordan? As we go forward, what can we expect? Prepare for? Be made aware of? Likes? Dislikes? Anything will help. I don't want to throw him playfully in the air if it scares him or turn off the lights if the dark frightens him. What games will he play? What foods should we prepare? Give us some advantage. Please."

"Keep your little girl nearby. She is incredible. I'm gonna try that shhhh technique. I read your book about *transcenditory* learning. You should add a paragraph about what happened today."

"I'll keep that in mind."

"By the way, I have your book and one written by Sandra. Could you sign them?"

"Sure. No problem. What about Jordan?"

"Jordan's had it tough. He's a good kid. Really is. He needs love. I have confidence you'll deliver that love. Do your best to put Guam out of his mind. The more he can attach to the life with y'all, the better. He likes *pho*. Who doesn't? Fish, hamburgers, popcorn. He enjoys puzzles. You'll see what he brought with him.

"I suggest you get rid of the clothes he has. Not soon. Smoothly allow the past to fade away. Try to replace what might remind him of bad memories with new, good experiences. Let him keep his pictures. They are good memories, friendly faces. I might be in one or two photos. As the years pass, the pictures will fade. He'll forget plenty. Some others … nope," Steele shook his head.

"You're good folks. Expect conflicts. Deal with him like you wrote in your book, 'would you rather be liked, or be a good leader?' Please, be good parents. You might need to get a little tough at times, you know."

"Thanks, Sergeant, for bringing Jordan to us. I'd like to communicate with you should a need arise."

"My duties are concluded, sir," he said with military zeal.

"Understood, Sergeant." Luke reflexively gave a slight salute.

Steele whispered as if to reveal a secret to a spy in a dark alley. "I accidently dropped a half-sheet of paper with my parent's names and phone number on the food table."

Luke laughed and patted Sgt. Steele on the shoulder. "You're a good man."

"As are you, sir. Some criticize your sense of humor. I do not."

With the customary final documents signed, instructions were given and best wishes expressed from Mr. Nguyen, Sgt. Steele, and the parents of the children. Everyone was kind, supportive, and gracious. Each communicated encouragement for Jordan with wonder and praise toward Phuong.

Sandra and Luke saw two very tired children in car seats behind them during the drive home. A stressful day for everyone—especially Jordan. Phuong calmed a storm and directed the family to a warm and pleasant first encounter. The new sister and brother soon fell asleep. As they did, Sandra and Luke opened a discussion.

"Sandra, what is your take on what happened today?"

"You mean Phuong and the way she quieted Jordan?"

"Yes. Remarkable."

"Mr. Nguyen didn't teach Phuong those Vietnamese words. Her awareness is beyond our comprehension. I am in awe," Sandra said, conceding to their daughter's gifts.

"Sgt. Steele called Phuong amazing. Something he never experienced, had never seen."

"It won't take her long. She'll lead this family, Church, the world," Sandra predicted.

"Who do we have in these children? We know there is some concealed force here, working, controlling, manipulating events," Luke speculated.

"We know that Mr. Nguyen is a part of it. I like the man. He's helpful, supportive. He and Ngo could be father and daughter. Their connections are eerily similar," Sandra said, connecting dots.

Luke directed the conversation back to Phuong. "What child can shhhh a volatile situation into a celebration? I'm astounded."

"Everyone was. I don't understand it. I will say, I'm glad it's us, Luke. I want these children. The Visitor, Nguyen, and Ngo are mysterious, but look at what we have." Sandra pointed to the backseat. "They have delivered special children into our care. I am committed to their destinies and our own. We will take advantage of the Consortium's powers and resources. Their organization, service, assistance, and intelligence are welcome. Needed."

"We have peculiar children. Bless Jordan's heart. He possesses gifts possibly as great as Phuong. When we met Ngo, it wasn't about adopting a child. We were already chosen for Jordan and Jordan for us. They used his biracial makeup as a ploy. Jordan responded to Phuong with great trust. There's a connection between them. It involves us."

"Whatever it is, Luke, we are obligated, but it's their destiny, within our own, for the time being."

"We're in a game of catch-up with Jordan. He will become accustomed to our hugs and touches. This will be the oddest of all possible families. Tightly knit, let's hope." Luke held her hand tightly. "I'm pleased you're our leader, Sandra. I'd be lost without you."

"Drop the drama queen routine. You're the divergent-thinking leader; I'm the convergent-thinking leader. Between the two of us, we make a functional Kirk and Spock, with a helluva crew in the backseat."

"We might need to purchase a van. Like other Mormon families."

"Please. No vans."

With that, the fourth hero took his place in the family. The years ahead were to be grand and eventful. Not without challenges and pain. *There ain't anything in this plan that is going to go right.*

Sundays were spent attending Sunday school, sacrament meeting, Relief Society, and priesthood classes. Phuong and Jordan learned mainstream Mormon cultural and doctrinal instructions with added contexts from their queer and questioning parents who attempted to settle affairs with reason over superstition. Balance is difficult with pretentious religious memes. —Apologies for the snooty words—Phuong and Jordan were taught to think, question, be bold, express challenges ... which they did.

The family created liaisons with Mr. Nguyen and Ms. Ngo. Reliable partners.

Mr. Nguyen, as a tutor, shared culture, history, language, arts, and customs with Phuong and Jordan. He became the sunshine of Vietnam with sounds, tastes, and smells. Their laughter and conversations as confidants became his gift. Mr. Nguyen, the beloved.

Ms. Ngo, not as visible, nonetheless profound, influentially engaged all questions Sandra and Luke asked with regard to religion, philosophy, science, or sundry matters. Ngo contributed guidance that pertained to Overlord. Her words and questions intrigued Sandra and Luke with images sordid, tender, gross, and most wondrous. Ngo possessed a rational mind. She was an antagonist you hoped would never leave and a partner who collaborated with Phuong and Jordan toward intellectual and moral skills. Ms. Ngo, the sage

The Visitor's presence seemed radiant, constant, though infrequent and unexplained. Luke held great hope to meet him again, understand his role, and discover his gifts. Nevertheless, assurances were given. The Visitor held to the same agreements with the Consortium: confidentiality and exchange of information, principally on behalf of Phuong, Jordan, and Overlord.

Singularly focused, the director of Southeast Asian Immigration raised money and placed immigrants. An administrator, not an angel.

Sandra tantalized as a speaker at Southeast Asian Immigration fundraisers. Her beauty captivated and persuaded. Skilled in the display of modest but eye-catching clothes, her spoken words equally enticed. "Each child comes to us from God with their own genetic codes. Luke and I do not have children who possess our DNA. In the Lord's wisdom, I am unable to contribute my DNA with Luke's. Heavenly Father knows we have tried."

Smiles from the audience.

"More often than can be counted."

Controlled, embarrassed laughter.

"Luke's efforts go beyond the expectations of most men and are greatly appreciated."

Laughter with applause.

"God, through providence, has blessed Luke and me with two unique, beautiful children. We love Phuong and Jordan with the same passion as though they are made with our own DNA. The real issues are with the newborns and toddlers who need homes. Families require sponsors. Food. Medicine. Clothes. Warmth from the cold of politics, war, and suffering these people have escaped."

Sandra and Luke used their voices to encourage adoption, sponsorship, and donations. Their private contributions were issued with a challenge to match or surpass past gains to benefit those who escaped oppression. It was a fair exchange for the information, support, and privileged confidentiality received from the Visitor, Mr. Nguyen, Ms. Ngo, and others who comprised the Consortium. Everyone behaved as supportive teammates in their causes.

The 1980s eased into the 1990s. New expressions found their way into world discussions. LGBTQ became a common descriptor for those within this classification. Sandra and Luke carefully walked narrow paths through LDS dogmas. They approached but never crossed possible lines of reprimand. Progression took place toward healthier standards of behavior: tolerance, compassion, and human reason. Yet violence, social harm, and intimidation stemmed from religious dogmatism and cultural traditions plagued the well-being of uncommon humans.

The Consortium collaborated with Sandra and Luke who wrote appeals to LDS and world interests challenging long-held tenets of discrimination. They specifically persuaded youth to explore ideas and practice inclusion in a diverse world.

Sandra received invitations from churches and associated groups to author articles. She spoke toward gender equity, women's issues, and family relations.

Luke published additional novels without a penname. He appealed for readers personal, emotional acceptance of characters beset with conflicts of uncommonness. He, too, was sought by churches and groups for his skills, including the Brethren in Salt Lake.

Videos were produced with manuscripts designed to enlighten families about interpersonal relationships. Phuong and Jordan assisted. The examples from their lives contributed valuable lessons. The challenges included family experiences. Illustrations with usable material related to ethnicity, crossed generations, gender, cultures, communication, history, and religious dogmas. Each prepared with charity, the pure love of Christ. Recipients were guided to become leaders, problem-solvers, decision-makers, and enabled thinkers within families and the makeup of organizations. Our heroes ably shared their talents with a global audience. Mormon or not.

Book sales, public rallies, and media exposure expanded. Popularity without paparazzi. Though well known, they were never menaced. The Consortium delivered on their vow for family normalcy while caring for Phuong and Jordan and simultaneously protecting Overlord.

Jordan's first years in America were challenging. New environment, routines, customs, language, and religion conflicted with his Vietnamese heritage and mixed ethnicity. The meager existence of Guam confused him with affluent family conditions in San Francisco. Jordan's uncommon qualities struggled with Sandra and Luke's discipline. Gradually, transitions met success. Phuong's enchanted skills were gratefully utilized.

Jordan unjustly endured racism from immigrant refugees in Guam. It was featured in his biracial face. He could not even escape the people from his homeland. Consumed with fear, his only means of survival was to fight. Tormented, without parents, his food portions had been stolen. Compassion, he learned, came from GIs on the island. Sgt. Steele, an angel, intervened with protection and friendship. The immigration camp on Guam was an island prison where Jordan survived but was unable to live.

Jordan's fear lessened his self-esteem. Hardiness[8] exercises helped Jordan become a liberated, free thinker. Hardiness is a learned behavior. Sadly, fear is also a learned behavior. It, too is acquired within most families, like public speaking.

Sandra and Luke designed challenges to develop family hardiness. They participated in rock climbing; jumps from platforms into water; delivery of speeches; meeting and greeting new, unfamiliar people; emergency care; pet care; and Sandra's favorite, math. Sandra and Luke created games of challenge that required resolutions to problems. Phuong and Jordan articulated their reasoning for each problem resolution. Always defended priorities. Discussions with feedback were constant activities at home.

Touches from Jordan's natural parents—forgotten. Touches, hugs, handholding, cuddles, two people wrapped in a blanket to

---

[8] Term and concept developed by Dr. Suzanne Kobasa who describes resilient traits young people and adults naturally learn, then engage, to confront social, health, and moral issues. Three personality characteristics anchored Kobasa's research of personal hardiness. Hardy individuals (1) choose commitment rather than alienation, (2) control rather than engage powerlessness, and (3) challenge rather than threat or danger. In each circumstance, but particularly challenge, it is a realization that change, rather than stability, is the normal course in life for achieving personal growth rather than threats to personal security.

watch a movie became common practices. Kisses never excluded. Fundamental behaviors required new memories.

Jordan's trust was earned and learned. He sat on the laps of Sandra and Luke, customary duties at movies, church, and home. Jordan learned that longer hair allowed him to receive hairbrushes from Sandra, sometimes Luke, and occasionally Phuong. His hair grew.

Resistance was strong. Given control over his environment, Sandra and Luke found food hidden in Jordan's bedroom and other parts of the house. Trust, they expected, would influence his behaviors. Jordan adapted. Food was no longer hidden. Through love he became receptive to family loyalty. He enjoyed music, picnics, rode his bicycle, and heard stories read by Sandra, Luke, and Phuong. They played games, hit baseballs, swam, observed birds, learned about sea life, held pets and insects, sang, and received hugs and kisses every night before bed.

> A fierce family forever.
> Phuong, the able prodigy.
> Jordan, the troubled challenger.
> She directed; he distracted.
> Dependent, one for the other.
> Each gifted; neither similar.
> Seeking answers in all moments.
> Adored by all who would hear.

"Jordan is speaking more. His grammar has improved. Unfortunate we didn't have him earlier," Sandra said, somewhat frustrated.

"Will he be prepared for first grade this fall?" Luke asked.

"I believe so," Sandra concluded. "It's an uphill battle and could take years to reach his classmates' levels. He's stressed. I worry about Phuong. Her concern for Jordan is sweet. This shouldn't be her challenge ... A real trooper." Sandra rubbed her eyes, somewhat fatigued. She, like everyone, wanted Jordan to have peace, communicate well, enjoy home and family without fear. Stress took its toll.

"Sandra, I received a call from the Church. I need to brush your hair tonight."

"Luke, are we being censured?"

"No. Possibly quarantined. *Secluded* is more appropriate. That's certain."

"What is it? Are they calling you as a mission president to Tibet or Antarctica? We can't do that. Not with Jordan. Not now."

"Whoa, Sandra. It's not bad. Nothing to fear."

"Luke, explain," she pled.

"The Church wants to know if I will accept the presidency of BYU–Hawaii. They want me to start when the new academic year begins."

"When is that?"

"July first."

"What did you say?"

"That I needed to speak with you. We make decisions by consensus."

"When must we reply?"

"In seventy-two hours. We have three days to discuss consequences." Luke smiled.

"It's time to speak with the Consortium."

"Sandra, I already thought of that. We have a meeting scheduled tomorrow afternoon. Mr. Nguyen will watch the kids."

"Luke, that is presumptive behavior. You should have spoken with me prior to scheduling my time." Sandra then smiled, followed with a firm, "Well done."

"I thought you would find my confidence sexy. Yes?"

Sandra kissed his cheek, placed her arms around Luke, and held him close. "You're always sexy."

They held each other. Luke continued their conversation. "One thought I had ... the advantage Phuong and Jordan would have in Hawaii. The number of Asians and ethnic variety is as strong, if not stronger, than San Francisco. Hawaii gives us limitations. Also, some control."

"Our work, research, consultation, and travel will be more difficult," Sandra said. "On the other hand, we can take useful advantage of the Islands. BYU–Hawaii is small, limited; then again, the University of Hawaii is nearby. I'm sure Honolulu has suitable recording and broadcasting studios."

"We speak like we've already decided."

Small footsteps were heard as Jordan turned the corner, followed by Phuong. Ribbons were tied in his hair. Sandra and Luke laughed at the children's mischievous deeds.

Luke went to his knee and opened his arms. Phuong and Jordan rushed to him with hugs. Luke fell onto his back, as if overpowered. He hugged, tickled, and kissed the little ones. Luke shouted, "Wow! Ain't the power of love grand?" Amid the pile, Sandra hugged, tickled and then embraced Luke with a passionate kiss to his lips. A fun family. Each understood the necessity of hugs, tickles, and kisses.

Sandra and Luke left Phuong and Jordan in the care of Mr. Nguyen at his office. As always, children played. Orders for ice cream were taken. In minutes, Sandra and Luke sat with Ngo at the offices of Southeast Asian Immigration.

"I understand you have received a call from Salt Lake City," Ngo said.

"Yes," Luke answered. "The Church wishes that I preside as president of BYU–Hawaii. Sandra and I have discussed the possibilities. We've discussed concerns this move will have for Phuong and Jordan. We see positive and negative consequences as it relates to our plans. We wish to discuss them with you."

"Of course. What have you determined?"

Sandra took the wheel. "We fear the distance between San Francisco and Hawaii. We see a great deal of good in Hawaii for Phuong and Jordan. At the same time, we feel comforted to remain in San Francisco. The readily available help from the Consortium— above all, the influence of Mr. Nguyen. The children love him. As Luke expresses, 'He's a godsend.'"

"What is your decision?" Ngo asked with obvious irritation.

"We haven't made a final decision; we need your guidance."

"You are damned irritating at times," Ngo fumed. "How often do we say, 'We're guardian angels. More guardian than angels?' We assist. At times, we protect. Neither our Heavenly Father nor we can tell you what is to be reasoned and concluded for yourselves. That's how revelation occurs. My God." Frustrated, Ngo recognized her error and gazed downward. "Forgive me, Lord." Turning her attention back to Sandra and Luke, she added, "We've discussed this."

"Our apologies. Sorry for the aggravation," Sandra said, appeasing Ngo.

"We are accepting the position at BYU–Hawaii," Luke hastily declared.

"May Allah be with us." Ngo crossed herself. "Look. I'm about fifty centuries ahead of you, so show some patience ... Please ... I'll make your path straight and smooth. If you need an 'iron rod,' hell, I'll get one. When you have discovered something, don't forget what you've learned, dammit. Revelation occurs from your own searches for discovery."

Sandra, Luke, and Ngo discussed duties and responsibilities that needed to take place in the weeks, months, and years ahead. Ngo asked questions. Breadcrumbs helped Sandra and Luke make appropriate decisions and recognize patterns and behaviors that would ensue. Conclusions settled. Problems solved. Decisions made.

"Whether it is San Francisco or Hawaii, we are nearby," Ngo affirmed.

Sandra and Luke returned to Nguyen's office with ice cream, toys, and treats. The children were ecstatic and playful. Sandra and Luke's hearts sank to see Mr. Nguyen.

"How was your visit with Ms. Ngo?" Mr. Nguyen asked.

"Beneficial," Luke answered. "We have news to share with you."

"You are moving to Hawaii. Congratulations." Mr. Nguyen happily applauded.

"How did you know?" Sandra and Luke asked. "Did Ngo call you?"

"Actually, we have known for some time. You made the best decision," Mr. Nguyen smiled.

"We feel bad about leaving. Phuong and Jordan love you. Luke and I love you. We feel horrible," Sandra confessed.

"No concerns. I will go with you."

"Wh—what?" Luke stuttered. "You have this office, your work, these children, all the people here who need you. What of your duties?"

"You are my duty. There are children, people, work, and offices in Hawaii. Angels are busy people wherever we go. We'll watch over your family when Overlord comes to pass. That's how you say it? Yes? Let us celebrate." Mr. Nguyen moved away.

"Whoa." Sandra stopped Mr. Nguyen. "Each of you in the Consortium is puzzling. What you know, Mormon expressions used, even everything everyone does. We approve. But how can you leave these people?"

"They know what they are to do, as do I. Causes and objectives are to be pursued. Your family is my interest. Please, let us celebrate this happy day. Melted ice cream cannot be enjoyed."

They celebrated.

Hawaii

The test of a first-rate intelligence is the ability to hold two opposed ideas in mind at the same time and still retain the ability to function.

—F. Scott Fitzgerald

IT IS A FAMILY effort for an individual to succeed. Phuong and Jordan joined the conference call with Sandra and Luke to express willingness to give BYU–Hawaii their best efforts. Each family member, no matter their age or experience, had equal opportunity to speak, cast an opinion, persuade, and vote. Consensus was the rule for this family. One is our family. Executive privilege held little value. Actually, none at all. Standards with exceptions were clearly understood. For the greater part, the policy functioned.

Our heroes visited the Islands to learn all they could about BYU–Hawaii. Sandra and Luke asked if the Church could house Mr. Nguyen, who would assist in duties related to the president's family. The short answer? No. However, Luke's contract granted remuneration from the university to assist the president in such matters. Sandra and Luke accepted their support.

Mr. Nguyen expressed appreciation for the assistance but said, "I know people. I have all I need in Hawaii. Take full advantage of my services for your family."

The university provided a home for the president that was adequately large for their family and university social gatherings.

With control over their own destiny, Sandra and Luke purchased property above the campus and built a home designed for their needs. A comfortable estate. Phuong and Jordan walked or bicycled to all campus sites and activities. The family lived well away from the commercial/tourist districts of Oahu. The home provided a suburban feel in their lives.

Luke governed well. He administrated student enrollment as well as faculty and academic achievement. Course studies, majors, and graduate numbers increased. He also governed the Church-owned Polynesian Cultural Center (PCC). A large number of the BYU–Hawaii students were employed by the PCC. It paid, in part, for their education.

Sandra and Luke valued the relatively small student population of 2,500, with an ethnic diversity ideal for their mosaic children. Phuong and Jordan loved the Islands and BYU–Hawaii. Their familiar faces traversed the campus nearly every day. The campus was their playground with all the arts, museums, sports, entertainment, and special activities that took place year-round. An idyllic home for children.

The two made frequent visits to Luke's office.

One day, Luke heard movements from the receptionist entrance. He looked to see Phuong at the open door.

"Hi, Dad."

"Phuong." Luke rose from behind his desk and stepped to her. As she approached, Luke went to a knee with his arms open. When they embraced, he fell back as if her hug overpowered him.

"Dad. I'm thirteen years old. Don't do that anymore."

"Hon, you knock me over with your love. Besides, quit growing, would ya? Look what it's doing to me. I don't wanna be an old fart."

The two giggled while getting to their feet. They sat in chairs near each other in front of Luke's desk.

"Where's Jordan?"

"Watching the rugby practice, or he went home."

"Gotta be tough to play rugby. Are we playing ball—"

"Is it okay for me to be here?" Phuong interrupted.

"Absolutely. No one will care what work was on that desk in fifty years. Besides, don't tell anyone, your mother and I make more money writing and through our appearances than they can pay me to sit at that desk. You are the most important person, Phuong. Actually, first is your mother, then you and Jordan, then baseball, of course. Sucking air is in the top ten, as is popcorn when we play games at home. What else is there?"

"Mom's right, Dad. You are goofy."

"Thanks. Takes one to know one," he said, smiling. "Would you like to know why your mother and I write so much?"

"Okay."

"When something is written, you have it forever. All you need is a bookmark when reading. When you return, continue to read, the words remain where you left them. That's why it was sad John Lennon died. The unwritten songs and lyrics in his mind. The same with Puccini, Einstein, and Hemingway. Your mother and I want families to read our ideas. Everything important to be understood when we're gone."

Phuong tensed and appeared alarmed. "You and Mom are dying?"

"Oh, Honey, we're not dying. Someday we will. I didn't mean to scare you. I have a rubber arm. A few million batting practice pitches to throw you, Jordan, and grandkids. Wanna hit today?" Luke limbered his arm with a hopeful expression on his face.

"Waiting for you to take the mound or hit some ground balls, pop flies. Later today?"

"My favorite thing to do. I'm good at doing those things." Luke still limbered his arm.

"You and Cy Young." Phuong paused … "Mom's different, isn't she?"

On alert, though unalarmed, Luke reasoned. *Phuong is precocious, astute, and inquisitive. She is disclosing her gifts. Uncommonly aware for one so young.* "Why do you say that?"

"Dad, in case Mom hasn't told you, I'm menstruating. She says my body is changing. I'm wearing a bra. Have you noticed?"

"Well, Hon, yes, I've noticed. Mom and I talk about such things. In some ways, I don't want you to grow. You're becoming an adult, a young lady. Can't be stopped."

"Mom has told me about Grandma having periods. When Mom first explained what's happening inside my body, she never talks about herself. Why?"

"You know Mom can't have a baby. That's a big reason why we adopted you. We love you like you are our own child. Is that why you are asking if Mom is different?"

"Maybe." She paused. "No, not really."

"What are you thinking?" Luke realized, *She's searching. An investigator seeking answers.*

"Mom understands what is happening to me. Not a word about herself, her own experiences."

"Well, Phuong, Mom has never menstruated. That's why we can't have a baby. We wanted a family. Found you. Later, Jordan. Your mom and I can't make our own baby." Luke struggled but failed to answer or divert Phuong's inquisitiveness.

"Okay. Mom is different. I thought you might have an answer for me." Fixed at attention, she awaited a response.

"The one thing I know for sure is that you and your mother are the most unique people I've ever known. Jordan is a close, third-place finisher. We're an uncommon group, yup, as different as light and …" Luke, unprepared for Phuong's determined quest for discovery, floundered.

"There's something about Mom. A reason why she doesn't have periods. Jordan goes to Mom. I am here, Dad. Talk to me." Phuong held her own.

Luke recognized her resolve. *It took courage for her to come this far and learn the truth.* "Phuong, you deserve to know. You're bold to ask. That tells me you should know the answer. I can tell you. But first, would you want your mother to tell you, or do you want me to? Either way, I believe your mother would like the three of us together. One day Jordan will learn. We'll make it a group of four when it happens."

"Is it horrible, Dad?" Tears grew in Phuong's eyes.

"No, Honey. It isn't horrible at all." Luke went to a knee at her chair, took Phuong in his arms, and hugged her. "Your mother will be pleased to share everything with you. She wants you to know. It will thrill your mother to have you know. Mom just doesn't want the world to know. One day the world will be told. You'll be with us when that happens."

"Now, Dad. I need to know what it is."

Luke went to the office door. Shut it. "If I tell you, your mother needs to be informed. Understood?"

Phuong nodded.

Luke sat again in the chair near Phuong, "You have been taught human genetics, correct?"

Again, Phuong nodded.

"You understand the human genome makes us what we are. Generally, there are Asian, Caucasian, and Black people. How am I doing?"

"You can be more specific, Dad. I understand."

"From birth, your mother didn't know that a genetic condition affected her. It's called 46XY androgen insensitivity. Your mother is genetically male. Everything else about her is female."

Phuong, surprised and stunned. "Mom is a man?"

"She is. Yes. Genetically, she is a man. I love her with all my heart."

"Really? Strange, but kinda cool."

Luke took in her reaction. "I told you it was nothing."

"No, you didn't."

"Keep it between the three of us for now," Luke said. "Don't tell a soul ... this is important to Mom ... promise?"

"Promise ... Mom is alright? She isn't hurt? Everything's okay?"

"Your mom is healthy. My hand to God ..."

"Rabbi Becker," they stated in unison, followed with laughs.

"That's good to know." Phuong was ready to play ball, "We're hitting this afternoon?"

"It's what we do."

"Great. I'll be ready. Just worried Mom might not be well. See you in a few hours."

"I'll be there." Luke gave Phuong a hug and a kiss on the cheek. She bounced to the door, opened it, and marched out of the office. Luke behaved as if par for the course. Impressed with her intuitions.

"Love you, Dad," Phuong called three steps out of the office as she walked past the receptionist's desk toward the exit.

"Love you too. My turn to brush your hair tonight," Luke shouted. He fell back into the chair, baffled. *How does this kid work? I tell her that her mother is genetically a man. She shoots out of here like, "So what?" Resilient, absolutely resilient. I wish I could share this with Dr. Kobasa.* For the next few minutes Luke ruminated then grabbed the phone and called Sandra.

"Mom, why do we go to church?" Jordan asked.

"Plenty of answers to that question," Sandra responded. "Why do you ask?"

"Most the time, I don't like it." He stared straight into her eyes.

"Well, don't tell your dad, but"—Sandra glanced around to check for anyone watching— "I don't like it either," she silently whispered. "I'll tell you what I *do* like. The good people and friends there. We're all part of a big community. Don't you like being with your friends? Seeing all the girls at church?"

"Yeah, that part is okay. Some of the girls are okay too. But it's dumb. I hear the same stuff all the time. It's boring."

"Immortality is boring, like going to church. Which is why the Church is true."

"Mom?"

"Sorry, Jordan. That's why we have families. I hope you don't find what we do here at home dumb or boring."

"Here is fun. We have games, a ballfield out back, things to do. You and Dad play with us. Church ain't fun."

"I need to get your father to stop saying *ain't*. Do you believe that fun is the objective for going to church?"

"It oughta be," Jordan demanded. "I'm not the only one. Other kids say the same. I don't like going."

"Heavenly Father would be disappointed if you didn't go."

"Everyone else is there. So, what difference does it make if I'm there?" Jordan shrugged.

"Heavenly Father loves us. Wants everyone to be there with Him."

"I don't see Him there. Never hear Him speak. Do I hafta go?" Jordan pled.

"You have the choice to go or not go."

"I choose not to go. It's like our family. I can choose for myself." Jordan tapped his head.

"Your choices have consequences. We have family rules," Sandra said.

"Like what?"

"In our family, if you don't care for what we agree to eat, you don't eat. Or you can fix your own meals." Sandra pointed at Jordan. "Try not to make a mess. If you make a mess, clean the kitchen."

"So, if I don't go to church, I can make my own church?"

"Historically, that's how much of it happened. For now, Heavenly Father says, 'It's my way, or hit the highway.' Does that make sense?"

"So, if I don't go to church, Heavenly Father will kill me?" Jordan stood; arms folded.

"Jordan, of course not. Heavenly Father wants you to attend the only true and living church on the face of the Earth. He wants you to be in the right place, with the right people, at the right time."

"When I was in Guam, I remember goin' to church. We hadta kneel and stuff. That okay? I heard people say if we did all that, we'd get to go to the USA."

"Oh, Honey. What happened there—what's happening here—" Sandra tensed. "They are similar but not the same. Can you give me time, give yourself time, to grow into a proper explanation?"

"I guess ... Do I hafta go to church?"

"We prefer you go to church with us. We will not force you to go. God will use threats and punishments and deny blessings. I won't demand you attend church, neither will your father. However, we should have a family discussion about this."

"Phuong is smart. She'll agree. Dad will talk to me about it on the field. Thanks, Mom." Jordan ran out the door onto the ballfield.

The phone rang. Sandra answered to hear an anxious Luke on the other end. "Sandra, Phuong was in my office. Are you sitting?"

"No. I just finished sparring with your son. How'd we get into this fix, Luke?"

"We need to talk. Soon. I'll be home right away."

"What happened? Did Phuong say something?"

"It's what she asked."

"How detailed should we be? I was unaware Phuong is this curious, that she observed us like a detective," Sandra motioned to Luke. "She's far more aware for her age than I considered."

"I'll say, threw me for a loop. Phuong is unreal. Wish I understood. We should ask her about doubts. She'd give us answers," Luke suggested.

"She might tell us what to do with Jordan. He doesn't want to go to church with us."

"Why?"

"Says it's not fun."

"It isn't," Luke said, voicing the same opinion. "It's repetitious, predictable, and boring."

"Exactly what Jordan said. He can't violate rules of behavior."

"Sandra, I'm certain he can. He's inexperienced and doesn't understand. But he's right. It's not enjoyable."

"It's the nineties," Sandra said. "These kids have computers in their classrooms. They don't write. They type on keyboards. Play Nintendo. The Church is competing with technology."

"As the Church should. That's why we play ball, ride bikes, and create thinking games. The Church is dependent on technology too. We have computers in our offices ... In our home."

"Luke, this technology is destructive."

"I'm not going to be Amish. I like the technology," Luke admitted. "It's Star Trek."

"We need to remain together. One is our family."

"Let's settle first with Phuong. Okay?" Luke prioritized.

Sandra nodded. "Phuong might have an answer for us ... what to do with Jordan."

Phuong, Sandra and Luke sat in their home study area. Jordan was with Mr. Nguyen at the Polynesian Cultural Center eating poi and enjoying the shows.

"Sweetheart, Dad said you visited him at his office."

"Yes," Phuong answered. "You are genetically male. I promised Dad, I'll never tell. It's personal for you."

"Thank you, Honey. I appreciate your confidence. What caused your curiosity? If you would like to ask questions, please do."

Phuong was accustomed and receptive to Sandra and Luke's intellect. Their nature to question. Not once did Phuong ever answer "cuz" or "I don't know" to questions. She never evaded them. She trusted the collective experience received through their love and behaviors.

"Mom, you didn't say a word about your menstrual cycles. Only about Grandma. I thought you might be sick with something terrible. I asked Dad because I thought you might be dying."

"Oh, Phuong. Should I be dying, I'll let you know ... I'm healthy."

"You are genetically a man. I never imagined something like that could happen. As I promised, I won't tell anyone. Why don't you want people to know?"

"Phuong, when I was your age, I saw classmates being teased. They didn't wear popular clothes at school. Others were different because of their religion or race. Suppose you are the only Asian in Hawaii and everyone else is white. You might be teased. That's why we live in Hawaii. More people like you and Jordan live here. Remember when we went to Utah for Christmas?"

"I didn't like the cold weather," Phuong answered. "It was okay there. Glad we live in Hawaii."

"We're all happy living in Hawaii." Sandra led the three in a small cheer. "Do you remember what you asked us in Utah?"

"I asked where the Asian, dark-skinned kids were. It's all white people who live there. Not like it is here."

"Phuong, we didn't want you teased because of your ethnicity. I was your age when I learned about my syndrome—being genetically male. It frightened me. If people knew what kind of person I am, classmates would tease me, never be my friend. I would not be included, even at church. When I told your dad ... my biggest fear was he wouldn't love me. He'd leave. I didn't want my heart broken."

"Dad loves you, Mom. He didn't go away."

"No, he didn't, Honey. He stayed with me. Look at us. We're a family. The most uncommon family of all families in the whole world. Black, white, Asian, and a mother who is a man. Very few can say that, but we can!"

"Mom, why would people tease you? Not be your friend?"

"People can be cruel, unkind. When someone is not what you expect them to be or want them to be—which is what I felt everyone would have considered me—they say mean, ugly, nasty words. I'm sure you've heard people say unkind words about homosexual people, even at church. Homosexual people are grouped with people like I am. We each possess genetic instructions that make us uncommon from others. Behaviors differ, as well. We've learned more about these matters, thanks to science. Please, Phuong, never speak badly of anyone. Honor everyone as a child of God, a star."

"Mom, really? People love you. Everywhere you go."

"Phuong, your mother belongs to a group of people that our Church and other religions continue to misunderstand. That misunderstanding might be purposeful. Your mother and I believe religions behave unkindly toward certain groups, those that are now called LGBTQ. You've heard people say, *You're so gay*. Call people *homo* or *fag*. Unkind words. Your mother is part of LGBTQ people who are misunderstood. She had no choice. Her DNA coding makes her look and behave like a woman, which she is. Genetically, however, your mother is male, like I am. That's why we couldn't 'shake and bake' a baby ourselves."

"Luke." Sandra mildly protested his humor.

"I get that. Yeah, it's weird," Phuong declared. "But I don't see why people would treat Mom like she's bad or something is wrong with her. She's smart, writes books, and is on TV every day. She's good to everyone. What makes people act that way?"

"The words are *bigotry* and *bias*. You understand those words, don't you?" Sandra asked.

"Yes. I hear them all the time. Dad also uses the word *ignorance* with *bigotry* and *bias*."

"Thanks for listening to your old man. It's obvious you've inherited my intelligence." Luke smiled.

"Dad, you're my father. Not my genetic provider," Phuong shot back.

"Whoa, Luke. Did you hear those words? She got you with that comment." Sandra laughed. They all laughed.

"Yes, she did." Luke chuckled. "But I'm on the mound today. First pitch is at your head."

"I'm wearing a helmet. Throw at me. I'm charging the mound." Phuong stared at Luke.

"Ooooh, I'm really scared." Luke feigned fear.

"Hey, the two of you can play your games later. We're having a discussion," Sandra said, trying to bring them back to topic.

"Yes, ma'am," Luke said, saluting.

"Don't call me *ma'am*," Sandra boomed at Luke. "It sounds old; I'm not old."

"The two of you can cool it. Let's finish this discussion so Dad and I can hit," Phuong said, taking the referee role from Sandra.

"Yes, ma—" Luke started to say before being pointed into submission by Phuong's finger.

"Okay. Where were we?" Sandra asked. "Ah, we were discussing bullying."

"Bullying?" Phuong and Luke simultaneously asked.

"Yes," Sandra exclaimed. "If people knew about my syndrome, I feared I might be bullied, another *b* word to go with *bigotry* and *bias*—bullied by schoolmates, Church members, Church leaders, and people everywhere. It scared me, Phuong. Still does. How would I be treated should relatives and friends know that I'm queer? I am extremely uncommon. Bless your father's heart. He fought through my fear with his love for me."

Sandra gazed at Luke. "I am so frightened of being hurt, bullied, teased, separated. I do not want anyone to know what I am. We've told you. Jordan will learn when it's his time."

"It's a secret?" Phuong asked. "Is that why you told me not to tell anyone?"

"Yes, it's classified. Top secret," Luke answered. "I learned of your mother's condition years ago. There are pros and cons. Consequences, as your mother says. I have learned it is wise to keep it a secret. The pros are increasing in today's world. Still far more cons. Phuong, the cons can be very bad. They can be directed at Jordan. You too."

"My influence, reputation, and value as an author, scholar, and counselor would be greatly damaged by bullies should people know I am genetically a man, part of LGBTQ," Sandra explained. "People would say horrible things about your dad too. I'd feel bad if the Church knew what I am inside, then forced your father to resign as president of BYU–Hawaii because of me. Phuong, that's why our family is to do our very best. We take cover in plain sight, so that one day people will understand they had no cause to fear or bully us … when they learn what I am."

"We three, and your grandparents in Arizona, are the only people who know our secret, besides doctors and other medical professionals who help Mom. Doctors cannot reveal what they know about your mother. We're protected by privacy laws. Geneticists, like all scientists, are guarded to reveal what they know about LGBTQ people. Bullies don't want to know; they don't care to hear it. Your mom and I, with a little help from our friends"— Luke sang a la The Beatles—"we intend to enlighten and change the world about these matters."

"Wow. I didn't realize it is so serious."

"Phuong, we hope this isn't too much for you to hear. Your mother and I fear people might tease and make fun of you and Jordan, if they knew this secret. However, there are stories you should read. People in history that you should know. Alan Turing and Elton John would be a good start. British and brilliant."

"God knows. God knows everything." Phuong lividly demanded, "God should tell bullies to stop being mean and cruel. They should love Mom like we do. People know how wonderful Mom is; they shouldn't be bullies."

"Few people know or understand that. God telling them isn't convincing proof for them. Once people learn and know, it should be obvious … It isn't for bullies," Sandra instructed. "When people quote scriptures, they never consult science to learn what the human genome does to uncommon people, like I am uncommon."

"Mom, you are special common. People and God should know it. Heavenly Father … Wait, isn't Heavenly Mother in on this? Grandma in Arizona would be telling bullies to 'Back off.'"

Giggles and smiles eased the atmosphere in their discussion.

"It would help if Heavenly Father **and Mother** told people not to be bullies," Sandra said. "But more is to be done. People need to understand for themselves. They watch too much television, believe scripture that is outdated, never trust science and fail to think and reason properly."

"Mom and I have learned that revelation from Heavenly Parents happens only when science, reason, and logic are understood by everyone. That's why there is so much religious confusion in the world," Luke concluded.

"In our home, we've discussed Black people and slavery," Sandra explained. "Our Church behaved badly toward Negro people in its first 150 years. The revelation of 1978 changed everything. People with noble reason make good things happen. Black people now enjoy priesthood and temple blessings. Jordan is free. He can marry in the temple like we did. The two of you will never be treated like inferiors because of your skin color or racial makeup, though some people try. Your father and I intend to stop bullies from harming LGBTQ people. We have angels who will help. They are around us, everywhere in the world."

"What is LG—whatever those letters are. I want to know. Angels?"

Sandra and Luke discussed with Phuong each letter in LGBTQ. They talked about issues of civil rights, civil behavior, compassion for those unlike the common, and the unwelcome or outcast. The benefits of the Consortium.

"Our Church is wrong," Phuong concluded. "I think we should write a letter to the prophet. Dad, you are right. People back in the day when the Bible, Book of Mormon, and Koran were written didn't know about genetics. Everyone is loved by Jesus and Heavenly Father, all people in the world. Shame on those unkind, uncaring people. It's been easy for me. Jordan is lucky to be alive now. He wouldn't be in our family if this happened before the 1978 revelation," Phuong hesitated. "You wouldn't have adopted Jordan. Would you?"

Phuong stared at Sandra and Luke. She narrowed her steely black, Vietnamese eyes. "Would you have adopted me?" she fearfully asked.

Time suspended itself. Please forgive me, dear reader, for my intrusion during this critical confrontation. I can. I must. Sandra and Luke found themselves challenged to respond to Phuong's blunt but valid questions. They long considered the need to explain this issue to the world and their children. How could a religion, a congregation of people who claimed an ear to God's mouth, fail so greatly in their compassion regarding race relations and ongoing affairs with LGBTQ people? How can a group of enlightened, spiritual men fail to grant full fellowship and inclusion for all God's children?

Sandra and Luke adopted the Captain Kohei Asoh defense:

On November 22, 1968, Captain Asoh piloted Japan Airlines (JAL) Flight 2 from Tokyo International Airport to San Francisco International Airport. He mistakenly landed a new Douglas DC 8 in the shallow waters of San Francisco Bay, two and a half miles short of the airport runway. None of the ninety-six passengers or eleven crew members were injured in the touchdown. No one even got their feet wet. All luggage and personal items were safely returned. When asked by the National Transportation Safety Board about the occurrence, Asoh simply replied, "As you Americans say, I f**ked up."

Captain Asoh, a capable, veteran pilot, admitted error and poor judgment. He was demoted to first officer and temporarily barred as a crew member on passenger flights. He received hours of extensive ground training then continued to fly, without incident, for JAL until his retirement.[9]

Sandra and Luke responded to Phuong. Detect in their heartfelt words the Asoh defense:

"We behaved righteously adopting our multiracial family. Phuong, we love you and Jordan unconditionally. You are our children," Sandra began.

"I'd cut off my throwing arm to keep you as my daughter and Jordan as my son."

"Each of you have made us aware of how badly we thought and behaved in our past. Forgive our slow, almost nonexistent learning curve. We erred. We apologize. Our intent is to do what is right and improve over past misdeeds," Sandra confessed.

"Phuong, we can't explain it. When we first saw you, we knew that you are unique. You do wonderous, impressive things. You mystify. There is much for us to do to change the world, particularly for those who are unique, like your mother and you. Our intent is to improve thinking. Help us discover problems. Solve these problems," Luke urged.

"We are here at this precious time. We are committed to this cause," Sandra strongly emphasized. "Failure to think properly harms everyone. To be uncommon is not a weakness. It is far better to be uncommon; that is why our family is strong. Please forgive us for all that happened before the 1978 revelation. Our improper behaviors. Thoughts of bigotry, bias, prejudice. I am sorry to say we were bullies toward Black people and others like you, Phuong. With your help, Sweetheart, humankind will understand our errors."

"Please, value our progression," Luke said. "Through our youth and teenage years, your mother and I were trained to say words, believe ideas, so we'd behave without challenge. To never

---

[9] The Douglas DC 8 was recovered from the Bay and refurbished. The aircraft flew until 2001. This incident occurred. *The Abilene Paradox* by Jerry B. Harvey differs from groupthink in that it is characterized by an inability to understand and manage agreement. When we agree, or believe we are agreed, we obey leaders when decisions, circumstances and numbers are wrong.

ask questions. Told, 'This is God's will. Obedience is the first law of heaven.' We realize our errors and mistakes of agreement. Our thoughts regarding race relations were clearly wrong, flat, nondimensional. Phuong, please, forgive us. Help us improve our behavior as we consider your mother's syndrome. To understand why we behaved as poorly as we did could take a long, long time to accept."

"Jesus is uncommon," Sandra declared. "Christians, LDS Church members, leaders, philosophers—all praise Jesus as a radical progressive. He displayed a will to challenge mistaken religious dogmas of His day. We want our uncommon family to follow that Jesus. We do not conform to blind obedience. We challenge. Question with reason. Like Jesus, uncommon thinkers are open-minded with a desire to become like our Heavenly Father and Mother. We no longer behave as sheep or chattel.

"Alexander the Great said, 'I am not afraid of an army of lions led by a sheep; **I am afraid of an army of sheep led by a lion.**' Phuong, we failed. Forgive our past misdeeds, our lack of courage to protest overly obedient behavior at a time when we should have been challengers, behaving as lions toward Church leaders and racist doctrines. Our family is a pride of lions. Lead with tolerance, compassion, and unflinching reason. Accept our apology, please."

Sandra and Luke awaited Phuong's reply. They hoped she would understand their guilt, transgressions, wrongful obedience, and unrighteous bigotry. Why they behaved as they once did.

Phuong silently stared at Sandra and Luke. Her beautiful Southeast Asian clarity and tone penetrated them. She assessed their honesty and sincerity. Finally, she held out her hands. "I will do my best to understand. I love you, with all my heart. Don't cut off your arm, Dad."

The three embraced.

"Phuong, we need your help. Jordan doesn't want to go to church. Is there anything you—"

"Shhhh, mom," Phuong said and placed a finger against her lips. "Jordan will be with us Sunday."

"Thanks, Hon."

"Can we hit now?" Phuong asked.

"Plenty of daylight," Luke said and excitedly rushed away. "I'll be ready in ten minutes."

Phuong was already on the go, retrieving her cleats and gear.

Left alone, Sandra silently reasoned their discussion. Discriminatory behaviors were the hallmark of race relations in the Church prior to the 1978 revelation. A direct bias toward Blacks with similar insults for Asians, Native Americans, and people with varied shades of skin. Battles for LGBTQ understanding and equity continued as the new millennium approached. Sandra felt pleased Phuong stood with Luke and her.

The three established a formidable influence.

Religions make mistakes. As do parents and children. Religions were created by imperfect men with little regard to possess an awareness of science, use of numbers, or skills of reason. Today, great minds with notable universities or institutions of free thought and behavior exist. Admit errors and faults. Move forward. Don't repeat mistakes. Learn. Improve. Display compassion and humble recognition to those who admit mistakes and error. Recover from an intolerant past. Such behavior is broadminded. Intelligent.

Land planes ... safely ... on sound runways.

Our heroes positioned on the backyard field with two buckets of baseballs and softballs for batting practice. Mr. Nguyen sat in a chair under an umbrella to watch the kids hit. Every bit a guardian angel. More angel than guardian.

Phuong stepped to the plate. Luke stood on the mound. Sandra and Jordan covered the outfield. Phuong, the little long-haired lefty, took a few warmup swings. She tapped the plate with her bat, dug her back foot into the dirt, and gazed at Luke for the first pitch.

Luke acted like he received signals from a catcher. Shook off two signs, nodded, and went into a windup. As he followed through, the ball flew over Phuong's head into the backstop screen. Phuong took a step toward the mound and threw her bat hard to the ground.

Luke threw his glove on the ground. Each stared at the other like two riled bulls. Phuong rapidly charged the mound as Luke ran toward her. They collided with their arms wrapped around each other. Arms swung as if they truly were fighting.

"Told you I'd throw the first pitch at you," Luke bellowed.

"Told you I'd charge the mound," Phuong yelled back.

They scrapped on the grass.

The two laughed and tickled. They delivered mock punches to arms and backs. Swiftly, Sandra and Jordan joined the melee assisting the brawl of fun. Everyone punched at Luke, who shouted, "Sandra, Jordan, you're my fielders. You shouldn't take swings at me."

Jordan responded, "Why are you throwing at a girl? Barely half your size."

"Yeah. Besides, you're more fun to tickle," Sandra said as the kids took advantage playfully beating on their father.

Mr. Nguyen laughed and looked into the bright Hawaiian blue sky and white clouds. Three children with gloves and a bat came into view. Mr. Nguyen smiled. He knew what they wanted; what children need.

Sandra and Luke were committed family people, intent on making home a refuge from everything that would tempt children to leave their family. They learned from Sandra's father. Make home a haven for hope, humor, and acceptance. Filled with music and laughter. No limitations. Any topic discussed, examined, with the purpose of being understood. Their home never became a place of ridicule or blame. - *Okay, maybe some of the time it did. But troubles were discussed and settled.* - Full-court basketball played across the driveway, complete with motion detection lights for late-night games.

Luke cautioned people in his congregation and colleagues at the university, "The Church will never interfere with batting practice or our family activities." It never did. Their home was known as the Field of Teaching Moments.

Sandra and Luke knew the value of the principle to which they testified so often: "Children will never get into the kind of trouble you wish them to avoid when you are with them. Should your children go into danger, **go with them**. It could be their last/only hope to safely return."

Home Is Fun

We don't stop playing because we grow old; we grow old because we stop playing.

—George Bernard Shaw

JORDAN APPROACHED THE AGE to receive the Aaronic Priesthood, pass the sacrament, and play a bigger role at church. He felt discouraged; church was, as he told Sandra, "Boring." He preferred to run free. Play ball of any kind. Swim the waters of Hawaii. He read well and enjoyed school. Far more compliant with Sandra and Luke's games to solve problems and make decisions. He enjoyed family discussions and activities. Of course, he loved the experience of Mr. Nguyen's compassion.

"Home is fun," Jordan said. Church was the antithesis of home, specifically on those occasions when people would look at Jordan then whisper.

Many Polynesians were darker than Jordan though few African-Americans were. Jordan found some acceptance from Black students in Laie. Plenty of Asians in Hawaii. Subtle enmity arose between Jordan and Asians.

He met biracial friends at school. Their associations tamed frustrations. Provided solace when words or actions suggested bias. Biracial assortments included Polynesian and Asian, Polynesian and Caucasian, and a few Caucasian and Asian, with the fewest Caucasian and Black. The rarest Asian and Black. Jordan was an extreme minority. Aware of this, Sandra and Luke discussed the circumstance with Jordan. They prepared him for consequences. Unfortunately, consequences became worrisome.

"Mom, I can pass the sacrament, but I don't think people want me to spend time with them," Jordan explained while he wrapped flowers into a *haku* crown.

"Really? What makes you say that?"

"I don't know. Things are cool at church, but some of the kids don't talk to me at school or play ball after school. I notice stuff like that." Jordan spoke as he adeptly weaved flowers.

"I notice the same stuff. We should use better words, Jordan," Sandra advised as she weaved her own flowers into a lei.

"You're trying to make me like Phuong. You and Dad say I am my own person."

"Yes. You are your own person. You'll serve a mission. It's never too soon to speak correctly. Speaking and acting as a leader is important. Are you bothered by how people act toward you?" Sandra experienced more difficulty with her *haku* braids than Jordan yet not keenly focused on their conversation.

"Being half-Black isn't good, is it? I've read some of the things you and Dad gave me. I like Martin Luther King, Douglass, Tubman, and Rosa Parks. She had grit, like Dad says. *To Kill a Mockingbird* is a good story. Thanks for reading parts with me." Jordan expertly braided and weaved.

"While reading the book, I considered Scout to be upright." Sandra struggled with her weaves.

"Yeah, like ya say, *perspective* ... Mom, I don't know if I like being Black. I think people look at me like I'm bad or something. Maybe it's cuz I'm Viet and Black. Though it could be something else."

"Jordan, it is what you are. Your blend of ethnicities is wonderful. You're handsome. Smart. Look at your braids. Excellent. Be grateful you are here rather than Vietnam. Mr. Nguyen has already told us how you'd be treated if there. Life is worthwhile here. Much better since the 1978 revelation."

"I wish the prophet explained things about Asians ... or other folks. He missed me. I don't think people understand what I am ... or what I feel in me."

"No, he didn't miss you, Honey," Sandra said. "The prophet loves you. Heavenly Father loves all His children. Especially you."

"Actually, Mom, I think Heavenly Father is pretty particular about who He loves. I ain't on His list for a lot of different things."

"Please, Jordan. I hope this makes sense to you. Heavenly Father's love is a perspective. It's not as meaningful. I am here. Your father is here. Phuong is here. We love you. Our love is the more meaningful love that sustains all of us."

"What do you mean, Mom?"

"God's love is like a long-distance love ... such as missionaries, soldiers, or lonely people who don't have what you enjoy. Isolated people who are away from their families. Ask your questions— describe your feelings to me, your father, or Phuong. Next time Heavenly Father or Jesus drops by for a visit, maybe we'll get an immediate response. He may have something to say to you ... us. Church is where we go to meet members who need group support. One is our family. Trust us above all others, even God ... I hope that makes sense?

"Okay, Mom. Don't get mad at me."

"I'm not angry, Jordan. I just become frustrated is all. It saddens me when we have done so much to keep the four of us united. I want you to feel our family is your greatest support for love."

"I know what y'all have done for me. It's appreciated. I ain't forgettin' it." Jordan smiled, placed his floral crown on Sandra's head. "You're beautiful, Mom. When needed, I'll speak well."

"Y'all and ain't. We should've moved to Alabama or Arkansas instead of Hawaii." Sandra grinned and gave Jordan a playful shove, then a hug.

"Remember what our *haku* teacher told us, 'An imperfect lei stands majestic, like a cliff on the neck.' Mom, let me be a kid for a while. I'll grow up."

"Prepositions ... Jordan, stay close to us, please." Sandra placed her braided lei around his neck, kissing each cheek with a loud smack. "I love ya plenty. Ya can't say it ain't so."

They smiled. Hugged.

Jordan was a challenge, Yet a person of joy. His value was dear… hugely misunderstood.

Diminutive Phuong grew with wit and class. Five feet, a few inches. Solid frame. Not skinny. Firm legs, arms, and stomach. She took advantage of every inch and pound socially and athletically. A natural left-hander, she played softball every day with able mentors. She threw with either hand. At second base, a righty. When asked to play the outfield, a lefty. She led calmly and argued her challenges with knowhow.

In contrast, Jordan behaved emotionally and was prone to neglect reasonable behavior. Athletics dominated academics. Possessed with a gifted, but undisciplined mind. He was easily distracted and disdained inflexible rules or discipline. Though not an achiever, Jordan did not embarrass himself. Did just enough. He was inclined to keep his intellect in reserve until needed.

Charismatic and pleasant to approach, Phuong truly charmed boys with the gifts of her royal blood. Socially adept, she gathered small groups near her and discussed ideas of interest or concern. Her intelligence was bold. Friends, teammates, and competitors were comfortable and drawn into her circle of influence. A leadership trait skillfully personalized from Sandra and Luke and her regal heritage.

Jordan acted rough. Intimidation a most useful tool. He took advantage of his striking first impression, Black features augmented with Asian mystery. Onlookers were stunned. At first glance, eyes stared, attempting to infer ethnicity. Curiosity yielded to uneasy whispers. At five-foot-ten, Jordan muscled himself, ready to "mix-it-up" if provoked, verbally and nonverbally.

When angered or determined, Phuong's slender eyes narrowed until two black orbs pierced your soul or stupidity. She was not easily intimidated despite her size. Luke enrolled her to be skilled in aikido, a self-defense martial art. When necessary, she stood on a dugout bench or upturned bucket amid ballfields with a hand on a teammate's shoulder.

Luke told Phuong and Jordan, "I can outplay your mother in baseball. Your mother will outplay the three of us in racquetball and intellectual arguments. She's the best player on our team. Not ashamed to say that, at all." The three recognized their gifts and potential. They also knew the function of a queen bee: star of the hive, well-ordered, dependent on her collection of workers.

Phuong, a junior in high school, confronted Luke in the outfield area on the ballfield behind their home. Friends on the field played with frisbees, kicked soccer balls, and bounced on the trampoline. "Dad, why don't boys like me?"

Ever-precocious, Phuong thought deeply. Her mind reflected on romance and sexual arousal. Luke led the task to explain how babies are created when the kids each reached age ten. He used a pen, notepad, and high school biology text that included detailed anatomical cross-sections of male and female genitalia. Phuong required an updated discussion.

"Boys like you very much, Phuong. Why do you ask?"

Phuong countered her father's statement. "I don't think boys see me as pretty. My friends are asked to movies. Why hasn't a boy asked me on a date?" Phuong was anxious in matters of mating behaviors.

"Phuong, you are intimidating. You played little league with boys. You play baseball better than most boys and have a near-perfect 4.0 GPA ... you are pretty ... your mother and I have discussed how gorgeous you are. All that is scary to boys. A boy who can climb his way over those walls will be special to you. Needn't worry, sweetheart."

"Dad, I think about boys, quite a bit."

"Really? That makes me smile."

"Smile? Why?"

"You have womanly instincts. You're behaving like a romantic person should. I'm happy for you."

"I've thought about kissing a boy."

"Anyone I know?"

"No. Daydreaming is all. No specific boy ... a few cute ones I know."

"I love daydreaming."

"Dad. You daydream?"

"All the time. About a ton of different things. When your mother and I were at BYU, I daydreamed about kissing her every day ... still do."

"Dad, has Mom's syndrome ever troubled you?"

"That she's genetically male? Never ... Honestly." He looked at Phuong and smiled. "She is what she is. Rare. Hope she never stops loving me. My heart would break to pieces without her touch and kisses."

"When did you first kiss Mom?"

"Your mother wouldn't let me kiss her for a long time. I tried. She literally pushed me away."

"Why?"

"Ask her. I'm handsome, humble, intelligent, athletic, self-confident—"

"C'mon, Dad, why wouldn't Mom kiss you?"

"Look at these arms." Luke flexed like a bodybuilder. "I'm strong, humorous, meek—your mother should've been chasing me for a kiss." He smiled.

"Dad, knock it off. Tell me when you first kissed Mom."

"Actually, we had two first kisses," Luke said.

"You can't have two first kisses," Phuong objected.

"Okay. There's nothing to tell. Wanna play catch?"

"Dad, I'm going to scream if you don't tell me when you first kissed Mom." Phuong smiled, became gently agitated.

"It's a story best told by your mother. She was with me both times," Luke said, continuing to tease.

"Augh, Dad ... Enough!" Phuong clenched Luke's forearm. Marched to the house with him in tow. They entered the house. "Mom ... Mom! I need you."

Sandra rushed into the family room. "Is someone hurt? What's happened?"

"Dad says you are the one to tell me when the two of you first kissed. He says you had two first kisses. How can that be? Mom, I need to hear this story." Phuong pushed Luke into a chair before landing in her seat at the family discussion table.

"I never wanted your father to kiss me," Sandra confessed.

"Dad said that. Why? How'd it happen?"

"I didn't want him to know of my syndrome. That I'm male. You recall my story. I—" Sandra paused. "I didn't want to be shamed. Bullied. I was afraid."

"When did Dad kiss you, Mom?"

"Your father was persistent. I really liked him. He's funny, a gentleman ... good-natured with me. I didn't know if he would love me ... understand what I am. My syndrome frightened me. I worried that when he learned, he might tell others. I'd be teased. So, I made a deal with your dad. We'd play a racquetball match—"

Sandra was interrupted when the door leading from the garage opened. Jordan came into the room. "Hey, troops. What y'all doin'?"

"Sit down. Be quiet," Phuong directed. "Mom's telling the story about when Dad first kissed her. They say they had two first kisses ... they're playing racquetball."

"Gotta hear this." Jordan threw his gear on the counter and sat with the family.

Sandra observed her children captivated with interest. Luke grinned, stared at Sandra, and bounced his eyebrows.

"Anyway," Sandra continued with a smile, "if your father won the racquetball match, I would allow him to romance me. If I won, your father agreed never to attempt any further romantic behaviors. He would leave me alone."

"Dad, you won. Good for you. Good for all of us," Jordan said.

"Sorry to disappoint you, Jordan. Your mother kicked my butt."

"Your father thought his athletic skill would defeat me," Sandra explained. "He didn't know how well I play. I needed one more point"—she lifted a single finger— "to send your dad packing." She pointed at Luke. "He was beaten ... exhausted. I had an eight-point lead. One point for the win."

"What happened? This is taking too long," a frustrated Phuong groaned.

"I wanted your mother to date and fall in love with me." Luke embarrassedly, "I hit the ball as hard as I could … I hoped to get it past your mother's reach. Instead, the ball hit the back of her leg, just above the right knee."

"Yowzers, Dad! Did it wipe her out? Mom?" Jordan turned, fixed on Sandra.

"It hurt like hell. I was in tears," Sandra said, touched the back of her leg. "There was a crimson-red splotch where the ball struck me. Thinking back, even now, I cringe."

"I was devastated," Luke sighed. "Defeated, your mother in pain. I hurt her. I thought she'd never speak to or ever see me again."

"First kiss, people. I'm waiting … *patiently*," Phuong said to quicken the storytelling.

"I was hopping around, thinking doctors would amputate my leg. Your father grabbed me and told me to lie face down on the court. Without words, I felt your father's breath. He blew several cool puffs of air on the wound. It felt wonderful … then with no alert at all, he kissed that ugly, red spot on my leg. The pain went away. It was gone. All of it."

"Is that when you fell in love with Dad?" Phuong asked.

"Yes, Phuong. I lacked confidence. That special moment changed me. Changed everything."

"When did you kiss Dad? — On the lips, I mean," Jordan asked.

"The kiss on the leg was the day after Thanksgiving, 1978," Luke explained. "We didn't have a full-on lip encounter 'til a month later, almost New Year's Day, 1979."

"Dad was doing his best, Mom. Why not give him a break?" Jordan inquired.

"Jordan, as you'll learn, I am an odd character. I needed to resolve a few issues."

"Tell us when you first kissed each other like people in love." Phuong insisted the story proceed. "I want to hear the good parts, please."

"Oh, Phuong. Your father's a champion … his words … stories. To ease my fear, he told me of coldhearted Turandot. We've told you about the opera, how Turandot avoided love. Everyone needs to earn love. Your father challenged me. I realized what I had to do.

I went to your father, held his face in my hands, and kissed him … passionately." Sandra placed a hand to her mouth and gently bit her fingertips. "Our lips pressed together. For the life of me, I cannot remember when we stopped kissing."

Sandra caught a glimpse of her children, rapt with an image of their parents engaged in a romantic first kiss. Phuong and Jordan returned from their reflections. "What happened next?" Phuong asked.

"Decided to marry," Luke answered. "You know the rest of the story, 'til now."

"It's cool that you can tell two first-kiss stories. The second one was best." Jordan raised a thumb.

"Dad's kiss on Mom's leg is important. It says more," Phuong added from her perception as an insider, dreamer, and daring thinker.

"Those kisses changed our lives," Sandra reflected. "Our family, us living in Hawaii—never would have happened without those kisses."

"That's true," Luke continued. "If we hadn't kissed, we wouldn't be having all this fun. The two of you would not be in our lives." Luke embraced the kids. Hugged and kissed them. Sandra joined the huddle.

"Those kisses created our ballfield. We wouldn't have all y'all to play with. You see what it did to me? I now say *y'all*, and end sentences with a preposition. Ain't life grand?" Sandra beamed.

Giggles everywhere.

Sandra and Luke were serious leaders, teachers, and counselors in Church callings. They shared insights and utilized accumulated experiences in all intellectual pursuits throughout their service in Church and organizational needs. Luke grew legendary for the combination of his Church callings with fun, family activities. Humor found itself along the way. Laughs and giggles occurred at unusual times. Other Church leaders throughout parts of Oahu copied Luke's example.

Of particular note, a Saturday morning as Luke pitched batting practice on the ballfield. Dressed in ball gear, he threw BP (batting practice) and at the same time conducted interviews on the mound as a stake president. The place filled with kids and a few adults. Between hitters, Mr. Nguyen helped a woman from the stake to a bench seat behind a large screen where Luke pitched.

"Thanks, Mr. Nguyen." Luke then turned to the woman, "You are safer here than seated in the celestial room at the temple. Guaranteed."

"I've heard of this," she nervously said. "It's not normal. I thought we'd have privacy."

"If you don't like it, don't stay. I do all I can to have the Brethren release me. Ain't happened yet. No worries. I've played baseball my whole life. I have good hands … Ask Sandra." Luke winked and smiled. "I have a capable glove. Years of experience. You'll be fine. No one can hear a word we say through all the chatter and activity… stay a foot or so behind the screen.

Luke flipped two balls from the bucket into his glove. He grabbed a third ball with his bare hand. "Heads up" he alerted, took a short windup and threw the ball. **CRACK!** The ball bounced past the mound into centerfield. At this distance, for the ages of these players, nearly all pitches are in the strike zone.

"Nice hit," Luke shouted. "Single, past the shortstop. Good swing." Luke lowered his volume and turned to the woman. "What is your work?"

With the next pitch, she reported, "I'm a CPA in Honolulu." **CRACK!**

"Really? You have a master's degree?" **CRACK!**

"I do. Required for CPAs these days," she answered. Luke took more balls from the bucket.

"Would you like a prestigious Church calling that is one of a kind, just for you?" **CRACK!** "Good hit!"

"What are you suggesting, President?" **CRACK!**

"Please, call me Luke. I don't like being called a title. We need a stake executive secretary." **CRACK!** "Foul ball. Jordan, keep an eye on it."

"That's a job for the priesthood," the CPA mildly protested.

"I've never read or heard anything such as that. Have you?" Luke grabbed three balls from the bucket.

"I guess not," the woman replied. "But it's not customary."

"You don't need the priesthood to balance numbers or allocate funds." **CRACK!**

"Well struck. If you accept, report at the stake center at seven Thursday night. We need your skills." **CRACK!** "For me, the best person for the job is a person. Gender is irrelevant." Luke let fly another pitch. **CRACK!**

The woman smiled, bewildered, as Luke placed three more balls from the bucket into his glove. "Are you prepared to break new ground?" Luke asked. "I can't do this without your willingness." **CRACK!** "Keep your back foot planted."

"You apparently want to challenge Church authority and gender policy?" the CPA asked. **CRACK!**

"Not my first time. The stake Sunday school president is a woman, a high school principal. Duhhh. Seems smart to me." **CRACK!**

Luke bent into the bucket for three more balls. "Married with children?"

"Yes, we have three girls." **CRACK!**

"Got under that one. Does your husband work?" Luke threw. **CRACK!**

"Works for the Maintenance Department, Laie City. Ten years."

"I believe your family would support this call." Luke's next toss skipped low into the backstop. "Sorry." Luke hurriedly picked three more balls from the bucket. "Do you accept? Hit this one." Held the ball above his head. He threw. **CRACK!**

"I struggle as a professional woman when I see gender disparity in the Church. I accept." **CRACK!**

"Whoa. Home run, buddy. Well struck, again. I'd trot around the bases hitting one like that." Luke circled his index finger like an umpire signals a home run. "The same to be said for you, Sister. Sorry, I detest calling you by your gender."

Luke wound and threw the ball. **CRACK!** "Off the end of the bat ... I understand you're good at what you do. Show your family and women of our stake there is no gender exclusion." He loaded his glove over the bucket.

"You gotta have some interesting conversations on this field," the CPA said. **CRACK!**

"I hear the strangest, funniest things. I could write a bestselling book of comedy and horror based on the confessions and tales I've heard." **CRACK!**

"Write the book," she encouraged. **CRACK!**

Luke ducked. "Line drive ... up the middle ... great job," Luke praised the hitter. He slapped the palm of his glove with his throwing hand. "One day, I'll try." Luke fished the bucket for the remaining baseballs. "You know Sandra, don't you?" **CRACK!**

"I do. She is standing by the house where the food is." **CRACK!**

"Good glove, Phuong. Please tell Sandra about your decision. She'll be happy to discuss it with you. She supports and encourages gender equity." Luke smiled. "Okay, last pitch." Luke waved the ball above his head. "Go out on a good one." He wound and threw. **CRACK!**

"Wow. Look at that. An extra base hit."

Luke snatched the empty bucket and hurled it toward the outfield. "Gather balls. Let's get the next hitter to the plate ... I need a full bucket ... where's my hug?" Luke turned to the plate with open arms. He awaited the hitter.

Two Polynesian children ran to Luke, an older 10-year-old boy and a smaller, young girl. The boy gave Luke a hug. The two placed their foreheads together. *Mahalo* exchanged between them. The little girl gave Luke a hug then ran back to her mother.

"There are plastic bats and balls for you," Luke shouted as she ran from him.

"You're good to these kids," the woman said.

"Baseball is good for young'uns. A game for all age groups. It should be played with adults and kids, no matter their ages."

"You feed them too," she said.

"Money well spent. You feed 'em, you make 'em better boys and girls. Ask Maslow."

Lessons from the Pali

Judge a person by their questions rather than their answers.

—Voltaire

PHUONG NEARED GRADUATION AND prepared announcements for family members in Utah, Arizona and childhood friends from San Francisco. Distant, treasured memories. Her immediate future? Play softball at the University of Hawaii. Leave the Islands. Pursue graduate degrees on the mainland.

Jordan's friends, mostly teammates, occupied his time. Able to date as a sophomore, he lacked interest in socializing. Uneasy, awkward, he blamed his biracial makeup. Sandra and Luke hosted parties for church groups, celebrations, and holidays. Social functions were organized so Phuong and Jordan could meet new friends and interact with others. Practical exercises in the rudimentary skills of mating. Sandra and Luke closely observed their behaviors.

Usually bright and inquisitive, but unnoticed, Jordan began to falloff in his studies. Unmotivated, removed, he flew below radar detection.

One blustery evening, Phuong found herself alone at home. Sandra and Luke were engaged in a Church/BYU assignment. One of those rare, quiet, solitary times in an otherwise active home. Phuong's mind explored.

She focused on Jordan, somehow compelled to find herself at his room. Reluctantly, she entered. Saw his collection of items and mementos. Baseball bats, balls of various kinds, a poster of Dale Murphy, another of Scotty Pippin, Steve Young, family photos, pictures of friends ... flowers everywhere. Jordan enjoyed the Hawaiian culture and Polynesian history. He was especially impressed with Hawaiian creations of *haku*, floral arrangements, like a lei, worn by tourists and Islanders.

Phuong smiled at a photo of Jordan engaged in a Maori *haka*, the rhythmic chest, leg, and arm self-flagellations. His teammates challenged rival schools with furious *haka* displays. *Bring it on. We will achieve our goal or die trying.* Jordan behaved proudly as a Polynesian. It resonated within his personal style of intimidation.

Phuong saw a handwritten paper on Jordan's desk. The light above it gave the note a glow. She hesitated to read something personal, but did. As she read, her senses tensed. She picked up the paper and devoured the message.

Fool, Phuong thought. *I know where he is.* She bolted from the room, flew through the kitchen, seized keys, grabbed a jacket, jumped on her Vespa and sped south toward the Old Pali Road.

The Battle of Nu'uanu was the bloodiest conflict in Hawaiian history. Seven hundred warriors forced to their deaths when pushed or jumped from the cliffs. Jordan sought to die with those warriors. Phuong pushed her Vespa to the windward side of the Oahu mountains. Her brother intended to end his life.

It took an hour for Phuong to reach the Old Pali Road. She forced the Vespa as far along the trail as it could go. Then abandoned it and ran in the dark without a flashlight.

Jordan praised the warriors who died high upon the Pali. Phuong knew he'd be there. The winds were strong and noisy. The warriors, he hoped, would accept Jordan's sacrifice from this treacherous cliff. She engaged all her athletic discipline to find Jordan. She ran the trail instead of hiking and finally, ahead, saw a figure on the cliff.

She strained with a few more sprints and lunges to reach him. "Stop, Jordan. Listen to me."

"Why are you here? Leave me to my own business."

"I read your note. Back away, now. Do it." Phuong demanded; her words issued like a military commander.

"You have no power over me. My choices." Jordan moved dangerously closer to the edge.

"You are unaware of the consequences. Back away so we can talk. C'mon, Jordan," Phuong pled.

"What do you know?"

"I know more than you. I know you're gay," she shouted through the wind. "I can't allow this. Mom and Dad have a purpose more noble than the two of us. Hear what I have to say," she screamed.

"You're the cherished one, Phuong. I'm the half-breed. I've taken more shit than anyone. A price will be paid."

Phuong tried to approach and stand next to him. He wore a Polynesian headband. He shouted angrily at her, "Get back or I'm jumping."

"If you jump, I go with you."

"Threats. That's all? No closer." He held up a hand and inched to the abyss.

"Mom understands. More deeply than you realize. Let me tell you what I know. Please," Phuong begged.

"I'll resolve my own problems," Jordan shouted and looked toward the ocean.

"Step back. We'll talk. Okay?" Phuong attempted to persuade through the winds.

"Reason won't work. It's gotta be forced. Blown up in people's faces. I have my—"

"Is this what Martin Luther King would do?" A third, unknown voice spoke amid the winds.

Phuong and Jordan taken aback. The Visitor unexpectedly joined their conversation.

"Who are you?" Jordan shouted. "How'd you get here?"

The Visitor calmly stood, silent.

"This is my protest," Jordan roared. His toes edged a thousand-foot drop. The winds pushed everyone.

"Answer my question," the Visitor pressed.

Phuong deliberately stepped inches toward Jordan. *I can grab an arm. Pull him back as that man distracts ... even help me. We need Jordan off this cliff.*

"Answer my question. Then jump," the Visitor shouted again into the wind, the dark night.

Phuong thought the man was a state employee. *Wearing a suit and tie?*

"Is this what Martin Luther King would do?"

"What are you asking?" Jordan snapped.

"Your words, 'Reason won't work. It's gotta be forced. Blown up in people's faces.' Is this what Martin Luther King would do?"

"I don't know what Martin Luther King would do," Jordan shouted.

"You've read King's words, heard his speeches. You have opinions. Do you not?" the Visitor questioned.

"Opinions mean nothing unless people listen."

"I'm listening. Phuong wants to hear your thoughts ... are you misunderstood?" The winds caused the Visitor to lose balance. He staggered.

"How do you know her name? The two of you are working together. Who are you?"

"I knew of Phuong and you long ago. Our first visit is tonight. Let's sit, away from this wind. Talk. Shall we?" He motioned for Jordan to withdraw.

"Mister, you're pissin' me off." Jordan sneered.

"Will you answer my question?" the Visitor demanded.

"King was blacker than me. That's his cause."

"Was King gay, like you, Jordan?" the man asked.

"Are you calling me a homo?"

"Why are you here? You prefer to die because you are homosexual? Is this your message?"

"How do you know what I wrote?"

"I'm a guardian angel."

"You'll say, 'more guardian than angel.' Huh?"

The Visitor stood silent.

"Leave me alone. Go away," Jordan yelled into the winds.

"You cannot answer a simple question. Why?" Despite Jordan's surly demeanor, the Visitor persisted and staggered to remain balanced amidst the winds.

"Shut up, Mister."

"Jump. If you are committed to it. Jump … jump now," the Visitor encouraged with a roar.

"Shut up. Leave."

"Jump. Go ahead. Do it." The Visitor laughed.

"I'll do it."

"Don't let me stop you. Are you a coward?" The Visitor smiled with great effort.

Jordan charged the Visitor with a raised fist.

Phuong undercut him. Although smaller, her athletic muscle upset his balance. Aikido training took Jordan out of action. She held complete control as she forced him into submission.

"I'll hurt you, if I must. Get yourself together," Phuong ordered. "Jordan, I read your note." She turned to the Visitor. "May I ask your name? You move fast … quietly … you couldn't have been that far behind me."

"Irrelevant. I need answers. Speak, Jordan."

"It's time for the bullet, not the ballot, Mister," Jordan shouted at the Visitor. Phuong applied her grip more tightly to quiet Jordan, who groaned from the discomfort.

"Was King gay? Like you?"

"Answer him. Now." Phuong applied pressure. "I need to get you home."

"Okay, okay. I'm gay," Jordan shouted. "I know myself. I don't know if King was gay. No evidence I know of. He married Coretta and had four kids. Some say he played around with women."

"Do you believe King's words of civil rights apply to homosexuals?"

"Yeah. Yeah, they do," Jordan finally answered.

"Phuong. Take him home. Your family has much to deliberate." The noisy winds gusted.

"Get on your feet, Jordan. I'm not releasing my grip until we're away from this cliff."

"I will stay with you until we reach your Vespa," the Visitor said.

Phuong felt great relief to reach the Vespa. No cliffs or steep thousand-foot drops. The winds were calmer. Phuong held Jordan in a tight grip to prevent his escape and started the Vespa. She adjusted the headlight to secure a clear vision of the Visitor. Then asked him to turn his head. She saw the scar. *He's the one who visited Dad.*

"It is a pleasure to meet you, sir," Phuong affirmed. "My father speaks of you with respect. Thank you for introducing our family to Mr. Nguyen and the others. We call your group the Consortium. Thanks for what you've done tonight. My mother, I'm sure, would like to meet you."

"Phuong, you know this man?" Jordan asked.

"First time I've met him. Mom never has. This angel first visited Dad in San Francisco when I wore diapers. Known as the Visitor. Without him, we never would've met Mr. Nguyen or other angels. Shake his hand, Jordan, or I'll break your fingers."

Jordan extended his free right hand to acknowledge the Visitor.

"Messages you need passed to our parents?" Phuong asked.

"No—Wait—Actually, there is. Tell your parents I will visit them sometime in the future. When I do, I want them to sign my collection of their books."

"Please, accompany us to our home," Phuong cordially insisted. "Do you have a car?"

"I have transportation," he told Phuong. "Your parents are concerned. Go to them. I am pleased to meet you, Phuong. You, Jordan. Quite the happy little family." The Visitor attempted a failed smile. "My colleagues say I should smile more. Others have greater confidence in those who smile."

What an odd man. Phuong and Jordan stared, but then, what's normal when a suicide is botched at Nu'uanu Pali?

"I will tell them." Phuong smiled. "Where is your car? Need help?"

"No." The Visitor looked directly at Jordan. "You will not trouble Phuong, will you?" He placed a hand to Jordan's face, whispered *"Shhhhhhhhh"* with a finger to his lips.

"No, sir," Jordan assured. "Not me."

"How did you get here, Jordan?" Phuong asked.

"Hitchhiked."

The garage door alerted Sandra and Luke that one of their two children had arrived home. They worriedly sat in the kitchen for the arrival of one, or both. They heard the garage close. The door swung open. Jordan entered followed by Phuong, who retained a grip on Jordan. Phuong was fierce in her intent to report events.

Phuong pushed Jordan toward their parents and boldly declared, "Mom, tell your story to this snot. He damn near killed himself tonight at Nu'uanu Pali. Almost jumped."

"What? Jordan, is that true?" Sandra doubted.

"Yes," he embarrassedly responded.

Phuong pointed at Jordan. "Don't let him out of your sight. I'll be right back."

Seconds later, Phuong handed Jordan's suicide note to Sandra. "You'll never guess why he was jumping."

Sandra started to read. Luke stepped behind Sandra to read the note. Sandra finished and passed the note to Luke who nodded and made eye contact with his son. "You couldn't have picked a better family, Jordan."

Luke turned to Sandra. "It all makes sense. How did we not recognize his sexual preference? Ngo and the Consortium knew. Black, yellow, white, gay, Hawaii—Jordan's a rainbow. Ideal for our home, our family, our purpose."

Sandra stood solemnly in thought as she reasoned. "I'm dumbstruck. We encourage others to think deeply. Discover problems. Solve problems before being sunk by an iceberg. Tonight, we were nearly torpedoed."

"Sandra, I mix metaphors. Not you," Luke calmly insisted.

During the stillness, Jordan expressed a complaint, "All that self-defense, aikido crap has done is turn Phuong into a bully. She—"

Phuong charged Jordan with the speed of a runner stealing second base. Luke surged for the combative Phuong, wrapped both arms around her waist, and lifted her off the floor. Phuong's arms swung and legs kicked. She screamed with a clenched fist, "Jordan, take interest in something other than your biracial excuses. Listen to Mom and Dad. You'll learn what a real bully is."

"Okay, everyone. Control your emotions," Sandra demanded. "We have miles to go before sleeping tonight."

"Mom, you didn't see him on the edge of that cliff in the noise of those winds ... darkness ... I'm entitled to one solid hit." Phuong shook a fist at Jordan from her position aloft in Luke's arms. "I love you, Jordan. You scared me to death."

Phuong's eyes dripped tears. Luke dropped Phuong to her feet, took a knee. He consoled her.

Luke gazed toward Sandra, caressed Phuong's head, wiped away her tears with his handkerchief. "We're handling this situation quite well. Don't you think, Sandra?"

Minutes later, each had changed into more comfortable attire, taken a potty break, washed faces, and grabbed a teddy bear, cat, dog, or pillow. Luke and Sandra prepared comfort foods—hot chocolate, toast, macadamias, apple slices, and other assorted fruits. They seated themselves at the family discussion table for an all-nighter to get their family back on track.

Luke began, "We apologize to our children. We should have recognized, but did not, our family circumstances. Jordan took us all—even Phuong—by surprise. Hid yourself well, Jordan.

"Phuong, your quick-thinking actions are noted. Commendable. The one complaint of your aikido self-defense uses has fallen upon deaf ears. Personally, I applaud Phuong's use of those techniques at Nu'uanu Pali, as they have been described. Every dollar spent at the dojo is justified. Jordan, you owe Phuong a great deal. She rescued you." Luke focused more on his son and said, "Jordan, we'll explain ourselves. But first, answer our questions."

Sandra asked investigative questions. "Please tell us, Jordan, when did you become aware that you are gay? Why didn't you tell us?"

"And don't say, 'I dunno,'" Phuong said, imitating a guilty six-year-old. "Truth."

Though uncomfortable, Jordan realized he would survive. He trusted his family and opened himself. "Before I received the Aaronic Priesthood ... passed the sacrament. I guess when I was seven, maybe nine." Jordan shrugged.

"What indicators—sorry, Jordan—how do you know you are gay?" Sandra kindly asked.

"Even in elementary school, I've been interested in boys and sex. Something I always thought about."

"On your tenth birthday, we discussed sex and reproduction. The big talk. We've had others since. Why didn't you say something? Tell us you preferred boys?" Luke asked with simple curiosity.

Jordan felt unease. "Gee, Phuong is here. Do I hafta talk about this in front of her?"

Sandra interceded. "Yes. Phuong saved you tonight. She had the same discussions with your father and me when she turned ten. Her presence is critical to our family, as you will discover. Why didn't you tell your father or me about your sexual feelings?"

"I was scared. I'm already a half-breed—"

Half-breed. All three came at Jordan like a full-blown avalanche.

"Turn a lemon into lemonade. You've never been harmed by your colors," Phuong roared.

"Stop making excuses. Justifying poor performance." Luke's tone was one of chastisement.

"Our family profile is uncommon. Racial considerations are not..." Sandra's voice trailed off before she finished her thoughts.

Finally, Luke gained control and spoke on behalf of the three. "Jordan, this is the last we will ever hear that expression used by you. **Ever.** You've used it far too much. Frankly, it's meaningless. Cowards speak those words, not you. You were given life; make the best of it. Why didn't you share your sexual feelings with our family?"

Jordan gathered his confidence. "I was afraid you'd punish me, even send me away, back to Guam. I hear what people say at church about homos, gay people. Places they ship kids like me to straighten them out when they need to be cured." Jordan emphasized his words. "You and Mom are high mucky-mucks at church. Everything you do. Everywhere you go. I love you and all, but I was too scared to say anything. People talk at church. I didn't want to be sent back to Guam for being queer."

The family fell silent. Luke turned to Sandra. "We hid ourselves far better than he."

"Jordan, you are almost sixteen years old." Sandra calmly spoke. "You know we'd never, could ever, send you back to Guam."

"I'll level with you," Jordan argued. "I underachieve. Yeah, I do it on purpose. A lot. You know it too. I have plenty of questions. I do what I do for a reason. I don't know when I'll need to hide food. I know you love me, but I hear stuff at church that scares me, knowing what I am. I'm homo. Can't change it. I went to Nu'uanu Pali tonight believing everyone, including me, would be better off if I jumped. Then Phuong and that creepy guy showed up."

"Mom, it's your turn. Jordan needs to hear your story," Phuong said, still agitated but with greater sympathy in her voice. She arose. "I need water. Can I get anything for anyone?" She walked behind Jordan, placed her arms around him, and hugged tightly, then she grabbed a container filled with ice water.

No one wanted water. Each person reached for nuts and fruit. Luke refilled his chocolate.

Sandra asked, "Who is the creepy guy?"

Phuong answered, "The Visitor. The man who talked to Dad after my adoption."

"The Visitor? How do you know?" Luke was impressed that Phuong identified the angel.

"He gave clues. I didn't know for sure until we got to the Vespa. I shined the headlight on him and saw the scar behind his ear. Looks like the other angels."

"The Visitor? On the cliff with Jordan and you?" Sandra asked.

"Yes," Phuong reported. "Wore a suit and tie."

"Like he beamed in or something," Jordan added. "He's kinda strange."

"He knew Jordan wouldn't jump," Phuong added.

"How do you know?" Jordan felt upset that Phuong would say such words. He wanted his threat of suicide taken seriously.

"He kept telling you to jump. You didn't. Scary as it was, he somehow knew you wouldn't. When you tried to hit him, coming off the cliff, I got a grip on you," Phuong said, taunted Jordan.

"Asked questions. All he could do," Jordan explained.

"Typical behavior of a Consortium member," Luke said.

"Took both of us to get Jordan off the Pali," Phuong said.

"Where did the Visitor go?" Sandra asked.

"Don't know. He said to leave. He'll soon visit the two of you. Wants your autographs." Phuong smiled. "I wanted to get Jordan home before he could change his mind."

"Jordan, are you ready to listen? I'll speak more than the others." Sandra smiled and nodded at him.

The next minutes became the most relevant time of Jordan's life. He listened as Sandra described her teenage years as a genetically masculine but beautiful girl. The rights of people who possess color. Black and Asian ethnicities. LGBTQ. Historical, religious, and social comparisons of bigotry and bias toward uncommon or minority interests. Phuong and Luke added their experience, intents, and perspectives in the purpose of Overlord.

A fire burned inside Jordan's mind and heart. Like he once again fell in love with baseball, tasted root beer, and considered himself Polynesian. He discovered purpose and allies with whom he could labor to free himself from oppression, senseless prejudice and separation. He understood the source of bullying.

Luke brushed Phuong's hair; an act customarily engaged during family discussions. While doing so, he said, "Mr. Nguyen will be in our home at eight tomorrow morning. He will maintain constant surveillance over your whereabouts, Jordan. You will not be allowed to remain alone or unsupervised. Not until this family trusts you will not harm yourself. Mr. Nguyen will remain until your mother or I return."

"Mr. Nguyen is gifted but elderly," Sandra said. "Jordan, you will respect him. Fall in line with his recommendations. A military-like practice of study for reading, written work, and research. Mr. Nguyen will oversee your schedule and activities. You will gain knowledge of topics related to LGBTQ issues, genetics, history, and world religions. You are now an active part of Overlord. Mr. Nguyen will assess your efforts and report to your father and me. As a family, we will hear from you. We will share our own experience with explanations of these topics. Do not lose your privileges to play, enjoy entertainment, group associations, friends and family activity. Do not fall behind. You could be left behind. One is our family."

"Pay close attention, Jordan. This is important and needed," Sandra ordered. "You will issue a heartfelt apology to Phuong for undue, careless stress placed on her resulting from the incident at Nu'uanu Pali."

Jordan looked at Phuong. She smiled coyly, wriggled her fingers, and winked. He smiled at her with a nod.

"Listen, please." Luke's subdued, apologetic voice stabbed at Jordan's heart as he stopped brushing Phuong's hair. "On behalf of the family, we love you, Jordan. Your brain is maturing into that of an adult. Now that you have heard your mother's story, we hope you have found the vision to assist our family in Overlord. In addition to your apology to Phuong, you need to express regrets for the distress you caused your mother from the incident at Nu'uanu Pali. I need no apology. I take responsibility for the failure to recognize your sexual preference. I failed to prevent all that occurred tonight. I should've provided the hardiness—"

Before he finished, Phuong and Sandra protested. "Dad, none of us saw it, you can't be responsible!"

"I was here too. You're not alone."

"Please," Luke persisted. His arms raised, hairbrush in hand. "I will be vigilant, more so than I have ever been in this family. In all I do. I want to prevent tragedy. I screwed up, Jordan. I landed this plane, our family, short of the runway. Don't allow me to do it again. Do you promise me, Jordan? I need a competent copilot in the cockpit. Will you keep me informed? Alert?"

"Yes, Dad. Sorry. Never again. Promise."

Four heroes. Uncommon, imperfect, distracted. Now more capable in their quests. Hawaii was now possibly too small to contain this team of characters. *Heads up* is stated to keep everyone alert. Unfortunately, the finest people never solve riddles, see icebergs, or anticipate or survive disaster. Usually, they are too intent to maintain tradition, harmony, or misguided agreement.

The most harmful? – Religious dogmas.

The Visitor's Visit

I never learn anything talking.
I only learn things when I ask questions.

—Lou Holtz

THE MORNING PROCEEDED TYPICALLY. No different than each Monday as president of BYU–Hawaii for well more than a decade. Administrative officers, trustees, and deans concluded their reports. Schedules were coordinated, graduation numbers were projected, and troubleshooting was completed. A closing prayer was offered. Luke prepared his labors for the remainder of the day when he heard a tap at the door. He saw a familiar face, absent far too many years. The Visitor.

Luke rose and stared at the mysterious person. No changes. Appearance, age, hair, not even his suit and tie. Luke approached the Visitor and offered his hand. They clasped. Luke saw the scar behind his right ear.

"Friend, it is good to see you," the Visitor said.

"For someone I have met but once, we've experienced much together."

"You speak of my fellow angels." The Visitor tried to smile.

"In part. Each distinct yet so much alike. Please have a seat." Luke gestured to a chair. The Visitor seated himself and placed a briefcase at his feet.

As the Visitor sat, Luke shouted a directive to no one in the reception area. "I will be busy with this person for some time. Make certain we are not disturbed. Thanks."

Luke rushed to his desk and made a phone call. "Forgive me, sir. There is someone anxious to meet you."

"Sandra, there is a Visitor in my office. How soon can you get here?" A silent pause. Luke nodded and uttered a few uh-huhs. "I won't let him leave. Yes. Sandra, I love you too."

Luke turned to the Visitor. "Sandra wishes you'd given us notice. She has gifts for you. But she'd like to make herself presentable." Luke smiled. "She'll arrive soon."

"Women have greater appeal in their forties," the Visitor said. "She is beautiful."

"I agree. More attractive, sexier now than ever. Brilliant too. I've wondered what she sees in me."

"Luke, you have gifts. You place smiles on Sandra's face."

"You didn't behave this kindly when we first met. You frightened me. Greatly."

"With a purpose. Sandra and you are to ascend a higher, more significant peak."

"What peak?" Luke asked, intrigued.

"You will experience it yourselves. Climb far." He encouraged.

"No questions? No clues to prepare us?"

"Sandra is not here. Patience."

"Yes, understood." Luke paused. "Your presence at Nu'uanu Pali is appreciated. Thank you."

"Phuong behaved well. Possesses great strength. Emotionally, intellectually. Her aikido is most impressive. Useful skills."

"Her size requires that ability. She needs every advantage in compromised situations. Never thought she'd subdue Jordan with it. Control someone larger, stronger than herself."

"She prevented contact between Jordan and me."

"Phuong lost her composure with Jordan when returning home."

"The experience challenged Phuong. She coped well with danger. Crisis is a teacher. She performed with skill. Grit. That is the word you use. Yes?"

"Was the incident designed for a purpose?"

"You ask? Follow breadcrumbs." The Visitor looked pleased.

"I wish I could see inside your mind. Speaking of breadcrumbs, it's been four years since Jordan made his attempt at the Pali. Phuong said you'd visit us. We expected you sooner."

"Time is relative. How is Jordan?" The Visitor redirected the conversation.

"Improved. Mr. Nguyen, who should be named Godsend, has performed wonders. Jordan is more curious. He's explored. Furthered his insights. Uses reason. Should you be responsible for Mr. Nguyen's salary, give him a raise. We've tried to reward him. Whatever he receives from us, we find in the hands of others. Mr. Nguyen is the definition of *good*."

"He enjoys his work. Has all he needs. The request for Jordan to be your copilot is commendable."

"How'd you know I—"

"Hello, gentlemen." Sandra stood in the doorway to the office. She wore sleek, long, gray pants, sandals, and a white summer blouse. Hair fell over her shoulders, braided at the crown to prevent strands falling over a bright face. A basket hung from an arm.

"I brought goodies." Sandra placed the basket on the round discussion table, turned to the Visitor, and offered her hand. They politely touched. Sandra was attractive and affable in her movements. Chairs were placed to accommodate the three in a conversation. Sandra and Luke, near each other, faced the Visitor.

"I have heard much about you; it is good to finally meet." Sandra politely smiled. "I'm certain there is an explanation for your presence."

"There is."

Sandra and Luke waited for him to continue. The Visitor stared back. Sandra leaned toward Luke's ear and whispered, "Did you see his scar? Are we speaking to the right Visitor?"

"The scar is there," Luke whispered into Sandra's ear.

"Are the two of you uneasy?" the Visitor asked.

"There is much that alarms us," Sandra expressed. "How do you explain your presence here with us today? We expected you long ago."

"What of Jordan?" the Visitor asked again with patience.

Sandra answered, "In the time since Nu'uanu Pali, Jordan exhibits greater confidence. He's more open and eager to learn, and he discusses a variety of issues. Mr. Nguyen has been tremendous. Jordan's homosexual disclosure, I believe, has given him a purpose. An interdependence in our family. We should have told him about me sooner. We had no idea he struggled and felt no guarantee we would understand to help shoulder his sexual feelings, or understand his daydreams. A blind person led by others blinder than he. We erred greatly. It requires a family commitment to share information and feelings. Especially when your community, or religion, is uncooperative. Against you."

"You have learned," the Visitor affirmed. "Hopefully, others will learn from your errors. Yes, you should have known that Jordan is homosexual. Investigated more thoroughly. Not good detective work or caretakers."

"I'm the worst detective," Luke admitted. "Like all parents, we fell short. Should've asked questions without criticizing responses. Children are to be sheltered with questions. No disapproval for their answers. Love unconditionally, with no regard to holy writ. We failed. We should've been discussing his issues. Not our own. We're fortunate we didn't lose Jordan. We acted like we knew, when we knew nothing at all. We are arrogant, self-important."

"You have stated the purpose for my visit," the Visitor proclaimed. "My work is done." The Visitor moved like he intended to leave.

"Whoa. Stay in your seat. I didn't hear what either of us said. Explain your purpose," Luke urged. "What did we say? In fifty words or less, why are you here?"

The Visitor settled back into his chair. "You will be asked to visit the prophet the week general conference begins. The two of you will attend. Take Phuong and Jordan. Challenges will be heard. Respond simply, honestly. Maintain Overlord. Carefully consider their offers. Changes will occur. Love. Reason. Happiness. Compassion. Families."

"What?" Sandra and Luke were lost.

"Fifty words or less. Correct? You're bright people. Think it through. You will succeed — What's in the basket? Will you sign my books, please?" The Visitor grinned ridiculously.

"Okay." Sandra stood. "I have sweet potato pie. All ingredients grown in Hawaii. I also have my latest book. It's not on the shelves yet. I will sign it. If you stay. Your name, please?"

"I like the moniker Visitor. Possesses a distinct, clairvoyant sound. Don't you agree?" The Visitor shook from laughter though his mouth fought the desire to grin. A happy occasion.

"You slice the pie. I will unpack my books for each of you to sign." His briefcase contained Luke's novels and copies of their more popular texts.

Their time together warm, delightful. The Visitor deflected questions as to where he lived, how he traveled, or spent his free time. He talked of children, principally Phuong and Jordan. Genuine in his concern for the well-being of people. A likable character. Just ... odd.

"You will visit us again?" Sandra asked, hopeful of something sustained. His visits were infrequent yet meaningful.

"I will. You are frequently on my mind. Willie Nelson. Correct?"

Sandra and Luke smiled. Nodded their heads. Luke said, "Good enough for who it's for."

"Thank you," Sandra praised. "We know you are out there, somewhere. It comforts us, especially when Phuong and Jordan needed help. Thanks, again, for watching over our family when we should have been there."

"My duty. Remember, the lives of people fall short of happily ever after. Only so much I, or anyone, can do. That includes Heavenly Father," the Visitor cautioned.

Sandra and Luke nodded their heads.

"I will speak words God will never declare," the Visitor warned. "Parents, children, all families expect happiness when it is not received or is unattainable. Happiness, like decisions, is a choice we make and is earned. Maximum rewards given from minimal efforts are futile. Birthrights, one's ethnicity, citizenship, or religious affiliation and membership never deliver happiness."

The Visitor ate a slice of sweet potato pie. Sandra and Luke autographed books. Sandra wrapped then placed treats in his briefcase, with additional slices of pie. A short, pleasant gathering. The Visitor walked away. Vanished.

"Sandra, the prophet's administrative assistant called today. He wants us to attend general conference in Salt Lake City. They will meet us Wednesday, prior to conference. I anticipate a call as a mission president. Maybe become a Seventy?"

"Have they heard you profane?"

"Hell, Sandra, please. Is this what the Visitor discussed?"

"Yes," Sandra answered. "We'll need to inform the kids what's on the horizon. They'll have questions."

"Phuong and Jordan will resist. Hawaii is heaven for them. Not once have they complained of island fever," Luke said.

"They've traveled with us," Sandra reflected. "They know what other parts of the world are like. They'll adapt. The Church probably wants to censure us for questions and challenges stated in our broadcasts and books. Until we know what the Church wants, we're guessing."

"We'll make our decisions after we meet the Brethren. Our staff and broadcast schedules will be disrupted, perhaps." Luke was sullen, lost in thought.

"We knew our days at BYU–Hawaii would end," Sandra lamented. "It's been wonderful."

"Phuong and Jordan are college students," Luke said. "Capable to go and do whatever they wish. Independent kids. Phuong more than Jordan. They'll choose for themselves. Phuong has one more season with Hawaii. She'll attend graduate school. If we accept a mission presidency call, neither will go with us. I wouldn't fault their decisions. They are adult decision makers. The Church may end our association with them."

"They've been with us nearly two decades. Can you believe that? I can't imagine them separated from us." Sandra sighed.

"They're the ages when we met at BYU. They'll discover their own loves. So much for families are forever."

"I wish we could stay as we are now. The four of us here. It seems to have been perfect at each age. Perfect as it is now. I don't want us to age, or for Phuong and Jordan to find their partners.

Time and marriage break up all families, even ours." Sandra's voice tinged with regret.

"We could reject what the Church proposes. Resign as president of BYU–Hawaii and conduct our research. We're independent. We'll subsist on television contracts, books, and speaking tours. Even with that, the kids will leave. Our existence with them ends far sooner than later. They've been taught to be self-reliant. Salt Lake could be Overlord's battleground. We don't know. Phuong and Jordan have their own paths, even in our cause. We will impact the world. Above all, you, Sandra,"

"So be it," Sandra said. "Call the kids. Let's get on with this. The Visitor advised us to carefully consider what the Church may offer."

Phuong and Jordan were briefed.

"I won't leave Hawaii," Phuong said. "I'll play ball then attend graduate school on the mainland."

Jordan asked, "Why does the Church control our lives? Decisions? I want to remain here."

"We can't solve problems 'til we know why Salt Lake called," Sandra said.

The family dispersed.

"Mr. Nguyen, is our family being separated?" Phuong asked.

"Your family is on a bold journey. Your mother will shine," he said. "Bright family colors."

Phuong exhaled then innocently admitted, "I enjoy what I am, my color, ethnicity. Yet, Mom and Dad are precious. All they have done for Jordan and me. I wish their DNA were inside me. I love them so much. They should have their gifts, best qualities, extended to a child of their own."

"Jordan and you are their legacy," Mr. Nguyen insisted. "I've heard them say they could never create anyone as wonderful as the two of you. They are happy. Better with you than without you. It began the very first moment they saw you at Camp Pendleton."

"You weren't there. Were you?" Phuong's beautiful eyes narrowed.

"Phuong, I'm an angel. They hugged and kissed you the first moment they saw you. I'll tell you a secret only guardian angels know."

"What's that?" she smiled.

"You can't disclose this to anyone. Once told, you must become a guardian angel for someone special."

"Sounds like fun," Phuong said, anxious to learn. "Explain."

"The more hugs and kisses you give your children, any child, the happier, more valuable that child will be. It's true. That includes hairbrushes and foot massages."

Phuong laughed. Playfully slapped Mr. Nguyen's arm like Sandra whaps Luke. "If that's true, I'm going to be on top of the world."

"It's true, Phuong. It's true. As your mom and dad say, 'Go test the theory.'" He smiled.

They hugged each other and laughed.

"If Mom and Dad leave Hawaii, stay with us, here. Please?"

"Guardian angels never leave. Not until our work is finished."

"Really?" Phuong asked.

"We'll test the theory." Mr. Nguyen smiled again. "I will remain as long as you and Jordan require my attention. Simple math," he winked.

Salt Lake and Beyond

Fear not those who argue, but those who dodge.

—Marie von Ebner-Eschenbach

OUR HEROES FLEW INTO Salt Lake the Monday ahead of general conference weekend. Luke used the available time to visit his parents and siblings, who volunteered guesses where he might be called as a mission president. Laughs with giggles a continual family staple.

Luke called the prophet's administrative assistant early Tuesday afternoon for the specific time Sandra and Luke would meet with the Brethren. The assistant instructed, "President Luke, go to the Church boardroom Wednesday morning; a member of Church security will meet you at 10 a.m."

"Where is the Church boardroom?" Luke asked.

"In the Church Administration Building. That's the building east of the Joseph Smith Memorial Building, south of the Church Office Building. Enter the Church Administration Building from South Temple Street."

"Thanks. Sorry. I didn't know the Church had a boardroom. Sandra will be with me. Is that expected?"

"Uh, yeah. If it isn't, I'll let you know. What's your number?"

Luke provided the hotel room number and expressed appreciation for Church efficiency.

Sandra and Luke walked to the Church Administration Building and were cordially met at the entrance by a "suit"—a plain-clothes security gentleman. The middle-aged white man sat behind a large, elevated, polished mahogany counter and wore a white shirt, dark suit, and tie. His haircut and overall countenance gave an impression of Mormon enforcement. He possibly packed a concealed weapon.

"Good morning, may I help you?"

"Yes. We have an appoint—"

"I know who you are. I've seen you on television." The man stepped down from behind the counter and approached Sandra and Luke with firm LDS handshakes. "I saw your names on today's schedule. I wish I'd known earlier; I would've brought my book for you to sign."

"Get the book here. We'll sign it," Sandra graciously said.

They acted like friends, unseen for years.

"Let me take you to the boardroom. We can't keep the Brethren waiting. They're probably just as excited to see you."

Guided by the Suit, they climbed a flight of stairs, went down a hallway, and passed through an open door. The building, carpet, photographs, and artifacts were old, out-of-date. It did not give an impression that a new millennium had entered. Rather, it was stale, dark, and musty. Like your elderly grandparent's home, late nineteenth century.

The Suit motioned his hand toward three men seated at a doublewide table designed for twelve, six seats on each side. At the top, a second table, as long as the width of the doublewide, with seats for three. Five sisters/women were seated in cushioned chairs against the wall under windows.

"Welcome." The prophet rose to his feet, along with his counselors. Each dressed like the Suit, akin to other Hassidic Mormons. Luke was not exempt. All men wore white shirts, ties, and primarily dark suits, with BYU honor-code haircuts. The ladies wore loose, modest dresses below the knee. Sandra wore a stylish, one-piece, sleek, V-neck, navy-blue, fitted dress that extended to the knees with three-quarter-length sleeves and moderate heels. It made her as tall as the men but fitter.

Sandra and Luke expressed thanks and offered a quick goodbye to the Suit with a pledge to sign his book. The two then stepped toward the three highest authorities of The Church of Jesus Christ of Latter-day Saints, bestowing them all customary expressions of courtesy for their positions and titles. The prophet turned to introduce the women in the room. First, the prophet's administrative assistant; the other four, the presidency and secretary of the General Relief Society. They mingled briefly and engaged in small talk with cordial regard.

"If you would allow," the prophet said, "we're separating the two of you for a time."

Sandra and Luke nodded. Felt uncertain. Tensely, they awaited the disclosure for their summon to Church headquarters.

"The Relief Society Presidency will take Sister Sandra on a tour while we chat with Luke. We'll all meet for lunch. Acceptable?"

Everyone nodded. Sandra was escorted from the boardroom. The administrative assistant closed the door behind them. The Brethren sat in the three chairs at the smaller head table above the doublewide. Luke sat across the table and faced the First Presidency, hands atop the table. The interrogation interview began.

"Luke," the prophet began. "We appreciate the work you have performed on behalf of the Church as president of BYU–Hawaii and as a stake president. You have acted as a good, faithful servant with a daring personality. Challenging gender calls."

Luke nodded slightly. He believed a sledgehammer would soon hit. However, a discussion of personal worthiness, detailed and deep, ensued. The sequence of questions was impressive. Their research into his life, financial assets, movements, and activities were thoroughly professional.

"Have you acted untoward with any person, sexual misconducts, Church funds in your care or within the purview of any Church business, contractual negotiations, or agreements?"

Luke pondered. "I snuck a small bowl of soup and a turkey sandwich into the BYU library back in 1978. I gave the soup and sandwich to Sandra so she could study at her carrel late into the evening. I've broken a number of rules purposely. I violate federal law by dropping Hershey Kisses in Sandra's mailbox. I want Sandra to know I'd risk myself for her welfare. Competent people know which rules to follow and those to be ignored. I do it often. I am confident Sandra has made that same connection. I love her. Only her since we first met. There has been no one else in my life. Just Sandra. I understand reports of LDS wrongdoings have found their way into public discussions. I'll say that I have faults. I err daily. I seem devilish, but I am no devil. I describe myself as fun-loving and open. I seek well-being for those who are uncommon, unaccepted."

"Do you lie?"

"Daily," Luke unapologetically answered. "To protect lives. Maintain confidences. Guard the self-esteem of children. Give peace to dying or disheartened people. A necessary trait of skilled leaders. Not that they lie. Some do not engage it properly. I'm certain you understand. You have your own experiences."

"Interesting. I'm surprised you didn't lie to me. Our investigators have concluded you are a skilled leader. You possess gifts. Capable behaviors," the prophet reported.

"Sandra and I know people who are efficient investigators."

"We may employ the same people," the prophet suggested.

"I would be fascinated." He stared at the prophet. "Quite scary, if true." Luke tried to smile. "You will like me much more once you know Sandra. She is a skilled, capable leader. Greater than I." Luke dissolved tensions.

"Sandra is our concern."

Luke froze. *They've discovered Sandra's syndrome*, he thought to himself. *They're irate.* He looked into the prophet's eyes but said nothing until asked a question.

"President Luke, tell us about Sandra," the prophet requested. "Her goals, hopes, intents. She is a progressive woman, persuasive. She's recognized by millions of people who watch her on television programs and from the books she's written."

"I do not speak for Sandra. She is highly persuasive. An accomplished media personality. She should respond to your inquiries herself."

"Very well. We will speak to her. For now, what are your impressions of your companion?"

"If not for Sandra, I wouldn't be where I am. She is why I have succeeded as greatly as I have. The world, Church members, recognize her talents and contributions. A terrific person."

"Her work and personality have been viewed by us. Our researchers," the prophet reported. "As noted, she is well-respected. Loved by millions of people."

"Again, you'll like me much better once you know Sandra, my best friend." Luke purposely guarded his words.

"What makes her happy?"

"Sandra is an open book, literally," Luke declared. "Read her books. She is what she has written." Luke remained brief. Protected Overlord. Guarded Sandra's true nature.

"We've read her books, as well as your own. We hope to confirm things about her."

"What do you wish to confirm?" Luke believed this would open the door for them to reveal their knowledge of Sandra's syndrome.

"Is Sandra as personable a leader as seen on television? Happy?"

"When I met Sandra at BYU, she told me the gospel made her happy. I hope I'm currently in first place for her happiness. Again, I shouldn't speak for her. She has her own voice. In my opinion, she's a fine leader. Our family refers to her, justly, as a prophetess."

The prophet bristled. "We know she is very supportive of women's rights, gender equality, and LGBTQ issues. The two of you make substantial monetary contributions to social and political groups for those causes."

"Your intelligence is correct. A matter of public record. Have your investigators told you we also contribute funds to BYU, Grambling, Stanford, UC Berkeley, Morehouse, the University of Utah, Greenpeace, Earth Day, Clean Water, Save the Whales, and the children of Kosovo, Vietnam, Southeast Asia, and Africa? That my grandmother thought Franklin Roosevelt walked on water and my mother-in-law is a Democrat? We also lend our voices in support of charitable causes to aid education, environmental concerns, childcare, drug abuse issues, suicide prevention … and other causes. We do not intend to end our support for these groups."

"We have skilled examiners," the prophet said. "You participate in humane practices. We are aware. We do not wish to have another Mark Hofmann[10] disgrace the Church. Sandra and you are well-known."

"Forgive my audacity. Are there moral issues to be considered while conducting Church investigations of its members? You compare Sandra and me to Mark Hofmann? A man who made fools of Church leadership—even living members of the Twelve—with his forged documents. A murderer. Where was revelation or your researchers then? Did your people or angels investigate Hofmann?" Luke's upper body straightened, placed his hands on the armrests, prepared to stand and leave.

"Sandra and you are not here to be compared to a murderer. I apologize for my words. Please, remain calm."

"I feel inclined to exit. Why *are* Sandra and I here?" Luke demanded. "To answer why we contribute funds and time to human rights, equity between genders, LGBTQ issues? How ghastly do we behave?"

"We need Sandra," the prophet confessed. "Her intelligence. Persona. It's essential for continued advancement of the Church."

"How so? Now you have my attention." Luke gazed intently into the eyes of the prophet.

"Sisters need direction, one of their own to show the way. The Church is in arrears toward independent social growth for women. Church character is maligned from of our lack of harmony for the circumstances of professional women. We have no visible spokesperson, no examples to guide LDS mothers who work to support families. How to act as leaders, at times, in careers outside the home with authority over men. The Church finds itself unbalanced. Our sisters need preparations to become mothers and wives while being paid incomes to support families. Luke, you called sisters in your stake to fill positions traditionally occupied by priesthood-bearing men. Did Sandra have any part in that?"

"Religions, including Mormonism, lag well behind in regard to racial and women's rights, gender equity, as well as LGBTQ issues.

---

[10] LDS document forger, counterfeiter and murderer of two people October 15, 1985 in Salt Lake City, UT. Forged the Salamander letter and many other Mormon documents.

Our Church is merely one of all religions that have not kept pace." Luke adjusted in his seat to attain height. "Sandra supported and encouraged my decisions. I called the most competent people to serve when gender or priesthood is not specified. Take my word for it, the best stake athletic director is a Polynesian woman, uh, sister. They don't take shinola from anyone—sorry. A female, um, sister CPA can balance the accounts of a stake or ward budget. A man with a degree in early childhood development can be a great Primary or Junior Sunday School president. Regardless of gender, call the best person for the job. Many will include the First Presidency, Quorum of the Twelve—"

"Don't speak critically of us, Luke. We need Sandra to be our voice. A face for Latter-day Saint women within the Church. We need her to design instructions preparing our daughters, mothers, and all sisters to be competent, as you have said. Our analysts believe that converts will increase, principally in North America and Europe, if we call her to oversee gradual changes toward gender alliances. Church members and global audiences see her, your marriage, your children, as a standard, diverse Mormon family."

"You speak of greater balance between the rights and powers of women and spouses in the home, as well as Church leadership. I don't believe I'm your *girl*. Your analysts are right. Sandra is the *man* you want. Believe me, she'll do the job for you. Men and boys in the priesthood will require this instruction. We're not in Kansas anymore, Brethren."

"Luke, you speak oddly."

"My words will make sense, given time. The Church, its members, will benefit from Sandra's gifts, once you know her, what she truly is. Why talk to me? Speak with her about this job. What's your proposal?"

"That's why you are speaking with us first," the prophet explained.

"I don't understand."

"We cannot call sisters to relocate their husbands, children, and family to Utah to do the kind of work is needed from Sandra, unless she lives near Salt Lake."

"Why not? I have research to do. Books to write. My ego is irrelevant. Honestly, my siblings and elderly parents all felt we'd be asked to go to Tooele as a mission president. You'd have us in Salt Lake for three years. If needed, we'll stay longer. I can take a position at the U of U, Westminster, maybe Weber State. Uh-oh, I almost forgot. Our kids don't want to leave Hawaii." Then, with excitement, he added, "Sandra can do the work from Hawaii."

"Luke, we need you to become a member of the Quorum of the Twelve Apostles. Should you accept, Sandra will be called as a member of the General Relief Society Presidency. Do you accept the call as an Apostle?"

Seconds of silence passed. Speechless, Luke weighed the suggestion. *Sandra and I are in our forties. I'm too old to play big league baseball. Too young to be an Apostle.* He looked at the Brethren. "Let me say, I'm certain you will see many first-time occurrences take place. You know that Sandra is a remarkable individual. I'm too young for this." Luke stated the obvious while he simultaneously considered all possibilities and ramifications.

"You are far from the youngest called as a member of the Twelve. God the Father and His Son, Jesus Christ, require your service to bring to pass the immortality and eternal life of man. For the sake of equity, with Sandra's talents, the eternal life of women as well."

"Interesting." He paused and thought, then quickly spoke, "I need to speak with Sandra. I won't say a word to disclose what you have told me. I would like a private conversation with her before she hears your proposal. A single minute—my word on that," he anxiously smiled.

The prophet motioned his hand to a counselor who stepped to the boardroom door. The counselor called for the administrative assistant, seated in the hallway. Luke couldn't hear the counselor at the doorway, but his nonverbal movements clearly indicated what the assistant needed to do.

As he returned, he asked, "Juice? Water?"

Heads shook.

The other counselor, a popular General Authority, said, "Hawaii is paradise. Will Phuong and Jordan really object moving to Utah?"

"These calls you want us to accept will separate Sandra and me from our children. Phuong plays softball at the University of Hawaii. She won't leave. Jordan considers himself Polynesian and enrolled at BYU–Hawaii. We'll talk with them. They understand consequences." Luke's mind bounced in ten different directions.

"Church calls strain family relationships," the counselor testified. "Involve challenges that require families to bend. The Lord needs special people to fulfill His purposes. Families are required to adapt with calls."

"Odd you say that … I hope the Lord intervenes. My opinion? Like soldiers in combat, we adapt. Personal hardiness takes over."

Luke and the popular counselor in the First Presidency fell silent and fixed upon the other's eyes.

"You know my children's names. I appreciate your preparation," Luke kindly responded.

"Very few members are unaware of Sandra, you, and the names of your children. Sandra is seen frequently on television, as are you. The four of you are pictured in magazines. Members read articles that mention you as a model Mormon family."

"Model? That's a joke," Luke argued with a chuckle. "We have our troubles and trials. Continual problems." He loosely shook his hands. "We love each other very much. Our greatest asset. We each are so uncommon and different. We don't see it. Every day, we fall in love like it's the first time."

"Seems like an ideal family in my estimation," the counselor offered.

Luke smiled and nodded as if to say *thank you for the compliment.* "Your expectations for Sandra are quite progressive for the Church. Long overdue. Uh, no criticism intended."

The Brethren began to respond when a knock rapped the boardroom door. The Suit stood next to Sandra, walkie talkie in his hand. Luke got to his feet, rushed to her. He thanked the Suit and wrapped his arms around Sandra.

"Luke? What's happened?" Sandra asked, perplexed by events.

Luke turned to the Brethren. "Is there a room? Somewhere we can speak privately? We won't be long."

Led to an office, Sandra and Luke closed the door behind them. Luke excitedly grasped her arms. "Sandra, they want you more than they want me."

"Luke?"

"The prophet will explain. Sandra, our being here is all about you. You're the prophetess we discussed back at BYU. It's complex. I needed to speak with you first. You'll be told what they want from you—sorry—us."

"As we walked, the women seemed confused. They don't know. I don't. What did they say?"

"There is a purpose in why we found each other, Sandra. Perhaps, divine. They're opening a door. We need to step through." Luke kissed her passionately. She returned the passion with her own mischievous flair. Breathlessly, the two broke apart. Sandra asked for Luke's handkerchief as they tidied themselves.

"Okay," Sandra exclaimed. "Let's face the music. I need to know!"

Back in the boardroom, the prophet repeated to Sandra, almost identically, the words he expressed to Luke.

"I'm surprised. I didn't expect this. I *am* intrigued, however. Actually, eager to participate," Sandra rambled. "This will mark a time in Church history for change. A new direction."

"So, Luke, do you accept your call to the Twelve?" The prophet leaned forward in his chair.

Sandra glanced at Luke, then back to the prophet. "I apologize. I spoke aloud. Violated protocol."

"We assured our children we'd receive their approval before I—we—accept a call. In this case, calls." Luke swiftly asked, "When must we respond? Our family customarily makes decisions by consensus."

"We hoped to receive your acceptances today. It's good we discussed this. We were unaware of your family policy. How much time is needed?"

"Sorry to disturb your plans. It's Sandra's fault." *Whap!* Sandra swatted Luke's chest. Luke fell back, cross-eyed, like he took a hit from Mike Tyson.

"Luke, stop. Your goofy sense of humor is not appreciated," Sandra said, scowling.

"I'm laughing," the prophet said, cackling.

"Good hit," one of the counselors said, chuckling. All three men were amused.

"If you encourage this, he'll keep doing it," Sandra sternly advised. The Brethren's shoulders bounced with laughter. She paused to see three generally staid, elderly administrative leaders enjoy themselves. Sandra smiled and shook her head. Luke reversed a tense situation and caused the three highest mucky-mucks in the Church to laugh aloud.

Sandra and Luke ate lunch with the First Presidency. They dined with General Authorities, staff, administrative assistants, and Relief Society officers. Conversations were cheerful.

People arrived to meet the popular Sandra and Luke, with books to sign. They consented. Nine books autographed. Last among them, a book from the Suit. Sandra and Luke took special care to write a personal message thanking him. The Suit appeared genuinely grateful for their attention.

Luke turned to a page that discussed hairbrushes. Asked the Suit, "Does your wife have longer hair?"

"Yes, she does."

"Do you have daughters?"

"Two."

"Their ages?"

"Twelve, fifteen."

Luke wrote in the book: *I have fewer conflicts with Sandra and Phuong when I brush their hair. An act of peace and love. A top ten of my greatest joys. Don't forget foot massages.* *Best wishes, always, Luke*

Phuong and Jordan waited impatiently in their hotel room for Sandra and Luke's return.

"We thought you'd be here sooner," Jordan said when the two finally entered the room.

"We're anxious to know where your call is, Dad," Phuong admitted. Typical, curious kids.

"Your mom will be the first prophetess in the latter days," Luke announced with confidence and smiled brightly.

"Dad, you're too easy," Jordan waved. "We can see through that. Is it Boise or Chernobyl? Either place, I ain't leavin' Hawaii. Go be a mission president without me."

Sandra stood in the middle of the room with her arms folded, "Your father had the First Presidency laughing uncontrollably."

"What did he do, Mom?" Phuong feigned a well-rehearsed, haughty attitude. "Will we all remain in Hawaii? If that's the result getting the First Presidency to laugh, I'll give Dad a hug. What happened?"

"Let's circle the wagons, kids," Luke said. "We have much to discuss. There is truth in what we've each spoken."

Chairs were circled. Water and treats were placed between them on a coffee table. In less than an hour the news and events were shared.

Jordan wanted to make sure he understood correctly. "Dad will be an Apostle. Mom a Relief Society leader ... to guide women in, what did you say, Mom? Self-reliance? Do I have it right?"

"Mom, you could become the most notable LDS woman in the new millennium," Phuong mused. "How can you allow this opportunity to pass you by? You must, Mom. You must. Like Dad said, a prophetess."

"Wait. Dad is well short of fifty. If he lives forty more years ..." Jordan's mind weighed numbers and possibilities. "Dad, you'll be the prophet one day. You and Mom – Prophets. It's unreal."

Phuong coldly interjected, "Probabilities have greater statistical chance. Too many variables to reason what possibly or likely will happen. Dad is certainly in the race to be prophet with fifteen men. We *can* say five—the eldest—are eliminated. It's callous conjecture," she reasoned. "None started at the same age. Mom and Dad can live only in the present. The future will get here when it arrives, today." She pointed downward. "Forty years from now isn't today. Likely? Possibly? Probably?"

"Phuong, you're no fun. If Mom and Dad haven't thought of it, they are now. Statistical probabilities being what they are, they have a strong chance to be prophet and prophetess, the first ones with a Black kid," Jordan said. Clearly exultant.

"That's why I'm going to graduate school," Phuong bit back. "Numbers are reliable. Neither religions, scriptures, nor prophets gave us medicine, rocketry, physics, or the Internet. Zeros and ones keep us alive and well. Know your numbers. And Jordan, you speak as a racist. I thought you, our family, are beyond that. We are human." She pointed at her own Asian face.

"Okay, enough. Your mother and I, along with the two of you, will meet the First Presidency at 8:30 tomorrow morning. What are our decisions and consequences?"

"I say accept the calls. Overlord is nearer, within grasp, serving here at Church headquarters in these positions," Phuong said.

"I agree with Phuong," Luke said. "The prophetess and prophet scenario are irrelevant. Your mother could influence generations of women. She'll make great things happen for men as well. This is a wonderful opportunity for her. I say accept the calls."

Jordan asked, "Because we're young adults, you'll allow Phuong and me to remain in Hawaii, at our home there, until we finish school at BYU–Hawaii and Phuong finishes playing ball with the Bows?"

"Mr. Nguyen will remain in Hawaii. He told me that as we left home," Phuong reported.

"Treat him well, Jordan. Do you understand?" Sandra stared directly into Jordan's eyes.

"Yes. I understand. Received and understood. I won't screw up again." Jordan opened his arms in surrender. "Accept the calls. I want Overlord to succeed."

"Mom. Do we have consensus?" Phuong awaited her answer, as did Jordan and Luke.

"Your father told me I was the brightest at BYU in 1978. He used the word *prophetess* to describe my skills to behave and think spiritually competing with men in graduate school. At the time, he didn't know of my syndrome … I am happy to be with him and make possible the inclusion of uncommon people in the Church and increase female competency and equity. Calls accepted."

As Sandra confirmed the family decision, they cheered and hugged like they just won the World Series. Long years of struggle and the challenge to scale a mountain far more challenging than Timpanogos towered ahead.

The next morning Phuong, Luke, Sandra, and Jordan stood at the entrance of the boardroom in the Church Administration Building, well-dressed and neatly groomed to meet the First Presidency. The door opened. The First Presidency rose to their feet as this diverse mix of Asian, white, male, androgen-insensitive, Black, domestic, female, heterosexual, foreign and gay family entered the room.

What did the Brethren see? A beautiful family of racial, intercultural, international diversity with unseen, unrecognized and misunderstood assortments. Characteristics this American Church of Jesus Christ of Latter-day Saints portrayed with difficulty—not just to the world, but to their own members.

The family sat across the table from the First Presidency. The prophet asked, "Have you made your decisions?"

Phuong rose. "On behalf of my father ... **One is our family** ... He accepts the call as a member of the Quorum of Twelve Apostles."

Jordan rose. "My mom is a prophetess within our family... and world. She'll lead as a counselor in the General Relief Society Presidency."

Silence.

Subdued laughter was heard. Luke embraced Sandra and lifted her off the chair with an enormous hug. Phuong and Jordan joined the family bear hug. The First Presidency and administrative assistant smiled their approval. Handshakes with congratulations followed.

A counselor asked, "What of Hawaii? Your children?"

Jordan responded, "Mr. Nguyen, our guardian angel, will oversee our home. We'll be fine. That man is really cool. The stuff he does. Can't believe what he pulls out of a hat or box. We love him."

The counselor looked confused. Luke said, "He's an amateur magician with a PhD from the University of Strasbourg, France.

We'll discuss him later." Luke smiled, shook the counselor's hand, and hastily moved down the line.

The Suit entered the boardroom. Guided Phuong and Jordan on a tour of the Church Administration Building and Relief Society Building. He showed them the separate offices Sandra and Luke would occupy.

Below the city is a place few members of the Church see. Structures/facilities connected by multi-tunneled paths between all Church-owned properties and businesses that branch underground from Temple Square outward in Salt Lake City. The Suit treated Phuong and Jordan to a ride on the prophet-mobile—a golf cart—to the furthest reaches of the impressive Church Underground.

Meanwhile, Sandra and Luke signed contractual documents, disclaimers, and vouchers. They provided passport information and received instructions regarding background services. General Authorities and officers receive compensation for their labors—living cost increases, interest-free loans, life insurance, medical/health care, housing, vacations, and miscellaneous benefits. Sandra and Luke negotiated a combined salary of $300,000. The collective amount awarded as scholarships or grants in their names and The Corporation of The Church of Jesus Christ of Latter-day Saints.

Sandra and Luke, non-beholden to the vast wealth of the Church for financial support, retained their authorship contracts, organizational enterprises, investments, holdings and media contracts. They took full advantage of the Church corporation, a marvel that assisted Overlord.

Church photographers snapped shots of Sandra and Luke, along with the entire family for media distribution and archival usage.

The sustaining vote occurred during the Saturday morning session of general conference. The prophet stood at the podium to sustain all "new and existing" calls among the General Authorities and General Auxiliary officers. Sandra and Luke were seated in the congregation near but not on the rostrum. After new General Authorities and officers are sustained, they climb the steps to their designated seats amid the General Authorities already seated before 21,000 patrons facing the rostrum. It was the final time Phuong and Jordan would sit with their parents in a Church meeting.

"It is proposed we sustain Sister Sandra as second counselor in the General Relief Society."

Sandra placed her left hand on Luke's leg and stroked his inner thigh. She turned her face to his ear and whispered, "Remember doing this at BYU?"

"Those in favor, please manifest it."

"Don't Sandra," he whispered, smiling like a stoic Apostle should behave. Each raised right arms to the square.

"Those opposed, if any, may manifest it."

She leaned into him, harmlessly teasing. "Sandra, thousands are watching," Luke tried to maintain some form of solemn composure.

"The vote to sustain Sister Sandra was unanimous in the affirmative."

"Still works," she whispered to Luke with genuflected satisfaction.

"It is proposed that we sustain Luke as a member of the Quorum of Twelve Apostles."

"A taste of your own medicine," Sandra teased.

"Those in favor, please manifest it."

"We're not kids at BYU. My goodness," Luke responded. Each squared their right arms.

"Those opposed, if any, may manifest it."

"My power is priesthood strong." Sandra grinned.

"The vote to sustain Apostle Luke was unanimous in the affirmative."

Luke clasped Sandra's hands and kissed them.

"Would those who have been sustained please take your seats on the rostrum."

Luke turned to Sandra. "Not sure I want to stand yet. We may never be seated together as a family again."

Sandra put her arms around Luke and whispered in his ear, "I'll lead us to our seats."

They rose, kissed innocently and affectionately as a series of "aaahs" was heard among the throng; they hugged and waved farewell to the kids as Sandra piloted their ascent to the rostrum.

Luke placed, his arm around her waist. At their point of separation, they looked at each other and kissed to another round of "aaahs." Luke placed her hands to his face, then released his grasp. She kissed his cheek. Sandra stepped to her seat among the General Relief Society leaders. Luke paced to his among the Twelve. A bit sideways.

The prophet spoke. "Brothers and sisters, I believe we have witnessed love, holy and pure. Welcome, Sister Sandra, Apostle Luke, to your new home."

Luke became acutely aware that each of the three new Apostles were white, reared and educated in Utah. *Not well considered by the Brethren*. Dismayed to think his multi-racial children could be unjustly exploited.

Luke, twelfth of twelve in seniority within the Quorum. Fifteenth of fifteen in line to become the prophet. Each man white.

Who keeps score?

Ways and Means

*Progress is impossible without change, and those who cannot
change their minds cannot change anything.*

—George Bernard Shaw

SANDRA AND LUKE ADAPTED, forced to reacclimate to the dry
cold and heat as Utah desert dwellers. Across miles traveled, they
understood techniques to adapt for different climates and locations.
All current travels, with little exception, were Church sanctioned.

Phuong finished her softball years as an Academic All-
American. Luke triumphed. She attended graduate school at
Stanford, her mother's alma mater, as a molecular biologist and
earned a research medical doctorate (MD-PhD) as a geneticist
from Harvard. Phuong surpassed her parents with a reputation all
her own.

Jordan attended BYU–Hawaii, awarded a BA in journalistic
writing. An advocate for civil, gender, and LGBTQ rights. Jordan
expressed, first-hand, his experiences with these issues. He felt no
restraint in his spoken or written arguments despite high-profile
parents in the Mormon hierarchy. Out of the closet when his parents
became Church leaders, Jordan demonstrated a commitment to free
himself from societal bias created by religions and their dogmas.
Without a mention of Overlord, he exposed religious LGBTQ,
racial and gender bigotry. He pled for tolerance and compassion.
He rarely ventured from the Islands. Mr. Nguyen remained Jordan's

mentor. Jordan expressed happiness that a Black-Hawaiian led the free world.

Luke met challenges as an Apostle. He tried to maintain an impression of like-minded conformity with the First Presidency and Quorum of the Twelve. He was compelled to honor other General Authorities, Church officers, secretaries, and constituent staffs.

He felt constantly at odds. Consider the First Presidency and Quorum of the Twelve. Fifteen men (Roman Numerable I-XV). Luke started his service among them in his mid-forties as Apostle XV in hierarchy to become The Prophet. Most others were in their sixties, seventies, and eighties, with three in their nineties; many lingered with pre-1978 opinions of race, gender, homophobic inclinations—iron rod biases from which Church leadership seemed unwilling to release their grips.

Political, social, financial, organizational, and doctrinal battles beset the Twelve and First Presidency. Church members greatly unaware of these walled in battles and struggles for power. At times, they were bitter with consequences. Professional and personal friendships strained. Directional guidance was often required prior to open, public events. One member of the Twelve described another, "Apostle III is like trying to stage manage a gorilla."

Unwritten and unspoken contracts governed the Brethren. Rules invoked to maintain a unified body of ecclesiastical leaders whether headquartered in the Vatican or Temple Square. Behaviors among leaders seemed benign. Nonetheless, they clashed to influence Church policies, money, and the behavior and minds of Church members.

Luke counseled, "Common consent is rare between fifteen power-absorbed men who appear to be of the same mind to uphold God's will." He followed with, "Great minds think alike. Fools seldom differ." The Brethren chuckled. Heads nodded.

Weaker members of the Twelve became pawns for the Presidency. Rarely, if ever, are the gray-and-white-matter advantages of female brains utilized. Struggles among these men extended to national and international policies and negotiations. The prophet held all aces and royal flushes. After all, he outlived his rivals to govern the Church.

Our heroes unknowingly stirred waters. Sandra and Luke met for lunch on Temple Square as often as occasion allowed. For them, to converse with sightseers on the Square was enjoyable. Visitors recognized them and introduced themselves to initiate conversations. Discussions were welcomed. Names, dates, accurate records of topics, problems, and issues were recorded. They were known, parenthetically, as 'accessible General Authorities.' Sadly, assignments and travel schedules made their public appearances with guests on Temple Square too infrequent.

Sandra and Luke ate lunch in the Church Office Building cafeteria. Employees gathered near them. They engaged discussions and took part in conversations. Sandra removed her pantsuit jacket and threw a loose shawl over her long-sleeved blouse. Luke placed his hand under the shawl to scratch or rub her back and neck. A member of the Twelve, II of XV, observed the group and their interactions. He took exception with Luke's behavior.

He entered Luke's office late the same afternoon. "It is wrong to touch your wife as you did in the cafeteria or anywhere in public. Members of the Twelve are not to be familiar with spouses in public. She is to wear a dress."

"Were we in error? Sandra dresses professionally. I do not dare to direct Sandra in her apparel. Is there a printed dress policy? Guidelines for apostolic-spousal behavior? Did you bring a copy for me?" Honest inquiries from Luke.

"I did not care—you touched scandalously in the cafeteria. It is also wrong to kiss your wife during sessions of conference. It's not a proper example."

"I beg to differ. The 'aaahs' during conference, feedback from members, and complimentary words from the prophet—we behave righteously. I love Sandra. She is not my property."

"You are a young General Authority. A greenie. Be on guard at all times. Practice continuous decency in your behaviors. We demonstrate a proper example to the world."

"Am I not to touch Sandra when we're in public? Among Church groups?"

"Handholding is okay. Do not touch other body parts like scratching backs or necks. Your behavior is suggestive. Young people, members, will get the wrong idea. It could excite them toward sexual violations. Avoid the very appearance of evil. Your wife and you have never had children of your own. If so, you would know the dangers open familiarity has on youth."

Luke kept his poise. "With all due respect, I am called as a special witness of Jesus Christ. Sustained unanimously by you and everyone in the Church. I did not ask for this call. Did not ask to be schooled by you in propriety. I respect your seniority—but back-off. Be grateful Sandra isn't here. I'd need to stop her from ripping you apart."

"Don't be insolent with me. I'm old enough to be your father. You should receive my words with appreciation. Obey as counseled."

What a self-righteous, controlling buffoon, Luke thought. "Heavenly Father, I surmise, created the condition that prevented Sandra and me from producing children. We deeply wanted our own children, a family. We adopted. You did it the more fun, traditional way."

"I don't appreciate your words."

"I don't appreciate words of condescension. You require help." Luke feigned concern. "Do you need a counselor, dietician, exercise regimen? I have empathy for you. I'll assist toward your recovery."

"Apostle Luke, you are out of line."

"March to your own drumline. Know this: I love Sandra. I'll kiss, hold, and touch her as we are inclined to do. We'll never have sex in public places; never join the mile-high club. I know my duties … leave … fulfill your own."

Luke pointed for Apostle II to depart. "Good day."

Sandra and Luke later found themselves in the boardroom, once again, with the First Presidency. Luke prepared for reprimand then release. *I'll own the record for the quickest dismissal from the Twelve in Church history.*

"You have a strong voice, Luke," the prophet said, visibly uneasy addressing the issue. "Words were heard by others. Apostle II will be here to apologize for his comments. Words hurtful to Sandra.

Please, will the two of you," he motioned with his hands, "make amends with Apostle II?"

The First Presidency opened their hearts and expectations more deeply toward Luke's duties. The Brethren also deliberated more openly Sandra's role and desired outcomes for the Church amid heightened issues of gender and leadership, abuse in LDS homes, and lastly LGBTQ. Their words confirmed The Church needed exemplars with faith to improve behaviors of current-day saints. Sandra and Luke anticipated it being a dark day. Instead, their hearts grew with hope, particularly as to scientific truth regarding people throughout time and eternity. In short, **science requires greater inclusion amid matters of faith upon our behaviors**.

"Sandra, Luke, The Lord blessed you with wondrous gifts and called you to labor in this magnificent endeavor," the Prophet said. "Your public image gives members a greater vision of how we are to be seen in the world. Our people lack righteous models within our global community. Show 'em how it's done." Then counseled with a smile, "But, please, be heads up."

Apostle II entered and issued an apology. Amends were exchanged. Sandra and Luke departed.

"Doors are opening for Overlord," Luke whispered to Sandra as they exited the boardroom.

"They are." Sandra held his hand and clutched his arm. "Let's go to your office. I want to kiss you."

Every general conference, Sandra and Luke were reliably observed kissing each other—innocently—on the rostrum.

Sandra exuded confidence and demonstrated independent decision-making in her duties as a member of the Relief Society presidency. To complete all the Brethren assigned her to do, she notified the First Presidency that autonomy was necessary for completion of her tasks. "I cannot run to your office for your approval or disapproval each hour of each day. I will resolve problems with my intellectual and spiritual abilities. The Lord called me to organize, prepare, and engage this guidance for members. It includes models and materials with instructions. I do not require constant inspection from male, priesthood supervision. I am equal among the three of the First Presidency and the Twelve. We'll reason through our disputes. Got that?" Sandra winked.

Luke looked at the Brethren with a shrug. "What she said."

Sandra organized researchers, writers, clerical support, and artistic designers. A number of Sandra and Luke's staff followed them from Hawaii to Salt Lake. The impact of their power and skills were immediately observed by astute onlookers. The Consortium assisted.

A new day grew brighter for changes in obsolete habits and beliefs.

When Women Speak

It is not that women are really smaller-minded, weaker-minded, more timid and vacillating, but that whosoever, man or woman, lives always in a small, dark place, is always guarded, protected, directed and restrained, will become inevitably narrowed and weakened by it.

—Charlotte Perkins Gilman

THE GENERAL RELIEF SOCIETY Presidency selected Sandra as keynote speaker for the BYU Women's Conference. Her first return to campus since 1980. She was determined to impact her audience, not with words alone, but her image as well.

Sandra's hair allowed her to weave, part, fringe, braid and wear a number of creative styles. Each style kept hair from falling over her eyes or onto her face. Hands never touched uncooperative strands as she addressed an audience or cameras. Her makeup was tasteful and smart.

Vibrant and in her mid-forties, she retained the shape seen at BYU decades earlier. She modeled affordable wardrobes for LDS women to wear. Modest for church yet captivating. Sexy? Yes ... never distasteful.

Sandra created sites where women could purchase attractive, low-cost, most feminine clothing. Women and girls in the Church commonly wore fashions displayed by Sandra, including similar makeup uses and hairstyles. Sandra's appearances and behaviors aided LDS professional women.

Beyond image, Sandra knew that public address skills required her to challenge old-fashioned female submission to male priesthood authority. The words of the prophet encouraged her preparations, *The Church finds itself unbalanced. Our sisters need preparations not only to be mothers and wives, but also while being paid incomes to support families ... with power and authority over men.*

She advised herself, *Pilot this plane like it's a fighter. My allied sisters and ladies must behave competently in a male dominated world, especially as leaders and teachers within our church. My speech must safely land this plane on a runway and be hangered where men thought women would never fly.*

Sandra addressed 1,200 women in the de Jong Concert Hall of the Harris Fine Arts Center; dressed in a dark-gray, tie-neck collar, knee-length, three-quarter-sleeve pencil dress with dark pantyhose and complimentary black high-heels. Her topic: **Latter-day Saint Women in the Twenty-First Century**. She controlled her independent thoughts. However, she suggested aspects of deviation while maintaining Church standards of patriarchal governance. *After all, do the Brethren really know best what women must do? Behave or dress?*

During the Q&A, a woman indicated an element of repulsion. "My husband never thinks of anything but sex."

Sandra's self-imposed safeguards crumbled, slightly. She responded, "Would you prefer he think more of murder? Abandonment? Suicide? Or adultery? Possible abuse?"

"Well, uh, I thought you'd say thinking of sex is wrong."

"You thought incorrectly. Why? Do you believe thoughts of sex are immoral?" Sandra asked.

"Sexual thoughts are impure."

Annoyed, Sandra asked, "Who said that? It's not true."

"We have been instructed not to covet another's possession—a wife. Sexual thoughts should never overtake spiritual devotion."

Mark Merkley

"*Covet* and *sexual thoughts* are not the same. Hear me … clearly. I covet Luke, my husband, in my sexual and spiritual considerations. Have you? I mean, not Luke, but your own husband?" Some of the women gasped.

"That's too personal for you to ask," another woman responded.

"I hope you **each** covet your husbands, and do so often. It would make them feel valued and special. That your eyes and heart desire him. That you long for him, shall we say, sexually? I confess to all who may hear my voice, I have consistent, ongoing sexual thoughts with Luke. A few are in my mind even now." Sandra smiled as her eyes flitted toward the balcony. Concluded with a sigh and a gratified smile.

Women in the hall made unsettled movements. A few smiled in curious anticipation as to what Sandra may next say. "Luke is a gifted athlete," she said. Giggled pleasantly.

"Ladies, your attention, please." She waved her hands to gather them to her. "I am a member of the General Relief Society Presidency. I'm married to an Apostle, a member of the Twelve. This speech presentation will be recorded and issued to all who wish to read or hear it. Sexual behavior is a wonderful pastime. It must neither be abused, nor maligned.

"Sex is not impure," Sandra continued. "It is the most intimate of all tactile behaviors. The greatest spiritual experience in which anyone will engage. Men want to pleasure women. Ladies, teach them. Show them what you need. Enjoy. Don't say, 'He holds the priesthood. He should know my needs in all things.'

"Ladies, be a helpmeet. Guide your man in righteous behaviors. Don't expect men to know your desires spiritually, sexually, financially, or as a parent. Speak, listen, and engage with one another toward more gratified performances and acts of kindness to make families happy. Such discussions are enlightening and highly pleasurable. Encourage them to openly express themselves without your criticisms or self-imposed biases.

"Lastly, each partner in marriage is equal. Neither is above the other. Remove yourselves from televisions or computers. Men appreciate carnal discussions while seated in a porch swing outside your home. Share an intimate sunrise or sunset conversation together.

"When with your husbands, be honest and direct. Share what is enjoyable, possibly expected. Tell them what hurts, physically and emotionally, in your sexual encounters, as well as any or all matters. Encourage rather than state harsh, critical, or bitter comments. Attempt to communicate meaning and understanding with your expressions. In practice, have safeguards ending unwanted behaviors and emotions. I will provide phone numbers for your assistance, if needed. Excellent counselors are available. They needn't be LDS to act as adequate guides or therapists.

"Yes, sex is engaged to create children and families," Sandra continued. "However, that alone is not the sole purpose of intimacy. As married couples, make the most of physical affection within bedtime play.

"A worthwhile marital sexual relationship is beneficial for everyone, everywhere you go. Sex impacts spiritual and interpersonal growth between spouses. Your interpersonal relationships among in-laws will improve, or as Luke would say, 'your outlaws,' colleagues at work, associates at school, your friends, and your children. Let your eternal companion know he is needed, enjoyed and loved by you. But only should your mind and heart say it is so."

Hands rose throughout the audience.

"Speak. I do not enjoy conversations with hands. Respect others seated in the concert hall." Sandra waited to hear what these women needed to express.

The first voice challenged, "When you were called, sustained... frankly, I was stunned. I've read parts of your books. Heard you speak on television for years. I thought, yeah, you're a Mormon. No way the Church will tolerate your independent feminist thoughts and feelings toward gender equality. Can we expect this while you are in this position? Did the First Presidency know you would say these words?"

"Let me ask ... as women, what do you want from God, the Church, the Brethren, or me? Which prayers do you wish to have answered?" Sandra paused. In her mind, she wanted to hear their views. She narrowed her eyes, like Phuong, just to see which of these women would courageously speak. She stared into their souls. Tested their mettle.

"I want more," a second voice said.

"More of what?" Sandra pushed back.

The answer came from a third woman. "Recognition."

"Power. I'll even say authority," a fourth woman added.

"Support. Who or how will our own interests, or my personal interests, be protected? Encouraged?" The fifth.

"Equality. For all women." The sixth.

"We already have that." The seventh.

"No, we don't." The eighth.

"This is not our way. Obedience is the first law of heaven." The ninth.

"Motherhood, homebuilding, babies." The tenth.

"Understanding. Do the Brethren honestly receive revelation from Heavenly Father as to the female perspective?" The eleventh. "Who reports our prayers to the Brethren?"

"Self-reliance. Less Old Testament scriptures. More survival instruction for current times." The twelfth.

"I want a temple marriage." The thirteenth.

"To be loved by my husband and children." The fourteenth.

"A job. Sufficient income for my family." The fifteenth.

"To pay a full tithe and at the same time afford my child's diabetic supplies and healthcare." The sixteenth.

"Happiness. I feel as if I'm alone. I am an obedient person." The seventeenth.

"What do I do with my teenager who is lesbian? I fear suicide." The eighteenth.

"My husband says he's gay." The nineteenth.

"Those problems go away, or never happen, when you pay a full tithe, attend church meetings—" The twentieth.

"I attend meetings … pay tithes … You self-righteous—" Fourteen through nineteen reproved.

"My bishop, who is also my husband, hits me." The twenty-first.

"There's abuse in our family." The twenty-second.

"My nineteen-year-old missionary was sent home. His next-door girlfriend carries our grandchild." The twenty-third.

"In the eyes of the Church, can you be a respected mother and pursue a professional career?" The twenty-fourth.

"I've followed the gospel plan in every way. Now my husband wants to join a polygamous group. What is wrong with me? My husband?" The twenty-fifth.

"I'm a single, working mother. Daycare is costly. Every LDS meetinghouse has a nursery and a kitchen. Please, I need help." The twenty-sixth.

"I've been falsely accused. What can I do?" The twenty-seventh.

"My husband is disabled from a fall he suffered and we have three children—seven, ten and thirteen years. His disability payments end in six months. I won't have my associates degree until a year from now. We paid a full tithe until a year ago. What choices do I—we have? The Church has billions of dollars in the storehouse." The twenty-eighth.

"I am Black and Latino, but feel second-class. Sandra, what do you say to your children?" The twenty-ninth.

Sandra raised her hands among the hundreds who wished to speak. "Please. Hear me. Write your thoughts and experiences. I want your names, a phone number, an email address if you have one. Print clearly. The Brethren need us. More than ever. Allow me to coordinate and lead this cause." She motioned for paper and pencils to be distributed.

"Finally, sexiness and body shape have a correlation with confidence. Women who speak with self-reliant voices are sexy. Intensely admired. Can I get an amen?" Sandra raised a thumb above her head, then closed into a fist.

A few amens were shouted. Not like those heard at Calvary Baptist Church. Mormons are too subdued and tentative. Yet, more was heard from these women than Sandra thought she'd hear. She admired their grit ... courage.

Women in the concert hall knew this was the Sandra they expected. A skilled pilot to lead them. No longer landing planes short of the runway. A lion to lead sheep. An uncommon leader, with uncommon gifts, expected to produce uncommon results. Sandra listened to each woman speak. Met privately, stood yards apart on the large stage of the theater to hear brief, personal disclosures. Each hoped Sandra, this woman who for years so often seen in media productions, whose books and articles they read, might have an alternative perspective. An influence upon the Brethren and the Church for their families and relationships.

An hour after the Q&A session should have ended, Luke walked onto the stage still crowded with women who clamored to speak with Sandra. Some clapped and others shouted when they saw him. Many expressed thanks and appreciation. He shared words with the women waiting on the stage. He finally reached Sandra and held her hand. Those who remained carried books for Sandra's signature. Luke said, "I need to take Sandra home."

Three women pointed. "She covets you," said one. Smiles were seen; giggles heard.

Luke responded, "I covet her *assets*, greatly. Please, don't tell the prophet."

Whap! Sandra let Luke have it.

Laughter splashed from the women; a few covered their mouths. Never before did general officers of the Church express openly such earthy, PG-13 behavior.

"I love it when Sandra does that to me," he said amid continued laughs.

A round, but attractive, mid-thirty-something-year-old asked, "Are the kisses you give each other at general conference for real?"

Sandra and Luke looked at each other, kissed, and embraced. While they kissed, Sandra curled her ankle behind Luke's calf and a hand gripped his hair. They demonstrated their love to be genuine. No faked words or behavior. When they finished, Sandra held Luke's face. "I love you," she said.

"Hold me tight, Sandra. Without you, I'll fall on me arse."

From that anecdotal event until their final act, the influence of Sandra and Luke became established as activists, lovers, and committed Church members. Relevant advocates for purposes among Church members. These imperfect, likable heroes advanced to the day they would grant the world their compassion for change with reasoned tolerance. They kissed publicly like eternal lovers— their true selves.

The Brethren utilized Sandra's supposed gender and intellect, with her illustrious character, to promote themselves without prejudice. She enjoyed leadership, conveying relief and promoting just causes that assisted uncommon characters. She was a worthy confidant who inspired women and led men in unexpected, innovative ways.

Discussions Among the Brethren

To be humane, we must ever be ready to pronounce that wise,
ingenious and modest statement "I do not know."

—Galileo Galilei

THE TWELVE MET TWICE each week in the expansive Quorum of the Twelve conference room in the Church Administration Building. The First Presidency also attended the mandatory gatherings. Few were not mandatory. Luke called them bull sessions. Fifteen potent bulls who rarely missed a single event.

Abundant space on a large, round table allowed for books, notepads, and a personal computer for each of the fifteen participants, plus guests. Distance was equally spaced so they could see and speak comfortably with one another.

The purpose for these sessions deeply extensive. To assign missions, determine distribution of funds, discuss current events, consider politics, analysis of Church audits, bestowed callings, clarification of gospel doctrines, deliberation of policies and procedures that included money, investments and financial disbursements. Negotiations were impassioned. Issues, at times, angrily argued. Profanities routinely heard, though discouraged. Political partisanship and social biases each clearly exposed.

Coalitions within the Brethren easily observed. Blocs of power were established within this august membership of men.

Additional people could be invited to bull sessions—like the Presiding Bishopric, members of the Seventy, and auxiliary officers, including Church accountants or architects. The sessions lacked professional inclusion. Amid deliberations, Luke would say, "We need correct numbers. A statistician. Sociologist. Psychiatrist. Researchers. Scientists. Let's give the U of U Medical School a call. Let's ask someone who knows—a physicist, imam, etymologist, rabbi, hygienist, biblical scholar ..."

Rarely were woman invited or a female perspective expressed.

In one exchange Luke boldly demanded, "Let's ask God. We claim two-way conversations with Him. He knows everything, including the future. Let's ask Heavenly Father or Jesus. Get a definitive answer. Catch up on what He knows, what I—we—don't know."

The Brethren looked incredulously at Luke in embarrassed silence.

"We assert great claims like access to the mouth of God to hear His words or His ear to seek His wisdom and direction," Luke innocently, boldly claimed. "We ask, 'Please, come down from Mt. Sinai or Park City with the answer.' With His holy answers we can report, 'So be it. It's God's word.'"

"It doesn't happen quite that way," Apostle IV waved off.

"Thank you. You've stated my point." Luke sighed. "Members of the Church know it too. Have we declared an untruth to our members? To the world? We claim the prophet is like Moses. That he converses interpersonally with Heavenly Father and Jesus Christ. Does he or does he not? Like members and other onlookers with questions, I am merely curious. We appear dishonest. Especially when innocent children say '**I know**' to dogmas of gospel truths they cannot possibly understand."

Silence answered Luke's inquisition.

"Brethren, please understand me. I have faith that Heavenly Father and Jesus live, but I cannot say I have seen either of them. I possess a testimony of the truthfulness of the Church. In spite of this, we live in the twenty-first century, not in an agrarian society of 1830 upstate New York. Our message and image need revision. We are losing members, not to mention influence, status, and prestige. Conversions are down in the United States. Retention of converts is less than fifty percent. The birthrate of members in Utah is the lowest it has ever been. Church membership is growing slower than the Earth's population.[11] We are in decline. Numbers do not lie. We have problems that need resolving."

The prophet stated to Luke and the Brethren, "I know Joseph saw and spoke with the Father and the Son."

"President, if Joseph Smith were alive—among us today with claims he received visits from an angel who once inhabited ancient America, used seer stones to translate golden plates, and conversed with God the Father and Jesus Christ in a grove of trees—he would be challenged, probably institutionalized."

"We have the Book of Mormon to testify of Joseph Smith's claims," the prophet countered.

"Yes, we do. That is why the Church must be prepared for challenges and arguments. Logicians are bright, persuasive. Secret meetings can no longer be hidden. The Book of Mormon and other scriptures should be sustained as spiritual creations. They are not literal or historic. Our young people and members are confronted with reasoned information." Luke ended his comments with research from BYU.[12]

The most recently called member of the Twelve approached Luke at his office door when the bull session ended. "I never realized discussions among the Twelve and First Presidency are so passionate, open, and greatly diverse. I believed it would be reverent,

---

[11] Peruse search sites regarding LDS growth compared to world population growth.

[12] Rachel Cope and J. Spencer Fluhman, "Keeping the Faith," *BYU Magazine*, Spring 2014. Cope and Fluhman write that a crisis of faith has increased with use of the internet, "The information explosion has exposed Latter-day Saints to a wider range of information about their faith and past"—including, among others, polygamy, women and the priesthood, sexual orientation/behavior, race and priesthood restriction before 1978, and translations of the Book of Mormon and Book of Abraham.

calm, more peaceful. Greater unity. Thinking alike; a unified body. I didn't expect what I saw and heard. Profanity?"

"Brother Brigham, George Q. and others profaned, more frequently than J. Golden," Luke said, snickering. "None of 'em could out-swear my grandmother." Luke, and newest Apostle XV laughed aloud.

"Don't be concerned." Luke patted his shoulder. Then added, "Sound decisions ought to be made. That happens when opposing views are allowed expression. — George Patton was a great general because he understood, 'If everyone is thinking alike, then somebody isn't thinking.' Patton didn't surround himself with yes men at the war table. That's what Hitler and all small leaders want—agreement and conformity. Should we as a group of leaders agree without opposition, the Church will ruin itself. We'll crash airplanes short of runways.

"Everyone should be aware that to be of one mind, thinking alike, is dangerous. It invites false agreement. What's needed? Unique, uncommon reasoning and courage to speak. – Critics will say feminists, intellectuals, and homosexuals are great enemies of the Church. They are, in fact, our best friends. Our means for salvation."

"Remarkable," Apostle XV mused.

"Never be afraid to state your opinions or share your knowledge. Express 'opposition in all things.' Best wishes, always." Luke winked at XV. "There's an adage that floats around this building. It says, 'You'll never know how wrong you've been as an Apostle until a new President is ordained.' It suggests verification that the Lord's will resides in the man who outlives the bulls. Few Apostles are remembered. Church Presidents are God-like."

Luke gave the Vulcan symbol with his right hand. "As Spock would say, 'Live long and prosper.'"

"Peace and long life," Apostle XV responded, doing his best to make the Vulcan hand gesture.

"Don't die too soon," Luke grinned. The two men laughed, shook hands with a hug, then parted ways. "Gotta run. I need to drop Kisses into Sandra's mailbox." Luke rushed away. "I could go to jail just to do what is right." Luke patted the Suit who chuckled as he passed.

Luke asked the First Presidency for Sandra to attend bull sessions. "She is a General Auxiliary officer," he argued. "Her leadership contributions and feminine viewpoint will add much to the decisions made by the Brethren." With that, Sandra became an active discussant with the Twelve and First Presidency. Her intelligence and spiritual power were far too valuable for God's anointed to have sit idle.

Sandra sat with Luke in all sessions. They became customary fixtures as proficient participants throughout years of discussions with the Twelve and First Presidency. She possessed decades of experience with men in academic, business, and scientific negotiations to resolve issues. Never intimidated by powerful men. She knew the source of power. It was not the priesthood or the physical makeup of men. She exhibited intelligence, logic, and reason with verbal skill. Luke, her greatest advocate.

Overlord now activated with two persuasive voices.

"Our purpose is to bring to pass the immortality and eternal life of man," Apostle III said. "That is done by producing families. A woman's primary duty is to bear and nurture children in the light of the restored gospel. A man must provide the seed and financial support for the family with the labor of his hands."

Luke thought, *His statement succinctly abridges generations of Mormon dogmatic bias and slavery – BS.* "You speak words reminiscent of 1843 Nauvoo," Luke countered. "We live in the twenty-first century with social, gender, racial issues and LGBTQ biases."

"Apostle Luke, how will you solve the issue of homosexuals if you and Sandra become President?" Apostle VI asked.

"Allow me," Sandra said. "Our decisions will come through the people, our own members. We no longer have home or visiting teachers, MIA, or other outdated customs. Our members know we've engaged inept behaviors with flawed dogmas and practices from our past. Particularly Blacks and the priesthood."

"Have you read Sandra's conclusions from ongoing research, and data? Usable numbers from years of inquiry?" Luke questioned. "Sandra has structured her questionnaires well. We must listen-in to hear the prayers of members. Problems they're asking God the Father to resolve. We are to enact God's will. It is our duty to listen, investigate and reason answers our member's prayers wish to have resolved."

"Jesus and the Prophet Joseph were progressive thinkers in their spiritual quests. Not keep it safe and barricaded. As Luke says, 'We ain't in Kansas or Nauvoo,'" Sandra added. "Look to the future. Lead with our eyes forward, not riveted to past biases."

"The majority among the fifteen Brethren (I–XV) agree with me," Luke said. "I am currently five of fifteen. I have four funerals ahead of me if the Lord decides to initiate changes to 'The Family: A Proclamation to the World.'"

"Apostle Luke, do you belittle us with your words?" the prophet asked.

"No, President," Luke explained. "The Proclamation was issued in 1995. The human genome was mapped eight years later. Since that time, geneticists have published dozens of research studies that explain sexual behaviors associated with genetic variants discovered in the genome. Phuong took part in these studies and identifying markers."

"There is no gay gene," Apostle II said, next in line to become the prophet.

"Correct," Luke affirmed. "Likely no such single marker will be discovered. Nevertheless, the genome, like God, is mysterious. Consider Down syndrome. Uncommon but easily identified. These people are given full fellowship in the Church. Everyone, members included, possess genetic factors, called variants, that affect behaviors. Sexual behaviors included.[13] Multiple genes, not one, play their roles. It makes some people, along with other factors, LGBTQ. Those with these markers are denied full fellowship in the Church and suffer indignities of social bias and bigotry. Bullied by our dogmas. LGBTQ people who are members of the Church, do not select their genetic makeup. Is that Christlike inclusion? Okay for one but not another?"

The Brethren were stone silent.

"Our silence is extraordinarily loud. We need a revelation," Luke stressed.

Sandra interrupted the stillness. "There is no gene for breast or ovarian cancer. Genetic indicators and variants do exist. BRCA1 and BRCA2 are genetic markers that inform women of the probabilities, lesser or greater, that they may contract ovarian or breast cancer.[14] These people can receive and undergo preventative care and treatment for these cancers.

"Like skin color, ethnicity, gender, or cancer, the human genome will trigger sexual behaviors in humans. It is not regulated by spiritual or scriptural laws or text. Science is, at times, difficult to digest, is it not? None of us in this room will argue our own heterosexual genetic urges. You cannot cure LGBTQ genetic codes with fasting and prayer or aversion therapy. The only cure is acceptance. No exclusions. Simply too many genes to say one among billions makes a person LGBTQ."

"You compare apples to oranges, Sister Sandra," Apostle II concluded. "Breast cancer and homosexuality are not the same."

"Correct, they are not," Sandra said. "Our use of reason is the issue. Why do we, and other religions, segregate people as spiritually condemned solely on DNA? As leaders of this Church, we admit individuals do not choose their DNA sequencing, any genetic behavior, including intellectual, or athletic skill. You can't

---

[13] Sandra Reardon, "Multiple new genes have been linked to same-gender sexual behavior, once again ruling out a single 'gay gene,' Associated Press, August 29, 2019.

[14] Mary-Claire King, professor of genome sciences and medicine, University of Washington, Seattle, discoverer of BRCA1 and BRCA2 genetic markers.

coach height, speed, or ability. Either you have it, or you don't.[15] No one chooses to have same-gender attractions."

"Okay. My point," Apostle II argued. "It is a mutation. It is not part of the natural order of families. A man and woman are to raise children. You have a choice as to your behavior. People cannot … must not act on improper urges."

"How well would each of us seated here behave if told never to act on our heterosexual genetic urges? How many members have illegitimate relationships and unwanted pregnancies acting on their heterosexual genetic urges?" Sandra asked. "At what age did each of us consciously decide to behave as heterosexuals? Got that? – It's already built within us—genetically."

The silence in the room shouted again.

"Multiplying and replenishing is a messy activity. Is it not? Consider this Apostle II, *mutation* is a genetic term," Sandra explained. "It means alteration, transformation, or as Church doctrines state, **transfiguration**. A thousand generations of genetic changes have modified/transfigured the way people look and behave. None of us today look like our ancestors did 200,000 years ago. We've **transfigured** or **evolved**. We'll look and behave differently 200,000 years in the future."

"There is a syndrome in God's DNA," Luke introduced to the Brethren. "It's called 46XY androgen insensitivity. A person with this genetic syndrome looks and behaves like a woman but is genetically male. It's rare. Generally, only one in 20,000 people are born this way. Almost the same rate as natural redheads.[16] What would you do as a bishop or stake president if a person with the 46XY syndrome presented himself-herself to you? Would you ordain that person to the priesthood or send him-her to Young Women and Relief Society?

---

[15] McKay Coppins "Love One Another: A Discussion on Same-Sex Attraction," *Buzzfeed News*, December 6, 2012; McKay Coppins, "The Most American Religion," *The Atlantic*, January/February 2021; Mormonandgay.lds.org

[16] melanocortin-1 receptor (MC1R) gene; 1-2% of the global population

Apostles III, VI, and IX confirmed from their computers the accuracy of the information shared by Sandra and Luke. Apostle VIII stated, "Dr. Phuong is one LDS cited professional. Do we have any BYU molecular biologists researching the human genome? Same-gender sexual behaviors?"

"Brethren, there are members of our Church with these genetic variants. Transfigured in the womb from males into females," Luke explained. "They love the restored gospel of Jesus Christ. Reason with me. All the letters of LGBTQ are entitled to receive every blessing and ordinance of the gospel. To create their own families **for time and all eternity**. Temple marriage."

A handful of Brethren spoke: "Apostle Luke, you are mad."

"It's not the Lord's way."

"What of children? Nuclear families?"

"Man, woman; husband, wife."

Luke raised his hands to settle everyone. "I understand. Brethren, we know that God's DNA is our own. That DNA doesn't always hit on all cylinders as we believe it should, whether it results in Down syndrome, cystic fibrosis, hermaphrodites, or genetic variants that affect sexual behaviors. There are no Book of Mormon, biblical, or latter-day scriptures to resolve these issues. Moses, Isaiah, Peter, Muhammed, Alma, Joseph Smith, or Brigham Young knew zilch, nothing, regarding quantum mechanics, an expanding universe, tectonic plates, or the human genome. Use our enlightenment. It's our time. We need to act! Sandra and I have done our best to explain it. We can't understand it for you.

"Our Church demands that science and spiritual intelligence are united," Luke pled. "Let's reason it. 'Choose the right when a choice is placed before you.'" Luke crooned the well-known LDS hymn. "The right is better than the left." He chuckled.

"How?" the prophet asked.

Sandra leaned forward and motioned to gather the men into her arms. "The Church sits on billions of dollars. At the same time, we counsel poverty-stricken families to pay a full tithe. There is a better balance to achieve. Far more we can do for those who are alive and desperately need God's care. Money paid to redeem the dead don't need it." Sandra passed binders to the Brethren.

"These pages include conclusions from ongoing research with recommendations and dollar allocations. Members will praise each of us seated here for our vision to resolve problems. Women in the Church, particularly, will acknowledge that the Lord heard and answered their prayers—I encourage altruism. Let's answer prayers by solving problems.

"Whenever a man from this group speaks with Heavenly Father, let me know what He says to you," Sandra continued. "He's already spoken to me. I don't need a vision, revelation, or a late-night visit from Moroni. I know what to do. It is inclusion, with equality, full fellowship for each person. All religions—Catholic, Judaic, Hindi, Christian, Islamic—adhere to archaic dogmas. Righteous change and progression occur when spiritual leaders think and discover problems, then resolve problems in real time. Today! As Luke suggests, do what is right. It's our future. Lead well. To save people, include them equally—all who appear uncommon to the gospel."

"It won't be today." The prophet waved his hands to conclude the discussion. "We are to reason longer. Our decisions require perfection."

"President, Sandra is a tremendous prophetess, seer, and revelator," Luke said. "Such women existed in biblical days. She is a leader superior to those of us in this room to make decisions. Fifteen men acting single-mindedly is myth. How do we manage our agreement?

"The Church cannot encourage legislation to ensure LGBTQ equality while simultaneously using religious freedom to spiritually segregate our LGBTQ members participation from temple ordinances or other shared activities.[17] Our doctrines, cultural practices are invalid. President, you see where our planes are landing—well short of the runway. Amen," Luke warned.

A few of the Brethren chuckled at Luke's words. Amens were heard. A closing prayer was offered. The Apostle who offered the prayer petitioned the Lord, "Please, dear Father, grant us the determination to understand the words discussed today. Let

---

[17] Spencer Burt – Latter-day Saint Church reaffirms support for legislation to ensure LGBTQ equality and religious freedom. Posted Feb. 27, 2021

us do what is right for all seeking blessings in our temples and homes. Keep our planes aloft. Land them safely, before our fuel is exhausted."

As they departed, several brethren approached Sandra. They smiled, exchanged hugs, and extended best wishes. They behaved amiably and respectfully toward this unique, astonishing female—or a person they supposed as female. One day, as they remembered Sandra and Luke's words, the Brethren **may** understand.

How unfortunate to listen with less than three-dimensional ears and thinking. Sandra, a lion amid bulls, leading flocks of sheep.

A poll conducted by *City Weekly* asked, "Which of the living Apostles would you most like to see become the prophet?" Sandra received an impressive 48 percent of the responses, her name written-in.

Luke made a point or two about the poll in one bull session. "Sandra is equally qualified, as much as any man here, to lead the Church. Why is gender a factor as to anyone's capacity to competently lead a business organization, government, or religion? Who will become the first latter-day prophetess in The Church of Jesus Christ of Latter-day Saints?"

Tensions increased. Apostle XI blasted, "Liberals will ruin this country. The Church must fight them."

"Fight? How? Clubs? Pistols? My hell, is that what you meant?" Luke asked. Visibly irritated. "A liberal promotes individual rights, democracy, and civil liberties. Will that ruin America?"

"You like to swear, Apostle Luke. I've heard your wife speak. A liberal," Apostle XI taunted.

"Luke speaks of a moral philosophy based on liberty and consent of the governed," Apostle VIII informed. "My computer states it right here. 'Liberalism is a political and moral philosophy based on **liberty, consent of the governed**, and **equality**.' Each person is equal before the law."

"What Sister Sandra and Apostle Luke have shared with us over the years is accurate. I've found several sources on my laptop confirming comments and definitions regarding their knowledge of these issues. How do you define *liberal*?" Apostle IV asked XI.

"Socialist, communist, government pays for everything. Forces people to change. Accepts homosexuals in society," Apostle XI replied. "If allowed to lead the Church, liberals will allow gay people to marry in our temples. Vile people who oppose male and female marriages. Families."

Sandra gripped Luke's wrist.

Luke calmly declared, "You have some gift to know how Sandra, or liberals, would lead. I suggest you never speak toward her decisions and leadership. As you know, Sandra and I, like gay men, cannot create our own babies. We adopted to become a family just as two gay men would do." Luke said casually, "Sandra and I are two men who reared our children."

"It's not the same," Apostle XI declared.

"It is exactly the same. You don't understand what you refuse to see," Luke forcefully said. He pointed at the Apostle and thundered his fist to the table.

Disaffection

Children begin by loving their parents; after a time, they judge them; rarely, if ever, do they forgive them.

—Oscar Wilde

JORDAN ASKED TO VISIT Sandra and Luke in Salt Lake. They scheduled to see a Triple-A baseball game. During this game, Jordan wished to disclose a path that would impact the lives of our heroes.

Jordan saw Luke seated two rows from the field, near third base. He took a deep breath and stepped toward his father. *This will be significant.* "Hi, Dad."

Luke jumped to his feet, opened his arms, and gave Jordan a bear hug. "We don't do this enough. I wish we all lived closer to each other." Luke recounted the years and experiences shared with Jordan. Teaching moments were memorable and cherished. More than father and son. Best friends.

"Too bad the Church isn't headquartered in San Francisco," Jordan lamented. "We'd be watching the Giants."

"Your mother is finishing business at Temple Square. This Church interferes with family far too much—at least our family."

"Dad, I miss what we were in Hawaii. You've made waves, but I miss the good days we had. I think Phuong does too. Better days are ahead, maybe."

Jordan expressed a hope Luke knew would never occur. A call as an Apostle is a commitment until death. What was good from the past could not return.

Jordan needed to confront his mentors.

"Dad, read this. I need your feedback." He handed Luke a single sheet of paper, a formal business letter addressed to the First Presidency. Jordan requested his name be removed from Church records and demanded that no court be convened, Church representatives never approach him, no attempts be enacted to persuade him to remain a member, and that his decision never be made public in ward, stake, or area meetings.

Luke finished, *Well-written letter. Impressive. Especially for a man who should be a returned missionary.*

Luke looked at Jordan. "Are you certain this is what you want?"

"No question, Dad. There is good in the Church. But the only true church? Please."

"You are free to make your own decisions. You're my favored son."

"I'm your only son," Jordan said, chuckling.

"Jordan, if you don't believe the Church is true, walk away. Why have your name removed?"

"I don't want my name associated with a church that treats homosexuals like Mormons do."

Jordan was distinctly eloquent. Luke felt shamed and simultaneously inspired, hopeful. "You are a better person than I, Jordan."

"The Church and its doctrines do not balance with social and scientific discovery. Ignorance keeps people from light. You're part of it. You want Church members to remain ignorant. Have you read this?" Jordan handed Luke papers; a dozen thick. Luke recognized the name Elder Mark E. Petersen. The title page read, "Race Problems—As They Affect The Church."[18]

---

[18] University of Utah Libraries, Special Collections. Collection number: Ms0376 special Collections, J. Willard Marriott Library, University of Utah 295 South 1500 East, Salt Lake City, UT 84112-0860, special@ library.utah.edu Speech delivered at Brigham Young University by Apostle Mark E. Petersen, August 27, 1954.

"I have read it, Jordan. The words it contains are offensive. It's part of a sad era in our history. An indicator of how far the Church has advanced. You know that families like our own, with deeper shades of color, are now included."

"The Church took its time. Spoken in 1954 at BYU," Jordan explained. "I get that people and Church leadership were bigoted, likely racist, in those days, but has the Church apologized for its past misdeeds? Crimes of thoughtless offenses toward Phuong, me? Petersen described Asians as 'Chinamen ... dark-skinned with all of the handicaps of that race to have little opportunity.' Dad, Petersen said Book of Mormon Lamanites 'shall become a white and delightsome people.' Yet he knew of 'no scripture that would remove the curse from the Negro.'

"You're an Apostle, Dad. Why assist the Church when it hasn't learned from its past? They treat LGBTQ people like Petersen spoke of Black-Africans and Asians back when he proclaimed this crap." Jordan flailed the pages at his father. "Petersen defended *segregation*, used the word more than two dozen times. Claimed segregation is an act of mercy toward people of color, including Polynesians and fellow Hawaiians. In 1978, a revelation given to Spencer Kimball includes people of color equally in the Church, making possible interracial marriages in temples, yet turns its powers of bias, bigotry, and segregation toward LGBTQ people. Mom. Me. Some act of mercy, huh? Kimball and Petersen were assigned the task to cure gays in the Church."[19]

Luke sat silently. He felt minimized, vulnerable, and terribly inadequate. He reflected how little his efforts for Overlord's success had been achieved. *Social, racial, gender issues are woeful in the Church. Have my acts improved the Church? For Sandra, Phuong, or Jordan?*

"I am dedicated to Overlord," Jordan confirmed. "But my journey will differ from yours."

---

[19] Apostles Spencer W. Kimball and Mark E. Petersen published a pamphlet, *Hope for Transgressors* (1970) Advocated techniques to remedy homosexuals from their grievous behaviors.

They heard Sandra's voice as she came down the aisle. "Hello. Missed much? How are the two most handsome men I know?"

Jordan turned, greeted his mother, and gave her a hug.

Luke, wounded, put on his game face. He smiled but was in need of Sandra's assistance. He hugged Sandra and whispered, "Just had the shinola kicked out of me."

"What?" Sandra awaited a reply.

Luke guided Sandra to her seat. "Jordan has a letter for you to read."

Baseball was played on the field. The real game clashed in the seats.

Sandra read the letter. "Well done. What's the issue?"

"Jordan, show her the other pages," Luke said.

"Mom, have you read this presentation by Apostle Mark Petersen?" Jordan handed her the pages. "It slams everything that I am, Asian and Black. Has the Church apologized?"

She recognized the document. "Petersen was racist. Clearly no three-dimensional skills."

"That's my point. Racism has been diverted toward us. LGBTQ is the object of the Church's bias. Religion is the bully. Oppression dumped on us. They believe we control the nature of what we are. You hide, Mom. I'm exposed. My skin and sexual nature."

Sandra felt his blows. "Jordan, I see your reasoning. Is this why you wish to have your name removed from Church membership?"

"As I told Dad, I don't want my name associated with a church who treats LGBTQ people as the LDS Church does. Have they ever issued an apology to people of color? Improved race relations? Their policies are still wrong."

"Have Catholics apologized for the purges, inquisitions, and crusades? Copernicus? Any of their abuses? Galileo wasn't absolved until 1992. Don't expect it," Sandra fired point-blank.

"When were you and Dad going to let Phuong and me know how deeply this garbage was so blatantly preached in our Church?"

"Okay. I apologize," Sandra answered. "It shouldn't surprise you that Lincoln freed slaves in America, but was a bigoted man. Told darky jokes, as they were called. Likely all Negro people would have been repatriated to Africa or into the Caribbean had Lincoln not been assassinated."

"Do Church members really care for racial equality and fairness?" Jordan asked. "Or do they just say the words since the 1978 revelation? Racism is rooted in this Church. Look how literally white LDS leadership is among the First Presidency, Twelve, elsewhere … everything in it."

"Jordan, revelation is painstaking. It arrives as fast as it can be understood and takes time. Like evolution, whether it is biology, social, economic—any kind of change. Homophobia and racism are pervasive and unconscious among all people, Mormons included," Luke explained.

"Bullshit, Dad. Phuong and I read Frederick Douglass. You and Mom read the books with us. We learned about slavery. Racism was—is—known. God knows. Joseph Smith ought to have known better. A short conversation between Heavenly Father and the Prophet Joseph or Brother Brigham could have brought the Church out of the literal dark ages sooner than 1978. The Church now points its bony white fingers at LGBTQ people—Mom and me."

"Jordan, your reasoning and arguments have value," Sandra said. "Your father and I battle Church authority to speak our considerations openly."

"Hell, Dad, you taught Phuong and me to think. This is wrong. Terribly wrong. You're an Apostle. A big shot with Mormons. Your job is to be a personal witness of Jesus. When did you meet Him? What does He look like? His skin color? Never married, that we're aware. Gay?"

Luke sat stone-cold silent. Sandra tried to intervene but was shushed by Jordan. "Dad, you know as well as I, if Jesus truly existed, knowing what we know today, He would have looked like me. So dark, Mark Petersen would never have approved. Is Jesus a white and delightsome resurrected being? Did he have a relationship with Mary Magdalene? John? Peter?"

"Jordan, you are unkind. You know your father does not advocate racist fantasies." Sandra defended Luke. "He doesn't know. We know so little. It is difficult to persuade those who lack reason or seek empathy."

"Reconcile," Jordan demanded. "Accept people for what we each are. Cease medieval thinking. Religious leaders like you need to tell unthinking followers the truth. Love is when you care for someone who's not quite the same. Someone you truly love. You married Mom—not who the Church said to marry. Who is worthy?

"Tests of faith Mom and I experience don't originate from a moral God. It's in our makeup. Our religion persecutes it. They're bullies disguised within good deeds. Defended behind the beauty of a uniquely designed temple. Dad, when will you testify of the Savior our family accepts? A God who will solve problems?"

Sandra argued, "Your father and I understand your frustration. It will take time and particular circumstances to effect change."

"Doesn't it make you angry, Mom? Young people are dying. The Church will not accept what we are, genetically. Men like Petersen shield themselves behind religious principles to justify segregation. Where is your allegiance, Mom? Human lives? Or Mormon theology?"

Sandra turned silent alongside Luke.

"Dad, we're short of the runway. I'm a competent copilot. Glad I didn't serve a mission."

Quietly, Luke opened himself. "I am failing to make things right for you and your mother. We're in the air with fuel. Leave the Church, Jordan. Don't leave our family, I beg you. You need to play catch with me when I'm old. Oh, wait, I'm already old, ain't I?"

Jordan smiled. "Mom, Dad, I love you dearly. I can't stay. Contradictions are too great. I am unwelcome. Best wishes to each of you."

"I wanted to get a foul ball. I'd like a bag of peanuts and a Diet Coke. What can I get for the two of you?" Luke, beaten but on his feet, was ready to purchase food and drinks. "Stay with your mother. I enjoy spending money. Do we all want the usual?"

Jordan understood. Luke needed to be with himself

Sandra and Jordan nodded. Luke walked the aisle to concessions. None of them watched the game ... an uncomfortable walk.

Sandra wrapped her arms around Jordan and placed her chin on his shoulder. She tilted her head against his. "Jordan, we're proud of you. Love you for the good you do. This will resolve itself. Your father plays a good game."

"I know." Jordan sighed. "So do you, Mom."

Sandra held her son. They spoke of baseball and enjoyed the beauty of the ballpark. The sky darkened; mountains faded into black beyond the fence. Later, Luke returned with two deacon-aged boys who carried kettle corn, drinks, peanuts, hot dogs, and surprises.

"These boys recognized me as a Hall of Fame baseball player. Asked if they could help me get this food to our seats," Luke said, placidly grinning.

"Uhnn-uhhhh. You're Apostle Luke," the boys protested. "You gave us money for popcorn to carry things here."

"Boys, this is my son, Jordan. I'm sure you know Sandra."

The young boys were courteous and shook hands. One said to Sandra, "My mom likes you, lots."

She nodded. "I'm certain your mother loves you as much as I love Jordan."

The boys grinned, nodded their heads, received hugs, said their goodbyes, and scurried away.

They enjoyed the remainder of the game sharing stories and memories of home, Hawaii, Phuong.

In the eighth inning, the deacons returned with a foul ball. They asked for autographs. Luke pulled a Sharpie from his pocket. He, Sandra, and Jordan signed the ball. Luke dated and cited the teams that played that night. "Coolest thing anyone has asked me to do. Thanks, boys."

A grand night at the ballpark despite the burden of loss.

Who Mourns the Fallen?

We stumble and fall constantly even when we are most
enlightened.
But when we are in true spiritual darkness, we do not even
know that we have fallen.

—Thomas Merton

"THE TWO OF US have a part in Overlord, Jordan. We don't know what it is we'll do or when." Phuong shuffled papers, tamped them evenly, and placed a heavy-duty binder clip to the clump.

"Mom and Dad are aging, D-Day must be near," Jordan said, seated next to Phuong at their home in Hawaii. "I see you, Mom, and Dad, the qualities the three of you bring into the equation. Not sure what I have to offer. Besides, I told Mom and Dad I'm on my own"

"Jordan, your writing is impressive," Phuong said, smiling. "Overlord has a credible voice in your pen. Mom's syndrome is secure. You should be pleased."

"Mr. Nguyen, without his skills ... well, I never could have written or spoken a word without him. I wish I could see it clearly," Jordan shook his head.

"Mom and Dad said there was an influence, a power, that drew them together at BYU. It involves us, the Consortium, experiences, people we've met ... Hawaii ... I'll include Mom and Dad's achievements."

"Phuong, do you hear yourself? You speak like Mom and Dad." Jordan smiled and held her hands. "I am part of this family, but my gifts are not like yours. My path is different, known only to me. I see what I am to do."

"Don't take that path too far away. Mom and Dad will likely never return," Phuong said, shaking her head. "They've changed many lives in their years. Especially in Salt Lake."

"The Consortium is a mystery. Ms. Ngo and the Visitor are riddles, and at the same time, so effective. Mr. Nguyen is wise, knows what to do and when things will happen. How do they do it?" Jordan sat perplexed. "Mom and Dad say they are truly guardian angels."

"Why should we doubt them?" Phuong suggested, hand upraised. "Jordan, you refuse to recognize your gifts. You speak well. Write persuasively. Your performance is admirable. I applaud you." She clapped her hands.

"You're too kind, Phuong. Thanks. When will you return to Harvard?"

"Two weeks," Phuong answered. "I took an abbreviated sabbatical. Here in Hawaii. The best place to make decisions. Personal issues need resolution. I need to finish my conclusions for the splicing research article. Publication deadlines. Facilitate clinic, clinic lab and hospital facilities—"

"What is it with you? You are so much like Mom and Dad. A degree from Stanford and a medical degree from Harvard. A geneticist. I'm not what the three of you are," Jordan said, lamenting.

"Yes, you are. Every bit," Phuong countered. "You've been a contributing participant in all our discussions. That includes three-dimensional thinking games you created. Those scenarios are printed in Mom and Dad's books, cited, and given royalties for your work. Look at what you and I have printed and produced together. Put your mind to it; anything is possible."

"Again, you're too kind—said more for encouragement than truth. Love you for that. You've been there for me, from the beginning. Shhhh." Jordan placed a finger to his lips and smiled. "You were at my games and activities and rescued me from the Pali.

Thanks, Phuong. I'll miss you when you're back at Harvard. But you plan to return—stay in Hawaii? Continue your research here?"

"After all that's happened, yes." She stilled for a moment. "Jordan, you are so sentimental. You're my only brother. Our whole family loved you since that first day in San Francisco. You've made our lives and family perfect," Phuong said. They placed their arms around each other, a seated hug at the table.

"Let's call friends. Hit some balls, or play a game on the field tonight," Jordan suggested. "We'll watch *Field of Dreams*. I cry every time Costner asks, 'Dad, wanna have a catch?'"

I cry too, Phuong thought, then clamped her papers.

Friends assembled early that evening. Like the good times, they played ball, shared stories, and laughed. As the sky darkened, a makeshift screen was set up on the field. Blankets, pillows, and quilts were thrown on the grass. Popcorn, pizza, and soft drinks shared as the movie played. Mr. Nguyen pulled a handkerchief from his pocket to wipe away a tear as the film ended. Father and son played catch on the enchanted ballfield in Iowa.

Or was it heaven?

The house was too quiet. "Jordan," Phuong shouted. No response. She shouted his name again. A third time. No response. The silence made her uneasy. She went to Jordan's room. Knocked. "Jordan. Are you awake?" Phuong cautiously opened the door. Found his room empty. The bed was made, room uncluttered, tidy. She stepped inside. The silence was clamorous. "Jordan. This is beyond teasing." She searched for clues and found a typed page. Her eyes swiftly absorbed the words. Her heart raced.

Phuong grasped the car keys and raced to the Pali.

She ran the trail to the cliff. The Visitor stood in her path. "Visitor, thank God you're here. Hurry. Jordan will jump. We have little time to save him."

"I am here to save you, Phuong."

"I don't need it. Let's move," Phuong shouted and maneuvered to bypass the Visitor.

The Visitor grabbed her arm. Stopped Phuong.

Phuong instinctively engaged aikido to release his grip.

"Your skills are defenseless with me," the Visitor stated without emotion.

"Please, let me go. Jordan will jump," she screamed. She struggled to escape and swung a fist that the Visitor deftly deflected.

"Both of you will fall should I allow it. There is a marvelous work you will do. This day cannot be your last."

"Our family will be broken if I don't stop him."

"Your family will end should I release you. Phuong, remain with me," the Visitor urged.

"What? Please stop him. Please," Phuong begged, falling to her knees in the struggle.

"Jordan has a purpose. Like all good sons and daughters in conflict, sacrifices are rendered," the Visitor explained. "His mission is conscious."

"He needs to know I love him. Mom and Dad love him. He can't leave. Not like this. This is not how it is supposed to be." She sobbed.

"He knows you love him. He knows your parents love him. Jordan has made a decision. Let his act testify of his love for each of you. The cause your family advocates to resolve."

"Jordan is to stand with us. Not buried beneath us," she shouted.

A gentle breeze waved shrubs and flowers. "It is played." The Visitor placed his free hand to Phuong's face, softly whispered, "*Shhhhhhhhh.*"

With a finger to his lips, he uttered a second "*Shhhhhhhhh.*"

A final, extended "*Shhhhhhhhh*" permitted Phuong to abide and be at peace.

"You are one with us. Finish your duties. Now, walk with me." The Visitor helped Phuong to her feet. The two walked slowly to the car. He asked for the key and released his grip.

"What will happen now?" Phuong asked.

"Authorities are notified. Mr. Nguyen awaits our return." The Visitor sat in the driver's seat, looked at the keys, and shook his head. "These contraptions still require thought before engagement." He looked at the floor, his feet, the panel, and the steering column. The Visitor inserted the key and started the engine. *When will they invent a voice-activated starter?* With a smirk, he said "Like riding a bicycle." *Hope no one hits us.* Clumsily, he maneuvered the car onto the road.

Mr. Nguyen stood under an umbrella as the Visitor parked the car. Again, Mr. Nguyen, where he needed to be, opened the car door and embraced a saddened Phuong.

The two walked into the house. Phuong asked, "Where's the Visitor?"

"With your parents," Mr. Nguyen answered.

Luke's cell phone vibrated.

"Luke speaking."

"Dad, I have disturbing news."

Luke's first thought, *Mr. Nguyen passed.* He listened intently.

"Jordan has fallen from the Pali. He is dead."

Luke heard Phuong's voice. *This is real.* Paralyzed, unable to speak, Luke sat frozen. He stared into emptiness. Tears filled his eyes. He shook with uncontrollable shudders.

Sandra, with the Visitor, stood at the door to his office. Her eyes were wet, tissues in hand.

"Dad, I tried—" Words failed her. "The Visitor is on his way to you."

Luke attempted to gain control. "The Visitor is here … with your mother … me … in my office … is Mr. Nguyen with you?"

"Mr. Nguyen is here, so are friends, Church members." *How can the Visitor be there?*

A long silence followed. Luke's eyes drowned themselves with tears. Spasms of weeping overcame him. His mind recounted memories with Jordan. The first minutes in San Francisco, games of catch, bike rides, books, baseball, family activities, laughs, arguments, conflicts, failures. Without awareness, Sandra sat on his lap, her arms around him. They wept together, unable to control their sorrow. Each felt failure. They failed to rescue Jordan.

"Luke, I am—was—his protector. We—I—should have been with him," Sandra said through her tears.

Where's my phone? Luke lost awareness of his bearings. He looked at his empty hand. "I was speaking with Phuong." Confused, dazed, he shook with grief.

The Visitor held his device and conversed with Phuong. He motioned for Luke to care for Sandra.

Luke buried his face in Sandra's hair and wept. "You sat on my lap years ago at your mother's home. Rescued me then and now." With uncontrolled shudders, through his tears, he said, "We did as much as we could. Or didn't we do enough? We need—we have Phuong. Her needs ..."

Their world changed. It looked the same, although nothing was the same.

Apostle XII and the Suit stood at the door, concerned. Their attention was captured by uncharacteristic movements from Luke's office. "Apostle Luke, what has happened?"

"Our son has taken his life," Luke responded, silently observing the movements in his office. "Please inform the First Presidency and Twelve?"

"Certainly. Anything I can do for you? What do you need?" XII anxiously asked.

"I need time with Sandra. Please close the door. We'll speak when we have collected ourselves. Thank you."

"I'll inform the First Presidency," the Suit said and rushed away.

"My sincerest regrets, Luke." Apostle XII closed the door.

The Visitor's voice cut through the silence. "This will be the saddest day of your lives. You will survive." He spoke without emotion, as if unaware of the loss Sandra and Luke felt.

"Jordan killed himself. Where were you?" Anger grew in Luke's stomach.

"I perform my tasks. As do the two of you," the Visitor answered.

"Jordan is dead." Sandra shouted with scorn.

"Is he? Your doctrines say Jordan is elsewhere. You will meet again. Families are together forever. Am I mistaken?"

"This is not a time for inconsiderate questions," Luke said.

"Why? Put into practice what you claim as truth. Death is meaningless should it truly be passing through a veil. One dimension to the next. Celebrate. Do not mourn."

"Visitor, I like ... respect you. Now you annoy me," Luke said.

"Have you no shame? No pity?" Sandra asked.

"Questions. Excellent. Let us reason, shall we?"

"This is neither the place, nor—"

"*Shhhhhhhh*. Grovel, should you believe tears will ease matters," the Visitor whispered. "Luke, do you enjoy tears, contrived or real, wept in church services?"

"Rarely. No," Luke answered ... justly agitated.

"*Shhhhhhhh*. Tears remain here when you depart this office. Leaders act. Leaders speak. Never weep before your people."

The Visitor's words were valid. Sandra and Luke sensed a power and reasoned awareness.

"Understood," Luke said like a good soldier. Sandra nodded her head.

"Sandra will deliver a speech that people with LGBTQ children will use to argue this cause of cultural bullies in their own families. Sandra is to speak at Jordan's memorial."

"I am a rhetorician," Luke said. "Allow me—"

"Luke," the Visitor interrupted. "Sandra will speak. She shall deliver this speech ... coach. Be a supportive contributor."

Luke nodded his compliance, disappointed his voice would not defend Jordan's final act, like Puccini's Butterfly.

The Visitor placed a hand on Luke's arm. He raised Sandra and Luke to their feet. The Visitor looked into Luke's eyes. As he did, he embraced him and held Luke tightly. "Not all heroes are buried under a monument or in a military graveyard. Jordan played his role. Play yours. Families with a Jordan in their home will pursue Sandra's appeal. Your time to speak will come."

With calm mastery the Visitor reached for Sandra as the three hugged and wept their final tears.

"*Shhhhhhhh.* Jordan's life was a sacrifice. Not an atonement, blood sacrifice, or as thoughtless as that," the Visitor said. "A protest for those harassed by religious oppressors. Mormons claim to be a persecuted people. Now they are persecutors. Religions are not benign. They create torment between worshippers with their own tenets, dogmas. Religions create bigots, violence, homophobia, racists, and bullies. *Shhhhhhhh.*"

A knock sounded at the door. The three separated and made preparations to meet the people. The world awaited. Luke opened the door.

Three Apostles and the Suit stared into Luke's office. "We heard voices. Everything went silent. Are you okay?"

Luke answered, "Yes. We needed time. Needed to gather ourselves. Jordan was conflicted. We're prepared to speak."

Men inched into the office.

"There is—was—an Asian gentleman here?" Apostle XII curiously asked.

"A guardian angel. We've known him for years," Sandra answered.

"Guardian angel? Are you serious? Where is he?" the Suit asked.

"Let me introduce you." Sandra turned. The Visitor was missing. She glanced behind the door. Under Luke's desk. "He left, apparently," Sandra said, puzzled. "Might be in the restroom. It has been—" She swooned, diverting everyone's attention.

The Suit rushed to Sandra, grabbed her arm, and called for assistance.

Men responded to calls for water, and sought a chair. "The stress of this news has been too great," Luke explained. "She'll be fine. She needs rest." Luke protectively embraced Sandra.

"Would a blanket help?" the Suit asked.

"There's one in my office," Apostle IX said.

"Please," Luke nodded.

Two Brethren left the office, saying, "We'll hurry."

Apostle XII approached and grabbed Luke's arm. "What's happening? I saw an Asian gentleman in here."

"Where'd he go?" The Suit searched. "Underground?"

"We'll explain when all this passes," Sandra whispered to him. She rolled her head toward Luke. "Jordan is smiling, watching this."

"If you weren't so beautiful, we'd be dead in the water." Luke lifted her into his arms as men rushed to help. "I admire your quick-thinking gall. Commendable."

"I love you too."

Briskly carried to a sofa, Sandra sipped water while minutes passed. Out of danger, emotionally, circumstantially.

The Suit, however, was frustrated, unable to explain the Visitor.

Jordan's services were staged outdoors at the family home in Hawaii. The outfield accommodated a sizable crowd that consisted of family, Church members, guests, and media outlets. A pool photographer, one camera shared by all outlets, eliminated restrictions to broadcast a service from Church property.

Sandra addressed onlookers:

"Jordan was tormented by two factors. First, a mixture of Asian and Negroid lineage. His racial blend with the history of social issues, LDS Church culture, and doctrines of race relations were great irritants. Second, his nature as a gay person created conflicts of faith and belief in the restored gospel of Jesus Christ.

"I request LDS Church members to think back. Consider the 1830s through June 8, 1978. The lessons taught in Sunday school, seminary, Relief Society, MIA, and priesthood quorums. Horrid years. Church members were instructed never to be inclusive of Black people, or homosexuals. My child and beloved son, in today's world was labeled 'multiracial LGBTQ.' Race and sexual behavior are social constructs. Genetics, such as epigenetic inheritance, is altogether more reliable and truer than outdated religious dogmas.

"Our teachings stated, in those bygone years, that 'one drop of Negro blood' disqualified Blacks from priesthood and temple blessings. Geneticists state that humans share 99.9 percent of our DNA with each other. That's a truth science revealed to us that Heavenly Father seemed unable to accept. Our long Church history of racism is a sad reminder that a mere drop of blood is ample cause for separation with assorted cruelties. Since 1978, the LDS Church has welcomed and proselyted Blacks into our folds, but has expressed no apologies for our prior acts of guilt.

"The Church disdains critical challenges toward their conclusions of accepted sexual conduct. We seek victims, once again. Sadly, full inclusion for all Church blessings has failed to find acceptance for LGBTQ. Heavenly Father smiles as He blesses each individual, no matter how uncommon a person may seem to the rest of us. Truly, all people 'are alike unto God' as the Church attempts to interpret with unintentional, though masked insults to Jordan and LGBTQ individuals. It has caused self-inflicted deaths... **and it must end!** Jordan should be in a mission home, not lying in a grave. Genetic proofs reveal that Jordan, as a gay person, is no more responsible for his sexual inclination than his skin color. Why demand to behave otherwise?"

Sandra concluded, "Protect those who fall. Care for those who are weak. The outcasts in our world. Every home has a Jordan somewhere within their families. Allow my son his place of acceptance and protection within our Church. 'All are alike unto God.'" (2 Nephi 26:33)

The funeral ended. Friends, Church members, and BYU–Hawaii LGBTQ students followed Jordan's casket to a secluded beautiful site approved for burial purposes. A location Sandra and Luke designated as their resting places. Jordan now included. Those who wished, participated in a farewell *haka*. Leis, *haku* crowns, and flowers placed near his place of rest.

Workers rearranged the field. Tables were spread with catered food. Bats and balls on the field. Basketballs with open hoops. Luke threw pitches. Children and adults took swings. Silly string memorials were abundant. Laughs and giggles buried grief and tears.

Sgt. Rulon Steele, now Lt. Colonel Rulon Steele, adjutant to the commander general of the United States Army Pacific, Fort Shafter, Honolulu, made the day brighter.

"Colonel Steele, good to see you again," Luke said, greeting the smartly uniformed officer. "Your service has kept you in the Pacific."

"Yes, sir. I express my condolences for your loss. My memories of Jordan ... a grim start. You gave him a good life. A fair chance."

"Please say hi to Sandra and Phuong," Luke said.

When Steele saw Phuong, he placed a finger to his lips, "Shhhh. Shhhh. Do you still do that?"

"On occasion," Phuong said, smiling.

"It's a reliable tool. Thanks for teaching me," Steele praised. "Many kids in Guam, some with their parents, where I used Shhhh... I'd walk the compound, and whole families would come up to me and say, 'Shhhh.' It works. My children have been recipients of the Shhhh practice."

Everyone smiled as Lt. Col. Steele shared the anecdote.

"You married, have a family?" Sandra asked.

"Yes, two boys," Steele explained.

Sandra asked, "I hope your wife and sons are here?"

"They are," Steele answered. "My wife hoped she might have a chance to meet you. We've read your books. Actually, we were baptized years ago."

"Where are they?" Sandra asked.

"Seated at a table near your home."

Luke snatched cans of silly string. "We're on our way. Lead us to them, Colonel."

Sandra and Luke never knew the number of people they influenced to join the Church, to become three-dimensional thinkers, to value *transcenditory* spiritual experiences, and to put aside religious obedience in lieu of virtues such as tolerance, compassion, and reason.

People celebrated. No one mourned. The sun's light faded. A homecoming ended.

Mr. Nguyen sat with Phuong, Sandra, and Luke on the patio deck, wearied from the day's activities. They were overjoyed to be together ... but distraught their reunion resulted from Jordan's fatal decision.

"I am leaving Hawaii," Mr. Nguyen sadly said. "My time is far spent. Jordan is gone."

"No," Phuong protested. "You are family. You can't go."

"Phuong, you are independent, a grown woman, a doctor. I am needed elsewhere." Mr. Nguyen sensed everyone's concern. "I will keep an eye on this family, always."

"Where will you go?" Sandra asked.

"Guardian angels are busy. In great demand. I cannot say where I will go. May I express, sincerely, this family has been the highlight of all my missions. Yes, there have been tears. Yet I have never laughed or smiled as much as with all y'all."

Everyone laughed to hear Mr. Nguyen's skewed grammar.

"It's my fault. Ya learnt that from me," Luke said, chuckling.

"Mr. Nguyen, don't tell anyone you began to use those words because of Phuong or me."

"We've tried correcting him. He's the bad example," Phuong said with a giggle.

Mr. Nguyen asked, "May we all return tomorrow to see Jordan's place of rest? The groundskeepers have finished their work. It should be lovely."

The morning's rays shone from the east as the group of four approached the site of rest. The groundskeepers' work was magnificent. Hardly a trace of the previous day remained. Simply an expanse of green with flowers and shrubs. Trees shaded all passersby.

"No gravestone or markers. No fences or walls," Sandra ordered. "When we rest with Jordan, the few who love us will know where we are. On resurrection morn, I don't want to stumble over tombstones or bump into other folks wearing cumbersome temple clothes."

"You're welcome to join us, Phuong," Sandra said. "You have others to consider, we know. Luke, Jordan, and I will be here, as beautiful as it is now ... look at the ocean, blue skies, white clouds, green landscape, mountains."

With her arms open, hands extended, Sandra spun in a circle to absorb the entire experience with all senses. As did Luke, followed by Phuong, and Mr. Nguyen until the four dynamos wrapped themselves in each other's arms.

"The four of us will know exactly where Jordan rests." Phuong gazed at the scene. "Some will throw a blanket on the ground. Enjoy a picnic. They'll never consider they are sharing space with Jordan. Great idea, Mom."

"Your father was in on it. He wanted to be buried near the peak of Mount Timpanogos in order to avoid the crowds in the valley. Everything here came from that. I think this place is far better than Timpanogos," Sandra concluded.

"Absolutely. Jordan's buried with his ball glove," Luke said. "He is ready to play catch with me. We're close enough to the field to hit balls. I'll have bats and baseballs in my coffin."

"Dad. Really? No softballs?"

Luke playfully chided, "Centuries in a grave, risen with a perfect body of flesh and bones, I'll strike you out with three pitches."

"With my perfectly resurrected body, I'll take it out of the park on your first pitch."

Mr. Nguyen chuckled.

"Okay, everyone," Sandra said. "Enough testosterone and estrogen for the day. Let's have breakfast. Get on with the day."

Luke caught Sandra's hand, then Phuong's. Phuong grabbed Mr. Nguyen's hand. The four walked home. A happy day. The only damper? Mr. Nguyen's departure.

Unlike traditional partings that include goodbyes and exchanges of phone numbers and addresses, guardian angels depart with no fanfare. They rarely return once an assignment is completed. Communication severed. A new angel may be assigned. How does one say goodbye to a much-loved, special angel? All three expressed their thoughts.

"Goodbye, Mr. Nguyen. Best wishes with your next assignment. Your love and kind words have been greatly appreciated."

"Thanks for your service. We are grateful. You are loved by us. Jordan loved you. Everyone in Laie and San Francisco."

"You are an excellent teacher and will be missed. Don't forget us... please return."

Mr. Nguyen reached the end of the line amid handshakes, hugs, and kisses. Mr. Nguyen walked away. Guardian angels are cool and unusual. It's beneficial to have them around. Their influence remains forever.

Sandra, Luke, and Phuong remained in Hawaii another four days. They needed the time to recover and adjust. Plans needed formulation. The home felt emptier without Jordan. It would be completely empty when Phuong returned to Harvard ... it would not be vacant long.

Sandra's speech was replayed among Media outlets. The Church felt discomfort from television discussions, editorial pieces, radio, newspaper, and internet archived social media displays.

In Salt Lake, Sandra and Luke found themselves, again, in the boardroom with the First Presidency. Familiar territory for challengers, questioners. Sandra neither amended nor retracted Jordan's memorial address. Each declared they would voluntarily vacate their positions as general officers should the First Presidency issue a reprimand for heresy. They assured the First Presidency that select Church administrators and personnel, whether financially indebted to the Church, or not, would exit with them should a reprimand be issued.

A coalition of Church employees, and a goodly number of general officers, held watch to balance power struggles within the hierarchy of corporate Church leadership ... Sandra and Luke, most persuasive within the power structure.

No punishments or restrictions from the First Presidency ensued. Sandra and Luke's Church membership and leadership as an apostle and Relief Society president remained intact.

Luke issued a statement to the First Presidency and Quorum of the Twelve:

"The playing field is unlevel, unjust for those deemed unworthy merely as victims of genetic statistical probabilities. Cease intolerance from such considerations of race, gender or LGBTQ.

Unequal inclusion is unjust. Sunday services requires change with our understanding of social and scientific discoveries ... line upon line, precept upon precept ... apologize and acknowledge past misdeeds. Keep pace. Lengthen strides. Prepared lessons must include historical racial discrimination, gender bias, and LGBTQ relations with notations.

Years passed as if only days. Our heroes aged gracefully. Nevertheless, they aged.

Broadened Horizons

All great truths begin as blasphemies.

—George Bernard Shaw

SANDRA HEARD A KNOCK at her office door. The Suit stood at the entrance. "Sister Sandra, you have a visitor." Sandra expected no one. Suits never allow anyone entrance into the office areas unless given adequate notification and clearance.

A vision as beautiful as Sandra appeared.

"Phuong!" Sandra clambered from behind the desk and rushed to her. They clenched each other, nearly lost balance. The Suit quietly exited.

"I remember when you'd run to your father at Berkeley. He'd kneel with open arms, hug you, and fall to the carpet. I'd join the hug. Now, I'm too old and you're a lady. A doctor. Still love you as much ... More!" Sandra smiled to see Phuong, her enchanted princess. Hugged her tightly.

Phuong nodded. "I love those memories. Made me feel special when the two of you'd say 'Your love just knocks us over.' Better not try that now. Dad's not here."

"I'll call him. He can be here in minutes. We weren't expecting you until tomorrow. Look at you, a medical geneticist, fit and toned, worldwide researcher, consultant. Wow!"

"Happy I don't live in this dreary place." Phuong hesitated before saying, "The Islands are calling you and Dad. Isn't it time to go home?"

"That's one of the problems with this damn Church. Won't allow us our freedom. Gotta stay here 'til Luke dies." Sandra punched numbers on her phone. "Luke, there's someone in my office you want to see … No, it's not the Visitor. Someone much prettier. Hurry … bye."

"Mom, I came as soon as I could. What's happened?"

Sandra, unprepared by Phuong's early arrival, became teary-eyed.

"Mom, what's wrong? Are you ill?"

"Sweetheart." Sandra took a moment to gain control. "I'm dying. Cancer."

Phuong covered her mouth, shocked by the news. "Oh, Mom. No. When did you learn?"

"Children have a tendency to bury their parents. This will be your first chance. Parents should never bury their children. It wasn't right we buried Jordan." Sandra faded amid her memories.

Phuong and Sandra stood silently as Luke arrived.

Phuong turned and embraced her father. Sandra closed the door. The three held tight until tears passed. "I gather your mother shared the news," Luke said as they took seats.

"Mom, what do you know about your cancer? I may have information that could be helpful. Genetic sequencing and genetic medical research are wondrous." Phuong listened with insight as Sandra explained her condition. The three spoke about cancer, genetics, and possible treatments for Sandra.

Finally, Luke said, "Phuong, we didn't ask you here for medical advice. We're planning, with the Consortium's assistance, to engage Overlord. We need your help to play a role during the final scene." Sandra and Luke discussed plans and contingencies for the execution of Overlord, scheduled Sunday of April general conference, just days away.

Phuong smiled and nodded. "I will participate," she pledged. "I have additional ideas to contribute. It's fitting. It will have an impact lasting more than a lifetime. Hear my thoughts."

Phuong needed a mere fifteen minutes to issue her proposal. Flawless. The three required further time to discuss the depth of their commitments. Nonetheless, an unparalleled context.

"Tears aside," Luke said. "I want to hear about Phuong's research. Genetic splicing, sequencing. It's fascinating. Hopes and dreams can be miraculously real."

"Phuong, it is good to have you with us at our farewell, final performance." Sandra clearly struggled. Her words, agony.

"Mom, I'm pleased to play my role. You'll undergo my proposals. I look forward to all of it. The impact will be remarkable." Phuong's support clearly eternal.

"Your research will change people's lives dramatically, including your own. Phuong, risks are high. Have you considered the consequences?" Luke asked, held her hand.

"Like the games you gave Jordan and me. You'd state, 'What are your decisions and consequences?' Each outcome, result, and conclusion challenged. You forced us to think three-dimensionally— critical, skeptical thoughts. *Semper ama* is my decision." Phuong's eyes, as brilliant as her intellect, flashed a *transcenditory* commitment. Accepted with no rebuttal.

"Your resolve to Overlord is remarkable. What you will do for us is noble." Sandra leaned toward Phuong and kissed her forehead.

Preceding general conference weekend, the Visitor and Luke stepped into Sandra's office.

"How do you feel?" the Visitor asked.

Sandra was weak, dreadfully uncomfortable … in pain. "Please Luke, take me home. I cannot make it through Sunday," Sandra answered.

"Not possible," the Visitor responded.

"Not possible! I've never felt so—"

"*Shhhhhhhhh,*" the Visitor said with a finger to his lips. He approached Sandra, continuing to "*Shhhhhhhhh.*" He touched her face with his free hand and whispered indiscernible sounds. A final "*Shhhhhhhhh*" uttered, the Visitor backed away.

"What did you do? I feel …" Sandra said. "Thank you."

"You will be well. Unimpaired until reaching the Islands," the Visitor assured.

"Sir," Luke asked, "is that technique an attribute of God? If so, where does that place Phuong in God's batting order?"

"I've told you; God is far from this place. With fellow compatriots on a journey of exploration, finding unimaginable life, new elements, better-reasoning civilizations, lesser-reasoning civilizations, and stories that are new. As interesting as Gilgamesh, Troy, Terracotta Warriors, and others."

"There is life after death?" Luke soulfully asked.

"Truth is … Luke," the Visitor said, nodding his head, "your attempts to make me err is commendable, quaint language and all. I admire your polish. Life to death is a mystery. As is nothingness to life. Yes, there are answers. Sandra will learn first. In due time, you will follow. Finish your memoirs, biographies. Accelerate your work. It will make a fine film. A love story, in parts. You, Phuong, Jordan, science, family, humanity, LGBTQ. Naturally, Sandra, 'protector, defender of man.'"

"You know the meaning of Sandra's name." Luke was impressed.

"I'm a know-it-all." The Visitor smiled, with difficulty. "I'm learning. I enjoy surprises."

"Get outta here. You are not God," Luke said.

"I'm an angel," the Visitor reiterated. "People of faith believe such. Isn't that what Mormons also believe?"

"Yes. You look nothing like a god or even an angel," Sandra suddenly involved herself.

"Neither did Gabriel, Moroni, Shoeless Joe in *Field of Dreams*, or the 101st Screaming Eagles. I love Sandra's sweet potato pie." The Visitor acknowledged Sandra.

"I'll be damned," Luke said, chuckling.

"Luke, that could happen to you." The Visitor successfully grinned.

"I want to ask about you, other angels," Sandra said, her customary self.

"There are countless angels," the Visitor assured. "Not easily recognized. You could be blessed with all angels know if you ask questions, speak with confidence, and increase your experiences.

Travel. Eat foods that seem inedible. Become friends with people most unlike yourself. You'll cross paths with angels. Fall in love as I once … I must leave."

"Please stay," Sandra urged. "Tell us your story."

"We shall talk. A long, long time from now. You have strength to complete your tasks." The Visitor touched Sandra's face one last time, a finger to his mouth, *"Shhhhhhhhh."* He took steps to depart.

"Are you an angel?" Luke hoped the Visitor would remain. "I see overwhelming fantasy in religions, but you seem real. I've touched you. Seen wonders, odd, ethereal. Are you immortal?"

The Visitor turned. "Religions are mistaken. God is the last option, never the first. When dams, armies, citadels fail, God is expected to intervene. Never has. Faith is valuable. Intelligence is far more meaningful. Phuong and Jordan were placed in your care. Not with God. Because God is not here. People with intelligence do the real work of God." The Visitor silently disappeared.

"Thank you, Teacher," they whispered.

Luke met with the First Presidency to disclose Sandra's illness. He asked permission to stand with Sandra during the Sunday afternoon session. Requesting their confidentiality, he provided a sheet of comments they would speak, accurate though undetailed. Luke requested the choir sing "I Am a Child of God," Sandra's sentimental favorite. "It will give me time to escort her home."

The Brethren consented.

Overlord activated.

D-Day

SANDRA AND LUKE WALKED to the podium. Their final performance. They made a noticeable pair, even in their advanced years. Each looked energetic and statuesque.

Sandra managed her self-assured, splendid image. Hair remained long, almost as thick, well-styled. Exercise and diet regimen created an impressive presence. She appeared regal, an angel adorned in a light lavender A-line, V-neck, asymmetrical, chiffon dress. Her shape was unaltered by the years. She was distinguished, in control.

Two elderly, intelligent, handsome people stood at the podium to surprise the world.

Sunday afternoon session of general conference. Possibly a million households, likely not, tuned to KSL Radio, TV, and the internet. Fewer than twenty thousand were seated in the Conference Center. But, whoa, the aftershocks.

Luke began:

"We are permitted by the First Presidency to stand together during our presentation. I intend to please everyone and speak fewer than four minutes."

The congregation responded with a customary, wholesome laugh. Sandra and Luke broke their hand clasp and placed arms around the other.

"I stand with my best friend. I love Sandra more deeply than God the Father or Jesus Christ, combined."

Stunned tension consumed the Conference Center patrons. Luke's words challenged Mormon customs. Unconventional statements from Luke, however, seemed commonplace.

"Sandra is the most gifted thinker and oft-quoted person on this rostrum." He gestured to the Brethren and Auxiliary officers. "Her work, writings, speeches, and interviews with public media on behalf of the Church have made her more greatly known than members of the First Presidency or me.

"My best friend will soon die from cancer."

The congregation released a unified gasp. Reverberations permeated in all directions. Luke heard sounds from closely seated members of the Quorum of the Twelve. Luke cared little for the Mormon tendency to display tears in speeches. He remained emotionally grounded, amid audible reactions. Complete attention focused on Sandra and Luke.

"I shall resign my position as a member of the Quorum of the Twelve to advocate on behalf of Sandra. Her wonderful accomplishments in life. The person she truly is." Further rumbles. Movements and a tense atmosphere thickened.

"I believe I am the first to freely abdicate his seat from the Twelve."

Acute listeners believed Luke would declare himself a cancer research proponent or fundraiser. No one expected his words.

"The highest godlike achievement is to understand those most unlike ourselves. Admiration and acceptance for supreme values within each of God's children. Walls cannot be built between what we do not understand and how we want matters, or people, to be.

"Change ... Adapt ... Discover science within the gospel," Luke stressed. "As a Church of revelation, timely surprises from leaders are expected. In fact, demanded to understand Jesus in the twenty-first century and well into the future. Prophets of God from the Bronze or Iron Ages knew practically nothing of the galaxy, medical achievement, or the human genome as we now do. Look to the future, not the unenlightened past.

"Sandra is a child of God, a quality greater than appearing as a man or a woman. President Russell M. Nelson, a thoracic surgeon, instructed that 'God's DNA is our DNA.'[20] And I say, what He, God, gives us ain't junk. Look at Sandra." He motioned his free hand toward her. Tall and elegant, her eyes focused on the congregation.

"Sandra is an extremely unique individual. More than anyone can fathom. Born with androgen insensitivity. A genetic transfiguration gives her the appearance as a female, though her DNA is male. She is a living miracle. A creation designed by our Father in Heaven. Research the topic with your home computers."

Rustling, tension, and confusion rippled through the audience, including media outlets.

"I encourage the First Presidency and Twelve: Reexamine our dogmas. Alter our actions toward those labeled LGBTQ. Reason together, with an understanding of Sandra's syndrome. My companion represents the letters TQ in LGBTQ. Sandra has done great acts of good for humanity ... and the Church. How will the Lord, the Savior of us all, receive these gifted stars in our Church? Sandra rose from the fragments of her syndrome to be the person she is. My love, mother to our children. A leader for billions ... and **she** is genetically male.

Gasps and tremors shook the congregation.

"We, as members, act more like Mormons than compassionate humans. Unwilling to understand people like Sandra, who are neither male or female, black or white, Jew or Gentile. Rather, we are children of God, each with our own singular genetic makeup that ancient prophets and Apostles knew nothing of. We are one. 'All are alike unto God.'" (2 Nephi 26:33)

Sandra spoke:

"We each sail aboard a ship called Death. Lives frequently torpedoed by enemies who believe men and women are not equal. Others, like I, thrashed in a hurricane of genetic transfiguration. I am happy to conclude my journey. Do not grieve my death. I

---

[20] David Noyce, *Salt Lake Tribune*, February 10, 2019.

survived the storm. I am a miracle. I admonish all people to think, discover problems, and solve problems. Women of the Church understand how this is done. Most competent leaders do so ... often.

"Heterosexual parents create children who are LGBTQ. Uncommon children delivered from our Heavenly Father who are unwelcomed and unaccepted by our Church. My parents created me. Trained me to be a follower of Christ. As a teenage young person, I was told by scientists and doctors that I am male. I thought I'd never meet or marry my love *for time and all eternity*. Shamed with no hope for full fellowship in the only true and living Church; or human society. I thought my life was destroyed.

Then ... I met Luke at BYU; we fell in love. I told him everything about me. We answered all questions truthfully and married *for time and all eternity*. We live as leaders, contributors, and full tithe-payers in support of our Heavenly Father and Savior, Jesus Christ. The prophet has a duty to seek after revelations calling for compassion and well-being for all who, like I, are richly uncommon. But we fail to understand LGBTQ, racism and gender equity while reading outdated scripture without 21st Century scientific enlightenment. Luke and I, our children, we each are uncommon. Black, white, Asian, LGBTQ, a man married in the temple to a man, albeit I am a womanly person," she said, smiling at the audience.

"Young people, like our son, Jordan, sacrificed their lives because they were conflicted with sexual feelings placed against antiquated scripture and Church teachings. Spiritual leaders, of necessity, should understand 21st Century science, the human genome, and how God's DNA rules our lives. Luke and I cannot abide acts of segregation. The separation of uncommon people, like myself and others grouped as LGBTQ. None of us were ever given a choice to be what we are. How we feel or behave ... or our ethnicity and gender.

"I am what I am, like unto God. All people are to receive full fellowship in the saving ordinances of our Father in Heaven's temples. Unconditionally. There can be no Church ordinance disqualification for genetic traits in our members. Our failure to accept LGBTQ is our failure to save them.

"We are children of God. I am a child of God. Stars in the eyes of our Heavenly Parents.

"Join Luke and me to reason with leaders who never question or challenge. We each possess the will to be honorable Latter-day Saints. Insults must end. Engage tolerance for understanding, compassion to solve problems, and reason toward justice. Luke and I will be condemned and simultaneously praised for what we are. What we have done. I'm saddened I will not live to reason these issues.

"'If it's not done this way, it cannot be done' is fatalism. Do not limit what God can do, or His Church and leaders. Humanity is more valuable than religion or its dogmas. Revelations are expected to justly act with known truths of our century and that of the future—Science with gospel reason.

"Einstein said impudence was his guardian angel in this world. Three special guardian angels blessed our family: tolerance, compassion, and the most trying angel, reason. Accept their invitation. Inclusion for all who are uncommon.

"In our prayers and within our gatherings, petition the Lord and spiritual leaders among all religions to hear and understand each person who desire the blessings, rites, privileges, and ordinances of Yahweh, Allah, and any and all Gods, even Jesus Christ. Amen."

Luke spoke again. "It takes courage to state that our trials are unfair. Sandra's courage is unprecedented. Hear her. I implore of all people, everywhere."

Sandra and Luke found themselves in each other's arms, locked in a kiss. Impressive for two lovers late in their lives. Admirable, actually. They separated and looked into each other's eyes. Luke leaned into her neck, blew a bluzzard. Sandra yelped and laughed. *Whapped* his chest.

Laughs, gasps, and 'amens.' Some applauded.

Others sat and struggled. *What just happened?* A member of the Twelve shouted a distinct, "Hear! Hear!" Followed by a second. A third. A final voice from the rostrum shouted, "Hear her!"

Voices, mostly female, chanted, "Hear her" from the congregation. The Choir sang **"I Am a Child of God."**

Sandra and Luke walked without fanfare from the rostrum as the choir continued to sing. Phuong awaited to chauffeur them from Salt Lake. They approached elevators behind the rostrum to escape mayhem.

The Suit blocked them. "Where are you going?" he demanded.

"To meet Phuong. I'm taking Sandra home."

"You can't leave. You're in deep trouble." The Suit appeared distressed and determined to use force to stop them.

"Sandra is ill. She cannot remain here." Sandra and Luke attempted to bypass the Suit. His outstretched arms blocked their way.

"I can't allow it." The Suit firmly gripped Luke's arm to detain them ... "News people have gathered at all exits. Even in underground parking. Come with me. I'll get you out of here." Hurriedly the three walked to service elevators, stepped in, and plummeted down.

"Call Phuong. I hope she has good cell reception." Although an old-timer, the Suit remained an arresting force.

The door opened. Luke said, "We're connected."

The Suit grabbed the phone. "Go to the corner of Regent Street and Second South. A block or so east, two south. Your GPS will get you there. Have the car pointed west, far-right lane on Second South." He gestured directions. "Look for me on the street. I'll have my hand in the air, trying not to draw attention. Hurry."

The Suit swiftly led them through a corridor that opened to a wide tunnel. Before them, the prophet-mobile. They all climbed on board as the Suit put the pedal to the metal and breezed off. "If Phuong's still on the line, tell her she'll see me on the street—three minutes."

"It's a go," Luke reported.

The Suit made turns from tunnel to tunnel then picked up speed on a straight path. "We're going downhill," he laughed, then braked, made a left turn into a corridor, and stopped in front of elevator doors. He inserted keys. The doors opened. In seconds, the elevator lifted them to a lobby. "We're near the Walker Building."

The Suit stepped out of the elevator. Like a soldier he scanned for the enemy. He signaled for Sandra and Luke to follow. A few steps later, they turned a corner and looked through glass doors at passing traffic on 2nd South, across from the Gallivan Center. "Stay inside. KUTV is nearby. I'll call you to the curb."

"Why are you doing this?" Sandra asked. "You're risking much."

"Doin' what's right. Heard and learned." He placed a finger to his lips. "Shhhh. Full of surprises." He winked and smiled. "God is with us. He'll be with you both 'til we meet again." Casually the Suit walked through the doors, a hand above his head. He acted nonchalant.

Almost instantly, Phuong braked near the curb. The Suit scanned for paparazzi. Seeing none, he beckoned them to come forward. The car idled as the Suit held open the back door. Sandra and Luke dived into the car. Phuong sped away from conference goers and Temple Square.

Sandra asked, "Did they blackout our speeches?"

"No," Phuong responded. "Your presentation aired in more than ninety-five languages on radio and television. It's everywhere. LDS translation facilities and staff are second only to the United Nations."

"What's happening now?" Luke asked.

"Confusion. Unbelievable how fast news people got to the scene. The session still has an hour to go. The plan's working. No one will know you're gone, thanks to the Suit ... I wouldn't want to be the next person to address the audience," Phuong smiled. "What will that person say ... or behave?"

Luke's curiosity was too great. "Phuong, did we succeed? Were we understood?"

"Wonderfully," she answered. Gave them a thumbs-up and asked, "Was the kiss planned?"

"Totally spontaneous." Sandra smiled.

"The bluzzard too?"

"Why soitenly," Luke answered ala Curly the Stooge, pleased with himself.

"Mom, hit him. When he did that to me, I hated it."

"No, you didn't. Phuong, you laughed."

Then came the familiar *Whap!* "That's for both of us, Phuong."
Silence.

Phuong looked in the rearview mirror. Her parents were locked in a kiss. Sandra raised the leg he kissed decades ago and placed it atop Luke's knees. His hand gently stroked her thigh. Their kiss continued. Phuong smiled. *They still act like kids, God bless 'em. Jordan should be here.*

Phuong sped through downtown Salt Lake en route to a private jet terminal near Salt Lake International. They quickly boarded and were in the air as the afternoon session of conference ended at four. The trio landed in Phoenix more than an hour later. Ms. Ngo awaited. Our heroes spent the evening with Sandra's mother. Her final embrace with Mom.

Neither Sandra nor Luke returned to Salt Lake.

Nightfall

Twilight drops her curtain down, and pins it with a star.

—Lucy Maud Montgomery

SANDRA AND LUKE SHARED tearful goodbyes with Sandra's aged mother as the doorbell rang. Stunned, Sandra and Luke froze. *We've been discovered.* Luke approached and asked through the door, "Who is calling?"

"I'm President Jameson … stake president in Surprise."

"Are you a journalist?"

"No. You sound like Apostle Luke. I must speak with you. I'm not here by coercion from the Church. I need your help. Please. I'm not a threat."

Sandra and Luke were bewildered. Phuong said, "Ngo will arrive soon."

Luke unlocked the door. "Enter." The man was alone.

"Please, take a seat," Sandra directed.

Jameson wore a suit and tie. He looked very much like a stake president. White, affluent, professional. He sat. Phuong rolled luggage to the garage exit.

"You need help? What is your concern?" Luke rushed him and then sat with Sandra on a sofa.

"First, is Sandra's mother well?"

Sandra nodded. "Doing more for us than we for her."

Jameson nodded back. His nonverbal behaviors suggested uneasiness.

"How did you know we were here?" Luke pressed.

"I didn't. Media outlets, Church spokesmen, no one knows a thing. You pulled off a great escape. You employ exceptional people. I only hoped you might be here."

"Why are *you* here?" Luke asked, hurrying the conversation.

"I want to express my sympathy, Sister Sandra, for the cancer you bear. I am saddened." His expression of sympathy was followed by a short, explosive tirade. "The surprising disclosure that you are LGBTQ. I need absolution. I am guilty of smugness. Indifference."

Sandra and Luke were taken aback by his outburst. They held hands. Stared directly at him.

"I listened to your presentation in Salt Lake. It's been on the internet less than 24 hours but has nearly one-hundred million hits. Six times Church membership and growing. People from Europe, South America, Australia, and Asia. Sandra's syndrome is a topic discussed on TV, radio, churches. I'm sure it will be a topic in classrooms."

Sandra and Luke thought the man sought retribution.

"Our Church and the world are changing. You cannot give absolution. But I plead for it," the man uneasily said. "I had a sixteen-year-old niece who killed herself. She left behind a note. A lesbian, with no hope to please the Lord. A fifteen-year-old Aaronic Priesthood holder in Surprise did the same. I failed both… sweet kids. Misunderstood. ***The Church's failure to accept them is our failure to save them.*** Just like Blacks and the priesthood."

Sandra and Luke sat frozen. They gripped each other's hands more tightly. Memories flooded them … the fateful day when Jordan wrote similar words then leaped from Nu'uanu Pali.

"We understand. Lives have been damaged, wasted. What is your occupation?" Luke asked.

"Provost. Arizona State—"

"A high mucky-muck," Luke said, interrupting him.

"Yes, I am." Jameson shrugged.

"Did you know my father?" Sandra asked. "He was an ASU faculty member before his death."

"I did not know him," Jameson expounded, "You have no idea what the two of you have done. Some are asking God to strike you both dead. Most want you to retain your position in the Twelve, Luke. *'God's DNA is our DNA. What He gives us ain't junk.'* Wish I spoke those words to my niece and that poor boy who took his life.

"Luke is being called the Martin Luther of Mormonism," Jameson continued. "Although you tacked no theses on the Salt Lake Temple doors, you stood in general conference, each of you, and threw down gauntlets."

Sandra and Luke sat silently, unsure what to say or do.

"Sister Sandra," Jameson continued. "You said that 'heterosexuals create LGBTQ people' but won't accept them. Your words generated a storm. People are arguing and talking. They are angry, most are sympathetic. Demands for a resolution have been voiced – balance scientific truth with religious claims. One member of the Twelve proclaimed Sandra as a latter-day prophetess. The mantra has grown."

"We haven't looked at the internet, media sources ... anything. Has the First Presidency or the Twelve spoken?" Luke calmly asked.

"Little from Salt Lake. Members of the Twelve who've addressed the media praise you. You've persuaded the majority, though not all. There's a rift. The relevant matter is Sandra," Jameson said. "Sandra is an example for women in and outside the Church. Now exposed as a male. The take most have declared is a simple truth: *whether a man or a woman, gay or straight, there is very little that separates us in our ability to perform tasks or lead.* Love is not consigned to gender or ethnicity, as your family has shown, as the two of you have proved."

"Seems to me there is much you can do," Luke said.

"What do you mean?" Jameson asked.

"Speak your thoughts," Sandra emphasized. "Share doubts, just as they are spoken to God in prayers. Open yourself to others. Encourage tolerance. Be compassionate. No lives sacrificed to make a point. Reason together. Question leaders. Be honest, sincere. We are all alike."

"I believe," Luke said, "when you read what Sandra and I have written, our words will have greater depth now that you know of Sandra's syndrome. Reason is in our words, more than most understand."

"Do you have plans?" Jameson asked. "Can I help?"

"President Jameson, don't tell anyone we were here until we've ridden-off into the sunset." Luke dryly said. "This is Arizona."

"He thinks he's cute," Sandra whispered toward Jameson.

Jameson smiled. "You each give smiles to millions."

"I hope Heavenly Father has a grin on his face," Luke said, smiling.

Jameson nodded, "From ear to ear. Not from your humor. From your sense of challenge and quest for equity. For everyone. You did remarkably well. Surprised us all."

"Thanks for the kind words," Sandra said. "We are leaving soon. Please respect our privacy. We cannot tell you more."

"We have no power of absolution," Luke said. "Your words have been heard. Include everyone with full fellowship. Have no prejudice toward any person for any cause. That includes gospel dogmas. Disregard any cause for separation. It is irrelevant."

"You have my commitment." Jameson departed.

Ngo idled in the driveway.

Sandra expressed a final farewell to her mother. Ms. Ngo chauffeured our heroes to Sky Harbor International, where they boarded a private jet to Burbank. Sandra and Luke granted interviews with trusted hosts and reputable news programs. The two days in Los Angeles were difficult for a weakened Sandra. She desperately wanted to be home in Hawaii.

Sandra and Luke accompanied Phuong to the UCLA Medical Center. Dr. Phuong gathered researchers, geneticists, and molecular biologists from the LA area. Sandra and Luke were pleased to see their princess lead fellow colleagues in discussions absorbed with advanced medical and scientific skill. Sandra and Luke provided blood samples for genetic studies and other uses. They hoped for Sandra's relief, her final days lay ahead. Hope and faith were urgently needed ... combined with fact and knowledge ... for solutions to problems.

Phuong helped her parents board a private jet to Honolulu. A sad farewell in the confines of an aircraft. The hubbub created during the previous days now gave way to other events, people, and issues that sought attention.

"Thanks, Phuong, for all you've done. What you will do. I wish to live long enough to see the outcome of your efforts," Luke said. He gave his princess-daughter a hug and kissed her head.

"Call me often. I'll return to Hawaii soon," Phuong said.

"Mom, I love you. You've made my life wonderful. There is much to be done in Boston. Our efforts will have no end. I'll be home shortly."

"Phuong, my sweetest, dearest little one. You are the leader of this family." Sandra embraced her only living child.

Phuong looked into her mother's face, riveted with pain no longer hidden ... or shushed away.

Sandra, going home ... to die.

In her final weeks, Sandra and Luke prepared memoirs titled *Queer and Questioning: Acceptance in a World with Religions that Are Not*. Sandra and Luke challenged, "Religions are allowed to violate human rights while granted tax-free status as recipients of government stimulus funds."

The book became the most printed and disbursed of all Sandra and Luke's bestsellers.

Sandra's Farewell

I love life more than I love death.
I want people to emphasize life before
death as opposed to life after death.

—Ayaan Hirsi Ali

"LUKE, WHAT CAN I do? My mind is racked. The pain is—" Sandra groaned from the duress.

"Take the medication, Sandra. You've done enough. Please." Pain relief injected. Seconds passed. The drug instantly acted.

"I can't reason. Oh, my ..." Sandra began to relax, her demeanor eased.

"You try to be too strong. Speak with me a little longer," Luke said.

"Spock would control the pain. I can't." She cried with disappointment.

"You don't need to ..." Luke kissed her hand he clutched between his own.

"People do not rush to a light when dying. They run toward death to escape pain," she said, squirming.

"Pain is temporary. You will—"

"Luke, I want to stay ... your name is Love." Sandra stared into an abyss. She whispered, "It is unusual." Her eyes fell asleep.

Sandra passed. Luke stood watch over her, shaken with loneliness. The room silent with her departure. "We agreed to struggle together. I hope we done good." Luke tried to make her smile or whap his chest. Luke's eyes betrayed him; tears fell like a soft rain. He stood alone, gazed at Sandra's stilled body, now peaceful face. He felt immediate loss.

Phuong placed a hand atop theirs. She stood next to Luke with a hand to his arm. Her head rested upon his shoulder. Loss fled. Nurses completed their duties, removed items, and covered the body.

Phuong and Luke turned to the door, prepared to exit the room.

Luke stopped. Not by a thought but rather a compulsion. He glanced back to Sandra, motionless on the bed. Her silhouette under the white sheet shone brightly from the radiant sunlight through the windows. The image struck him. "She looks like—she is Timpanogos."

"Something *transcenditory*, Dad?" Phuong asked, holding his hand.

"Perhaps," Luke answered. "I wounded her. As I kissed that smarting, red welt, everything changed. Your mother shed tears that we would never pass our qualities to a child." He kissed Phuong's head and held her with calm assurance. "Give humanity the best of us, Phuong. Through you, we will continue."

Luke took steps back to the bed, bent, and gently kissed the sheet draped over Sandra's quieted leg. "You are legend, Sandra. Saved, loved me. With clean hands and a pure, enormous heart."

Phuong's eyes melted. She saw a Hershey's Kiss atop her mother's leg.

Luke lived only a short time after Sandra's death. He missed her greatly. Luke compiled Sandra's biography with his autobiography. The legacy of their lives included audio and video recorded messages from each. They spoke of their journey and the mountains climbed to change lives and achieve peace for those unjustly harassed. Simply for being the least common of our Heavenly Parent's creations.

They lie together, near Jordan, overlooking the blue ocean, white clouds, clear skies and rugged green landscape of Hawaii. Nearby an engraved stone reads **One is our family**.

Phuong later gave birth to a healthy, fully *Caucasian* girl.
A wonder in an age of scientific miracles.

Epilogue

THIS STORY IS TOLD exactly as it happened in a parallel universe. An abstract within the laws of physics gives credence to the parable printed here. The allegory is an illustration of inept behaviors on an isolated world that places illogic before logic. Fear ahead of concern toward specific individuals we separate, enslave, or segregate, predominantly in religious contexts.

There are more dimensions than three. Think into and beyond each dimension to love all people with charity. Life is precious. Intelligence respects life, equally and wholly. We are more intelligent today than yesterday, more intelligent tomorrow than today. Two hundred years from now, humanity will deem early twenty-first-century thinking as unenlightened. Questioning people thrive and succeed. Awaiting answers from holy revelation is slow, inapt. It makes us inactive and bonded too greatly with creeds and doctrines which create religious acts that bully. Empathy cannot wait for religious leaders to reveal truth. Spiritual leaders within all religions learn it, like the rest of us, from research, experimentation, thinking and rational thought. Do the math.

Brilliant thinkers with rational discussants discover then reveal truth. Again, ***do the math!***

Love every child without separation or spite. It is wise to be intelligent with inclusion of the uncommon, those unlike ourselves. Consider each child as a bright, shining star. Not equal in brilliance. Equal in hope, the right to acquire our Heavenly Parent's blessings and love.

> … Please help my people
> The poor and downtrod
> I thought we all were
> The children of God?
> God help the outcasts
> Children of God
>
> —Stephen Schwartz, lyricist

Every religion requires specific behaviors and thinking patterns from worshipers. These behaviors with thoughts patterned from untried, unchallenged traditions are roots that become fruits of unknowing actions: righteous fanaticism, hardheartedness, and senselessness. To seriously regard religion as superior to humankind, or any single individual, is a terrible, terrible fascination. Leaders, beware your actions.

As Sandra would question, "Got that?"

God, the Narrator

Meet the mystery outfielder determined to make a good impression at Mariners camp

March 15, 2024 at 10:00 am Updated March 15, 2024 at 10:00 am

Sun City, Ariz., resident Mark Merkley, 71, is a fixture at Mariners spring training, commonly seen shagging balls in the outfield during batting practice in spring training. An infielder in his college days at Brigham Young University, moved to Arizona from Salt Lake City three years ago, and plays in local baseball and softball leagues. (Dean Rutz / The Seattle Times)

By Adam Jude
Seattle Times staff reporter

PEORIA, Ariz. — There's a veteran ballplayer who reports to the Mariners' spring-training complex each morning and takes his usual place in the outfield grass on Practice Field 1. No place he'd rather be.

The guy's a bit of a mystery, but he does look the part: Mariners shirt, Mariners cap, gray baseball pants, black belt, black spikes, well-worn Rawlings glove.

On a field with a number of nonroster invitees, he stands apart. Call him a nonroster interloper.

No one seems to mind, though. He looks like he belongs, at least, even if you'd be hard-pressed to unearth any sort of scouting report on him (we tried).

Best shape of his life?

Mark Merkley laughs.

No, not exactly. At 71 years old, Merkley is past his peak playing days, and two years removed from surgery to treat bone cancer in his left forearm.

That doesn't stop him from volunteering each morning to shag fly balls during Mariners batting practice. Most days, it's the best part of his day. Some days, it's even more than that.

"I tell ya, coming out here every day is the highlight of my life," Merkley said.

The Mariners offer a Shaggers Program to anyone interested in stepping on the field during spring training. Shaggers are

336

required to have at least played high school baseball or softball, and they must sign a waiver releasing the Mariners (and the city of Peoria) from any injury liability.

A handful of other regulars join Merkley in the outfield most mornings, and they've become their own little community, these silver-tipped shaggers sharing a field with big league ballplayers.

"We're all just kids out here. All of us," Merkley said. "It's like we're 8 years old again."

As Mariners hitters spray batting-practice balls all over the field, Merkley usually sets up in shallow center field, behind a large net. As other shaggers field the balls in various parts of the outfield, they'll throw them back in toward Merkley, who gathers the balls and piles them in a bucket.

Once the bucket is full, he'll carry it to the pitcher's mound for assistant coach Carson Vitale, the regular batting-practice pitcher.

Merkley played shortstop and third base in college at BYU. In retirement, he moved from Salt Lake City to nearby Sun City, Ariz., three years ago — largely because of the pull of baseball. He joined a year-round men's senior league baseball team, and he plays on a coed softball team, too. He just wants to play, for anyone who'll let him.

Once he discovered the Mariners' shaggers program, he committed to showing up as often as he could. The cancer diagnosis was a setback. In surgery, healthy muscle and skin tissue from Merkley's leg was used to rebuild his left arm, and recovery kept him off the field for several months. He still doesn't have complete range of motion in his left hand.

"Every once in awhile, I notice when a ball comes into me, it'll hit the front of my glove because I just can't get my hand all the way back. But, hell, I'm 71 years old, what am I going to do?" he said with a laugh.

He's still confident in his glovework, though. He's had a few close calls with 100-mph line drives flying by, but he's also had his share of highlights.

"Last year I caught one right here," he said, clenching his fist and slamming his right hand into his glove, "and, man, it was a screamer. I went down to one knee and caught it. Man, it shook my glove, and all the guys around the [batting] cage were cheering."

The ultimate highlight?

Without a doubt, he says, it's getting to "play" next to Ichiro every morning.

The Mariners Hall of Famer still reports to camp daily, and even at 50 years old, Ichiro still looks like he could play a Gold Glove right field. Part of Ichiro's morning workout routine at spring training is to shag fly balls during batting practice, alongside Merkley and the other volunteers.

"The first time I came out here, it was so fun. I was in the outfield and here comes Ichiro trotting out," Merkley said. "And I thought, 'My gosh, I'm sharing the outfield with a Hall of Famer — with the greatest hitter who's ever played the game.'"

The volunteer shaggers are asked not to engage with Mariners players while they're on the field, and that generally applies to Ichiro, too. Merkley couldn't help himself one time when he looked on in wonder as Ichiro made a nifty behind-the-back catch on a high fly ball (something he loved to do during BP in his playing days too).

Merkley says he's spent some time in Japan, and knows a little bit of Japanese, and he just couldn't resist — he had to say something after that behind-the-back catch. So he hollered across the field to Ichiro: *Subarashii, masuta sensei.*

Which loosely translates as: *Well done (or wonderful), master teacher.*

In return, Ichiro turned toward Merkley and offered a deliberate head nod.

"What a thrill," Merkley said.

Just a couple of kids playing a kid's game, no end in sight.

Adam Jude: ajude@seattletimes.com; Adam Jude covers the Mariners and other teams for The Seattle Times.

www.ingramcontent.com/pod-product-compliance
Lightning Source LLC
Chambersburg PA
CBHW022033120726
47899CB00001BB/168